Acknowledgements

Brian Wroe Chief Superintendent, and a former
Divisional Commander, with Greater Manchester Police.
Anthony Phillips FFS.DIP, former Senior Scene of Crime
Officer at New Scotland Yard, and Visiting Lecturer at
Thames Valley University. Joan Rogers, Barbara Caterall,
Chris Beswick. Julie, Nathan, and James at
1885, The Restaurant. Google Earth.
Lindsey Small, Mike Atherton.

And, not least, the amazing City of Manchester.

The Emperor of Ch'in
Shih Huang-ti
Built a wall
From the hills to the sea.
He built it wide,
He built it stout,
To keep his subjects in
And the Tartars out.
The Emperor of Ch'in.

Meng Chiang-Nu, one sad day
From her own dear home
A thousand leagues away
To the wall did come.
Weary and worn
She wept and she cried:
"Where is my dear love
Buried inside?"
She wept and she cried
And her tears did fall
Till down, down tumbled
That great big wall.

Traditional Chinese Children's Nursery Rhyme
www.activityvillage.co.uk.

*"If you don't go into the cave of the tiger,
how are you going to get its cub?"*

Chinese Proverb

1

He felt the truck come to a halt, and heard the hiss of the air brakes, and the engine cutting out. Then there was silence. After what seemed an age another vehicle pulled up beside them; a lorry perhaps. He pressed the button on his wrist watch. It was nine twenty seven pm. Five minutes later he heard the squeal of the bolts as they were withdrawn.

The heavy steel doors swung open. The narrow beam from a torch stabbed through the dark, bouncing off the roof to light their way as they squeezed on hands and knees between the wooden pallets piled high with crates. They jumped in turn from the container, several of the weaker ones twisting around, cramped limbs protesting, to lower themselves gingerly to the concrete floor of the haulage depot. The seven of them stood shivering in the cool night air.

'Now, go clean yourselves off, and do whatever else it is you have to do.' the courier told them, massacring their dialect. He motioned to Wu Ling, the only girl among them. 'You first, over there.' He pointed to a stack of containers off to the left, and handed her a plastic litre bottle of water from the bag at his side. 'And be quick'. Then it was the turn of the men.

Feng Yi marvelled at the steam rising before him. Suddenly his arm was seized in a vice like grip. 'What did you do that for?' he hissed. 'Look at my shoes!'

'Don't say a word,' Zheng Hu whispered urgently. 'Just listen.'

Awkwardly, Feng Yi zipped his trousers with his left hand. He strained to hear what had caught his friend's attention. On the other side of the stack the courier was deep in conversation with another man. He guessed that they were speaking in English – certainly not his own Fujian dialect nor Mandarin, nor Cantonese. It might as well have been Japanese for all that he could understand it.

The hold on his arm tightened. He found himself being dragged away, towards the furthest end of the passage between the rows.

'What are you doing?' he hissed.

'Saving your life.' Zheng whispered. Then he released his grip, turned right, and sprinted ahead.

Feng Yi was confused and reluctant to leave the girl, Wu Ling. He heard a curse, the sound of angry voices, and running feet. His mind made up for him, he set off in pursuit of his friend. His legs were weak from lack of exercise, and the days and nights of confinement in cramped spaces. It was inevitable that they would catch him; that the sound of his feet ringing on the concrete would betray him. At the next junction he stopped, panic rising in his chest. An arm beckoned from behind a seven high double stack of rusting containers.

He squeezed into the narrow gap between the two stacks, backed in until Zheng's knees dug into his back, and held his breath. He heard their pursuers pause at the junction, and pictured them listening for the sound of flight, considering their options, deciding it was a lost cause. Just as he felt his lungs would burst, that the pounding of his heart would give them away, he heard the sound of retreating footsteps, the mutter of recrimination, the swearing of vengeance.

They waited, fearful that the men would return. Instead they heard the familiar sound of the flat bed container truck that had brought them here starting up, and driving away. Breath recovered, palpitations eased, Feng Yi began to move. His friend pulled him back down.

'Not yet,' he whispered.'

'What about Wu Ling?' Yi said. 'I promised her parents.'

'She'll live, believe me,' said Zheng Hu. 'I'll explain later. There's still the lorry. We have to wait until it's gone.' He rocked back onto his heels, biting his lip as he played back in his mind the conversation he had overheard; wondering how much of it to tell his friend.

'Why did you transfer them to this container?'

The newcomer had asked angrily in English rather than his native tongue.

'Because we had a tip off that Customs would search the TIR when it arrived in Hull.'

Their courier had answered.

'But why the hell did you choose this one – with the company's name splashed across its side?'

'Because there was no time to wait for instructions. I couldn't risk trying to get them out of the terminal, or finding somewhere to hide them in Rotterdam. The place was crawling with search teams with CO_2 monitors. Don't worry, there wasn't a problem. We put a reusable electronic seal on the TIR after we'd got them off, shifted the other

cargo, and put another seal on this one. They won't suspect a thing.'

'But did you blindfold them before you made the change over?'

'No. We didn't have time. Anyway, it was dark.'

'But there were lights in the terminal?'

'Yes, but there was a lot of shadow, with all the trucks and containers…'

'Did they see the logo on the side of the container?'

The courier had faltered; Less certain now.

'It's…. possible.'

The newcomer had paused. When he spoke his tone had hardened.

'They saw it. If not there, then here…just now.'

Another pause.

'How much do they still owe us for their passage?'

'Another five thousand each.'

'Thirty five thousand. But then the rest of the cargo is worth fifty times as much.'

'What will you do?'

No pause this time.

'Kill them. Not the girl. She can earn back what the rest of them owe us. Transfer the men into the back of the lorry. Tell them to get their heads down for an hour or so. Tell them that in no time they will be safe and sound in Manchester

'What about the girl?'

'Gag and bind her, and put her back into the container. Then get it out of here.'

That was the point at which he had grabbed his friend and told him to run. To justify his actions, he would have to tell him some of the conversation. Yi would understand; but what to tell him about the girl?

Back in the lorry with the other men Jin Chen wondered what the angry voices could have meant, and where Zheng Hu, Feng Li, and the girl, could be. He convinced himself that it was none of his business. They had, in any case, kept to themselves throughout the month long journey. At least this lorry – for all that it had seen better days – was dry, and smelt of nothing worse than cabbages. He closed his eyes, and tried to doze. The engine started up, and began to idle. He imagined himself listening to the sound of the torrents of the Nine Turns Stream as it crashed over the shoals of stone on its way to the crystal clear, dark green pools in the heart of the Wuyishan valley. Sleep sucked him into the vortex at the centre of the swiftly flowing river.

He dreamt that he was drowning, fought his way to the surface, and awoke fighting for breath. Close by, someone was retching. Jin Chen attempted to stand. His head swam, and his balance failed him. As he started to fall, he clawed at the side of the lorry. His head crashed into the corner, and he slid limply to the floor.

The only sounds were the hum of the engine, and the hushed whir of the fan high in the roof.

2

Manchester was on the cusp of spring. The only signs, here in the city centre, were the yellow and white trumpets of narcissi forcing their way through the winter pansies in the hanging baskets outside the Ox gastro pub. There would be more, Caton knew, around the Cathedral, and in front of the Town Hall. Before the week was out, the vast public gardens the Victorian fathers' of the city had mapped out for the workers in the mills, the factories, the warehouses, and docks, would be ablaze with daffodils, their heads nodding in a light wind that would barely cease until summer.

It was still cold enough for his breath to condense on the inside of the windscreen. As the lights changed to red at the junction with Deansgate, he wiped the patch his blower had been struggling to clear. Would the day ahead become any clearer? The Chinatown investigation had dragged on for seven months. It had already run into the ground when it was given to his team. Not so much a hard case, as a dead end. Tomorrow he would hand it over to the recently formed Serious and Organised Crime Agency; SOCA, or The Agency as it was becoming known. It was disappointing after all the effort they had put in, but at least it meant that Detective Superintendent Gates would have to find something else for them. Almost anything would be better than watching his team bang their heads against a brick wall. Caton grimaced. That was, after all, precisely how the case had started. The lights changed. He shifted into gear, and followed the stream of traffic weaving past the Beetham Tower, heading for the Mancunian Way.

They sat around the conference table in Caton's office. Seven squeezed around a table designed for six. Detective Sergeant Carter, and Detective Constable Woods, arms folded across their chests, pulled their chairs out, allowing Duggie Wallace, the senior intelligence officer and analyst, to squeeze in. It gave them the excuse to stretch out their legs, reinforcing just how little consequence this meeting held.

'When's the hand over Boss?' DS Carter asked.

'The day after tomorrow.' Caton replied. 'There's an Agency seminar at the Radisson. We're doing a presentation on the case.'

'The Radisson, very nice!' Detective Inspector Sarah Weston exclaimed, flicking her newly feathered neat blonde bob in case there was anyone who had yet to notice.

Carter chanced his arm. 'Would you like someone to go with you Boss?'

Caton smiled. 'Nice try,' he said. 'Sadly, as Gordon did the bulk of the work on this, he's already booked his place.' Caton understood the mood in this room. Mixed feelings; glad to get rid of the case, disappointed not to have sorted it.

'Look,' he said. 'Whatever impression we make at that seminar is going to reflect on everyone in this room. I know we've worried this to death, but let's just give it one more go; make sure we haven't missed

11

anything. If nothing else, let's show SOCA that we've been thorough.'

He glanced around the table. Carter drew his legs in and sat up, the rest of them were nodding. Only Woods lounged in a manner just short of insolent. If he really wanted to spend his last few years in uniform that could be arranged. Caton would take it as a personal failure, but there were plenty waiting to take Detective Constable Dave Woods' place.

'Are you joining us, DC Woods?' he said.

The detective constable uncrossed his arms, sat up, and made a decent fist of looking interested. 'I'm all ears Boss.' he joked, trying to make light of it.

The rest of them stared down at the table, their silence eloquent.

'In that case Gordon,' Caton said. 'Takes us through it. If anyone has any questions, or thoughts, please hang onto them until Inspector Holmes has finished. That way we won't spoil his train of thought.'

'The Chinatown murders.' Holmes began. 'Just under two years ago - April sixth - the body of Michael Han, victim number one, was discovered in South Pump Street. Forensics revealed that his head had been smashed repeatedly against the wall beside which he had been found. Two days later - on the eighth - the body of James Lee was fished out of the Rochdale Canal; at the Ducie Street junction, beyond Back China Lane and the Dale Street car park. His head had also been smashed repeatedly against a wall; a different wall as it turned out - Accrington brick, as opposed to those from the Daubhill brickworks.'

No one laughed; they had heard it all before. Unabashed, he carried on.

'There were no signs that either victim had attempted to defend himself. Since nothing had been taken, robbery was ruled out as a motive. The victims didn't appear to have any connection with each other. Nor were they known to the police. Michael Han, thirty six years of age, of Cantonese origin, was a legal immigrant who arrived in Britain from Hong Kong ten years ago. Married, with three children, he lived in a council flat in Longsight, and worked as barman in the Arch Casino on Portland Street.'

He checked his notes again, although Caton knew for a fact that he'd memorised them.

'James Lee, forty six years of age, was British born; in Crumpsall Hospital to be precise. His parents arrived in the late fifties and worked their way to a decent standard of living; the father as cook in the restaurants in Chinatown, the mother on the checkout in a Chinese supermarket. James joined the Inland Revenue at eighteen, and worked his way up to higher grade inspector, based at New Century House on Upper Bridge Street. The investigating team followed three lines of enquiry. Not unreasonably, given that it was just nine weeks after the death of all those Chinese cockle-pickers in Morecambe Bay, they wondered if there might be a connection. They tied up with Operation Lund, which was working on that case, but after months of work drew a complete blank. The fact that Han worked in a Casino led them to check if he gambled, owed any money, might have been caught fiddling the till, or passing insider secrets. Another dead end. Their last hope revolved around the fact that Lee had received threats – to himself and his family – as a direct result of a tax investigation he'd been leading. The Revenue had discovered a big hole in the accounts of a major international corporation with its European Headquarters in Manchester. The Hang Xian Lo Corporation based in Shanghai, is one of the largest, and oldest post war companies in China, controls interests in the import and export of clothes, electrical goods and components, and oriental supermarket supplies. It has its own Panama registered shipping fleet, and has recently diversified into real estate in Shanghai, and Southern China.'

'You'd think they'd be able to afford a decent accountant then,' DC Woods ventured. Carter kicked him under the table.

'What?' Woods exclaimed, looking at his assailant with a pained expression. The rest of them glared at him. DI Holmes took the opportunity to clear his throat, and have sip of water, before carrying on.

'As the only Mandarin and Cantonese speaking inspector in the whole of the North West, James Lee drew the short straw. It was obvious to him from the start that, at the very least, he was looking at a major piece of tax evasion. Hundreds of thousands of pounds, possibly millions, unaccounted for. Within weeks of setting up his first meeting with HXL he got the first phone call. Back off before your wife and children get hurt. He reported it to his boss, who passed it on up the line. Lee soldiered on. Two weeks later his wife gets stopped in the street when she's out shopping. Tell your husband this is his last chance. He comes home to find her in a right panic. Tells his Boss he wants to be taken off the case. Our lot are called in from Barton Street to investigate the threats, but they're chasing shadows. In the meantime, the

Revenue suddenly abandons the case. No explanation, just a directive from London. The only justification given, that there was no likelihood of a successful outcome; whatever that meant. This is six months before Lee is killed; so, no obvious motive there. After that, the investigation team had nowhere to go. It ended up on our lap. We reviewed the case, and came up with the same conclusion. No suspects, and no obvious motive. It was also clear that the original investigation team had chased hypothetical leads rather than following the evidence, such as it was. So we started with what we did have.'

He ticked it off on his fingers.

'Both victims died in the same manner; they were both of Cantonese origin; both resident in Manchester; and there was one identical set of DNA found on the clothing of both victims. Mr Wallace ran the MO through the Police National Computer, and came up with three previous: one in Birmingham, one in London, and one in Liverpool. All within the past five years.'

He paused, and looked around the table to check that they were still with him.

'Whoever our perp' is, he gets around. The same DNA turned up on all of these other victims. Two of the victims were of Chinese origin – one of them Cantonese, the other, an illegal from Fujian. The third was Montenegrin. All of those cases also hit a dead end. Apart from the MO and the DNA there was no obvious link between the victims. No obvious motive. No one willing to talk. It was beginning to look like a professional hit man with a head banging fetish…or a random nutter. The Cantonese theme led us to take a look at Triads operating in those three cities. The Wo Shin Wo Triad, who are strong here in Manchester and in Birmingham, and the older 14K Triad running, among other things, loan sharking and extortion in Liverpool and in London. We got loads of help, but no concrete leads. It was suggested we ask the FBI to run the DNA through their database.'

'Remind us,' said Caton for the benefit of the newest member of the team. 'Why was that?'

'They have a much larger problem with the Triads, especially in San Francisco, New York and Los Angeles. They did as we asked; no joy there. Then the guys heading up Operation Lund suggested that we might like to go out to China with them. The Chinese Government were smarting from all the bad publicity around the Morecambe Bay disaster, and the international unease about the expansion in people trafficking, and agreed to co-operate. The Boss and I went out there. We hung around in Beijing, and then for a few days in Shanghai, waiting for permission, papers, and an escort. We finally got an internal flight to Hong Kong, where we were allowed to interview relatives of Michael Han and James Lee. Nothing doing. It wasn't that they were hiding anything – there was clearly nothing to hide. So we came home, and now it's up to SOCA to see what they can do with it.'

He pushed the file away from him, and took a sip of water.

'Thanks Gordon,' Caton said. 'So, what have we left out?' He scanned their faces. They shook their heads and shuffled in their chairs. 'In that case, put yourself in the place of the agents who are going to be grilling us tomorrow. What do you need to know?'

Detective Sergeant Carter put his hand up. 'What's your gut feeling Boss? Were these random, or a hit of some kind?'

'Gut doesn't come into it,' Caton told him. 'The evidence suggests they were all hits. The absence of any theft, sexual activity, or trophy collection, points that way. As does the fact that all of the men were found in places they were never known to have been before, and when there was no obvious reason why they would go there.'

'This doesn't have the hallmark of a Triad execution though, does it Boss?' DS Stuart asked.

'No it doesn't Jo,' Caton replied. 'We'd expect knifing, slashing, chopping...or more rarely, shooting.'

'And it's far more likely the body parts would be scattered to the four winds,' added Holmes grimly.

'What about street gangs?' DI Sarah Weston ventured.

'That's a possibility, but they'd have beaten them to death, or knifed them.' Caton responded.

DC Woods leant forward. 'In any case, they only found two other sets of DNA. With a gang, surely there would have been more?'

They stared at him in genuine surprise. Why the hell couldn't he make the effort to be like this all of the time, Caton reflected. There was a sharp knock on the door, and Ged the office manager popped her head in.

'I'm sorry sir. It's North Yorkshire Police on the phone asking for you. They say it's urgent.'

'Chief Inspector Caton? This is Chief Superintendent Speed, North Yorkshire Police.' The voice exuded authority, and just a little too much emphasis on the words Chief Superintendent. 'Officers from the Serious and Organised Crime Agency are on their way. Their Agent, Ray Barnes, thought you might be interested. He asked me to give you a call, and invite you to join him.'

'Where is this exactly sir?' asked Caton.

'Do you know the cooling towers, just to the East of Ferrybridge, on the M62?'

Caton saw them in his mind's eye. Eight massive concrete towers, belching steam at the side of the motorway, like some demented giant egg timers. Hard to miss.

'Yes sir.'

'Well that's Eggborough. You leave the motorway there at the junction with the A19, and head south, signposted Doncaster. Take the second right. Whitefield Lane. We've got a patrol car there. It'll bring you straight to the sand pits.'

'What is this incident exactly?' Caton asked.

Caton heard the slow intake of breath. He imagined Speed puffing out his chest, relishing the drama of the moment.

'We have a number of bodies here Chief Inspector. Five to be precise. The cause of their death has yet to be ascertained. Not to mention how they came to be here.'

Five dead bodies, almost sixty miles away, in a Yorkshire sand pit. A long way from Caton's patch.

'I'm curious Chief Superintendent,' Caton said. 'What does it have to do with me or GMP?'

'Good question.' Speed replied. It sounded as though he was sucking on a lemon. Caton guessed that he was seriously put out that the Agency had turned up, and that he now had Greater Manchester Police getting in on the act.

'Mr Barnes assured me that you would want to join him.' Speed continued. 'Just tell him, he said, these victims...they're all Chinese.'

3

Caton moved into the centre lane, shifted into fifth gear, and turned on the radio. He liked this motorway. On a fine day there was a kind of majesty to these moors at the heart of the Pennine range. On a bad day - and there were plenty of those on the highest motorway in the country - spray brought visibility down to ten metres or less, and cloud and mist obscured the hills on either side.

This morning the sky was clear, blue, and empty but for criss-crossing condensation trails from jets bound for Europe and beyond. He glanced to his right at the brooding heights of Saddleworth Moor still in its brown winter coat. Spikes of green rush stood out against the broad sweeps of heather. Occasional slashes of rich black peat scarred the hillside, exposed by the fierce wind and rain that swept across these grit stone uplands.

Each time he passed this spot Caton recalled the three small bodies retrieved from shallow graves on the side of the moor, and the one that lay there still; undiscovered, but not forgotten. On his eighteenth birthday Caton's aunt had presented him with a replica copy of the Manchester Guardian, for the day on which he was born; July twenty third, 1963. It was how he learned that he had entered the world on the same day that Pauline Reade, the first victim of Ian Brady and Myra Hindley, had gone missing. It probably explained why he had chosen the notorious Moors Murders as part of his final dissertation at University, and helped to explain why he'd decided on the police service as a career. Six years later, in 1987, he was a young PC in South Manchester when the body of Pauline Reade was finally recovered, and reunited with her grieving family. Five young lives cut short, four of them consigned to moorland graves. Now here he was, twenty years later, with five more bodies waiting to be brought home.

He pressed the CD disc button, and turned up the volume. The opening chords of Hotel California filled the car, and wrapped around him. He checked the outside temperature on the onboard computer. Three degrees centigrade. California this was not.

The concrete cooling towers reared up before him. Eight plumes of steam, trailing west, bore testimony to the bitter East wind that had swept in from the Urals, unimpeded on its journey across the flat lands of northern Europe, and the North Sea, before driving up the Humber estuary. Three of these towers had collapsed back in the sixties; inherent design faults exposed by turbulence on the leeward side. Looking at them now, planted solidly, it was hard to credit. Just as it was hard to believe that someone had chosen to dump five bodies here.

The motorway sign for the A19 and Eggborough exit told him there was a half a mile to go. He glanced across to the right beyond the westbound carriageway, and glimpsed a clutch of vehicles with the blue and yellow markings of the Yorkshire force, strung out beside two hill-like mounds incongruous in this agricultural landscape of level fields.

At the bottom of the slip road diversion signs had been set up. Caton joined the queue as it crawled around the roundabout. At the fifth exit a motor cycle policeman was directing the traffic away from the road to Doncaster, across which his bike had formed a temporary barrier. Caton placed his portable blue light on the dashboard, and switched it on. The patrolman waved him forward, and leant towards the open window of the Octavia.

'Detective Chief Inspector Caton. Greater Manchester Police.' Caton told him, reaching awkwardly over and behind his seat, trying to extricate his warrant card from the inside pocket of his jacket, hanging from the rear grab handle.

'It's alright Sir. I was told to expect you.' The patrolman smiled, stepped back, and waved him through.

At least someone's pleased to see me, Caton reflected. By comparison, the two officers in the patrol car at the entrance to Whitefield Lane gave him a hard time. Grim faced, they insisted on seeing his ID, and examined it together as though it was somehow alien. They made him wait while they radioed through to Chief Superintendent Speed for confirmation that he was bona fide. This wasn't attention to detail Caton decided. This went back six centuries or more. The Wars of the Roses; The White Rose of Yorkshire versus the Red of Lancashire. This was the kind of stunt that DC Woods would have pulled. Eventually, grinning like idiots, they waved him through. He watched them in his mirror as he drove away. One of them gave a mock salute, and both of them burst out laughing. If he had been in two minds before, this had decided him. Detective Constable David Woods would have to go.

The lane cut back towards the motorway between neatly portioned fields, until it ran parallel to the westbound carriageway. Three quarters of a mile on, where it merged with another lane, he found his way blocked by incident tape. Beyond it, he could see the cars and vans that had caught his eye from the motorway. A woman sergeant in uniform approached him, clutching a clipboard and pen.

'Good morning sir,' solemn, but not unfriendly. 'Can I have your name please?' She found it on the second sheet, ticked it off, and recorded the time in the third column. 'I'm afraid you'll have to leave your car here sir. If you could just pull off behind the van in front of you. And I'd be obliged if you could leave a gap of about five metres.' She stepped to the side, and lifted the tape high enough for the car to pass under.

Caton could see immediately why he'd been asked to leave a gap. This was the last of a line of three mortuary vans. Five bodies into three vans, and no cross contamination? Caton didn't see GMP scene of crime managers standing for that. He emptied the pockets of his jacket of everything but his biro, notebook, and voice recorder. The rest he placed in the glove compartment. He climbed out of the car into a vicious wind chill. He put on his jacket, released the boot, and opened his incident bag. He had no idea how far he would have to walk, and decided against putting on his overshoes and Tyvek all in-one, until he reached the search cordon. He shut the boot, locked the car, and set off. On the way he passed the vans, a mobile incident room, and a small mobile kitchen from which drifted the tempting smell of freshly brewed coffee.

The lane curved away from the motorway; more of a surfaced track now than a lane. It circled the base of the spoil heap of a large sand pit. On the right, he passed a much lower mound, perhaps a quarter of a mile in circumference, enclosing three, perhaps four, circular expanses of water; empty pits, now full of rainwater. Rounding the southernmost slope of the larger of the mounds, he came upon a hive of activity.

A narrow corridor of tape marked the common approach that led to a large, rectangular, white gazebo like structure, several metres from the track, on the lower slope of the grass covered mound. Three people stood with their backs to him talking at the corner of what he took to be the leeward entrance to the tent. Two others stood on the track itself, holding plastic covered clipboards, and a mixture of paper and plastic evidence bags. Twenty metres further on, two figures on bended knee were working on a small patch of land that had been taped off at the side of the track. Along the summit of the mound, and down its side, a dozen or so officers he assumed to be Tactical Aid, were advancing slowly, head down, line abreast. All wore their lightweight polythene fibre clothing, including masks; as much, he suspected, against the cruel wind as the possibility of contamination. Caton found himself shivering. He climbed into his protective suit, and pulled on his hood. He took a moment to commit the scene to memory, and then approached the tent.

'And you are?'

The voice, bluff, pompous, and commanding, was unmistakeable; This would be Chief Superintendent Speed. The Tyvec, presumably borrowed at the scene, was at least two sizes too small for him. The hood clung tightly to his head, and the elasticated waist strained to contain a stomach yet to recover from seasonal excess. Thin beads of sweat carved narrow paths through the steam on his lenses. At five feet four inches tall, he had the appearance of a demented gnome. Caton held out his hand.

'Detective Chief Inspector Tom Caton, Greater Manchester Police.'

'Oh yes. Caton, GMP. I'm Speed.'

They shook hands, latex against latex.

'The pathologist and the photographers have been and gone.' Speed told him. 'Our scene of crime crew is doing their thing. You'd better come and meet Yeadon. She's the senior investigating officer.'

Caton was struck by how much Detective Superintendent Sally Yeadon resembled his immediate boss, Superintendent Helen Gates. The same trim build, the same intelligent searching brown eyes, the same loose black curls poking out from beneath her hood, the same air of tough, no nonsense, professionalism. At five foot eight she was a good deal taller, but in every other way, the double of Helen Gates.

'I gather from Agent Barnes that you're working an investigation that may be related?' she said. 'He'll be with us shortly by the way.'

'I don't know about that,' Caton replied. 'Both of mine were of Chinese heritage, but the deaths were separate in place and time, and the manner of death was singular.'

Her eyebrows arched. 'Singular? In what way?'

'Their heads had been smashed repeatedly against a wall.'

She smiled grimly. 'That's definitely not what we've got here.'

'What have you got?'

'Come and have a look.'

She pulled back the flap. 'Hang on a minute guys,' she said. The two SOCOs sat back on their haunches, giving him a more or less unrestricted view. A pair of lights clipped to the plastic struts cast shadows across the macabre scene.

The smell was overpowering. He was used to the stench of death, but it was not just that. There was also the unmistakeable odour of human vomit. He felt the bile rise in his stomach, and put his hand to his mouth, fighting back the gagging response.

At first glance it was difficult to tell how many bodies there were. He could make out two on the extremities of the group, arms akimbo, legs splayed. Another lay in the centre, on top of one more body, perhaps two. Then he remembered. Five bodies in total; so it must be two. They all wore woollen jackets and trousers, and sturdy boots or shoes. On the face that he could see most clearly there was a strange colouration to the cheeks; cherry red. The others looked as though they had spent time in a freezer, so pale were their skin and lips. The youngest looking had blisters around his mouth. Caton put their ages at between twenty and thirty; everything to live for. He already had a pretty good idea what he was looking at. Illegal immigrants in search of a better life brought here on the back of their families' life savings, not to mention a pile of debt to be worked off. Only to have those hopes and aspirations snuffed out, at a disused sand pit, in a foreign land.

'The pathologist can't be sure till he gets them back to the mortuary,' DS Yeadon told him. 'But it's almost certainly carbon monoxide poisoning.'

Caton had guessed as much. He had seen that discolouration once before. In a supposedly empty council flat in Collyhurst. A family had been squatting there. Thieves had stripped out some of the copper piping, and the debris had blocked up the only flue from the gas boiler. Six dead, four of them children. They had been dead for three days before they were discovered. He had seen some things in his time, but the sight of that had never really left him.

'Could be poisoning from another source,' she continued, 'But his money's on carbon monoxide.'

She let the flap fall, and stepped back a few paces, allowing the SOCOs to return to their grim task.

'They were dumped here then?' Caton said. It was more of an observation than a question. She nodded.

'There are tyre tracks in the grass back there where it came off the lane. It looks as though they thought about dumping them in the deep water at the centre of this pit. There are two sets of footprints in the grass leading to the top of the mound, and you can see where they turned the lorry round about a hundred yards further on. Must have decided it was too difficult, or panicked. Either way, it looks as though they just them hauled out of the back, and then literally slung them up here,' she paused for a moment, picturing the scene. 'Like infected carcasses.'

'Why not the pools at the end of the lane?' Caton wondered. 'No hills to climb there.'

'Too close to the Motorway,' she said. 'They'd probably have shown up in the spill-out from headlights. All it would have needed was a lorry cutting back into the inside lane at just the right place, and they'd have been lit up like a Christmas tree.'

'Who found them?'

'Three young lads who got mini dirt bikes for Christmas. They come up here to race them. It's about the only off-road site for miles. They're not supposed to be here of course, but it's better than having them doing thirty miles an hour, unlicensed and uninsured, on the roads and pavements of the villages round here.'

'What time was this?'

'Quarter to seven this morning. Seems they were hoping to do a spot of fishing first. Caught more than they bargained for.'

'How long have the bodies been there?'

'Overnight. We know that, because these lads were here until dusk yesterday, which was about quarter to seven. There are also people who walk their dogs up here of an evening, so it's likely someone would have spotted them if they'd been dumped any earlier.'

'When did they die?' Caton asked, rather than when were they killed. However inhumane the disposal of these bodies, there was always the possibility that it had been an accident. It wouldn't be the first time.

She looked at him, and smiled knowingly. 'He won't tell us that until we get his post mortem report. But his initial stab at it is sometime in the twelve hours before he got to examine them. Not more than twelve hours, and not less than four.'

'What time did he examine them?'

'Just before eight o'clock this morning.'

Caton was wondering what to ask next when Speed arrived, accompanied by a man about half his width, and a head taller. In his early fifties.

'This is Mr Barnes,' he said. 'From the Serious and Organised Crime Agency. I hope you two gentlemen aren't going to keep Detective Superintendent Yeadon too long? She has a lot to attend to.'

'It's alright Sir,' she assured him. 'It helps to have colleagues asking questions like this. Even retelling the story helps to clarify things in my mind.'

Caton warmed to her even more. Speed muttered something unintelligible, and turned on his heels.

Caton and Yeadon introduced themselves.

'I'm sorry I'm late,' Ray Barnes told them. His voice was deep, and measured. 'I had to make the final arrangements for the seminar tomorrow. In any case, SOCA has no intention of hijacking your case Superintendent. It's just that it's clearly in both our interests to work together on this one.'

'No problem,' Yeadon told him 'Something like is always going to fall within your remit. And it's obvious to anyone that SOCA can save us time and effort.'

Probably not obvious to your boss, Caton was thinking. She turned to him.

'Look, Tom, why don't you go on back to the incident van and get a warm drink. It's freezing up here. I'll run through it again with Mr Barnes, and then he can join you there.'

29

Tom already. 'What about you?' he said. 'Can I get them to bring you a drink up, you must be frozen.'

She smiled. 'No thanks, not if the others aren't having one. I'll call a break shortly, and we'll all come down together,' she struggled to push back the elasticated cuff on her sleeve, and checked her watch. 'Eleven thirty five. Didn't get breakfast either. We'll be just in time for brunch. Tell them to get the bacon on.'

They sat inside the mobile incident room eating bacon barms, and drinking strong Yorkshire tea. Caton wiped a dribble of ketchup from the side of his mouth. It didn't seem right somehow. Stuffing their faces in the warm interior of the van, while those five young men lay out there, twisted, cold, alone.

'That's the most likely,' Agent Barnes was saying. 'Came in on a truck, probably through Hull. Dead on arrival. It's happened before. Dover in 2000. Sixty Chinese illegal immigrants in a truck that had just arrived from Zeebrugge. Fifty-eight of them died, two of them women. Only two survived.'

'That wasn't CO_2 though was it? Didn't they suffocate?' said Sally Yeadon.

The agent nodded. 'Combination of that, and the heat apparently. They'd spent the afternoon before in a sealed container on the docks in Belgium. The temperature had rocketed into the mid thirties centigrade, and someone had turned the cooling system off. Probably to save money. Not only that, but the air vent had been closed.'

'Why the hell would anyone do that?' Yeadon asked him.

He shrugged. 'They never found out. My guess is they didn't want to risk anyone hearing that there were people inside.'

They drank their tea in silence, trying not to think about the scene inside that container in the hours before they died.

'Those five out there. Some of them had been sick.' Caton mused. 'Could that have been a sea crossing, or the carbon monoxide?'

'Either, or both, I would think,' Barnes replied. 'What difference does it make?'

'Well, if it was because they were sea sick, then that suggests they were still alive when they arrived in England. In any case the carbon monoxide would probably have come from the engine exhaust. And, you're not allowed to run the engine while the ferries are at sea. And if the pathologist is right, then they died sometime between eight o'clock last night and four o'clock this morning. It's unlikely they died abroad, or at sea.'

Sally Yeadon put her mug down. 'So either there was a leak from the exhaust that found its way into the main compartment, while they were travelling, or someone deliberately poisoned them.'

'After bringing them half way across the world, and almost certainly having further payments to collect from them.' Caton observed. 'Why would they want to kill them?'

None of them had an answer to that.

'One thing is certain,' she said. 'Whoever dumped them here is either local, or regularly travels this way. It wouldn't be an obvious place to choose in the dark. Anyway, we've got the tyre tracks. Finding that lorry would be a start .'

4

It was gone two in the afternoon when Caton arrived back at the station. Holmes had already prepared a draft Power Point presentation for him to look at. Caton was impressed, not just by its quality, but with its brevity. He knew that had it been left to him it would have been a third as long again. Not only that, but it marked another stage in Gordon's transition, from old style cop to twenty first century detective. Holmes drummed his fingers nervously on the table top.

'What do you think Boss?'

'It's good Gordon. Really good. Better than I would have done.'

A boyish grin suffused the inspector's face. It took several decades off him when that happened. 'Do you reckon there's any connection between those bodies, and ours Boss?' he asked.

'I've no idea. If we knew a bit more about what led our two to their deaths, I'd be able to make an educated guess, but as it is…God knows. Anyway, after tomorrow I don't suppose it'll have anything to do with us. I'm just about to see what DS Gates has got lined up for us.'

Holmes hauled himself to his feet. 'I'll leave you to it then,' he said. 'Finish boxing up the case files. I just hope we get something fast. There are several SIOs lining up to bag this incident room. I don't fancy having to trawl across to the other side of the patch, to some box room.'

'That's not your real problem though is it?' Caton said mischievously. 'You just don't like the thought of your precious Mondeo sitting unprotected in some back street behind a suburban nick.'

Holmes settled for closing the door a little more heavily than he might otherwise have done. A hollow victory, but just about all that was left in this bounded world of hierarchy and political correctness.

'You did your best Tom,' Detective Superintendent Gates told him. 'Sometimes we just have to admit there isn't enough evidence, and put it on the shelf until something turns up. You know that.'

Caton did. That didn't stop him from waking in the early hours from time to time wrestling with a dormant case that had got under his skin. Usually it was a child or young woman. But not always.

'This Yorkshire thing,' Gates said tentatively, 'There's no way you're going to get caught up in that is there?'

'I doubt it Ma'am' he said. 'They've already got The Agency involved, the last thing they need is another force muddying the waters.'

She wasn't convinced. 'SOCA must have known that, so why did they send for you?'

'I assume, because there was an outside chance there might be a connection. That, and because I'm delivering the presentation tomorrow. But I doubt that it will lead anywhere.'

She nodded. 'Good, because we could do with some help with the Ramsbottom Rapist.' She paused long enough for him to guess that she was working out quite how to put her next question. 'Your Kate Webb is involved in that isn't she?'

Your Kate Webb. Caton could tell that she was covering both the professional relationship between them that had started with the hunt for Bojangles, and the more personal and intimate one that everyone in the force now seemed to be aware of. He knew exactly what was worrying her. He and Kate had made a great team, but it had nearly ended in disaster. Gates was wondering how it might affect their judgement, and how other people would feel having to work with them in the same team. He decided to face it head on.

'Yes, Kate has been consulted on that one. It shouldn't be a problem working together again. It wasn't last time'

'I've already spoken to the senior investigating officer,' she said. 'Tony Burton. He doesn't have a problem with it, so it's decided. You can start the day after tomorrow.' There was another pause. This time more pregnant than the last. 'I'm afraid your team will have to move over to the Bury major incident room; they'll make room for you.'

Caton should not have been surprised, but he was. 'Vacate Longsight? For how long?'

'How long is a piece string?'

Great, he thought. They're going to love this. Playing second fiddle on someone else's investigation, and having to move out of a place that had become like a second home.

'Very good Ma'am,' he said, through gritted teeth.

He sensed her smiling sympathetically. 'Don't worry Tom, It's only until something better crops up.'

Caton had to hand it to her. She was not only the youngest, fastest promoted officer in GMP, but also a damn good detective who also understood the politics of modern policing. And she could read your mind over the telephone. A skill Caton was still honing.

'Let me know how you get on tomorrow,' she said, and ended the call before he could think of a suitable response.

'Why the hell didn't you tell me!'

Caton held the phone away from his ear. He looked at his watch. It was only ten minutes since his conversation with Helen Gates. Chief Superintendent Hadfield, Head of the Greater Manchester Major Incident Team must have just got off the phone with her. He was spitting feathers.

'I did tell Superintendent Gates,' Caton said mildly, sending a torpedo, hitting him broadside. He could picture Hadfield red in the face, reflecting on the chain of command about which he was so obsessed. There was no way he was going to criticise her to a junior officer.

'Only after the event.' Hadfield managed finally.

That wasn't true, but Caton decided not to push his luck. He held his counsel and let Hadfield surge on.

'I've just had the Chief Constable of the North Yorkshire Force on the phone, wondering why one of my team is meddling in one of their investigations.'

That will have been Speed, Caton decided, no surprise there.

'I was asked to attend by SOCA, Sir,' he said. 'And the invitation came via the Yorkshire force.'

'And that's another thing,' Hadfield pressed on.

'When were you going to tell me about this seminar?' He was on overdrive.

'I did tell Superintendent Gates, Sir.'

This time he heard the sharp intake of breath, and the slow exhalation as Hadfield pulled himself together. Caton was beginning to weary of these exchanges. It made him feel like the archetypal stroppy detective in a crime novel, justifiably attracting the ire of his senior officers. The only difference here was that he never saw himself as stroppy. If anything, he actively avoided being difficult. And since when had Hadfield needed a reason to go off on one? He imagined him sitting back in his chair, tugging his jacket down over a spreading waist. Measuring his reply more carefully, trying to recover his dignity, seeking some gravitas in his parting words.

'I expect a written account of that seminar on my desk the day after tomorrow. And you don't make any promises on behalf of GMP, Caton. Not in relation to your time, nor that of anyone else. Do you understand?'

'Yes Sir.'

But then understanding is not the same as complying, Caton reminded himself. Everyone knows that.

It was nearly six o'clock by the time Caton had cleared the backlog of emails, emptied his in-tray, and reduced his work pending to Dave Woods' final appraisal review, a couple of surveys, and three written reports. With tomorrow taken up by the seminar his in-tray would be overflowing again in no time. He would be kissing goodbye to much of the weekend. But at least there was this evening to look forward to. He turned off his computer, put the briefing papers for the morning in his lap top case, locked the door, and left. On his way to the car park he met DS Stuart coming the other way. She gave him a wide grin.

'Someone loves you Boss. There's a great big bouquet at reception with your name on it.'

'They're not for me,' he said. 'It's Kate's birthday. She's not at the University today so I had them delivered here. I'll spring them on her later, when she thinks I've forgotten.'

'Taking her somewhere nice I hope?'

'I don't know. It's a surprise. Her choice.'

She raised her eyebrows in mock surprise. 'Shouldn't that be the other way round; you surprising her?'

'I don't know that she trusts me to choose.' Caton told her. 'The important thing is I'll be paying.'

'Make sure you do Boss. And have a good time.'

'Don't worry,' he said. 'We will.'

Feng Yi was beginning to regret having left the security of their refuge. His friend Zheng Hu had found the Bolton takeaway with surprising ease; his passable English had helped with the two lorry drivers that had given them lifts. The greeting from the owner of the takeaway - the brother of Zheng's father-in-law - had been ecstatic. Until, that was, the real reason for their visit had emerged. Although some bedding was found, and it was arranged that they should sleep in a rear storeroom, there was obvious tension in the family. They were visibly shaken. But not as much as the two kitchen hands, fellow illegal immigrants from elsewhere in Fujian. Anyone could tell they were scared witless. Feng understood. They had borrowed from the snakeheads half the sum they needed to get to Britain. Two years down the line, and not yet halfway through paying back the loan, the last thing they needed was these fugitives hanging around; hunted by a gang like theirs that came to collect each week. And so he had slipped away in the night.

If Feng had felt guilty about putting those people in danger, how much more responsible he felt for Wu Ling whom he had promised to protect. And now she was God knows where. He had brought shame on his mother and father. If it turned out that he had abandoned her his parents would never be able to face her family, or the rest of the village. He had rung them to say that he had arrived safely, and told a pack of lies about a job and shelter. He had even lied about Wu Ling being fine, but he knew her family would soon become suspicious if she did not call herself.

At first the logic had been crystal clear. As clear as the waters of the Flowing Fragrance Gully. Manchester had been their original destination. They had been promised work in Chinatown. Wu Ling would have been brought here. She was pretty, very pretty, and a new arrival. He had only to ask around among fellow Fujianese in Chinatown he reasoned; show them the photos he had taken of her on his mobile phone. Someone would have seen her. Once he knew where she was, he would work out how to get her away to a place of safety.

Faced with the reality, he was no longer sure. Chinatown was so much smaller than he had expected. It was a rectangle of streets, five blocks by three, teeming with restaurants, supermarkets, banks, bakeries, and herbalists. He had taken the precaution of coming in the evening to lessen the risk of discovery, only to find this the most colourful, brightly lit, part of the city. The biggest surprise came as he turned the corner into Faulkner Street, and was confronted by the Imperial Chinese Archway.

He stood transfixed, staring up at the magnificent structure towering above the narrow street. A small group of tourists, fellow countrymen and women, appeared as if from nowhere, pushing forward, surrounding him as they pressed to take their photographs. Their guide stood to one side, her closed umbrella raised above her head; one moment a rallying point, the next a pointer.

'This is the only true Imperial Chinese Archway in the whole of Europe,' she began. 'It is even more magnificent than the more famous arch in San Francisco, America. This unique Ching Dynasty Arch, a gift from the people of China to the City of Manchester, was built, erected, and decorated by a team of craftsmen and engineers from Beijing. In recognition of the magnificence of this gift, it was officially opened by his Royal Highness Prince Philip, Duke of Edinburgh, Consort to the Queen of England.'

With open-mouthed, drop-jawed surprise, and shrieks of disbelief, they pressed closer, almost suffocating him. An elbow struck him above his right temple as a mobile phone was thrust high to capture the moment. He found it impossible to move.

'Note the exquisite decorations of the arch which include areas of Chinese ceramic, lacquer, paint, and layers of gold leaf. This arch symbolises the hopes of the People of China for the peace, prosperity, and health of the city.' The umbrella whirled several times above her head before stabbing to the right. 'Behind me are the ornamental gardens, and the two pavilions in which we are invited to rest. But we do not have time to rest. First, we must eat.'

Umbrella aloft, she turned on her heel, and marched off. With an excited cheer, the crowd surged after her like a swarm of chattering locusts. For a moment he feared they might carry him with them. Instead they swirled past, leaving him standing dazed and alone.

Uncertain of his bearings, he turned right beneath the arch and headed on up Faulkner Street past the New Hong Kong Restaurant. Hunger caused his belly to rumble; fear caused the pulse in his neck to begin to throb.

The taxi dropped them at the corner of Charlotte Street and Portland Street. Caton paid the driver, and stepped back onto the pavement. Behind them lay Chinatown, ahead was the start of the Gay Village.

'OK,' he said. 'That narrows it down. We're talking Mediterranean, Asian Fusion, Japanese, Chinese, Indian, Thai, Vietnamese, or Italian. Probably not Indian, because then we'd probably be in Rusholme on the Curry Mile.'

Kate grabbed his arm, and slipped her own around it. 'You're so clever, Tom Caton. I'm amazed you never considered becoming a detective?' She whirled him round, and started off down Charlotte Street.

Caton began to check off the possibilities. There

were three restaurants here that he had previously brought her to for lunch. There was another new buffet style one that he knew she rated for the same purpose. But for dinner, there were only three that had become firm joint favourites. As they crossed the junction with Faulkner Street he glanced West at the Imperial Arch, gleaming red, gold, and green in the reflected light. She led him left into George Street towards two strong contenders; *Pacific* with its Chinese and Thai cuisine each on separate floors; and his personal favourite, the *Little Yang Sing*. Kate watched his face as they sailed past.

'Getting warmer,' she said, squeezing playfully.

They were forced to step smartly into a doorway as a babbling crowd pressed past, led by a formidable young woman, holding aloft a furled umbrella.

The field had narrowed considerably. If he was a betting man he would have put his shirt on it. 'Why don't I take us the rest of the way?' He suggested smugly.

'Just for that, I may very well change my mind and take you somewhere else.' She said.

'What about the reservation?'

She laughed. 'No problem. It's in your name!'

Feng Yi had quickly discovered that it was pointless trying the front entrance to the restaurants. The front of house staff were all British born Chinese or Cantonese. The majority of the customers were not Chinese, and those that were did not come from Fujian province. Instead, he had worked his way around to the narrow dark alleys behind the restaurants, where the black plastic bags of rubbish had begun to pile up, and clouds of steam billowing from the open doors and windows carried the familiar smells of cooking oil, rice, and spices, into the cold night air.

Occasionally, one or two of the kitchen workers would emerge into the alley for a breath of air, or to have a quick smoke. Then he would approach, show them the photograph, and ask if they had seen her. Always he was eyed with suspicion. On several occasions he sensed their reticence was more to do with fear than ignorance. Just when he had begun to doubt this strategy, he saw in the eyes of a young man about his own age, a glimmer of recognition. He pressed him further, and felt sure he was about to tell him something when one of the cooks appeared in the doorway, and shouted something in Cantonese, causing him to hurry inside. The cook made it clear by the tone of his voice, and the wave of the cleaver in his hand, that Feng was not welcome there, and so he pretended to walk away. Once the door had closed, he crossed the alley, melted into the shadows, and began to wait.

'Great choice.' Caton told her. 'Even better than the last time I was here.' He lifted a plump piece of braised duckling from the spicy yellow and black bean casserole. 'I like the way they've refurbished it too. I'm surprised they didn't do this after it was rebuilt following the fire.'

'I don't think modern 1930's Shanghai style décor was the rage then. ' Kate replied, using her chopsticks to deftly wrap a whirl of Chinese greens around a succulent piece of monkfish fillet.

They ate for a while in silence, savouring the food, comfortable in each other's company.

As the meal reached its conclusion, the conversation drifted inexorably to their work.

'I don't know if DI Burton's told you,' Caton said. 'But I'm supposed to be bringing my team over to work with his.'

'The Ramsbottom Rapist?'

'That's not going to be a problem is it?'

'No, of course not.'

'That's what I told Hadfield.'

'Was it his idea?'

'No…Helen Gates'. There's nothing in the pipeline for us, so I assume she went for the one with the highest profile.'

Kate smiled thinly. 'Well she was right there. Three women, and two girls, raped or assaulted in the space of six weeks, and not a lot to go on.'

Caton took a sip of his Tsing Tao beer. 'He must have left traces?'

'Oh, there are plenty of those, but you know the score. They're not much use without a suspect.'

'Which is where you come in?'

'Precisely,' she said. 'No pressure there then.' She made to top up her jasmine tea and finding the tea pot empty removed the lid, as a signal that it needed refilling.

'So what have you got?' he asked.

Kate shook her head. 'Oh no you don't!' She said. 'This is my birthday. Do you really think I want to spend it talking about a rapist, and his victims. You'll find out soon enough. Until then, I'm sure you can come up with a more appropriate subject,' She leant forward into the light pooling in the centre of the table, her auburn hair a shimmering contrast to the gold and blue cushions on the banquette. 'Like how very young, and beautiful, I am.'

They crept from either end of the alley, keeping to the shadows. They were almost upon him before he saw them. Only at the last moment did a shaft of light slanting from an open window flash on the blade of a knife, and alert him to their presence. There were five of them, armed with knives and cleavers. Resistance was futile. His arms were pinioned behind his back. Masking tape was wrapped several times around his mouth, and across his eyes. They dragged him to the end of the alley where a large black 4X4 with tinted windows waited. They bundled him into the back, climbed in, and closed the doors.

'Thank you for a lovely meal,' Kate said as they descended the steps to the pavement. 'For the flowers, and for these,' she fingered the string of pearls around her neck. 'They're beautiful.'

Caton kissed her lightly on the lips. 'Not as beautiful as you,' he grinned. 'Not that you were fishing for compliments of course.'

She laughed; a deep, sexy, throaty laugh. 'I hope that wasn't the only present you were thinking of giving me tonight?'

'In that case,' Caton said. 'I'll get a taxi.'

She raised the collar on her coat, shook her shoulder length hair loose around it, and reached for his hand. 'Don't do that. I need to walk that meal off. We wouldn't want to hurry things would we?'

They waited impatiently by the traffic lights at the junction with Portland Street. As the lights changed to amber, he tightened his grip, and held her back as a black 4x4, with smoked glass windows, cruised past, heading South, towards the University Precinct.

5

'Wake up lazybones.'

Caton rubbed his eyes, forced them open, and peered at the vision slowly forming before him. Kate's face was in shadow. The light around the edges of the blinds cast her auburn hair into a flaming halo, accentuating, even in the half light, the porcelain paleness of her skin. Three months into their relationship he still could not believe his luck.

He forced himself up onto his elbows.

'What time is it?'

She put the mug of tea on his bedside cabinet, and sat for a moment on the duvet, making it impossible for him to move.

'Six forty five. I told you, I have to be away early. I want to call at my place before I go in to work. Your seminar doesn't start till ten, so I thought I'd let you lie in.' She leant forward, her musky smell intoxicating. She kissed him lightly on his lips. 'By the look of you, you need all the sleep you can get,'

'As I recall,' he said. 'We didn't get too much last night.'

'And as I recall, I rather think we did.'

'Sleep I mean.'

'The trouble with you, Tom Caton, is that you want to have your cake, and eat it.' She sat back, allowing him to sit up and reach for his tea. 'That's the thing with Chinese food, all that carbohydrate for energy,

46

and the other stuff to get the hormones flowing.'

Caton grinned. 'So that's why you chose the Yang Sing. So you could have your wicked way with me?'

She pouted her lips, and put on a faux French accent. 'A girl has to do what a girl has to do.'

'I can't argue with that,' he said. 'Perhaps this girl should feel free to do it more often.' He switched on the bedside light, the better to see her. Her green eyes flashed provocatively.

'That all depends on how this girl is treated,' she said.

'More flowers and presents?'

'That wouldn't go amiss; plus respect, and admiration, and a little awe,' she paused. 'And rapt attention on shopping trips.'

Forgetting the cup in his other hand, he grabbed a pillow from her side of the bed and threw it at her. As she sidestepped hot tea coursed down his bare chest. He cursed, and rubbed his chest with his free hand.

'That serves you right,' she said from the doorway. 'Have a good day, I'll see you tonight.'

Caton heard her collecting her things from the kitchen table, walking down the hallway, closing the door behind her. He put the mug down carefully, sunk back onto the pillows, and closed his eyes for a moment, recalling the passion of the night before; luxuriating in the afterglow. Not since the start of his relationship with Laura, and the first year of their marriage, had he experienced anything like this. Perhaps not even then. Although Laura had been his first lover, and his only wife, the impact of her affair, and departure, and the years that followed when he found himself unable to commit to another woman,

47

had built up in him both a hunger and a doubt verging on despair. Kate, he realised, had assuaged the first, and swept away the second.

Gordon Holmes stood pointing at his watch on the pavement outside the Edwardian Radisson Hotel.

'What time do you call this Boss? I thought you said half past nine?'

'Five minutes late isn't so bad,' Caton countered.

'Not when I've had to walk across town. I suppose you've parked on the Great Northern rather than use the tram?'

'You never know when we might get called out. Someone has to think about these things.'

'True, but not very green.' Caton looked up the façade of the imposing stone building with its classical Palladian arches and pediments, and the Wedgwood blue historical plaque marking the infamous Peterloo Massacre. In August 1819, here in St Peter's fields, a crowd estimated at between sixty and eighty thousand had come to protest peacefully at the Corn Laws. Magisterial incompetence, poor communication, and lack of discipline among the mounted yeomanry, resulted in eleven dead, and scores of wounded; slashed by sabres and trampled in the rush to escape. In its day the furore that followed had been greater than that after the 1989 Hillsborough disaster.

'Did you ever come here when it was The Free Trade Hall?' he asked

'Just the once. The wife bought us tickets for my birthday. It was Tom Paxton; the American folk singer.'

'I didn't know you were a fan of folk?'

'I'm not. Marilyn is.'

'Where did you go for her birthday?'

'I thought Manchester United versus Arsenal, and a meal afterwards at The Old Grapes. She thought My Fair Lady, and a meal afterwards at the Siam Orchid.'

'And?'

'She won. Just to rub it in, United won too.' The hurt was still etched on his face.

'Birthdays, Gordon,' Caton said to cheer him up. 'Who needs them?'

'I suppose you came here a lot Boss?'

'As a matter of fact I did. My father used to play with the Halle, and with a brass band. My mother brought me a lot. So I was introduced to classical and brass from an early age. After they died in the accident I couldn't face it. So I turned to rock instead. Do you remember the Anti-Section 28 Rally in February '88?'

Holmes pulled a face. 'Do I beggary! I was on duty in Albert Square. There were two hundred thousand gays, lesbians, and students like you lot, squeezed in there. It was a bloody nightmare.'

'A peaceful nightmare.'

'Go on, I'll grant you that.'

'Well there was a star studded concert here,' Caton said. 'And I had a ticket. And I was here in 1994 for the "Fender Stratocaster 40th Anniversary" concert. There was Frankie Miller, Irish Rock legend Rory Gallagher, and when John Verity performed "Stay With Me Baby" it brought the entire audience to its feet.' He saw the glazed look on Gordon's face. 'You don't have the faintest idea of what I'm talking about do you?'

'To be quite honest, Boss, no I don't.'

'There were two gigs though,' Caton continued.

'I would have given anything to have been at. The first was the night that Bob Dylan ditched his acoustic guitar, went electric, and was heckled from the crowd as a traitor to folk. The second was in June 1976. In the upstairs room– the Lesser Free Trade Hall – there was a concert by the Sex Pistols which most people believe started the whole punk and new wave movement. There were only about forty people there, but among them were Tony Wilson, Mick Hucknell, Morrissey, Ian Curtis, Pete Shelley, and Peter Hook. You must have heard of them?'

'OK, Tony Wilson of the Hacienda, and Factory Records. Mick Hucknell, he's Simply Red. Morrissey, lead singer of The Smiths. But I've never heard of any of the others.'

Caton found it difficult to credit. 'You're kidding me! The Buzzcocks, Joy Division, New Order, Happy Mondays?'

Holmes shook his head in equal disbelief. 'I never took you for a punk Boss.'

Caton grinned. 'It was a kind of affectation. We wore it as a badge at Manchester Grammar. To be honest it was a sad sort of rebellion. I wore one uniform during the day, another one in the evening. Everything except the shaven head; I never would have got away with that. My Aunt thought I was going mad. In a way I suppose I was. There was a lot of anger bottled up after my parents died. I suppose The Smiths summed up a lot of what I was feeling.'

'Heaven Knows I'm Miserable Now?' Holmes suggested.

Caton nodded. 'I suppose,' he said. 'That, and 'The Boy With The Thorn in His Side.'

An uneasy silence lay between them. Caton acknowledging that he had still not completely exorcised some of those feelings, Gordon Holmes embarrassed, and not a little surprised, by his boss's apparent vulnerabilty.

Holmes attempted to lighten the mood. 'Don't you get enough of dates and facts at work, Boss?' He said.

'Not really,' Caton admitted. 'I think that history's fascinating; it's about our roots.'

'Well, don't take it personally Boss,' Holmes grinned to take the edge off it. 'But to tell you the truth, it does my head in. Shall we go in?'

They ignored the lift, and made their way up the broad staircase, past the impressive statues, paintings and other artefacts retained from the Free Trade Hall, to the second floor Business Centre.

The room had been set out cabaret style with six tables, each accommodating six people. According to the seating plan they were on separate tables. Caton had no option but to trust that Gordon would keep his views on the Agency to himself. He doubted they'd be pleased to hear that it should have been strangled at birth. More used to a room full of self-important suits, Caton found it refreshing that at least forty percent of those present were women. Including the one at the lectern waiting patiently for them to fall silent.

'Good morning everyone,' she said. 'And welcome to the Radisson Edwardian, to Manchester, and to today's seminar. My name is Barbara Bryce. I am a Deputy Director, Operations, with The Serious and Organised Crime Agency. My role today is to welcome you; to briefly introduce the Agency to those partners whom we have invited here today; and to set out the agenda for the day. So let's get straight to it. A lot of hype and speculation has surrounded the formation of the Agency. Not least, the suggestion that we are the poor man's FBI.'

Polite laughter rippled around the room.

'A kind of superior police force racing around the country, with special agents muscling in on all the juicy cases, magically tracking down serial killers, foiling diamond heists, smashing drugs rings, and making gangland Britain a thing of the past.'

She paused for effect, leaning forward, making eye contact with every table.

'If only!' This time the laughter was full on. 'But it's true in parts.' She said. 'We shall expect to make a major impact in all of these areas, less so in relation to serial or multiple murders, but not by magic, nor by doing the work of the various police forces. But through our partnership with the police and other enforcement agencies, here, and abroad. In particular, through providing the joined up intelligence resources that have been so sorely lacking. Which is why today, we have invited representatives from local police forces, from MI5, and MI6.'

Impressive so far, Caton reflected. And long overdue. Also impressive was the fact that Barbara Bryce didn't have a single note to hand.

'What you may not realise, is that SOCA - and no, I'm not going to continue to use that acronym, it's too like SOCO for my liking, so I'll just use The Agency - is an executive, non-departmental, public body. That means that although we're sponsored by a Home

Office that controls the thirty or so police forces and the judicial system in this country, we remain operationally independent from it. It has been suggested, somewhat cynically in my view, that all that means is that when we get it right the Home Office will take the praise, and when we get it wrong, the Director General will get the blame.'

More laughter and nodding of heads.

'The Agency has been formed from the amalgamation of the National Criminal Intelligence Service, the National Crime Squad, that section of Her Majesty's Revenue and Customs dealing with drug trafficking ,and associated criminal finance, and a section of the United Kingdom Immigration Service dealing with organised immigration crime. A formidable partnership, I'm sure you'll agree. This is an intelligence-led agency with law enforcement powers aimed at reducing the immense damage caused to people, and communities, by serious organised crime. And nowhere is that damage greater than through the trafficking of Class A drugs, organised immigration crime, and large scale fraud.'

Caton found himself nodding along with everyone else. It was a recorded fact that more than eighty percent of the crime on the streets of Manchester was down to these closely linked activities, and that the majority of that was committed by the members of just eighty families.

'For that reason, our immediate priorities, to which sixty five per cent of our work will be geared, are the trafficking of drugs; primarily those in Class A – heroin, methadone, cocaine, ecstasy, LSD, amphetamines prepared for injection, and processed magic mushrooms

– and organised immigration crime. Twenty five per cent will focus on individual and private sector fraud, and other organised crime, including counterfeiting, hi-tech crime, serious robbery, and the use of firearms. Underlying all of our work will be an emphasis on recovering the proceeds of crime. Crime shall not go unpunished, nor shall it pay.'

She stepped back a pace to signal the end of the introduction. It was an impressive performance that drew a warm and genuine round of applause. Caton could see that even Gordon Holmes had joined in, if a little less enthusiatically than the rest.

The Deputy Director stepped forward again. 'Today we are here to examine, and to share intelligence about, one area of criminal activity that does harm to the community from which it emenates, as well as the wider community. Namely, organised crime associated with those of Chinese origin. China is one of the worlds fastest developing economies. It is predicted that within a decade its wealth will eclipse that of both the United Kingdom and America. Serious and organised crime is growing in China at an exponential rate, causing grave concern to its Government. But the problem is not only a domestic one; crime is one of its undesireable exports. One that is also expanding. Before you begin to listen to the inputs, and join in the discussion, I want to make it clear that the Chinese community here in Britain is, and always has been, one of the most law abiding and self-regulating sections of the community. Much of that has to do with the importance accorded to family, to respect, and to "face". Unfortunately, that also makes it one of our least penetrable communities, and that presents a major problem in dealing with serious crime. Between now, and lunchtime, you will hear a series of inputs dealing with the key areas of activity. This afternoon, Chief Inspector Caton of Greater Manchester Police, and his colleague, will present a case which highlights the problems of gaining intelligence within the Chinese community, and then you will be invited to discuss possible ways forward. I hope you have a productive day.'

The first of the Agents to speak was a tough looking bruiser in his mid forties, looking just as uncomfortable in his new blue suit as Holmes did in his. Almost certainly a member of the specialist anti-gang section of the former National Crime Squad, he spoke with authority about the Chinese gangs.

'You take almost every one of the forms of criminal activity listed by Mrs Bryce,' he said. 'And there is a Triad controlling its operation. I want to be clear; there is a hierarchy here. Big business interests and corrupt officials may sit at the top of the pile, initiating the activity, providing the funding, and taking the greatest profit, but the members of Triads will make it happen. Beneath them, at street level, there are street gangs; average age sixteen to twenty five, often of illegal immigrants, many of them Fujianese unable to find legal employment. They'll do the dirty work, as much to build up "face" among their peers as to make money. These are the ones we tend to catch. There's a parallel here with those black and white working class kids, and increasingly Asian, and mixed race ones too, pushing drugs on mountain bikes for the heavy dealers on our inner city streets. Only there's more chance you'll find the Chinese street gangs distributing pirate videos, CDs, and counterfeit goods. As well as providing muscle for the protection rackets; an activity they try to give a veneer of respectability up here in the North by referring to it as taxing.'

A hand went up. 'What's the difference between a Triad and a Tong?'

He took it in his stride. 'Good question. The Tongs tend to have a longer tradition. They started out a bit more like our guilds, supporting craftsmen, and businesses, with a common interest. Nowadays, I suppose the nearest parallel would be a Masonic lodge, or a Round table; A bit more like a club, or a charitable organisation. The majority of them are respectable, and not involved in crime at all. The Triads on the other hand have only two purposes: to become wealthy through crime; and to protect each other, and the organisation, to the death. Their four key areas of activity are drugs, people smuggling, counterfeiting, and extortion. Because of the need to shift the profits from these activities into respectable funds, they also engage in money laundering and gambling – legal and illegal. They also act as conduits for money laundering on behalf of business corporations.'

Another hand went up. 'Why do people refer to them as snakeheads?'

'That's a stereotype, based on the tattoos that identify the different Triads, and groups within them. It's a bit more complicated than that. From the early 1950's until the early 1980's most of the Triads were members of the 14K Triad; either directly or through affiliation. They were pretty low on the radar of our law enforcement agencies, and were based mainly in

London, Liverpool, Manchester and Birmingham. Drugs, especially heroin, flowed in through Amsterdam but when things got too hot for them over there, and in Hong Kong where there was a crack down on corruption in the HK police force, two other well established Triads fled to Britain: the San Yee On; and the Wo On Lok, the largest of all the Triads.'

This time it was a woman on a table near the front who raised her hand.

'Didn't that lead to in-fighting with the 14K?'

He was impressed. 'Yes it did, and with each other. But rather than start a turf war, the Wo On Lok had the sense to settle for those parts of London where there was least competition, and also Southampton, where they had no competition at all. Although there's still the occasional clash that hits the headlines, most of them are more worried about their other rivals – the Turkish gangs in North London, and the new kids on the block; the Albanians, Russians, and Croatians. Our intelligence on the Triads is mixed, but generally poor. There are two reasons. Firstly, almost to a man they are first, second, or third generation Hong Kong Chinese. They speak Cantonese, and have built on family ties over the generations. Not unlike the Mafia in Italy. Secondly, induction into the Triad is for life, and any betrayal of the Triad, or any member within it, is punishable by death.'

He paused to grab the attention of anyone whose mind had wandered, and to add emphasis to his point. Not that any was needed.

'And not a very pleasant death either. There are three manners of death in the common Triad Oath: the death of five thunderbolts; the death of a thousand swords;

and the death of a thousand knives, sometimes known as the death of a thousand cuts. If you ever get to see the results of a ritual Triad execution, take it from me ladies and gentlemen, you won't have any difficulty recognising it. Unless, of course, they've gone the whole hog, and scattered the body parts to the four winds.'

Another hand went up. it was Gordon Holmes.

'The others seem pretty obvious,' he began. 'But what about this death of five thunderbolts? What does that mean?'

'Also a good question. Mainly because I don't have an answer. Maybe in the old days they stuffed fireworks in their orifices, but it's more likely it refers to multiple shooting.'

'What about being beaten to death?' Holmes persisted.

'I suppose that's possible.' The speaker grinned. 'To be honest, we do see it more frequently than the fireworks option.' That drew a nervous laugh from around the room, but Caton could see where Holmes was coming from. He was thinking of the victims in the Chinatown investigation. What if their heads had been banged against a wall five times? Wouldn't that be interesting?

The next speaker reminded them that the British Empire had been the world's leading drugs trafficker throughout the nineteenth century, and had waged Opium Wars against successive Chinese Emperors to protect the opium smuggling that offset the cost of buying tea from China.

'Before you start to moralise about this dreadful trade,' she cautioned them.

'You might want to reflect on the fact that they were fighting to rid their country of the evil of heroin addiction, and that Queen Victoria dabbled with heroin, and created James Matheson, the second largest landowner in the country whose fortune was built on heroin, First Baronet of Lewis. When we finally left China, it was physically and morally debilitated, and badly governed. That left the way open for the Japanese to flood Manchuria with heroin throughout the Second World War, so that by the end of that war, over one third of the population were estimated to have become addicts.'

She looked up from her notes. 'You could say that we had sowed the seeds for the harvest that is now being reaped in the cities and towns of this country. There are fifty thousand registered addicts in the UK, and probably as many again unregistered. Research suggests that to feed his or her habit the average addict commits one thousand offences a year, to a total value of more than forty thousand pounds. Do the figures for yourselves. And that's only heroin.'

She went on to catalogue problems with cannabis, and designer drugs, including crystal meth. Caton had heard all of this a dozen times before, and found his attention wandering. He opened the bottle of still table water, offered some to the colleagues on either side, and filled a tumbler for himself. He had just raised the glass to his lips, when the speaker sat down, and a break was called.

6

Fortified and refreshed, with less than an hour to lunch, Caton resolved to concentrate. The first of the three remaining inputs was the one about which he thought he knew most; mainly because it had been an obvious, if unproven, point of connection between the deaths of Michael Han and James Lee. This speaker, like Han, had worked in the Inland Revenue Investigations Branch, before moving to the UK Financial Intelligence Unit, now subsumed within the Agency's Proceeds of Crime Unit.

'I want to begin,' he said. 'By looking at those activities that only rarely hit the headlines, but represent the most lucrative form of criminal activity. Those carried out by businesses of one form or another. I'm talking about tax evasion, illegal contract procurement, copyright theft and copyright evasion, industrial espionage, and money laundering.

'For Chinese companies – just as for any other companies registered abroad, and operating in this country - tax evasion can be an issue for both the country of registration, and the UK. The resources they will employ will be crooked accountants and lawyers. To be honest, this is really the domain of the Inland Revenue, rather than ourselves. These companies do enter the remit of this Agency except where they draw on the resources of the Triads and other criminal organisations.'

He tapped the laptop computer on the shelf attached to the lectern. A title slide was projected onto the screen. One after another he used the slides to highlight the key activities.

'Major contracts can be procured illegally through two principle methods: the offer of rewards, inducements, and bribes; and through the threat - of violence, sabotage, or extortion.'

The speaker turned briefly to industrial espionage, and then to counterfeiting, or intellectual property right infringement as it was more correctly known. Something which Caton already knew to be at crisis levels in the Democratic People's Republic of China.

'The problem is four fold,' the speaker was saying. 'Companies do not take sufficient steps to protect their patents and copyrights in the first place; the People's Republic of China does not have appropriate procedures in place in its civil or criminal justice system; there is a lot of corruption among officials, especially in the provinces; and finally, there are too many people in this country willing to buy counterfeit DVDs, CDs, clothes, and high tech goods. There are whole towns, cities and regions in China where the economy is based on the manufacture of counterfeit goods. This is not a problem that is going to go away overnight.'

He clicked the final slide, and checked his notes .

'And finally, there is money laundering. Money gained illegally, will always attract attention. For that reason, it is fair to say that none of the activities we are discussing today could exist on the scale that they do, without ways of turning the proceeds of crime into respectable funds. Effectively, making dirty money, clean. Eighty percent of the world's profits from illegal drugs are laundered. With interest payments, we are talking over a thousand billion pounds. Some of you will remember the BCCI scandal when the London branch of the bank was raided and we discovered vast sums held there for General Noriega, and the Columbian cartels? Since then it has become harder for criminals to use the banks, so the preferred mechanisms include passing it through small service sector businesses, or shell companies; into gambling casinos; or claiming it as the proceeds of gambling. Increasingly, ill gotten gains are being invested in legitimate businesses that have a good reason for not asking questions about the source of those investments, especially if they are close to insolvency. And this gives the Triads, in particular, a motive for gaining a foothold within respectable businesses by one means or another.'

Caton chewed the end of his pencil. And Manchester had been fighting it out with Blackpool for the dubious honour of hosting the UK's first super casino. Now that would have been a money launderer's dream come true. Next up was a woman who had joined the Agency from the Immigration Service.

'According to the latest census,' she began. 'There are close to three hundred thousand persons of Chinese heritage living in the UK. In the absence of any official figures it is impossible to say how many live here illegally. There are a significant number of asylum seekers who are allowed to work here legally, and close to seventy thousand Chinese students who are studying at College or University. We know from the number of illegal entrants detected at our ports each year and those, tragically, who are found dead in the back of container lorries...' she paused for effect, scanning the room, inviting them to make the connection. '...that there is a constant tide of such people desperate to find a better life. Today there are probably more who arrive at our airports with false papers, than in the back of a lorry, or in the hold of a ship.' She paused to consult her notes.

'Only the occasional tragedies, such as the fifty eight found dead in a tomato lorry at Dover in 2000, the twenty three cockle pickers who drowned in 2004, and yesterday's discovery in West Yorkshire, alert the public to the scale of the problem. The reality is that each year thousands of people are paying upwards of twenty thousand pounds, to travel fifteen thousand miles across Asia, through Turkestan, Uzbekistan, Turkmenistan, Iran, Turkey, the Balkan states, and finally via France, or the Netherlands, to Britain. And when they do arrive here, to the Promised Land, they find themselves in the clutches of the snakeheads, or gang masters, until they've paid off the remainder of their loan. For those who don't find work – for example in one of the nine thousand takeaways – then their only recourse is to join one of the street gangs selling counterfeit goods, or carrying out dirty work for one of the Triads. Many women and girls find themselves tricked, or forced, into working in backstreet brothels.' She took a sip of water.

'The majority of them are from the province of Fujian in the south East corner of China, where there has long been a history of emigration to other parts of Asia, to America, and to Europe. Fujian has not yet been touched to any significant degree by the economic boom in mainland China. Wages average fifty pounds a month. Many of those who come here are among the better educated, and are able to borrow from family, and local moneylenders associated with the Triads, to fund their trip. Within five years they hope to have paid off the loan and be sending money back home to lift their family out of poverty. For many that happens. Others die on the way, or live a wretched life here as a fugitive and wage slave.'

She picked up her notes and looked out across the room.

'The work of the Agency in this field is to support other partners – including the People's Republic of China - in cutting off this trade at source, and rescuing those who have become victims of it.'

The Deputy Director rose to her feet and looked at her watch. 'I am afraid that we've run over time this morning. Nobody's fault, but lunch has been set out in the Brasserie, and I wouldn't want it to get cold. I propose that we take just forty five minutes, then we can finish on time. Any objections?'

Lunch was a hot buffet. Holmes hurried to join Caton in the queue,

'What do you think then Boss?' he asked. 'That bit about turning dirty money into clean was interesting. Puts a whole new meaning on the phrase Chinese laundry?'

Before Caton could reply Ray Barnes appeared at his shoulder, plate and serviette in hand.

'Hello Tom, mind if I join you?' He held out his plate for the pork casserole. 'I've got some news for you about the Eggborough Five. It seems they may well have been heading for Manchester. A lorry's been found burnt out, and three quarters submerged in a quarry, at Newhey, just off the M62 Junction with the A640 near Rochdale. The fire probably destroyed most of the trace evidence that might tie it down to the Yorkshire victims, but they should be able to get some kind of lead on ownership from the engine number on the block and chassis, even if they've filed them off. Unless of course they've used an angle grinder.'

'Do you know if the Agency is going to become involved in the investigation?' Caton asked.

'Not directly. That's still down to the Yorkshire Force, but we will be providing them with as much intelligence as possible about the routes and carriers that may have been involved. This one has an international dimension, and we're already pulling together a lot of sources, here and abroad, that might be able to assist them.' He opted for the rice, and collected cutlery for the three of them. 'That was a good question you asked by the way DI Holmes. You may not have done your presentation yet, but you've already been noticed. Won't do you any harm.'

Not unless Chief Superintendent Hadfield finds out, Caton thought. So much for keep your heads down. Lunch flew past. Gordon Holmes divided his attention equally between the food, and an unconventionally attractive female agent. Her name was Rebecca Sharp.

'Sharp by name, and sharp by nature.' Holmes confided as they made their way back to the seminar room. 'A real looker, but she'd cut you to ribbons if you made a false move.'

'Make sure you don't then Gordon,' Caton warned.

'Marilyn will have something to say about it too.'

Holmes winced at the thought.

'I'm doing the introduction and taking the questions,' Caton reminded him. 'The rest of it's all yours.'

'Absolutely Boss. Only I hope you're as nervous as I am.'

Caton doubted it. This must be his umpteenth presentation, and his inspector's first. Gordon would be bricking it.

Rebecca Sharp was not at the table. Caton didn't have to wait long to find out why. As she strode towards the lectern, it was immediately apparent that it would be far too high for her. A technician appeared with the intention of lowering it, but she waved him away, and sorted it herself. She stood confidently, without notes, lap top, or any form of visual aid. At five foot two, in a neat two piece suit, slimly built, with cascading curly black hair, and elfin-like features, she looked anything but your typical law enforcement officer.

'I was going to ask you,' she began. 'Approximately how many young women and girls you think have been smuggled into this county in the past five years for the specific purpose of sexual exploitation. But then it occurred to me that some of you would know, because it's your business to. And the rest would be so far from the mark that it would be embarrassing. So I'll tell you. Twenty five thousand. That's up to six thousand every year, sold into sex slavery.'

She paused to let it sink in.

'The total number of women from other countries forced to sell themselves, here in the UK, to as many as thirty men each day, is estimated at around fifty thousand. That's approximately ten per cent of the half a million women trapped into this trade in Europe as a whole. And that could well be a conservative estimate. Auctions are held at our airports and ports, where unsuspecting arrivals, who have come for regular work, or on the promise that they will be students of English, are sold directly into sex slavery. We know this, because in the past year over three hundred police operations, resulted in over a thousand arrests, and the recovery of more than four million pounds. And that's the tip of the iceberg. Only six months ago, here in Manchester, two initiatives – Operation Pentameter, - a national anti-trafficking operation - and Operation Talon, involving Greater Manchester Police's Sexual Crime Unit, came together to release a number of young women from a sauna on Cheetham Hill Road. Those arrested were three Czech men, and an Albanian woman. In a raid in Birmingham, nineteen young women were freed. Lured here on the promise of work as waitresses or nannies, they came from Greece, Latvia, Turkey, Poland, Italy, Japan and Hong Kong. Not all of them will be illegal immigrants, but every one of them will have been falsely trapped, or coerced, into this living nightmare.'

She moved to the nearest table, and calmly poured herself a drink of water.

'As far as the Chinese community is concerned, we have two issues. Firstly, there is reason to believe that girls of Chinese, and other Asian origin, are being held, and groomed, for two specific sets of tastes: European men attracted to Asian women; and Asian men. It is proving extremely hard to gain intelligence about these activities. Secondly, girls and young women of Chinese origin are turning up in brothels, saunas and massage parlours operated by Russian, Latvian, Albanian, Czech, Croatian and English gangs. Here at the Agency our work will include the development and provision of intelligence to help the Sexual Crimes Units, and Vice Units, of UK police forces, to tackle both these outlets for what is a most vicious, cruel, and immoral crime.

The Manchester example shows how closely woven are the strands of people trafficking, and sexploitation, and how important it is that we all work in partnership. Thank you.'

The applause was immediate and genuine. Only when it had subsided did Caton remember that he and Holmes were next up.

'I've had a word with the Deputy Director,' Agent Barnes told them. 'She was very impressed by your presentation. But the reality is that as far as your two deaths are concerned – just like the ones in Liverpool, Birmingham and London – the absence of a clear motive means that none of them fall neatly into our brief. In any case, as you'll have discovered today, we are really about providing better joined up intelligence, rather than taking over the work of individual police forces. So it's still your investigation, even if it means putting it into moth balls for the time being. Now that we've got a better idea of what's involved you can be sure that if anything comes up on our radar that might give you a lead, we'll let you know.'

'What do you reckon on that Boss?' Gordon asked him as they stood on the edge of the Great Northern Square, watching the rush hour traffic inch its way forward.

'Well it's not the answer I wanted to hear,' Caton told him. 'But at least it's confirmed we've done everything we could. I suppose we'll just have to get it designated a cold case, until something turns up.'

'Does that mean we'll still have to move out of Longsight, Boss?' There was an air of pleading in his voice.

'I'm sorry Gordon, but yes it does.'

Holmes shrugged his shoulders 'Can I give you a lift back?'

Caton looked at his watch. It was hardly worth it. Better to go in early in the morning when it was quiet, rather than snatch an hour now while the rest of the team were busy loading files into boxes. In any case, the seminar had set his mind whirling.'

'Thanks,' he said. 'But I need some time and space. I'll see you in the morning. And Gordon, that was a bloody good job you did in there today.'

He crossed to the other side of Peter Street, turned right onto Deansgate, and walked the hundred yards to Katsouris, his favourite cafenion and delicatessen on the corner of John Dalton Street. A mug of coffee, and a tasty Greek pastry, would set him up nicely. After all, he reasoned, why else do I bother sweating it out at the Y Club?

Three miles to the south, Feng Yi had lost all sense of time, and place. Even the pain had reached a level where it no longer seemed to register other than as a continuous scream inside his head. His body began to shake again; a violent shiver that reminded him that he was both cold and wet. He was no longer able to distinguish between that which came from his bladder, and that which seeped relentlessly from his capillaries, and veins. He tried to remember if he had told them what they wanted to hear. He no longer remembered what it was. He just needed it to end.

7

Zheng Hu cupped his hand around the luminous dial of the wrist watch. One thirty am. Apart from the tremulous snoring in an upstairs bedroom, the house was silent. The shop had been closed for the past hour and a half; the kitchen hands long since returned to the squalid terrace they shared with seven others.

The moment he'd discovered that Feng Yi had gone, he had known that he could no longer stay here. The others had known it too. Although nothing had been said, it hovered between them like a spectre. His companion would have gone in search of Wu Ling. The chances of finding her would be remote. That Yi would be taken, was certain. It was pointless regretting that he had come here to the takeaway, or that he had brought Yi with him. Only action counted now. All that remained was to put as much distance as possible between himself and this place. He had said nothing to his hosts. He hoped that when it became clear that they didn't know where he had gone, the snakeheads would leave them alone.

Two hours later, in the north west of the city of Blackburn, in long established landscaped gardens set back among the trees on Beardsworth Brow, Zheng Hu stood at the entrance to the drive of a large detached house. Surprised by its grandeur, he checked the address for a second time. This was indeed the address the uncle of a school friend had given him when he left home, making him promise to deliver a small package to his nephew, an accountant, when he got the chance. He felt for that package, safe in the inner zipped pocket of his jacket. It was too small to be drugs. Diamonds perhaps, or some jewellery. Whatever it was, he hoped that it would be enough to get him sanctuary. His watch said three thirty am; too early to rouse the occupants. He started up the drive, keeping to the grassy border to avoid the gravel, pulled his jacket tighter around him, and disappeared among the bushes.

Twenty three miles away, as the crow flies, the driver of the white Peugeot Boxer cut the engine, and cruised quietly past two short rows of terraced houses, before coming to a halt alongside a stretch of derelict land. His front seat passenger climbed out, and walked softly forward, the hood of his parka low over his forehead. He stared at the globe of the CCTV camera suspended high on the factory wall sixty metres away. Judging it not to be a threat, he returned to the van, and tapped lightly on the side. The door slid open.

Two men, identically dressed in hooded parkas and black jeans, climbed out, and took up positions facing the interior. Their two companions inside the van slid towards them a long package covered in a dark green ground sheet, until it was finely balanced between them on the edge of the van. They climbed out, supporting the package until it was clear of the vehicle. The front seat passenger leaned in, took a large can from the interior, and slid the door closed.

He led the way, followed by the four carrying the package, two at the front and two at the rear, across a jumble of bricks and weeds alongside a breeze block boundary wall. The path narrowed. Beside a clump of bushes it became wet and slippery under foot. They walked slowly, and carefully, in the half light this side of dawn, stopping only once, to lift the package over a small iron gate.

After fifty metres, they emerged on the grassy bank of the canal. The package was laid end on, close to the water's edge. The tarpaulin was removed, and carefully folded into a two foot square. The man who had led took a box cutter from his pocket, bent down, and sliced open the short end of the bag closest to the canal. He rose, stepped back, and watched as the others grasped the bag, and eased it forward until it overhung the water. At a whispered count of three, they raised the rear end of the bag. The contents slid smoothly out, dropping silently the short distance into the shallow water.

The bag was bundled up, and carried several metres into the bushes where it was thrown onto the ground. They peeled off their heavy duty latex gloves, and threw them onto the bag. Their leader waved them back to the van. When they were out of sight, he unscrewed the can lid, poured its contents over the bundle, threw it onto the pyre, and stepped back. From a safe distance, he took out a hoodless cigarette lighter, lit it, and threw it into the centre of the pile. Ignition was instantaneous; accompanied by a soft explosion. Orange and yellow flames leapt several feet high, flaring blue as the fuel burnt off. He waited long enough to be sure that the fire had done its work, and turned away. Behind him, a pall of acrid black smoke rose towards the night sky.

In the grounds of Claybrook, a hundred yards beyond the opposite bank, Gaz Butterfield drew deeply on his cigarette, the tip glowing briefly in the dark. He heard the muffled crump of a small explosion. Like a Molotov cocktail, or a can of fuel. After seven years in the Lancashire Fusiliers, including a spell in Northern Ireland, and another in Iraq, it was unmistakeable. He pressed the button on his radio phone.

'Control, this Golf Bravo. Come in Control. Over.'

'Roger, Golf Bravo, this is Control. Go ahead. Over.'

'Control. I've just heard what sounds like a small explosion. Could be some kids starting a fire of some kind. I'm pretty sure it's on the other side of the canal rather than the back of the building, but I'm going to have a look.'

'Roger that Golf Bravo. Keep this line open, and Gaz... no risks alright?'

'Roger that Control. No risks.'

He left the car park and walked briskly across the field until he reached the corner of the main building where, between the railings and the trees marking the boundary with the canal, there was a partially restricted view. The intermittent glow of flames was barely visible low down among the sparse bushes beyond the opposite bank. The crackling sound, and the plume of smoke curling lazily in the light breeze, confirmed his suspicions. He looked to his right, past the building, to the narrow bridge across the furthest lock; the only point at which someone could cross

74

with ease to this side of the canal. Neither there, nor on the opposite bank, was there any sign of movement.

'Control. This is Golf Bravo. Over.'

'Roger Golf Bravo. This is Control. Go Ahead, Over.'

'Control. Some idiots have started a fire on the north bank, on the waste land, in among the trees. Looks like they used an accelerant, 'cos it's fading fast.'

'Do you want me to call the fire brigade?'

'No point. It'll be out before they've left the station. There's no property nearby, and whoever did it will be long gone. I'll just keep an eye out for a minute or two, to make sure they don't come over this side. Can you see anything on the monitors? Over.'

'Nothing on the monitors, Golf Bravo. Over.'

'Roger that Control. Golf Bravo, over and out.'

He listened for a minute or two to the sound of the water bubbling its way through the sluice channel. A little further away, the arterial traffic on Ashton New Road was beginning to pick up; a gentle stream in its own right that within the hour would sound more like the roar of a river. He lit another cigarette, unclipped the torch from his belt, and began to walk east along the rear of the building. Glancing to his left, he could see that the fire had died down. Only tell tale wisps of smoke remained.

He was contemptuous of the games he was forced to play; hated the pretence that carrying out a nightly check on these premises could be likened to a military or covert operation. True, the use of army protocols gave a semblance of professionalism but it was as far from the real thing as the moon was from Manchester. Even if there were people who would murder their mothers to get their hands on what was locked up here, it was safer than mowing the lawn. Boring as hell.

Mandy, the brindle boxer bitch, held the stick between her teeth. Saliva bubbling from the sides of her mouth hung like liquid stalactites. Her stubby tail wagged incessantly, willing her master to take the stick and throw it. She was out of luck. Patrick Molloy was beggared if he was going to turn up late to work with a cock and bull story about his dog going into the canal. Be even worse if she went into one of the locks along this stretch. Mandy moved to the water's edge and began to bark. When she failed to respond to his call he went to pull her back.

Less than three feet away, wedged into the mouth of the narrow sluice channel that ran beside the lock, floated a naked body; head down, arms pinioned between the gritsone walls, legs flailing helplessly in the turbulent flow. Even in the dim light of early morning he could see the livid red and purple slashes against the pale flesh. He fought back the urge to vomit.

Caton was in his car, turning into Liverpool Street, when his pager went off. He pulled into the first vacant parking bay alongside the Museum of Science and Industry. It was Helen Gates. When he rang the number there was no preamble.

'Where are you Tom?'

'In the car, on Liverpool Street Ma'am.'

'Well get yourself over to Bromlow Street, on the boundary between Openshaw and Clayton, between Ashton New Road, and the Canal.'

'I know where it is Ma'am.'

'I'll meet you there.'

And that was it. No details. Ever since it had become clear that people could hack into an infra red hands free conversation, they had either been using police channels, or keeping the details vague and the conversations short. Whatever it was sounded urgent. He called the office, started the engine, and set off.

As Caton reached the corner of Bebbington Street, he could see Gordon's silver titanium Mondeo parked halfway down Bromlow Street. He and DI Weston were busy putting on their Tyvek suits. It could only mean one thing. He pulled up behind them, and took his murder bag from the boot.

Suitably kitted up, they gave their names to the officer with the scene of crime log, ducked under the tape, and picked their way carefully over the rubble strewn common approach.

'Why did they go to all this trouble?' Holmes wondered. 'It must have been a nightmare in the dark.'

'It doesn't look so bad over there.' Sarah Weston replied nodding towards the line of tape beside the ten foot high breeze block wall.

'I don't know about that,' he countered. If their love lives are anything to go by, I'd say there was plenty of trouble around here; unless they're into threesomes.'

Caton stared at the graffiti on the wall neatly sprayed in vivid turquoise blue; Daniel loves Amy, Amy loves Dwain. The paint looked fresh.

'Maybe they were here last night. They might have seen something.' DI Weston suggested.

The approach path skirted another square of tapes around a small area of blackened earth, and the charred remains of slender trees, before emerging on the grassy bank of the Ashton Canal. Helen Gates was deep in conversation with Jack Benson, the Senior Scene of Crime Officer attached to the Force Major Incident Team, and Superintendent Stephen Graveney, the sub-divisional commander at the Grey Mare Lane station less than a mile away. A photographer, and a member of the video unit, waited patiently up stream towards the higher lock, checking the footage they had already taken. Beyond them, Caton could see several police vehicles at the top of Crabtree Lane, and a dozen or so members of the Tactical Aid Unit busy kitting up at the side of the Strawberry Duck. At first sight it was impossible to discern the reason for all of this activity until Gates and Graveney turned, and stepped apart revealing the portly figure of Mr Douglas the pathologist kneeling beside a body laid out on a clear plastic sheet. Helen Gates' greeting, her face a shade or two paler than normal, was characteristically brusque.

'You all know Superintendent Graveney, I think?'

They did, and exchanged nods.

She stepped sideways to give them a better view.

'It looks as though he was dumped in the canal at some time during the night. We think just about there.' She pointed five metres upstream where parallel lines of tape emerged from beside the wall, and out onto the bank. 'It's also possible that we have a time. At exactly four forty three, a security guard doing his rounds in Claybrook heard a sound, and came down to the boundary fence to investigate. He saw a small fire in the bushes over here, but nothing else.'

They stared across at the low red brick wall and blue slate roof of the brand new Claybrook complex, secure behind iron railings, and a maturing screen of conifers.

'Were they taking the piss, or what?' Holmes said, voicing what the rest of them were thinking. Who, in their right mind, would choose to dump a body this close to the GMP Force public order training unit, and firearms range.

'More likely a coincidence. Unless you knew about it, there'd be no way you could tell from here.' Graveney suggested.

Caton was less sure. The information was available on the web. And the locals, and most of the workers on the Clayton Industrial Estate would know what went on there. In this day and age of freedom of information, there was no such thing as a public sector secret. In Caton's view it was a double edged sword.

'Did he report it in?' he asked.

'Yes. But since the fire was already dying down, and posed no threat to life or limb, they didn't bother the fire brigade.'

'Probably as well,' Jack Benson said. 'That lot trampling all over the evidence wouldn't have done us any favours. As it is, we've got a really well contained site. All of our approaches have been down this bank, or along the sanitised common approach, whereas the perpetrators came across this derelict land along the side of the wall. There are footprints where they came out onto the grass, some more where they dropped him in the canal, and a set where they started the fire. They must have parked up on Bromlow Street, which is why we asked everyone to park so far back.

The pathologist stood up, raised his shoulders, and stretched his back. He bent again to retrieve his bag, and came to join them.

'I'm done here.' He said. 'If you get him back to the mortuary before lunchtime, I can have a look at him later this afternoon. If not, then tomorrow morning. I just need to know, who's drawn the short straw?'

'Chief Inspector Caton is the Senior Investigating Officer?' Helen Gates informed him.

'Well Mr Caton, you've got a particularly nasty one here.' He stepped to the side as they turned to face the body.

In life, this had been a young man in his twenties or thirties, of South East Asian origin; almost certainly Chinese. His hair was matted with pieces of flotsam from the water; twigs, pieces of plastic, and other debris. Mercifully, his eyes were closed. The most striking feature was the mass of wounds, between three and six inches long, crisscrossing his entire body. The action of the water had only served to widen these cuts so that the flesh was revealed, like so many ripening figs, split open in the sun. The fingers on both hands appeared foreshortened, ending in pulpy stubs where they had been severed. Because the body had floated face down, lividity had caused the remaining fluids in the body to pool in purple blotches, stark against the unnatural whiteness of the skin.

'Before you ask,' Douglas began, 'I can't be sure of the cause of death. But, I don't believe that he drowned. He was almost certainly dead before he hit the water. Those cuts – which incidentally are carried on across the rear of his body – together with the amputated fingers - could have been sufficient to kill him; loss of blood, or shock, or both at once. But then he's also sustained several blows to the back of his head, possibly on the side of the canal, possibly beforehand.'

'And the approximate time of death?'

He smiled. 'I can always count on you, Mr Caton, to exercise a little patient professionalism; a nod towards an understanding of the unreasonable expectations so often placed upon our work. Approximate indeed. Made even more so by the fact that he was in water, and the water was still only five degrees Celsius when I got here. So I have that, as well as the air temperature, to take account of. But I can safely say, unless he was kept in a freezer, that he died at some point not more than fourteen, and not less than six, hours ago.'

'So, between seven pm yesterday evening, and one o'clock this morning?'

'If you say so.'

'That would tie in with when the fire was started.' Holmes pointed out.

'Providing that they didn't kill him here.' Sarah Weston reminded him.

'At first sight, that doesn't look to be the case,' Jack Benson told them. 'Looking at those cuts there must have been a mass of blood, and so far there hasn't been a trace anywhere on their approach route, or here by the canal.'

'How do we know those footprints, and the fire, are connected?' Gordon Holmes wanted to know. 'What if they're just a coincidence? A bunch of kids messing around? For all we know, he could have been dumped off the bridge by The Strawberry Duck, and floated down here.'

'We don't,' Benson replied. 'Not for sure. But it's unlikely. The canal is pretty still up by the bridge. It doesn't form a current until much further down, near here, where it gathers force as it tries to squeeze through the narrow channel of the sluice. Secondly, if it did drift down this far, it would be more likely to come to rest up against the lock gates. Thirdly, the canal is so shallow at this point, that I reckon that it would only be likely to float into the channel if it had only just gone into the water.'

They looked beyond the body, to the canal, testing his reasoning.

'That's for you to work out. I've got enough worries of my own,' the pathologist told them. 'Will I see you at the post mortem, Chief Inspector, or the delightful Inspector Weston?' Although this time his smile verged on the lascivious, all of them knew him to be harmless, if totally unaware that there had been a revolution in political correctness.

'DI Weston, I think,' Caton told him. 'But we may come together.'

Douglas pulled his coat tight around him. 'I'll see you there then; I look forward to it,'

The sad thing, Caton reflected, as he watched him go, is that he probably does.

'Just in case you were in any doubt Tom,' Helen Gates was saying. 'This one is yours. And unless I'm mistaken, it will mean unpacking the Chinatown investigation.'

'Does that mean we can stay at Longsight Ma'am?' Holmes was quick to ask.

She turned her gaze upon him, the smile playing on her lips betrayed by the steely glint in her eyes. 'Yes it does Detective Inspector. But it also means that the bodies are piling up, and it's time we had a result.'

'Those slashes on his body, Boss,' Holmes ventured. 'Death of a thousand cuts?'

'What is he talking about Tom?' Gates asked.

'It's a ritual form of execution used by the Triads,' Caton replied. 'Usually reserved for those who've betrayed the group in some way. It was mentioned at the SOCA seminar we attended yesterday.'

'Another co-incidence?' she said.

'Like you, I'm as interested in the blows to the back of the head. If that proves to be a link to the other two deaths, and maybe the ones in Liverpool, Birmingham and London, this could be the break through we've been waiting for.'

'Not for him it wasn't,' Sarah Weston observed. 'Poor beggar.'

Content that Caton had it all in hand, the two Superintendents left. One, to return to the fraught routine of a sub divisional commander, the other to forewarn the Chief Constable, and make sure that the press office was getting its act together.

Caton took stock. The photographer was busy recording the remains of the fire. The Tactical Aid Unit had already begun their inch by inch search of the area under the direction of Jack Benson acting as the Crime Scene Manager. Two of his scenes of crime officers were preparing to bag the body. DI Weston had been sent back to Longsight to open up the Major Incident Room, and lead the team in unpacking the Chinatown files. DS Stuart would be tasked to oversee the house to house enquiries in the area, DS Carter to retrieve the footage from any CCTV cameras in the vicinity, including the one on the factory wall that Caton had spotted when they arrived. From there he would work outwards and see if there were any others in the vicinity that might have picked something up. At the same time, DC Dave Woods would look at the feed from traffic cameras on Ashton New Road; the only possible access point to the streets lining this side of the canal. Then he'd turn his attention to traffic movements in and around Chinatown in the early hours of the morning. By lunchtime, the Force Underwater Search Unit would have begun the unenviable task of searching this stretch of canal for anything that could be remotely relevant. A request had gone to the Greater Manchester Fire Service to send out one of their fire investigation officers. There was nothing left for Caton here but to follow DI Holmes up the towpath to The Strawberry Duck where they had been told that Mr Butterfield, the civilian security guard from Claybrook, and Mr Molloy, the dog walker who had found the body, were waiting to be interviewed.

Caton paused, and turned for a moment on the lane at the top of the rise, between the pub and the bridge. The wooden picnic tables in the pub's canalside garden looked forlorn in the weak morning sunlight; the canal itself, a bleak and grey expanse of water. Straight ahead, beyond the line of officers in black working their way down both sides of the canal, the City of Manchester Stadium, triumphant host of the Commonwealth Games, stood proud against the horizon; the best and the worst of the city brought into stark contrast on this spring morning.

Caton turned towards the doors of the Strawberry Duck. A notice in the window declared that no children were allowed in this pub after 6pm, and that no baseball caps, hoodies, or Under 21s, would be allowed to darken its doors. Another poster confirmed, that this weekend "No Boudarys" would be performing hits by Stone Roses, Franz Ferdinand, Stereophonics, Razor Light, and The Killers. By then, Caton reflected, speculation on the corpse found close by would have grown stale, and moved on to City's chances of staying in the Premiership. A young Chinese man would pass between the tables hawking cut price DVDs, until the landlord spotted him, and turfed him out. No one would see any connection. Caton opened the door, and stepped inside.

8

Caton peered through the safety glass panel in the door of the incident room. Desks had been pushed together; two additional tables, and an extra whiteboard, had been shoehorned in. Sarah Weston was busy directing operations. He decided to leave them to it.

His own office suddenly seemed inordinately large. It was his practice to hold as many operational meetings in here as possible, to make life a little bearable for those like Ged, Duggie Wallace, and the Receiver who recorded and redirected information and evidence as it came in, and the Allocator who allocated tasks and kept a record of who was doing what, all of whom had to spend most of their time bound to their desks, and computer screens. He knew from experience that even a walk down the corridor and a change of scene helped relieve the stultifying routine. Caton had two calls to make. He checked the first of the numbers in his BlackBerry, and rang it. Agent Ray Barnes answered straight away. It took less than five minutes for Caton to bring him up to date.

'So you won't be putting the Chinatown Investigation to bed after all,' Barnes said when Caton had finished.

'Well there's only a tentative connection at this stage, but I have a gut feeling about this one. I'm going to need everything you've got on Triad executions bearing those characteristics.' Caton told him.

'You'll find they've all been entered into HOLMES2. All the domestic ones, that is. The only additional data we've got covers similar murders, and grievous bodily harm, committed abroad; mainly in Asia, Europe, and especially in the US. It may not give a lead to specific suspects, but it is likely to confirm, or eliminate this, as a Triad MO.'

In Caton's view the new and improved second generation Home Office Large Major Enquiry System had already proved a godsend in providing a single interactive database system for all major incidents, across all forces, in the UK. Gordon Holmes made a habit of telling new staff – particularly female ones – that it had been his brainchild, hence the name. None of them fell for it, but it broke the ice.

'What I can do,' the man from the Agency continued. 'Is send you a link to all the on-going and cold case investigations related to the Chinese community in the North West, North, and Midlands. That may throw up some new names, and it'll give you the contact officers your people will need to delve any deeper.'

'That'll be a great help.' Caton told him.

'That's what the Agency is all about,' he said. 'Better intelligence, joined up, and there when you need it; that's us. Look, I've got go. I'm emailing that link right now. Keep in touch, alright?'

Caton speed dialled the next number.

"This is Kate Webb." Even on the answer phone the sound of her voice gave him a sense of calm and warmth; an anchor in a sea of storms. Sometimes he dialled just to hear her voice message. When he'd told

her that she'd laughed and said. *"Voice massaging! Perhaps I should charge for it."* Caton had pleaded with her, without success, to change the message after the Bojangles investigation. Her obstinacy, and sense of invincibility, appealed to him as a man; as a detective whose work revolved around murder and abduction, they were a source of constant anxiety. He spoke quickly to stay within the limits of her voice mail.

'Hi Kate. Something's come up. You'll probably have heard by now that I won't be joining you on the other thing, and unfortunately I'll working through till late tonight, so I won't have the pleasure of your gnocchi con pesto e chorizo either. With any luck I'll be able to make it up to you sometime over the weekend. If you need to contact me, send a text or email. I Love you.'

That done, he began to attack his emails with a clear conscience.

DI Sarah Weston turned as Caton entered the incident room. Behind her, a virgin whiteboard waited for the first photographs to be selected from the fifty or so laid out across two tables.

'We're just about sorted Boss,' she said, advancing to meet him. 'I've put the Chinatown review boards over there, at the back; as a reference point mainly. The rest of the files we've left boxed, because they're already catalogued and indexed, and no less accessible than if we took them out, and used a load more space.'

She pointed to the new boards. 'I take it you want to make this one a separate investigation?'

Caton nodded. 'Until we identify a connection.'

'Ged has set up a new log,' she said. 'And the Receiver has begun to sort the data we've got so far. We just need to know what you want to call it.'

He thought about it. Something simple, until they had a name.

'Lock 12. That's where the body was found. Lock 12 on the Clayton Flight.'

She crossed to the whiteboard, picked up a marker from the ledge, and printed it neatly across the top.

'Where are we up to with the post mortem?' he asked.

'I'm afraid SOCO took a bit longer than anticipated. They wanted to make sure they had all the forensic evidence before they moved the body. It means we've missed this afternoon's slot, but Mr Douglas has promised to schedule it for first thing in the morning. Do you want to be there?'

It was a genuine offer. As the team's forensic liaison officer it went without saying that Sarah would be there. He knew that he could trust her to ask the right questions. Everything would be in the Pathologist's report. But sometimes it helped to see it for yourself. It was never something he took a vicarious pleasure in. But it always stiffened his resolve. And, of all of the team, DI Weston was the least likely to feel undermined by his presence.

'If you don't mind Sarah, I think I will.'

She smiled broadly. 'Of course I don't. It'll make a change to have some company.'

'Right. Then let's get this started. Is everyone here?'

'DS Stuart is still co-ordinating the house to house in Clayton and Openshaw. DS Carter is on his way in. Everyone else is here.'

'OK. My room in five minutes.'

'I'll tell them to bring a drink with them,' she said. 'The machine is on the blink again, and the canteen will be chocker block by now.'

Caton's office hummed with energy. He could almost feel it, like static. There was nothing to compare with the first twenty four hours of an investigation. The revulsion at the deed, the sense of determination to right a wrong, the urgency and excitement of the chase. As the hours turned into days, and the days into weeks, he knew that tiredness and frustration would take over. The ability of the senior investigating officer to keep the momentum going, to maintain morale, to re-energise the team, would become paramount, but for now, in these golden hours, it would be enough to keep them focused. When they were seated, Caton began.

'DI Holmes and I have spoken with Butterfield, the security guard over at Claybrook who heard the fire starting, and with Mr Molloy, the man who found the body. They haven't been able to add anything to what we already know. We don't even know if the fire was related to the deposition of the body.'

'We may have something on that Boss,' Holmes interrupted. 'I've just checked where DS Stuart is up to with the foot patrols conducting the house to house enquiries in the area. There's nothing so far, apart from a report from a woman in one of the terraced houses on Bebbington Street; a Mrs Sutton.'

He pointed to a row of terraced houses on the Google Earth printout of the area surrounding Lock 12. It was the last row of houses running at ninety degrees to Bromlow Street. The backs looked out over the derelict ground on the north side of Bromlow Street, towards the factory.

'She heard a vehicle starting up around five o'clock. Her husband is a long distance lorry driver and she doesn't sleep too well when he's away. She remembers looking at the alarm clock, so she's fairly sure about the time. Reckons it was a diesel engine, and says it sounded like it did a three point turn. Reckons she heard a bump, and a scrape, as it mounted the curb on the other side. It's littered with bricks, and pieces of stone, over there. Then it drove off, and she went back to sleep. That ties in with Butterfield's statement. His first call to Control was timed at four forty nine, and thirty five seconds. By the time he'd walked down to the canal the van would have just left.'

'How come he didn't hear it then?' Carter asked.

'Well, it was on the other side of the canal, and over a hundred yards away. We did ask him if he heard any vehicles, and he said yes, but he assumed they were on Ashton New Road.

'Where was she sleeping?' Caton asked him, staring at the photograph. 'In the front or in the back?'

'In the back. But she didn't get out of bed, so she didn't see anything. Even if she had, they would have had to have been parked well down the road near the factory, and there are no street lights on that section.'

'It ties in with the forensics,' Jack Benson told them. 'So far, we've turned up three different partial sets of tyre prints in the mud in the gutter at the side of the road. One of them is a car, one looks like a van, and the other a large van or a lorry.'

He pointed them out on the photograph. The car was up by the factory gates; the lorry outside the last of the terraced houses on Bromlow Street before the start of the derelict land. The van was ten metres on, towards the factory, just a few metres from the start of the rough path that led down to the canal, and Lock 12.

'We've also got seven different footprints,' he continued. 'Unfortunately, most of them are layered one on top of the other, and badly blurred. One set is quite distinctive, and leads from the grassy bank just upstream of the sluice, to where the fire was started. The initial analysis of the fire has thrown up an oil can that had been filled with an accelerant – almost certainly petrol. The charred remains are largely hard molten globules of some kind of plastic material. The Fire Service Investigator reckons most likely a heavy duty clear plastic bag or sheet of some kind; possibly PVC. There are also quite a few fibres and small bits of material, including animal fur, snagged on the bushes and trees alongside the path from the street to the canal. We're gathering samples of the grass from the canal bank. The Force Underwater Search Unit have only just arrived. I'll be going back out there after this meeting.'

'What about pollen and spores from around the path, in case we need to bring in a palynologist at some stage?' Caton wanted to know. Traces of specific pollen or plant spore provide a unique signature for deposition sites, and scenes of crime, that can be compared with traces on the person, clothes and possessions of suspects. It had worked for the Soham investigation, linking Ian Huntley to the Thetford

Forest site, and on his own Head Case too. It would only add to the cost of the investigation, and Caton would only sanction the analysis if they had a suspect or suspects who needed tying down to the scene. But it was best to get the samples straight away.

The Senior Scene of Crime Officer nodded his head. 'We're doing that too.'

'Have you found any traces of blood?' asked DI Weston.

'No. Not so far. What ever they carried him in must have been watertight. No drips on the way there, and none on the way back. It's not often we get that. Which brings me back to the fire. The fire investigation officer says an accelerant has definitely been used; almost certainly petrol. Probably brought in the can. The remains are of some kind of heavy duty plastic. Most of it has congealed in molten lumps, but there are small pieces that were thrown clear when the can exploded. He thinks it was either plastic sheeting or a plastic bag.'

'That's how they got the body there without leaving any traces.' DC Woods announced, as though it couldn't possibly have occurred to anyone else.

'If they've gone to all that trouble, why bother to leave the body where anyone can find it?' Asked Duggie Wallace, the Senior Intelligence Officer and analyst.

'Perhaps because they wanted the body to be found, but didn't want to risk getting get any of his blood or fluids on themselves.' Gordon Holmes suggested.

'Why would they want the body found?' Woods wanted to know.

'Because if it was a Triad execution it would be a pretty dramatic reminder to others to keep their mouth shut.' Holmes told him pointedly.

Detective Sergeant Nick Carter entered the room holding a DVD wallet. The grin on his face signalled that this was going to be worth seeing. He pulled up the remaining chair, and sat down; immediately the centre of attention.

'Go on then DS Carter. Enlighten us.' Caton said.

Carter slid the shiny disc from the wallet, and held it carefully between his thumb and middle finger. 'Footage from the factory at the bottom of Bromlow Street. It's not brilliant, but it's pretty dramatic.'

'Do you want to do this next door Boss?' Holmes asked, shuffling his chair back in anticipation.

Caton stood and reached over to lift his lap top from the side of his desk. 'It's alright; we'll have a look at in here first.' He said. Two minutes later, the lap top had booted up, the disc was in place, and they were glued to the screen.

They could make out the top of the factory gates and the street beyond it. To the left, as far as the start of the open derelict land, stretched a high wall. In the centre was part of Bromlow Street, and, to the right, the other patch of concrete base, and spare land. The digital clock across the bottom of the screen read four fifty one am, and counting. Suddenly, a hooded man, head down, came into picture closely followed by two men, and then another two, carrying between them a long and heavy package. They turned to their right at the beginning of the wall, and disappeared out of sight. Carter pressed fast forward, pressing play again just as four men re-appeared, made their way back down the road, and out of sight. A minute later a fifth man came into shot, and followed them. The clock read four fifty nine, and seven seconds.

'Well,' Caton remarked. 'Even when we get that enhanced, it's not going to give us anything on those five other than their build. But at least it confirms the timing in the reports from Butterfield - the security guard - and Mrs Sutton. Presumably they got in a vehicle with a diesel engine, just out of camera shot.'

'Probably a van, a people carrier, or a small truck.' Carter pointed out. 'They'd never all get in an estate car with the body as well.'

'So we we've got a time frame, and a pretty good idea of what we're looking for,' Caton said. 'So what have you got on the traffic cameras DC Woods?'

They all turned to look at Dave Woods, who was doing his best to be invisible.

'Well actually, I started with the ones in Chinatown,' he said apologetically. Gordon Holmes made a grunting sound that required little translation.

Woods pretended not to have heard, and blustered on. 'But then I got all the stuff from the Ashton corridor. I can show you it right now. I just haven't had time to analyse it.'

They had no alternative but to follow him into the incident room, and perch themselves around the screen.

'Let's start with the three minutes before those five started walking down Bromlow Road, and the three minutes after we lost sight of them.' Caton said. 'DC Carter, and Mr Wallace, you keep a note of the times and vehicles. One of you can call them out, and the other record them.'

95

To anyone unfamiliar with the life of a city, the amount of traffic on Ashton New Road at five o'clock in the morning would have come as a surprise. To Caton, however, it did not. Freed from the deadening routine of shift work, he still remembered that the task of feeding not just the city, but the entire region, from the markets and wholesale suppliers, was a twenty four hour operation that seemed to accelerate in the hour and a half before the rest of the world got in their cars, and headed for work. There had even been talk of white vans and trucks being excluded from the city during daylight hours, forcing all essential deliveries to be made between dusk and dawn. He had no doubt that when it came in the congestion charge would do just that.

In the three minute windows Caton had selected they counted nineteen vehicles that had been driven, either East or West, on Ashton New Road, within two hundred yards of the only point of access to Bromlow Street. Seven of the vehicles were cars, and were temporarily discounted. Of the others, two were Tesco lorries, two were petrol tankers, one a Royal Mail van, one a police patrol van, one a butcher's van, and another a greengrocer's van. All of the remaining four were apparently anonymous white vans of one description or another. Of all of these vehicles, there was only one that appeared in both time slots. Caught heading East, away from the city and towards Ashton Under Lyne, at four forty six, and then, in the opposite direction, at one minute past five o'clock.

'That has to be the one,' Gordon Holmes declared excitedly. 'Take it back and let's freeze it so we can get the plates.'

The picture froze on the rear of the van, showing it to be a Peugeot Boxer with a 2004 registration plate. Duggie Wallace got up, and went to put the number through the Police National Computer. While they waited, Dave Woods ran the sequence back, and froze it this time on the front of the van. As he zoomed in they were able to see, quite plainly, two men sitting up front. Both the driver and his passenger had their wind screen sun visors down, and were wearing hoods over their heads that completely obscured their faces. Woods zoomed in further, this time concentrating on the tax disc.

'This will have been automatically picked up somewhere by one of the special cameras for identifying cars without current tax discs,' Woods said. 'I can track that footage down for us if you want.'

'No need, Dave, 'Nick Carter told him. 'Just focus it up a bit, so I can read the registration.'

With the picture clear, and enlarged, it was obvious what they had done. The tax disc was current – not due to expire for another four months - but for another vehicle entirely; a BMW M5 500 series.

'Probably a stolen car.' Holmes observed. 'Luxury car like that will be out of the country by now, so they've used the disc to hide the identity of the van. Good enough to avoid getting stopped at night, just so long as they didn't park it up where a warden or a foot patrol could read it. Cunning bastards.'

Duggie Wallace returned, confirming their deductions. 'They're false plates. Probably stuck on top of the real ones so they can peel them off easily, and quickly.'

'Taking a bit of a risk there though weren't they?

Sarah Weston said. 'Any patrol car deciding to run a PNC on their plates would have picked it up straight away.'

'A calculated risk,' Caton reminded her. 'Not many patrol cars cruising around at that time – and we've just seen for ourselves there's nothing suspicious about a white van early in the morning. A couple of hours earlier perhaps, but not around five o'clock.' He stood up and stretched for a moment. 'So if we aren't going to be able to identify the van, at least we can see if we can find out where it came from, and where it went. Grab yourselves another drink and come back here. This is going to take some time, and I want everyone wide awake.'

Twenty minutes later they had tracked the van from Ashton New Road, onto and up Alan Turing Way, and then lost it shortly before it became Hulme Hall Lane. Two cameras out of action had not helped. They pored over the enlarged map of East Manchester. There were only three ways they could have gone, each with a range of possibilities. They had driven it up a ramp into the back of lorry; they had turned off onto Philips Park Road, which could have taken them either into town or Holt Town, or up into Miles Platting; or they'd turned off into Stuart Street, round the back of the velodrome, then into Clayton, and out towards Oldham.

'Why would they do that – its just doubling back on themselves?' Holmes pointed out.

'Why expose themselves to the cameras on Alan Turing Way in the first place?' Sarah Weston responded.

The six of them stared at the map in silence, quartering it section by section, waiting for something to jump out at them. Caton was the first to stir.

'That van,' he said, turning back to look at the photographs that Wallace's team had already pinned to one of the boards. Is that a vent grill on the roof?'

They all turned to stare at it.

'Yes Boss.' Carter agreed.

'So it either carries animals, or it's refrigerated.' Caton pondered out loud. Turning back to the map he traced his finger from the National Cycling Centre, up Bank Bridge Road, and left into Riverpark Road, stopping at the large circular building, and its complex of smaller buildings, taking up the entire area between Riverpark, and Briscoe Lane. He stabbed it with his finger.

'The Abattoir,' he said. 'There will be dozens of vans going in there at that time of the morning, loading up with meat for the markets, butchers, supermarkets, restaurants. What better way to convey a corpse. Those vans do it day in, day out.'

'And you can bet there are facilities to hose them down, and steam clean the interiors.' Sarah Weston added with her forensic hat on.

'Nice try Boss,' said Holmes. 'But I can't believe you two didn't know the abattoir's closed down. It's just got approval for a re-development project.'

'So what's there now?' Caton asked.

'It's mainly derelict. I think there's some haulage firms use it for parking up overnight.' Carter told them.

'We'll check it out anyway,' Caton told them. 'I'll go with DS Carter. There's likely to be security. We'll get their CCTV footage if any, and find out if there was anyone there this morning with a vehicle fitting that description. Especially, anyone of Chinese heritage.' He had to think for a moment. 'If the abattoir's closed down, where do the shops and restaurants get their fresh meat from now? Does anybody know?' Nobody did. 'In that case,' he said. 'Find out Duggie. I want a list of abattoirs, and meat wholesalers within a ten mile radius. And the same goes for fish wholesalers.'

'What about Smithfield Market, Boss?' Dave Woods chipped in. 'On Ashton Old Road. That's only about a mile away from where we lost them, and they do fish wholesale.'

'It's even less than that from Bromlow Street though,' Gordon Holmes said, pointing to the map. 'All they needed to have done was turn right, and go down Edge Lane. Why the hell would they set off in the opposite direction?'

'He's right though,' Caton said, 'It could have been to throw us off the scent. We have to cover every angle,' He turned to his constable. 'DC Woods, you can widen the search on the cameras now. See if you can spot them heading out of the city, or doubling back on themselves. When you've done that, go back to before they arrived in Clayton, and see if you can track that vehicle back to where it came from.'

They were already on the move when Ged appeared at Caton's side.

'I'm sorry Sir,' she said. 'It's Mr Hymer on the phone for you. He doesn't sound very happy.'

Larry Hymer, senior crime reporter at the Manchester Evening News. Larry was rarely happy, least of all when his photographers couldn't get near the deposition site, as had happened this morning, and even less so when he had just been fobbed off with a bland statement from the Press Office at Chester House.

'Tell him I'll be with him in a minute Ged,' Caton said. 'I'll take it in my room.'

He stared for a moment at the photos of the body on the board; then at those of the van; and finally at the map with pins tracing the actual and supposed route from Bromlow Road towards the city abattoir; long since pawned to the gnomes of Zurich. He checked his watch. Eleven thirty six am. Less than five hours into the investigation, and only an hour and forty minutes since the body was discovered. This time they were not so far behind. He had a good feeling about it. The arrogance these men displayed, might just be their undoing.

9

Caton could tell immediately that the guy on the gate had something to hide. He was fine until their warrant cards came out. Then his eyes narrowed, and his mouth shut like a clam.

'I'll ask you again, sir,' Caton said, eying the four monitor screens in the cabin. 'If you can't be a little more forthcoming I'll have to speak to your boss, and then I'll have a look at your CCTV footage. If I find you've been telling porkies, or holding something back, I'll take you in for obstructing a murder enquiry. And if it does turn out that our suspects have been through here, you'll be looking at aiding and abetting, or even conspiracy.'

The words murder, and conspiracy, seemed to have the most effect. The man's pupils dilated both times. Right now, they were pinpoints as he weighed up the pros and cons of saying nothing, or of revealing his little earner on the side. It was a no brainer.

'OK,' he said reluctantly. 'There was a guy come in here with his van, about that time. Took it round the side, left about half an hour later.'

Caton took his notebook out. 'What time exactly?'

'I dunno. But I can find out from the tape.'

'You do that. And then I'll be taking the tape away with me. So, describe the van.'

'It was a white Peugeot. One of those refrigeration ones.'

'Model?'

'A Boxer, innit.'

'Registration?'

The man rolled his eyes. 'Am I a train spotter, or wot?'

'Not the whole number, just the year?'

'I dunno. Fairly new, 04, 05, somefin like that.'

Caton watched his eyes flick up to the left; accessing his visual memory. Almost certainly constructing a truthful as opposed to a fabricated reply.

'Yeh that's right, PG04 was the last bit. My woman's initials.'

'And just a driver? No passengers?'

'I di'nt see none.'

'Can you describe the driver?'

The man shrugged. 'Chinese.'

'Asian then?'

He sneered. 'I'm Asian pal, he was Chinese.'

'So what did he look like?'

'Chinese.'

'Can you be a little more specific?'

'He was Chinese looking.'

Caton gave him the evil eye. 'If you're about to say what I think you're about to say, don't!' he warned.

The man looked aggrieved. 'Well they do,' he said. 'To me, anyway.'

'And if I said that about people from your part of the world, how would you feel?'

'My part of the world?' He sneered. 'You mean Cheetham Hill?'

Caton could see this accelerating down a blind alley. 'How tall was he?'

'Short. Five four maybe.'

'Hair colour?'

'What you'd expect.'

'I'm warning you.' Caton said, beginning to lose his patience. Beside him Carter was grinding his teeth.

The eyes flicked up to the left again.

'Black, medium length, straight, shiny.'

'What shape was his face? Oval, round, square?'

He thought about that for a moment. 'More round than oval.'

'Build?'

'Slimmish.'

'And what age would you put him at?'

'Late forties, early fifties.'

'Has he been here before?'

'A couple of times?'

'Does he work here?'

'No.'

Caton could see him beginning to clam up again. He clearly had something to hide. 'Look,' he said as reasonably as possible. 'I'm here on a murder enquiry. If you've got some kind of scam going on I'm not really interested – unless it turns out to be a serious crime, in which case I'll find out anyway. So, let's try again. What was he doing here?' He saw the shoulders sag, heard the exhalation like a sigh, and watched the defences collapse. He knew exactly what was meant by that phrase about taking the wind out of your sails.

'People sometimes come here to use the truck wash. It's high power, and there's a steam hose as well.'

'And they slip you something for the privilege?'

The man gave a defeated nod.

'Two quid. They just give me the money and drive on through.'

'Well that's between you and your employer. I'm not interested. I just want to know about this man, and this van. How often does he come?'

'Twice a week. Usually late afternoon, early evening.'

'After he's finished his deliveries.' Caton guessed. 'So what was he doing here this morning?'

'Well that's the odd thing. He was only 'ere last night, about five thirty. So why would he need to come again so soon? Not only that, but this morning they tell me he was steam cleaning the driver's cab. Took him half an hour to wipe it dry.'

'Who told you?'

'Couple of the haulage drivers. One of them took pity on him, and loaned him a wash leather.'

'I want their names and details, and anyone else who may have seen or spoken to him. Have you got any idea where he lives, or who he works for?'

The man shook his head. 'Sorry mate, no idea. He never speaks. Just gives me the money and drives on through.'

Caton put his notebook away. 'Let's start with the CCTV tapes.' he said.

'I'll have to speak to my manager.'

'Then do it. And tell him it's a murder enquiry, and if I don't get them now I'll be back with a search warrant, and turn this place upside down.'

While the man reached for his phone Caton flipped open his own, and dialled.

'Gordon' he said. 'Looks like the van was here. And it sounds like they'd whipped off the false plates. I'm getting the CCTV tapes right now. DS Carter is going to find out if anyone saw anything.' He ended the call and turned back to the booth. 'Have you got those tapes yet? I haven't got all day.'

The plates were genuine. It took less than fifteen minutes to establish that the van was on lease to a Chinese supermarket, and that the key holder was fifty one year old Lee Quon, who had been one of their drivers for the past ten years. They were given a list of the deliveries he was due to be making. Twenty minutes later, he was arrested coming out of the kitchens of a restaurant in Chorlton. The van was awaiting full lift retrieval to preserve the evidence. Lee Quon was waiting in interview room three at Longsight station. Gordon Holmes, who had brought him in, briefed Caton before the pair of them began the interview.

'He's Cantonese, been over here legally for thirty two years, no police record, highly thought of by his employers. He lives in Higher Broughton, with his wife, a daughter, and a son, both in their teens. And one way or another he's in it up to his armpits. Because he's not just nervous, he's scared shitless.'

'What has he said so far?'

'I've no idea. He just keeps shaking, moaning, and gabbling in Cantonese.'

'Speaking in Cantonese, not gabbling.' Caton said firmly. 'Just because you can't understand what he's saying, that doesn't mean he's gabbling.'

'Point taken Boss. Let's just say he's talking very fast, in a highly excitable manner.'

Caton had no idea if he was being smart, or giving an accurate description. He decided to give him the benefit of the doubt. 'Have we got an interpreter?' he asked.

'There's one on her way. Having said which, Quon has been resident here for years, and both of his kids have been through the state system, so I'd be surprised if he didn't speak some English.'

'But if he chooses not too, we'll have to have an interpreter here anyway. We'll have to question him under caution, so you'd better get the duty solicitor as well. If nothing else, that may just impress on him how serious his situation is.'

Holmes raised his eyebrows. 'I don't think he needs any reminding that he has the right to remain silent, Boss.'

'In which case,' Caton said firmly. 'it can't make matters any worse can it?'

There was a nasty smell in the room, of fish, and fear, commingled. Lee Quon shook uncontrollably. Sweat glistened in his hair, ran in rivulets down the sides of face, and pooled in the hollow at the base of his neck. The woman interpreter had one arm around his neck and was speaking to him in soothing tones. The duty solicitor had yet to arrive.

'We can't interview him like this,' Caton decided. 'I want the police surgeon to have a look at him. When he's deemed fit to be questioned we'll try again. And Gordon, we don't tell him what it was his van was used for. Not yet. If he doesn't know, finding out will only spook him even more.'

Fifteen minutes later, they had the all clear. Although the van driver had regained a degree of composure it was obvious that he was still terrified. The breakthrough came after fifteen minutes of fruitless questions, to none of which Quon had replied. Caton had called a break, turned off the tapes and was about to get up when the interpreter, unbidden, said something to their suspect that caused him to look up at her for the first time. An animated exchange took place as the two policemen and the solicitor looked on. Sensing that something was happening here, Caton motioned Gordon Holmes to sit back down. Finally, Lee Quon turned to look at Caton. His eyes were bloodshot, and his cheeks streaked with dried up tears. His expression stood on a brink between desperate pleading, and the abandonment of hope. The interpreter nodded to Caton. He switched the tapes back on.

'This interview recommences at one seventeen pm. Present, as before, are Mr Lee Quon, Ms Jenny Chu interpreter, Jaswinder Singh duty solicitor, Detective Inspector Gordon Holmes, and Detective Chief Inspector Tom Caton. Mr Lee Quon remains under caution. Does Mr Quon understand that he is still under caution Ms Chu?'

She checked. 'Yes he does.'

'And is he now willing to answer our questions?'

'Yes he is.'

Caton hesitated, framing words carefully in his mind. 'Before we begin, Ms Chu I have to know what it was that you said to him that persuaded him to talk to us. I hope that you won't take this the wrong way, but I have to be sure, for the record, that he is doing so freely, and not under duress or promise of any kind.'

She smiled nervously. 'Of course. I told him that if he was frightened because someone who had threatened him would know that he was speaking with the police, it was too late for that. They would already know because he was arrested in public, and his van had been towed away. Whatever he told them they may not believe him. Perhaps he needed to consider how best to protect himself and his family. If he did not co-operate, it is possible that he could still be arrested, and then neither he, nor the police, would be in a position to provide such protection.'

Smart woman, Caton reflected. Why the hell didn't I think of that? He understood why she was nervous. Strictly speaking she had stepped outside her role as an interpreter. But since Singh, the solicitor, seemed to have no objection, and she had done both the police and the suspect a huge favour, it seemed churlish to point that out.

'Thank you Ms Chu,' he said. 'Now could you please ask Mr Quon if anyone other than himself has used his van in the past twenty four hours?'

Caton waited impatiently as the answers began to come; frustrated that the exchanges between the suspect and his interpreter always seemed so much longer than the answers they received.

'Yes. He says that his van was boxed in yesterday afternoon in Boothstown when he was on his way to make a delivery in Tyldesley. Three men got out of one of the cars, and told him that they needed to borrow his van overnight. He would be paid. He was to leave the keys to his van under the front wheel arch on the driver's side before he went to bed. He was to tell no one – not even his wife. If he did so then his wife and children would disappear. They would die; but not immediately. First they would suffer terribly.

Then they would be returned to him, packaged like the meat and fish he carries in his van.'

It was obvious to Caton from the expressions on Lee Quon's face as he listened to the interpretation, that he understood every word, and was reliving the experience. His refusal to speak English was giving him time to think, and to keep a barrier between them.

'Can he describe these men?' Caton said.

She asked the question. The answer was telegraphed by the shaking of his head in advance of his reply.

'No. He says that they were wearing hoods and balaclavas.'

'What about the cars. What were they like?' Holmes prompted.

This time the shrug of his shoulders was unconvincing.

'He doesn't really remember. He says he was in shock.'

'Tell him to take his time. To think about it. Tell him we've got all day.' Holmes said.

Caton knew that Holmes was banking on the man beginning to worry more about what would happen to his family the longer he was in here. It seemed to work.

'He says one was a big black four by four. The one behind it might have been a BMW. He didn't really pay attention. He was too frightened.'

'Where did this happen exactly?' Caton asked.

'On a back road just off the East Lancashire Road. He doesn't know the name. It's a short cut that he uses.'

'And he did as they said?'

'Yes, he was terrified. He knew that if he didn't, they would do exactly as they had threatened.'

'So how did he get the van back?'

'They were going to drop it back outside his house, but he had a phone call at five o'clock in the morning, telling him to get a taxi to Riverpark Road, where he would find his van. The keys would be in the same place he had left them. He was to immediately power clean the van inside and out, like he always did, including the wheels, tyres and underside, but also steam clean the driver's compartment. If he failed to do this, or spoke to anyone about this, they would carry out their threat.'

'So what did he do?'

'Exactly as they told him. The van was waiting there. The keys were under the wheel arch. The van was empty, there was no damage to it. There was an envelope on the floor with two hundred pounds in it. He says it was still in the glove compartment when you stopped him.'

'So what did he do then?'

'Drove into the haulage compound, cleaned the van, then made his way to Smithfield market to collect some fish that had been ordered. Then he went on to a meat wholesalers. Then he had some breakfast at the supermarket. Then he began his rounds.'

When it was clear that he had nothing else to tell, or at least that he was prepared to tell, they went over the questions a second time, searching for additional facts, or discrepancies. The fact that there was an interpreter made in that much harder. There was always the danger that she would repeat what he had said the first time, or even remind him of his original version. That was unlikely, Caton knew. She was trained to do this after all, not just plucked off the street. But it would still be necessary to have someone else listen to the tapes, and verify the translation.

'It is plain that Mr Lee Quon was an unwilling party to whatever it is you are investigating Chief Inspector,' Jaswinder Singh said when they had finished. 'So, unless you propose to charge him, I assume that he will be free to go home to his family. It is clear how distressed he is, and how distressed they must be.'

Caton waited for the interpreter to finish translating, and then replied.

'This is a murder enquiry Mr Singh. By his own admission, your client is an accessory before, and after, the commission of the crime. Even if he was unaware of what it was, he must have known that his van would be used to carry out a crime.'

'But surely Mr Caton,' the solicitor protested, 'His involvement was no different to that of a bank manager whose family are held hostage to induce him to assist in the robbery of his branch?'

'That would be for others to determine. In any case, I'm not certain that he has told us everything that he knows, and so far the version he has given us is uncorroborated. I intend to hold him for further questioning.'

'But surely you can't expect him to…' the solicitor began, but was cut off by a fearful cry, as his client threw himself towards the table, and began gesticulating with both arms at Caton. Caton and Holmes leaned back out of reach, waiting for Singh and his translator to calm him down, secure in the knowledge that the camera was still running, and he had nothing with which to harm them, or himself. When Quon was back in his seat, Caton raised his eyebrow quizzically.

'Would you care to tell us what that was all about, Ms Chu?' he asked. 'Unless of course he cares to do so himself, since he clearly understands English.'

'Mr Lee Quon protests his innocence, and is worried about his family. He says he has to be with them. He says he must take them away for their own safety.'

'Which is precisely why I cannot just let him go. He is after all currently the only witness we have to a very serious crime. And now he says he intends to leave Manchester.'

'Perhaps it is time you told us what this crime is Chief Inspector,' said Singh. 'I think my client has a right to know.'

Caton looked at Holmes, inviting him to reply.

'Murder,' the inspector said. 'A particularly brutal murder, involving a fellow countryman of your client.'

Ms Chu paled as she translated, but he had already let out a wail, bowed his head, buried it in his hands, and begun to weep.

'I think.' Singh began, 'That you can see from my client's obvious distress that this has come as a complete surprise to him. I think that you ought at least to be prepared to release him on bail, with a condition that he does not leave his current place of residence.'

Caton shook his head. 'I'm sorry, but I can't do that at this stage. What I will do – and I'd like you to tell him this Ms Chu - is send a family liaison officer to stay with Mr Lee Quon's family until we've been able to satisfy ourselves with regard to his statement.' He waited until she'd finished translating. The effect on Lee Quon was less dramatic than he might have hoped, but at least the crying began to subside. 'And now,' he said. ' I propose to terminate this interview to allow Mr Lee Quon to have a break, something to eat and drink, and an opportunity to consider what else he might find it advisable to tell us.'

'What do you think Gordon?' Caton asked as they walked down the corridor towards the incident room.

'I reckon he's telling the truth. But it begs the question, why on earth would they go through all that rigmarole rather than just steal a van for the night? I can see the point in using a van that wasn't going to attract the attention of a patrol car, but then why go and stick false plates on it?'

'Good question. Maybe they just wanted to show how easy it was to intimidate a member of the community. Or maybe they didn't want the hassle of having to dispose of it afterwards. Either way, we won't find out until we catch them.'

'It doesn't look like he's got any more to tell us, even if he does suspect who they might be. And I doubt the family will know anything. That was a good move of yours though Boss, sending a family liaison in. There's a chance one of them might tell us something to get him back home.'

'That's not the main reason I did it,' Caton replied. 'I think they may really be at risk. Given how brazen the killers have been so far, I wouldn't put it past them to give our Mr Lee Quon a reminder that he'd better keep his mouth shut,' he pushed open the door of the incident room. 'What better way than through his family?'

'They might get some fingerprints and DNA from the envelope, and the notes,' Holmes pointed out. 'Although I wouldn't hold out much hope on the van, not after he's steam cleaned it

Caton thought he was probably right. 'Show him photos of car makes, starting with BMWs, and 4x4s, and see what he comes up with,' he said. 'See if you can pin down exactly where he was stopped, and at what time. I'll ask the Allocator to get someone to have a look at the cameras on the routes to and from that point, and see if they come up with anything. And we need to see if Dave Woods has come up with anything from the cameras around Chinatown. This time we need him to be looking for black 4x4s. There can't be that many of them around.

'You'd be surprised Boss,' Gordon told him. 'And it's not just the drug dealers and would be pop stars either. There's the footballers, their wives and girlfriends, and then there's the Cheshire set wannabes.'

'True,' Caton said. 'But how many of those do you think are likely to be of Oriental appearance?'

10

Caton checked the incident room clock. It was five past eleven in the evening. Paper cups, takeaway cartons, and paper pizza plates littered the room. Everyone looked exhausted. Lee Quon had been interviewed twice more; his version of events unwavering. His attempts to identify the vehicles that had blocked him in had simply complicated matters. For someone who drove for a living his inability to distinguish between a Rover, a Jaguar and a BMW beggared belief. They fared no better with the 4 by 4s. So far he had identified a Nissan, a Mitsubishi, a BMW, a Chevrolet, and a Cherokee Jeep. Caton was convinced that there was no way Lee Quon was going to provide any information that he might later have to confirm in front of the killers. He decided to keep him in overnight, and have one last go in the morning.

Over fifty officers had been involved in house to house enquiries. The family liaison officer, accompanied by a British Chinese uniformed officer had been at the house since four pm. They were convinced that none of the family knew anything. Caton had two armed officers in an unmarked car watching the house. If as much as a suspicious drive-by were to happen, they would call it in. One of the administrative officers, and a detective sergeant, had volunteered to sit out the night shift in case something urgent came in. They would also follow the Receivers instructions in relation to the mounting pile of paper that still had to be sorted, to save their colleagues time in the morning. Caton decided there was nothing more to do, except hope the following day would bring some leads; from the post mortem, or forensics perhaps.

'OK everyone,' he said. 'Listen up. 'Thanks for everything you've done today, and for staying this evening, but right now we all need a good night's sleep. I'm afraid I need everyone back here for eight o'clock in the morning. So don't be tempted to hang around here. Straight home please.'

He waited to make sure that they were logging off before he made his way back to his own office. As if by magic, his in-tray had filled up again with paper unrelated to the case. There were thirteen fresh emails. He went through them one by one, logged off, collected his coat, and left the office. A quick check confirmed that only the night detective, the administrator, and a couple of stragglers remained. He shooed the stragglers out, and followed them into the car park.

The sky was clear this evening, a colder night in prospect. A sea of stars twinkled, despite the blanket of light above the city. Caton wondered if Kate might be at her window watching them. It was too late to call her. He took his BlackBerry out to send her a text. At least she would know he was thinking of her. If she was up, perhaps she would call. It would be reassuring to hear her voice

The car cruised slowly past. A light from the kitchen in the rear washed across the unlit serving counter, throwing eerie shadows onto the plate glass window.

The clock above the counter showed forty minutes past midnight. But for the car, the street was deserted. The front seat passenger spoke into his mobile as the driver executed a tight turn, mounted the pavement, and pulled up outside the takeaway. He left the engine running, and stayed at the wheel. The three other doors opened simultaneously. Four men got out. Each wore a black parka with a hood; balaclavas covered all but their eyes. Two of them carried pick axe handles in black gloved hands, one of them a short handled cleaver, the fourth a short sword with a black handle. Gold and silver rays cut through the darkness where the light above the window struck the brass habaki and the differentially tempered steel blade. A single kick tore the door from its frame, and left it hanging inwards.

Across the road a light came on in response to the shouts and screams from the little takeway. A curtain moved in an upstairs room. Momentarily, a woman's face appeared, wide eyed as she watched dark shapes disappear into the shop. A large hand grasped her shoulder, and pulled her back. The curtain fell into place; the light went off.

Caton was sitting on one of those folding canvas chairs you can get at motorway service areas for less than a fiver; a stainless steel flask on one side, a keep net on the other. The rod rested serenely on its tripod. He watched the float bobbing idly in the barely moving waters. Suddenly it dipped beneath the surface. The rod bent wickedly, its tip waving erratically from side to side. He leapt to his feet, seized the rod, and began to reel in. It was massive, possibly a carp or a pike, not at all what he would have expected in these waters, and not fighting back, just dragging heavily against the line. His heart beat faster with the exertion. Only when it came within five metres of the bank, and broke the surface, could he see it for what it was. The wide eyes stared at him accusingly, as the cruelly lacerated body, bleached white, twisted and turned in the ebb and flow. A siren began to sound.

He awoke in a sitting position, his arms outstretched behind him supporting the weight of his body. His heart was racing. It took a second or two to register that it was the phone. He switched on the light. It was five past three in the morning.

'I'm sorry Sir,' the night detective said. 'But you did say if anything came up, to ring you. Bolton have been on. There's been a disturbance at a Chinese takeaway on their patch. One dead and another seriously wounded. They thought there might be a connection.'

Caton rubbed a hand across his face; pushing back the sleep, erasing the nightmare image. 'When was this?'

'About two hours ago.'

'Who's dealing with it?'

'Detective Chief Inspector Renick is the SIO, Sir. It was him that phoned.'

'Did he say where it was?'

There was a pause, and rustle of paper. 'Yes Sir. The Drum Mountain, on Plodder Lane. He says he'll either be there, or at the hospital. They're only about a half a mile apart.'

Caton pushed back the sheet, and swung his legs over the side of the bed. 'Tell him I'm on my way.'

There was no need for the SatNav. Caton recalled a painful and intimate acquaintance with Plodder

Lane when he ran the British Pony Marathon. He had been twenty one, in his final year at University. After the death of his parents he had gone through a phase of having to prove himself. He had trained for over six months, and had recorded a good time. Three hours and four minutes, on the most gruelling course in the country. The hardest point had been the final uphill two mile stretch, along Plodder Lane, and Smethurst Lane. At the corner where the two roads met, St John's Ambulance personnel, and paramedics were busy tending those whose legs and hearts gave out as they took the right hand bend, and stared into the face of hell. For many, after twenty five miles, and the cruel plod up the eponymous Plodder Lane, Smethurst was an Everest too far. Somehow Caton had found the strength to make it to the top, and known the pure exhilaration of the down hill run to the finish on Hulton Lane Fields. In some ways it had been a rite of passage. Until that moment he had always felt the truth of the phrase in Andrew Marvell's poem that he had studied in the Sixth Form.

"And at my back I alwaies hear, time's winged charriot hurrying near."

Before the marathon he felt he had been running from death; from the heightened sense he had of his own mortality. Now he was running because he wanted to. That had been his most important achievement of the day; the second was surviving Plodder Lane.

'I'm sorry sir,' said the Sergeant with the incident log. 'But Detective Chief Inspector Renick has gone over to the Royal Bolton Hospital to question the survivors. It's only half a mile up the road.'

'I'd like to have a quick look before I go over and join in.' Caton. said.

The Sergeant looked distinctly uncomfortable. He had obviously been given his orders. Under Caton's authoritative gaze he appeared to relent.

'I suppose it will be alright, sir' he said. 'As long as you stay on the outside, and within the marker tapes. SOCO have got their work cut out in there. They'll be here all night and most of tomorrow I reckon.'

Caton began by looking through the front window. Scene of crime officers were busy sifting through the remains of the long fronted glass counter cabinet. Behind them, pools of blood on the floor, and streaks and smears of crimson brown on the walls and kitchen door frame, told their own tale. It was the kind of carnage that left you wondering how anyone could possibly have survived. He walked around the outside of the end terrace, and into the ginnel at the back from which it was possible to see where the gate into the small back yard, and the rear door to the house, had both been smashed open. They lay splintered on the stone flags, witness to the force of the assault. He walked back to his car and drove to the hospital.

Nick Renick had been with Caton on the Management of Serious Crime HYDRA course for Senior Investigating Officers; a simulation exercise that both of them had found extremely challenging, but enjoyable. He was in his early forties. Tall, dark, and athletic, very much a slightly older version of Caton himself. Except that he had been married for nine years, was not divorced, and had three children. Had Caton still been married, he felt sure they would have become firm friends. Renick was in a room reserved for relatives; a Chinese woman, a boy and girl in their early teens whom Caton guessed would be her children, and a woman in her mid thirties, sat facing him. The children, eyes wide with bewilderment and terror, leaned in towards their mother, whose arms encircled them protectively.

'Give me a couple of minutes Tom and I'll be through here,' Renick said in the doorway. 'Grab yourself a drink in the canteen and I'll join you there.'

Renwick pulled up a chair and wearily slumped down. He picked up the cardboard cup holder, blew across the surface of his coffee , and took a cautious sip.

'I bloody hate these cases,' he said grimly. 'Not so much the savage nature of the injuries, or even the pitiful innocence of the victims, but more so the fact that you know they aren't going to give you anything. Not one single, tiny shred of information. It's like starting a jigsaw with a blank frame, and no pieces.'

He shook his head despairingly, and took another sip.

'What happened?' Caton asked.

'That at least we do know. They were clearing up in the back, mopping the floors, and washing down the sinks, when all hell broke loose. The front door and back door to the kitchen were broken down simultaneously. The back door was actually unlocked but they didn't bother trying it, just kicked it in. Men – they can't agree on how many exactly - dressed in black, with hoods over their faces, came at them with kitchen cleavers, pick axe handles, knives and a short sword. The owner and his wife were threatened. Two of the kitchen workers stupidly reached for their own cleavers. One is dead. Had his head virtually severed from his body. The other is in intensive care. They may to try to sew his right hand back on, but they don't know if he'll survive the gashes to his head. The two children upstairs started screaming. After a bit more shouting, yelling and waving of weapons, the gang left; seemingly empty handed. It took this lot five minutes to dial 999, and another two for the ambulance to get there. The control room alerted all mobile patrols but you know how many are actually on the streets at that time of night. Most of them are in the city centre, in the station booking in drunken drivers, or on a break. In any case, they had no idea what they were supposed to be looking for.'

He blew on his tea and took another sip.

'We got an interpreter through the Bolton Council emergency contact, and she was here within the hour. It took another hour just to get that much out of them. At first they claimed it was an accident following a misunderstanding, then, when we pointed out the consequences for the wounded men if they survived, the owner admitted it was an attack. Of course they had no idea why, and they didn't know who, nor can they identify any of their attackers.'

'What about the neighbours?' Caton asked.

'I got the house to house underway, starting with the neighbouring houses – most of whom had their lights on by then. So far, everybody heard the noise, but nobody saw anything. Unless they went through any of the traffic lights on red, we're not likely to get anything from cameras in the immediate area, because we haven't got any. There are at least four routes they could have used to get to the shop, and we haven't got any idea what vehicles we're looking for, so it's likely to be a long haul identifying the vehicles they came in, if at all. We might get a better idea from descriptions of the comings and goings over the past few months.'

'You might want to look out for any 4 by 4s with smoked windows.' Caton told him.

'Is that what was involved in your incident yesterday?'

'Looks like it.'

Renick put his coffee down. 'As for motive,' he said. 'We tried all of the usual ones on them. Protection money not paid, gambling debts not settled, repayments not met by the illegals working in the shop. Revenge is always a strong one, but I don't see this family having posed any threat. Then again, they could have made the mistake of paying protection to a rival gang. We tried all of those, and drew a blank on every one of them. As far as all of these victims are concerned the attack came out of the blue. They have no idea who their attackers were, or why they chose to attack them. And it's obvious that every last one of them is lying. Even the children know something they're not telling us. As for suspects, the favourite has got to be one of the Triad gangs. Except that one of the kitchen workers let slip something that suggest his attackers were from Fujian. According to the interpreter she heard him say to his colleague, 'We are from Fujian too. Why attack us?' Then his mate told him to shut up, and he did.' He shook his head. 'Completely. Haven't had a word out of him since.'

'Sounds naïve to me. What made him think that coming from the same region would protect them?'

'I don't know, but it tells us they probably weren't Cantonese, or from Northern China, and therefore less likely to be Triad'

'True,' said Caton. 'But they could be an affiliated street gang doing their dirty work.'

Renwick grimaced. 'More than likely. And you can bet they'll be completely invisible. No national insurance numbers, no names, nowhere on our radar.'

Caton had a thought. 'Can you try something for me Nick? Ask them if anyone has been staying with them, or left them, lately.'

'So you're thinking this may have something to do with the body you pulled out of the canal yesterday?'

'What was one of the first things they taught us when we joined up? Don't discount the possibility of coincidence, just don't believe in it.'

Renwick grimaced. 'Like Doubting Thomas? Lord I believe, help thou my unbelief?'

'Exactly,' Caton said. 'And a little divine intervention wouldn't go amiss right now. I don't know about you but I could do with some fresh air.'

They stepped back as a patrol car, siren wailing, lights flashing, swung into the semicircular entrance, closely followed by an ambulance that backed up to the double doors of the Emergency Room. They watched as the Casualty team appeared as if by magic, and the paramedics lifted the stretcher into place. The patient's face was partially covered by an oxygen mask, but it was obvious that he was in his late teens or early twenties. His neck was braced and his body strapped securely into position. One of the paramedics held a drip high. It had all the hallmarks of a car crash. Within seconds the group had disappeared through the double doors, the sirens silenced and the lights dimmed.

'Well that went well,' Renwick said in a voice heavy with sarcasm as he followed Caton outside.

'I don't know,' Caton replied. 'OK they may have denied it but their faces spoke volumes, especially those children. I'm betting that someone was there, and whoever it was, this gang was after him, or her.'

'The guy you've got in the mortuary?'

'Certainly not him, he was already dead. There must have been someone else. And if we don't get to that person before they do...'

Renick turned up his collar against the sudden icy drizzle. 'Unless they just did.' He said.

It was agreed that they argue for the two investigations to be run separately but in tandem. It would double their resources, at least in the short term, and bring two sets of minds to what could be overlapping crimes. There would be a total sharing of information on an ongoing basis – something which the creation of the Force Major Incident Team had facilitated. Different SOCOs and pathologists would ensure that there was no cross contamination of forensic evidence. Caton would liaise with the Serious and Organised Crime Agency. He was already wondering what Agent Barnes would have to say when he told him. Two dead already, one grievously wounded, another five over the border in Yorkshire. And that wasn't counting the ones on the Chinatown file. Whatever this was, Caton felt that it was running out of control. And that was almost certainly what Chester House would conclude, and the media delight in trumpeting.

Dawn had broken, and the traffic was just beginning to build up as Caton reached Salford Crescent, an equidistant mile from his home and from the city centre. There was no point in going to bed. He decided to have a shower and a shave, grab a quick breakfast in Katsouris, and head for Longsight. Sometime in the next twelve hours he would snatch a power nap. It was one of the skills that hospital doctors and detectives seemed to have in common. Right now, he was too tired to remember what the other ones could possibly be. Only the adrenalin was keeping him going, and when that leached out it would be worse than running on empty.

11

'I knew we'd be early.' Sarah Weston said, as she held open the door into the viewing gallery.

There was no-one in the room beyond the long glass window, where the post mortem table shone under the overhead lights. Alongside, instruments lay ready on a mobile trolley, gleaming impatiently.

'Better early than late.' Caton responded. 'Our Mr Douglas was never one for being kept waiting. Anyway I could do with a moment or two to get my head straight.'

He chose a seat in the centre of the viewing gallery, and watched as DI Weston placed her shoulder bag over the seat in front, sat down, and stretched out her long slim legs. The short brown jacket that she unfailingly wore to post mortems had been replaced by a smart black one, over a fitted white shirt, and black Armani Jeans. She saw him watching her, and smiled grimly.

'Dual purpose,' she said, her blue eyes cool, and slightly distant. 'Funerals and post mortems. And God knows they're coming thick and fast.'

They had been friends as well as colleagues ever since they'd taken the inspector's course together. But for the fact that she'd been married for the past fourteen years, they could quite easily have been an item. As it was, their relationship had gone no further than a little mild flirting when they were on their own, careful formality when not, and a sympathetic ear when needed. He sensed that this might be just such an occasion.

'Are you alright Sarah?'

She searched his face, wondering if, and how, to reply.

'I never could hide anything from you,' she said at last.

'Nor I from you,'

Her fingers played with the buttons on her jacket. 'It's nothing really. Just something Mike and I are going through.'

It was the last thing Caton had expected. Mike worked long hours, and gave far too much attention to his property development business, and in Caton's view too little to his wife; but that had always been the case. And who the hell am I to talk he thought. But as for cheating, he couldn't envisage either Mike or Sarah doing that. She glanced at him, reading his mind.

'Not that you idiot!' She looked down at her feet and waggled them nervously. 'It's just the old biological clock ticking away.'

Caton had never thought of her as a potential mother. Glamour model, good time girl, fashionista, and damn good detective; only not a mother. He wondered if all along she'd been putting up a front; hiding behind a confident, engaging, controlled exterior. It would explain why she'd shown no inclination to go beyond her current rank.

'Does Mike know how you feel?'

'Oh yes,' she said without looking up.

'And?'

'I don't think he understands. He thinks it's some

kind of hormonal thing…which of course it is. He thinks it's going to pass.'

'And is it?'

She lifted her head. There was a trace of wetness in the corner of her eye. 'I don't think so. The trouble is he's hoping so. And even if it does, I'm not sure I'll ever be able to forgive him.' She reached for her bag, took out a tissue, dabbed her eyes, blew her nose, and put the tissue back into a side compartment. She closed the bag and put it back on the seat. She turned to face him full on. 'Or myself.'

'You have to tell him exactly how you feel. Make him understand.'

She put a hand on his knee.

'I know.'

'He'll come round.'

He could tell she wasn't convinced.

The speakers crackled into life.

'My, but you two are here bright and early! I hope I haven't disturbed anything.'

They turned like naughty school children caught in the act. Douglas, the duty pathologist, strode, as best he could in his protective suit, towards the mortuary table. Behind him, trailed Dr Jean Hope his assistant, her serious brown eyes acknowledging them behind the plastic face shield, and behind her Zahood – they had never learned his second name – photographer and audio visual technician, clutching an SLR camera with micro lens attached. Bringing up the rear, came the long lanky figure of Benedict, the mortuary technician, pushing the trolley on which lay the stark and motionless corpse of the victim from Lock 12.

Caton and Weston found their eyes drawn inexorably to the red, blue, and purple gashes crisscrossing the chalk white body like the work of a crazy abstract artist. Dr Hope moved to set out the slides and specimen containers at the work stations. Zahood switched on the projection unit, and watched the whiteboard screen as the technician in the control room at the rear of the banked viewing gallery in which they sat, began to test the digital cameras that would record every detail. Benedict pushed the trolley beside the post mortem table and slid the body across, adjusting it until it was in the right position. He moved the trolley away, and raised the table to the perfect height and rake for this pathologist. His final action was to switch on the integrated down draft system to minimise the smell, and the fine spray that body fluids released by the scalpel would exude.

'Not yet please Benedict.' the pathologist commanded.

He waited for Zahood to finish a series of shots from both sides, and either end of the table, signalled for the recording to start, then stood over the head of the corpse. He smiled up at the two detectives.

'Smell,' he said. 'The first tool of the pathologist. Not that I think it likely that it will tell us much in the case of this poor wretch, but you just never know.' He leaned forward until his face was within a few centimetres of the lips, and pulled the mask away from his face. His microphone caught the sound of him breathing in, and out again. He replaced the mask, stood, and shook his head. 'There is nothing to indicate any noxious substance administered or ingested orally, but I assume, Chief

Inspector, that you'll want a full toxicology, whatever the cause of death?'

Caton spoke to the microphone hanging from the ceiling above them. 'Yes please Mr Douglas. We'll need to know as much as possible about the circumstances of his death.'

'You and the Coroner both,' Douglas replied. 'As you will be aware, ever since the Shipman Enquiry we are all required to address three elements on every death certificate: the sequence leading to death; the underlying causes; and any contributory causes. He's put us to a lot of trouble has Dr Harold Frederick Shipman.'

'Not as much as his two hundred and fifty victims, and their relatives,' whispered Sarah Weston.

'I heard that, Detective Inspector,' the pathologist said as he shifted position to get a good look at the victim's eyes.' 'Got your lot a hell of a mauling too, if I remember rightly.'

Caton let it pass; grateful that neither of them had been involved in the original investigation, or the official enquiries that had followed.

The pathologist began his external examination of the body, punctuating the flow of technical terminology with short asides intended for the detectives. It was these for which they listened intently, making their own notes as they went along. The eyes brought nothing of significance. Not so the torso.

'These soft tissue injuries crisscrossing the skin,' he said. 'I'd say they were caused by several different weapons of differing size and shape. The only thing they have in common is that they are all razor sharp.' He pulled open, and prodded, one gash after another.

'This is a wide, deep, blade, at least three millimetres thick. This one, however, is barely thicker than a razor blade or a box cutter.' He moved to the mobile trolley, selected, and held, up a small scalpel, and what looked like a butcher's knife. 'These instruments create similar effects to those I've just indicated,' he replaced them on the trolley and moved back to the post mortem table. 'This one here...' he pointed to a long slash that appeared to begin at the centre of the right shoulder, cross the chest and abdomen, and finish above the left hip. '...was probably done using something both wide and long. Probably a right handed person standing in front of, or over, the body, and slashing downwards from left to right.'

'Could it have been a sword?' Caton asked.

'That's entirely possible, but I can't speculate, only describe the effect and direction of cut,' Douglas reminded him. 'You will be interested to learn however, that in my opinion all of these wounds, the cuts that is, were inflicted either perimortem or more probably post mortem; close to or immediately following death.'

He turned his attention to the centre of the body, the stomach and the chest. 'A shape has been incised on his abdomen.' He said. They watched on the screen as his finger traced a cut over two centimetres wide that started flat, low down to the right, just short of the pubic bone. It curved from side to side, snakelike, becoming ever narrower as it crossed the stomach and finished in a tiny spiral beneath the left hand rib cage.

'Again, someone right handed, practised with a knife. Interestingly, I believe this was almost certainly inflicted ante mortem, as suggested by the significant degree of haemorrhaging.' While Zahood moved in to take a close up, the pathologist turned his attention to the pubic region.

'There are indentations on either side of the scrotum. They are also blackened and burned, consistent with the application of something that has been heated, or... the delivery of a powerful electric shock'. He probed a little further. 'The indentations are large, and serrated.' The cameraman moved in again. They stared at the screen transfixed as much by the pictures in their mind, as those before them. Douglas's voice came through flat, matter of fact.

'The last time I saw something like this was in Northern Ireland. It was caused by jump leads used for starting cars.'

He examined each arm in turn, and then turned his attention to the hands and fingers. 'There are bruises to the upper and lower arms, consistent with him have been punched, and held roughly, and deep indentations around both wrists suggesting that he may have been restrained. The depth and width of these indentations are more consistent with plastic ratchet ties commonly used for computer and electric cables.' Behind the mask, he smiled to himself. 'I use them myself in the garden.' He paused for a moment, straightened up, and looked up at the gallery. 'I don't need to remind you two of course, that when I say *consistent with* I mean exactly that; could have been, not *definitely was*.' It was an unnecessary statement. More for the record Caton knew, than for the two of them.

'The fingers on both hands have been severed at the second knuckle, the thumbs are still intact,' he picked up a magnifying glass and leaned closer.

'Although the cuts are clean – straight through the bone in one go – the fingers are badly bruised, and the edges flattened, consistent with his fingers having been beaten with a flat implement, certainly after, and possibly before, the fingers were amputated.' He smiled up at them as he turned and moved down to study the feet. 'If you can find me those fingers, we should be able to tell you what was underneath his finger nails. Assuming of course that they didn't remove them first.'

The feet were probably the only part of the body that seemed to have escaped assault. He moved to the head, lifted it gently back, and pulled the jaw forward and down

'As you can see, five of his teeth have been torn from their sockets. He waited until the cameraman had finished taking photos.

'Right, let's have him over.' He said.

Benedict sloped forward, and expertly turned the body so that it was facing down. The same pattern of slashes scarred the back and buttocks; less so the arms and legs. There were also purplish red blotches on the skin that both Caton and Sarah Weston knew to be yet more lividity. It was the first thing that the pathologist remarked upon.

'There is significant lividity, here between the shoulder blades, the sides of the buttocks, on the thighs, and in the well behind the knees, that suggests that he was supine following his death. Given the amount of lividity on the front of his body, I would conjecture that he was moved from his back onto his front; after the blood and fluids had begun to settle, but before they had congealed.'

135

How long would that be, Mr Douglas?' Caton asked. 'That window between the fluids settling, and congealing?'

The pathologist stopped what he was doing, and gave it careful consideration. 'Now that's a hard one. Livor mortis generally begins somewhere between 20 minutes to 3 hours after death, and the fluids begin to congeal in the hour or so after that. It can take up to twelve hours before it's complete. Or quite a bit less than that. A lot depends on the temperature, the manner of the death, and the clotting factors present in the individual.' He looked across at Jean Hope who was listening carefully. 'In this case, a reasonable estimate would be between one and five hours after death.' His assistant nodded her agreement, and turned back to the computer.

'So he could have lain where he was killed for several hours on his back, and then been moved to the vehicle in which he was transported to the canal, and then dumped into the canal, where he ended up floating face down?' Caton reasoned.

'Yes,' said Sarah Weston, 'But he could equally have been kept for a longer period where he was killed, and then placed in the van face down, before he was dumped.'

Douglas's voice cut through their conversation 'Conjecture. And I don't see where it gets you.'

'It gives us an approximate timescale within which they moved the body after they'd killed him.' Caton told him. 'That tells us something about their movements. What we need alongside that is an approximate time of death.'

'All in good time Chief Inspector. And I'm glad

you said approximate.' He moved to examine the upper back. 'This is interesting. Zahood, let's have some close ups, I'm sure the officers will want to take some away with them.' While the photographer snapped away, the digital video camera zoomed in, revealing on the screen in front of them a tattoo of a bird of some description on the right shoulder blade, and a set of marks beneath it that looked to Caton like Chinese italic script.'

'Could be his name.' Sarah Weston suggested.

'Or the name of the bird.' Caton said. 'Or both his name, and the bird's.'

'Like Freddy?' The pathologist said.

'Like Mountain Eagle.' Caton replied. All Chinese given names have a significance, many of them with nature. Some of the family names as well.'

The internal examination, confirmed that death was not by drowning, and that the victim had eaten nothing for over eighteen hours. Finally, the table was raised at an angle, and the skull cap removed. Douglas carefully laid the hemisphere of skull on the examination bench. They could clearly see the jagged edges where the bone had splintered, and the indentions and cracks where blows had been struck, There were two overlapping holes, three centimetres across, where the bone was missing altogether, and a third where a piece of bone was hanging inwards, as on a hinge. The pathologist picked the skull cap up, and rotated it slowly, examining the interior.

'There are a number of large fractions to the skull, on and around the occipital protuberance. Several of these fractions are depressed. They are consistent with heavy blows delivered across the inferior and superior suchal line. Radiating fractions indicate repeated blows at marginally different angles of impact.' He placed it back on the stainless steel tray, and turned his attention to the open cavity. He signalled for another set of photographs, and took a pair of tweezers from the instrument tray.

'There are several pieces of bone and tissue embedded in the surface of the brain.' They watched on the screen as he removed the slivers of bone and placed them in the tissue container held out for him by Dr Hope. He placed the tweezers in a second tray, and turned to face the gallery.

'What we have here Mr Caton, Mrs Weston, are classic effects of severe blunt trauma to the brain. There is bruising caused by the impact of the soft tissue of the brain against the surface of the skull. There are tears in the brain as the soft tissue is torn apart by the force of the impact, including at the front and mid-section of the brain. Finally, there is swelling from the ruptured blood vessels, and from the tissue surrounding these injuries as the body attempts to relieve the pressure. Unfortunately, the confines of the skull itself prevented that from happening, and simply increased the pressure. Which is of course, what killed him.'

'The blows to the head killed him. Not the cuts?'

Douglas nodded sagely. 'Oh yes. The majority of the cuts, as we have already seen, were post mortem. The injuries to the head were ante-mortem; or more accurately, perimortem. The scalp bleeds freely. In this instance there is less than might have been expected. The same is true of the bleeding and swelling in the brain, but there is sufficient to be sure that he was still alive when the first blow was struck. Any one of the blows that crushed his skull with sufficient force to embed those fragments would on its own have been sufficient to kill him.

'How many blows were there?'

'Impossible to tell, until we see more x-rays, and I attempt a reconstruction. But just with the naked eye I can see multiple concavities. I would say three at least. There may be more, because some will have had an almost identical point of impact.'

'How do you know?' asked Caton.

'Because on the scalp on either side of the head above each temple, there are identical patches of haematoma where the hair was held and pulled. There are several wounds where the hair was actually torn from its roots. That, and the nature of the fractures to the skull, are consistent with someone grasping his head and smashing it repeatedly against a wall or a concrete floor.' He turned and faced Caton, miming the action, rocking an invisible head to and fro. 'As you can see the act tends quite naturally to be a repetitive one, back and forth, not side to side,' he paused, and a different tone crept into his voice; softer, more humane. 'Someone has held this young man's head, smashed it repeatedly against an immovable object, stared into his eyes, and watched him die. We have been here before Mr Caton, you and I.'

'Chinatown?'

'April 2004; Michael Han, and James Lee. Contrary to what you all imagine, Chief Inspector. I never forget a face, nor a name.

At least we have a time, and a cause, of death,' Sarah Weston said as they walked across the car park. 'We know they must have held him for some time before they killed him, because he hadn't eaten. And since all that stuff with his genitals, teeth, and fingers, took place sometime before he died it can only have been to extract information from him.'

'Or to punish him,' Caton speculated. 'And they could have chopped his fingers off and pulled his teeth out to try to frustrate our attempts to identify him.'

'We can still use his fingerprints, DNA, and the rest of the teeth, to do that.'

'They may not have known that.'

She shook her head as she climbed into the passenger seat. 'Do you mean there's someone left on this planet who hasn't seen Crime Scene Investigation, or CSI Miami?'

He started the engine. 'At least they left us one thing; although if they really wanted to hide his identity, I can't think how they overlooked it.'

'That tattoo?'

'Probably not unique, but there can't be too many of those around. I wonder what those Chinese characters are going to tell us.'

'Gordon is going to want to change the name of this investigation,' she said as they headed for the motorway. 'The Clayton Flight Bird Man. Good name for a film.'

Caton stopped at the pedestrian crossing by Newall Green High School, and waited for the lunchtime stragglers to meander across.

So long,' he said. 'As it doesn't end up in that series of Great Unsolved Murders.'

12

Caton sat on the corner of the table, and scanned the progress board again. All around him there were ringing phones, and the incessant chatter of computer keyboards. The house to house enquiries in Bolton and Openshaw, Clayton and Chinatown, continued to draw a blank, as had analysis of the street cameras, and the CCTV. It was rapidly becoming clear to him that everything would come down to the quality of the intelligence they could amass about the dead man, and potential assailants. Given the dead ends they'd reached on the deaths of Han and Lee, he drew little comfort from that. The only glimmer of hope he could see was that Ray Barnes was coming over to see if there was anything to link this death with those in Eggborough; and what more the Agency could do to help. Perhaps there was something in the SOCA databases that might just hold the key.

Ged waved at him from across the room, one hand over the mouthpiece of the phone. 'Superintendent Gates for you Sir,'

For once, he took it at her desk. If it proved problematic he would have it switched through to his own room. Had it been Hadfield, Ged would have done that automatically.

'Ma'am.'

'Tom. Thank you for leaving me the message with the initial findings from the PM. Nasty business. All the more reason why we need to catch them fast. I'm trying to work out how much we dare release to the media about the manner of his death. It's only a matter of time before they find out anyway. I'm afraid that the Press Office tells me that Hymer is already pushing for full disclosure.

'Given the fact that he's made it clear that he's hacked off with me for refusing to speak to him, I won't be surprised if it's headlines in the morning edition.' Caton told her.

'Well right now you've something else to worry about,' her voice sounded edgy, less composed than usual. He wondered if she was fielding yet again the pressure that would otherwise have borne down on him, and on his team.

'The Chinese Business Forum has requested a meeting today. It seems they're concerned about the negative press surrounding this investigation, and certain tensions surfacing within the Chinese Community. I've emailed you the contact details. I want you to get back to them straight away, and get over there, with Agent Barnes, before this goes higher up the food chain. And just in case you're wondering Tom, I'm talking about Chester House, not Chinese Cuisine.'

They were greeted courteously by a young man wearing a smart black suit, with a white cotton shirt, and pink silk tie. He took them through to a room at the rear of the ground floor restaurant. Four men, and one woman, stood as they entered the room. Sergeant Howard Green, Caton recognised from Barton Street police station, and his liaison work with the Chinese community. The others Caton knew from previous meetings in connection with the Chinatown case. All of the men, bar the policeman in his uniform, were smartly dressed in business suits, sharp ties and expensive shoes. The young woman wore a cream open neck blouse beneath a classic two piece suit. They shook hands one at a time as Caton introduced the members of the Forum. Robert Yu, the Chairman, in his mid fifties; Michael Wang Deputy Chairman, the youngest of the men in his early forties; Larry Ying, member and owner of two supermarkets and a restaurant; and Carol Wang, Secretary to the Forum, sister of the Deputy Chairman, and assistant manager of a local casino. The fact that this was an emergency meeting would account, Caton guessed, for the uncharacteristically low attendance.

'Before we start, Detective Chief Inspector,' Robert Yu began,' I would like to formally welcome Agent Barnes on behalf of the Chinese Business Forum. You are very welcome sir. I would also like to suggest that we take tea throughout this meeting. I know that you enjoy our teas Detective Chief Inspector. Mr Barnes, how about you?'

'Thank you Mr Chairman,' he replied. 'I too am partial to Chinese tea.'

They made polite conversation while the tea was served. Caton blew on the surface, and took a sip. It was surprisingly mild, sweet, and fragrant, almost nutty, with a soft coconut flavour. Not like anything he had tried before.

'Drum Mountain White Cloud,' the Chairman observed. 'Very low in caffeine, so good to drink in the evening. You will find it in any of our supermarkets.' The Chairman told him.

'But you will find it freshest in one of mine.' Larry Ying said leaning forward across the table, drawing a chorus of laughter.

'Drum Mountain?' Caton's surprise was genuine. The same name as the Bolton takeaway. Another coincidence?

'Drum Mountain White Cloud is a famous Chinese tea,' the Chairman was explaining. 'Originally grown by the Buddhist Monks at a monastery in Northern Fujian. But it is time we got down to business I think.'

He opened a small file in front of him, and took out a piece of paper. It looked like a speech had been prepared, and so it proved. He cleared his throat, and began.

'We, the Manchester Chinese Business Forum, have worked closely with the community, the City Council, Greater Manchester Police, and many other partners, to develop Manchester Chinatown as one of the most important, welcoming and vibrant parts of the city centre. We have worked tirelessly to promote trade between companies here in Manchester, and those in The People's Republic of China. It is only a little more than a year since the Lord Major re-launched Manchester Chinatown following the major improvements designed to make it a more attractive, and a safer place for visitors, for businesses, and for residents alike.'

He nodded to the Deputy Chairman on his left, who took over without the use of notes.

'We believe,' he began, 'That our relationships with the Greater Manchester Police have been consistently cordial and productive. Not least, I suspect, because we have the lowest incidence of recorded crime of any community in the city. We welcome our regular meetings with Sergeant Green, and his colleagues. Police presence is always sufficient and good natured during our festivals; for the Chinese New Year, and the Dragon Boat Race for example. We were also very greatly reassured by the successful prosecution by Greater Manchester Police of the violent kidnappers in this region who fled to London. We are disappointed, however, that our concerns regarding the activities of illegal immigrants from Fujian have not been properly addressed. We have no need to employ people here illegally. There are many students willing to work in our restaurants. But there is still prostitution, the illicit selling of illegal CDs and DVDs, and of cigarettes. And, more worryingly, there are still two murders unpunished.' He stared directly at Caton. 'And now there have been two more. There is much fear, and disquiet, within the community.' He cleared his throat, and moved his gold rimmed glasses onto the bridge of his nose. 'There has been much publicity,' he said solemnly. 'Some of it hysterical in nature. This has disturbed the community, frightened some of the residents, and troubled the Consular General, here in Manchester. We are hoping that you will be able to assure us that there will be a speedy resolution of these matters.'

Carol Wang stopped writing. Her pen poised in mid air. Caton felt all of their eyes upon him; the weight of their expectation heavy in the air.

'No Mr Chairman, I am afraid that I cannot,' he said bluntly. 'I can assure you that we are doing everything in our power to catch the perpetrators as quickly as possible, including drawing on national and international agencies to help us. That is why Agent Barnes from the Serious and Organised Crime Agency is here with us today. But I am sure you know from our previous conversations that we have several serious obstacles in our way.' He could tell from the look on their faces they knew exactly where this was going. Before anyone could protest, he hurried on.

'Despite the impression given by cinema and television, ninety percent of detection still depends on information received from the public, and on the evidence of witnesses. When communities are reluctant to provide information, for whatever reason, we have to recourse to covert, undercover, intelligence. There are communities where such intelligence gathering is particularly difficult. Unfortunately, yours is one of those.'

Uneasy movements around the table presaged a torrent of response. Before anyone else could reply, the Chairman raised one hand. He waited for the others to settle in their seats.

'Detective Chief Inspector, we have been here before. You know that I am going to remind you that our community is used to settling its own difficulties. That it has a traditional suspicion of the police, not just here in Manchester but in China too. For that reason, recruitment into the police force is historically low, and we appreciate that that makes intelligence gathering difficult. Above all, however, we are talking here about extremely dangerous men. The real obstacle is fear.'

Caton found himself nodding in agreement. 'I appreciate your honesty, Mr Chairman, and agree completely with your analysis. These are deep rooted and longstanding issues which cannot be changed overnight. We hope that the work of Sergeant Green and his team will begin to overcome some of the suspicion of which you speak. That future generations of young people will begin to see a career in the police service as a way of increasing the security and harmony of your community. But such improvements will not come in time to remove the immediate fear of which you speak. The only thing that will do that is the arrest and conviction of the men responsible for these murders. And to achieve that, I am afraid that we do need active co-operation from the community. Something I know we have always been able to rely on from the Manchester Chinese Business Forum.' The room was silent for a moment as his challenge lay before them.

'And how exactly do you believe we can help, Detective Chief Inspector?' Robert Yu, the Chairman asked.

Caton unzipped the slim black document case on the table in front of him and took out two sets of photographs. He passed a single copy of the first set to Ray Barnes, and gave the remainder of the set to Carol Wang to hand around the table. He waited until everyone had a copy in front of them.

'You may well have seen this photograph before. My officers have been showing it as part of their door to door enquiries here in Chinatown. Sergeant Green and his team have also been carrying it with them throughout their shifts.'

The photograph was of the face of the victim from Lock 12. It was less horrific than would otherwise have been the case because this had been the only part of his body to escape the brutal cuts, and the mortuary technician had done an excellent job. The image showed him almost in repose; a far cry from Caton's vivid memory of the vacant eyes and gaping mouth.

'Yes we have seen it before,' said Deputy Chairman Michael Wang. 'But what can we tell you? He is not known to us, and without the clothes it is impossible even to guess from whence he may have come.'

'The hair, the bone structure, is there nothing here that might suggest a region of China perhaps?' Caton asked.

'Look around this table Mr Caton. True, several of us are related. And all but one of us are from Hong Kong or Guangdong Province. Do any of us have an identical bone structure? Have you any idea of the migration of peoples across the centuries in China? Much is made of the fact that over sixteen million men, now living in lands that were part of the former Mongol Empire, are believed to share the genetic signature of the Emperor Genghis Khan. But there are one point six billion people resident in China, and there are another thirty three million of Chinese heritage, just like us, around the world. Contrary to the stereotype still clung to in the Western world, our heritage is not characterised by uniformity Mr Caton, but by infinite variety.'

Caton decided not to dig himself deeper. Instead he passed the second set of photos to Carol Wang.

'Perhaps this may help,' he said.

The photo showed a close up of the tattoo on the shoulder blade of the deceased. In the top right hand corner the cruel v of one end of a diagonal cut was just visible, and the image had been distorted slightly by the puckered skin. Barely distinguishable as a bird, this creature had a large bill, a snakelike neck, the back of a turtle or a tortoise, and the tail of a fish. Stylised feathers of fading black, white, red and gold radiated from its sides. It was impossible to tell what it was that it carried in its bill. The Chinese characters beneath the image were in black ink. Caton watched as the men around the table became animated, leaning towards each other, pointing to the photograph, speaking all the while in Cantonese. Finally they were agreed, and settled back, waiting for their Chairman to respond.

'Feng.' He said at last.

'Feng?'

'This bird is Feng; the phoenix. In Western mythology I believe that the phoenix lives for half a millennium, is consumed by flames, and then rises up again from the ashes of its own funeral pyre. Life after death, the setting and the rising of the sun, immortality; a powerful image. In our mythology it represents the union of the elements, of Ying and Yang. It symbolises power and prosperity, great virtue and good grace.'

'And the characters beneath it?' Caton asked.

'Also Feng. The name of the creature. Also a Chinese family name.'

'Have any of you seen this tattoo used before?'

'No.'

'Could it be the sort of tattoo that would be used to identify members of a criminal gang; a Triad gang, for instance?'

He sensed a stiffening around the room.

'For that, Mr Caton, you would have to ask someone who knew about such things. Our knowledge would not go beyond the films of Bruce Lee and Jackie Chan.'

'I think I can answer that question.' Said Agent Barnes 'This is nothing like the insignia tattoos traditionally used by Triad gangs. It looks more like those used by many young men of Chinese heritage to express their personality, or the personality they would like others to believe they have. Or it could simply be an affirmation of his membership of the clan; the family of Feng.'

The Chairman smiled. 'Thank you Agent Barnes. You are well informed.'

'Mr Chairman,' Caton said. 'I understand what you had to say about the dispersal of the Chinese population over time, but if this was just that, a family name, might it tell us anything about the possible region, or regions from which the victim may have come?'

Once more there was a brief discussion between the members of the Forum.

'Bearing in mind what you say about this being little more than a guess,' the Chairman said. 'We can say that it is unlikely that he was from the province of Guangdong, or from Hong Kong. He was probably of Han Chinese origin, although since they make up the majority of the population of mainland China that may not be very helpful to you. It is possible that he was from Fujian province, where this name is not uncommon. Taken together with the not unreasonable assumption that he was an illegal immigrant - which would explain why no one has come forward to identify him - that would seem most likely.' He waved to the waiter standing patiently at the far end of the room. 'More tea Detective Chief Inspector?'

'I thought you handled that quite well.' Ray Barnes speared a pan fried pork and prawn dumpling, swirling it slowly in the dipping sauce.

'Apart from those occasions where I managed to give offence.' Caton lifted his spoon of Beijing hot and sour soup, blew ripples across the surface, and savoured the clash of flavours; yin and yang.

'I wouldn't be too hard on yourself,' the Agent crunched through the crispy shell, into the soft and succulent flesh beneath. 'There was quite a bit of dissembling going on in there if you ask me. It stood out a mile that he was Fujianese, or at the very least not from Hong Kong. It was just a way of keeping you on the back foot.'

'Well at least we have a name, and symbol to go at.' Caton held his spoon suspended above the bowl. 'And why do I have a feeling you've been saving something up to tell me?'

Ray Barnes grinned. 'Three of the bodies at the sandpits also had tattoos. None of them identical, but the same kind of thing; family or given name in representative form.'

'You bugger!' Caton said a little too loudly, drawing startled looks from customers on nearby tables. He lowered his voice, and leaned forward. 'You knew all along, and you let me go through all that.'

'Better that way. It meant you couldn't give anything away. I wanted to see how much they suspected, without letting them know too much about the other investigation.'

'So the two are connected?'

The Agent turned his attention to a shredded duck roll in bean curd leaves. 'It looks that way. And another thing; from the clothes, and a few personal possessions the perpetrators overlooked, we have no doubt those five were newly in from Fujian Province.'

Caton let the final mouthful slide slowly down his throat, put down the spoon, picked up his chopsticks, and stabbed the air with them to make his point. 'Too much of a coincidence. And didn't you say you were surprised that there were only five bodies. Barely enough to make a shipment worthwhile?'

'Exactly so...I tell you what though, this food is seriously good.'

They ate in silence for a minute. Enjoying the food; considering the options.

Caton was the first to break the silence. 'We have to track this back; like they did with the guy who was kidnapped from that restaurant a few years ago. If we can find out how they got here, we stand a chance of discovering why they were killed, and by whom.'

'My thoughts entirely. And this time round it should be a whole lot easier. Ever since those cockle pickers died in Morecambe Bay we've had a liaison officer attached to the embassy in Beijing, an agent in Shanghai, and we've started exchanging police officials with the Chinese to target human trafficking. There are also several Chinese Ministry of Public Security Officials already working over here with the Home Office to try and identify illegal immigrants. I'm arranging to get the photographs of the Eggborough five sent down to them; your man too. You'll be cracking on with investigations at this end?'

'Of course. But if we don't make any progress soon I can see another trip to China coming on.'

'Well that shouldn't be too difficult to arrange. And if we can't get you a fast visa through the Consul General, I bet the Chinese Business Forum could.'

A waiter appeared with the final two dishes. He placed them on the table with due ceremony.

'Steamed pieces of chicken, with fish maw; Chinese mushrooms and crab stick; steamed tripe, marinated with oyster sauce. Please enjoy.'

Caton stared at the small attractive dishes with a rising sense of guilt. His team were slaving away, and here he was indulging. He consoled himself with the thought that it would be late evening before he ate again, and raised the chopsticks. Barnes got there first. The tripe squirmed between the ivory sticks, slipped back into the sauce, and peppered the tablecloth with spots of reddish brown. It reminded Caton that there were probably others still out there, hunted by the men that had put Feng in the mortuary. He wiped his mouth with his napkin, and finished the mineral water in his glass. His appetite had deserted him.

13

Evening. Close to sunset. An ethereal glow backlit the inky vastness of the High Peak. Ten miles west, it flamed the windows of the twenty story block, and painted crimson the concrete cladding. Wu Ling stirred on her bed in the box room of the tenth floor flat. It was several hours since the sharp prick of the needle had been followed by a sudden rush, and a surge of inexplicable euphoria. The heat flooded her veins and warmed her skin; her mouth was dry, her limbs heavy on the bare mattress. For the last hour or so she had drifted in and out of sleep. Never fully awake, she lived in a dreamlike state. Dragons and tigers populated her dreams. They chased her through deep ravines and sparkling mountain streams, across wooded slopes of fir, and pine, and rosewood. Each time she fell, her father would lift her gently to her feet and urge her on; his voice morphing into that of a younger man who told her to call him Johnny. In the distance, her mother's voice intoned the nursery rhyme that had so amused her as a child, but now sent a chill through her like the wind on the highest slopes of Mount Wuyi.

This little cow eats grass
This little cow eats hay
This little cow drinks water
This little cow runs away
This little cow does nothing
But just lies down all day
We'll whip her, let's whip her, let's whip her.

She tried to turn on her side, but the silken ties binding her to the frame of the bed cut into her hands and feet. Exhausted, she lay back, and drifted into sleep.

Beyond the metal plate, secured by an external bolt into the reinforced door jamb, her captors played Sic bo. This was a rehearsal for the more promising arena of the casino; as though practice could replace good fortune, and dictate the vagaries of chance. Their leader placed the three dice into the plastic cup. Shaking it twice he turned the bowl, and watched as they tumbled to the floor. Three fives. He cursed. He had bet on Big, and despite the high total, he had lost; disqualified by the triple. One of his two companions leapt around the room, howling, ecstatic. The triple had given him a hundred and eighty points. Just as well, Johnny reflected, that they were only betting ten pence a point. He looked at his watch. It was time.

He rose from his haunches, and stretched. She had been on the heroin for five days now. Enough to have developed the level of dependecy that he needed. He would give her another fix, wait for her to enter the perfect state, and begin her education. He took a small wooden box from the ageing fridge in the open plan kitchen, unlocked the padlock on the bedroom door, withdrew the bolt, and went inside. The shape of her pale body shone pearlike in the half light seeping through the cheap cotton curtains.

'It's me,' he said softly. 'Johnny. Everything is good. Nothing to worry about. Johnny is here. Johnny will look after you.'

They met at one of the Agency's forty offices. The former North West Headquarters of the National

Crime Squad. Less than thirty minutes from Longsight, for Agent Barnes it was currently home.

'Who wants to kick off?' he asked, settling into his chair.

'Since we both got here early,' Caton replied, 'I took the opportunity to bring Superintendent Yeadon...'

'Sally.' she reminded him, smiling encouragement. The black curls which he had last seen trapped beneath the hood of her Tyvek shone as brightly as her teak brown eyes.

'To bring Sally,' he said. 'Up to date with the Manchester scenario: the Lock 12 victim, the Drum Mountain clash, the Chinatown investigation, and our meeting with the Chinese Business Forum.'

'In which case, Sally, I guess it's your turn.' Ray Barnes said, pouring himself a glass of water.

She flipped open the leather document case and passed them each a copy of a single page of print.

'That shouldn't take too long,' she said. 'The five dead males were definitely illegal immigrants. The most likely points of entry were Hull, or Immingham. We're waiting on details of every lorry and container that entered those docks in the two days prior to the discovery of the victims.' She looked at Agent Barnes, who swivelled his chair to face Caton.

'SOCA has a list of all the companies and shippers that we suspect may be involved in illegal human traffic. We also have a list of those we are either investigating, or seeking to build intelligence about, that may be involved in other forms of smuggling; drugs, counterfeit goods, and banned substances. I'll see you get them.'

'Both North Yorkshire Police, and the Agency,' Yeadon continued. 'Are certain from the appearance, clothes, and several personal possessions recovered from the dump site, that the victims originated in Fujian province in South East China. The cause of their deaths has been confirmed as carbon monoxide poisoning. In two cases they had actually drowned in their own vomit, but the common factor was CO in their blood streams. Forensics are still working on the remains of the lorry found on your patch Tom, but there's very little to go on. What we do know, from the tyre tracks leading into Newhey Quarry, is that the vehicle was also at Eggborough sand pits. The tax disc was missing, and the license plates had been cloned. The lab is not confident that it can recover either the engine number or chassis number. Even if it could, I'd lay a pound to a penny the vehicle was stolen in the first place.'

She poured herself a glass of water, and waited for one of them to comment.

'It seems to me,' Caton responded. 'That you and I are in much the same position. Unless someone comes forward with some information – and let's face it there isn't exactly a brilliant track record when it comes to cases like these – we haven't got a lot to go on.' He turned to the agent. 'Is it true Ray, what those businessmen told us about not employing illegals? About having enough Chinese students from the Universities willing to work the evening and weekend shifts, and right through their holidays? '

Barnes nodded. 'Broadly speaking, yes. It's true that they do employ a hell of a lot of students, just as they said. But almost all of those work out front as waiters and waitresses, or in the offices. Very few are willing to work in the kitchens. They may do some of the prep work, but not washing up, or cleaning the floors and equipment. We know the top restaurants have tried hard to avoid employing illegals. It's too much of a hassle, and the new wave of illegals stand out – both in appearance, in language, and traditions. They don't fit in well with the Cantonese, and the well established British Chinese.' He drained his glass and placed it on the table, rocking it from side to side, examining the reflections it threw across the polished table top.

'And there's another factor. Ever since the cockle pickers died out on the treacherous sands of Morecambe Bay the gang masters have turned increasingly to supplying the takeaways, and the sex trade. But when it comes down to shortage, needs must. Let's face it, how many English hotels do you know that are staffed by British born? And of the rest, how many do you think are here legally? The new East European migrants may be legal, but they've had a knock on effect that's causing a real headache for the Agency. Employers have started switching to these legal migrants, and displacing those who have been working illegally. So what are the displaced now going to do to survive, if not more serious crime? And how are the Triads going to respond to increased competition squeezing out their human traffic? Your two investigations may just be symptomatic of some of this. An early warning if you like.'

'Do you think the two are linked Ray?' Caton asked.

'You tell me. You've both heard about each others' cases. What do you think?'

'The Eggborough Five are a real puzzle,' Sally Yeadon said first. 'On the one hand, it could have been an accident. In the past decade there have been a score of multiple deaths like this, here, in Europe, and America. Illegal immigrants desperate to avoid detection; likewise the carriers. Sealed in airless over-heated containers. But most of those have involved death from asphyxiation, overheating, or dehydration; and very occasionally from hypothermia. So far there is nothing to suggest that the exhaust on the lorry was faulty, or, that even if it was, the fumes could have entered the main compartment. Perhaps it was a cynical decision to take the money, and not have to provide work or bed. But why not do that from the outset, rather than trail them a third of the way across the world? And why forego the money still owing? There must be more to it than that.'

'Perhaps they thought they were in imminent danger of discovery,' Caton suggested. 'And wanted to cover their tracks. To silence potential witnesses. Especially if they were only one part of the cargo. That would certainly tie in with what happened to Michael Han, James Lee, and the one at Lock 12.'

'What about the Drum Mountain?' Barnes asked him. 'Would it hold true for that as well?'

Good question. Caton had been wrestling with that ever since he'd arrived at the takeaway. 'I'm not sure,' he said. 'If they had wanted to silence anyone, I'm prepared to bet no one would have been left alive. Not even those children. I think they wanted information, which would also explain why the bird man was tortured before he died.'

Sally Yeadon stared at him quizzically. 'Bird man?'

'Feng. It means phoenix. You remember I said he had the name tattooed beneath the image of a Chinese phoenix? The team preferred bird man to the victim at Lock 12.'

She smiled. 'Can't say I blame them.'

'So,' he concluded. 'We need to know why, across two counties, at least seven people, probably eight, have been permanently silenced, and everyone at the Drum Mountain takeaway is scared witless from speaking to us.'

'And what it is,' Sally Yeadon butted in. 'These people are so desperate to find out.'

'I have a feeling,' Caton said calmly. 'That it's the whereabouts of one or more people whom they still need to silence. The problem is, that if we can't find the answers here, the only chance we may have of saving them is to fly halfway round the world.'

'A third of the way around the world.' Yeadon corrected him.

'My suggestion is that we cover both ends between us,' Barnes told them. 'I and my colleagues can work with your team Sally to firm up on the port of entry, and the possible carriers. There is no way that lorry will have brought them across the channel. The most cursory inspection would have given them up. So there must have been a switch. What we'll try and do is identify known and suspected carriers. Then we can work through Europol, and the police in the Netherlands, to take it a stage further. If you two feel you can leave the domestic side to your team, you may be better served firming up the identification of your victims, and see if you can get a hold on the snakeheads who were paid to bring them here.'

Caton and Yeadon looked at each other. 'I think I can manage that,' she said. 'Although it would help if the Agency could apply a bit of pressure on DCS Speed.'

'I don't think I'll have a problem either,' Caton told him. 'I have every confidence in my team. My boss will be supportive, and DCS Hadfield is so desperate to get it sorted he'll probably agree to almost anything; especially if it has the Agency behind it.'

'Easily impressed then?' Barnes asked.

'Yes, but it's more than that. I think he sees it as his way out of the politics and bureaucracy.'

The agent laughed. 'He's in for a big surprise then. Marginally less politics perhaps, but just as many targets and tantrums.'

'My visa is still current,' Caton said. 'What about yours Sally? It can take months.'

'Given our special relationship,' the Agent said. 'With the crime enforcement and home security agencies of a maturing, and politically anxious, Democratic People's Republic of China, I'm sure we can get that sorted straight away.' He seemed suddenly to notice the words printed across the front of his file. 'And by the way. The powers that be have agreed to upgrade this to operational status within the Agency. We're calling it, Operation Tiger's Cave.'

They both gave him the same quizzical look.

'That's the thing about being in the East Asian section;,' Barnes continued. 'We have a number of experts with a Chinese Studies background. Apparently, it's from a traditional Chinese proverb: If you don't go into the cave of the tiger, how are you going to get its cub?'

Caton had no problem persuading Helen Gates, and she had no problem in exercising her magic on Detective Chief Superintendent Hadfield. His one tricky decision was who to leave in charge. Gordon Holmes was the older of the two, but he and Sarah Weston had equal seniority, and had both been promoted to Inspector at more or less the same time. In the event Sarah made it easy for him.

'It's alright Boss,' she said. 'We've talked it over. Gordon kept the Chinatown investigation going all the time we were tied up with Bojangles. And he went out to China with you last time. It's only right that he should head this up while you're away.'

And so it was decided. Gordon Holmes agreed that he would involve his fellow inspector in all of the key decision making, and make sure the rest of the team knew that. It took a weight off Caton's mind.

Caton insisted on stacking the dishwasher. There wouldn't be time in the morning. He had to be at Manchester airport by six thirty, to get the shuttle to Heathrow. That meant leaving the apartment by six. Kate had offered to do all that, but this was his apartment, and he didn't feel they'd reached a stage where he could just expect her to. While he cleaned up, Kate made the coffee, and poured them both an Armagnac.

'How's the Ramsbottom Rapist going?' he asked as they settled down on the sofa.

'Well, there isn't an obvious suspect,' she said. 'So they've decided to start voluntary DNA testing.'

'Based on the profile you gave them?'

162

'Based on my profile, on what limited descriptions they got from earlier incomplete attacks, and from two later attacks which were fended off. They're going to test all males between eighteen and forty within a three mile radius of the attack sites.'

'And anyone who refuses, will be come right under the microscope. Have their lives picked inside out.'

'Within the limits imposed by the Police and Criminal Evidence Act.' she added playfully.

'Of course. Surely the main problem won't be people refusing. The big problem will be impersonation,' he said. 'It's happened before.'

'That's why they're going to demand photo ID. A passport or driving licence. What they're really worried about is the perpetrator taking off as soon as he finds out.'

'Which would be as good as confessing.'

'Only if his name is on the electoral register. And if someone close to him isn't prepared to lie about him having left.'

She took a sip of coffee and changed the subject. 'What about your investigation. How's that going? You haven't told me where you're up to. Only that you have to go to China.'

It took him fifteen minutes to go over all of circumstances surrounding each of the deaths, and the actual events as he understood them.

'So what do you think?' he said at last. 'Professionally speaking? What are we looking at here?'

She put her cup down and steepled her fingers.

'On the face of it, it presents as a series of assassinations. Crime related. In the case of the third victim, gang related. And we know that serial killers tend to operate alone, or at best in pairs. However there is something about the MO of all three that appears to be consistent with the behaviour of a serial killer. Characteristically the serial killer gains much of his, or less frequently her – satisfaction, through the process of seeking out and selecting a victim. For them the thrill of the hunt is as satisfying as the kill itself. There is also the satisfaction to be derived from a well executed plan. The victim has to be taken at exactly the right moment, and in just the right place. Has to be subdued, controlled, quite possibly abused. And finally killed. The kill may be the climax – often sexually as well as emotionally and intellectually – or it may be incidental. Then there is the manner in which the body is concealed or displayed. We saw that with Bojangles. For him, display was far more important than the kill. In his mind, his victims were already dead when he took them. And finally, there is the taking, or not, of a trophy.'

'Which in this case the killer did not.'

'You can't know that for certain. But on the face of it, it looks unlikely.'

'So given all that, what's your conclusion?'

'In the case of your three victims, there is no question that they were carefully selected. They were taken without any witnesses, and in places where they would not normally have been. No attempts were made to hide the bodies. In that sense you could say they were deliberately, and publicly, displayed. And finally, there is the manner in which they were killed. The repeated smashing of the head against a hard surface, required – as your pathologist pointed out –

close, personal, hands on contact by the killer. There was no intermediary to come between them; no knife, or gun, or other weapon. Just the killer and the victim. And the killer looking directly into the victims eyes, watching the light in them go out.'

'You say they were displayed? They looked dumped to us.'

'There is an element of display – especially in the last one, the one in the lock. Basically it's a statement. The FBI would call it a signature. The killer wants you to see what he's done. He's telling you that he's proud of it; of how he's mastered, and tortured, his victim. He's not afraid of you. On the contrary; he's the one to be feared.'

Caton was unconvinced. 'You keep saying he, and yet we know that there were a number of assailants involved in the slashing of the last victim, and in dumping him in the lock.'

She shook her head. 'But you told me those cuts were made after his death. And the purpose of the canal was probably to make it even harder for you to get forensic evidence.'

'So what are you saying?' he asked.

'That I'm sure your killings are just what you think they are. Assassinations related to serious criminal activity. Gangs may well be involved, but in every case the actual death has been identical. I think you're looking for a paid assassin. A psychopath who, if he wasn't engaged in this particular trade, would probably be a serial killer.'

She could see Caton going over it in his mind. She pulled the cushion from behind her back, and began to hit him with it.

'You beggar, Tom Caton. The only reason you asked about the Ramsbottom Rapist was so you could pick my brains about your case. And for free! I've a good mind to bill GMP for my time.'

'They know we're seeing each other,' he managed, between fending off the blows. 'They might think it's for special services over and above the call of duty. It's against the law, soliciting, you'll get us both sacked.'

He wrestled the cushion from her hands, pushed her back onto the sofa, and smothered her giggles with his lips.

'What's this Superintendent Yeadon like anyway?' she wanted to know, plumbing the pillow up behind her; pulling the single sheet up over her naked breasts. 'Rock solid Yorkshire copper worked his way up through the ranks, or a Grand Worshipful in the Masonic Lodge?'

'Where the hell did that come from?' Caton asked as he padded back into the bedroom with two glasses of Armagnac he had recovered from underneath the black lace underwear strewn across his coffee table. He handed her a glass, and climbed back into bed beside her. 'All that stuff about the Masons is years out of date, and anyway she is…'

'She?!' Kate cut him off. 'Since when was he a she?'

'Since she was born I guess.' Caton said, hanging onto his glass with both hands as he dodged a prodding elbow.

'What's her name? How old is she? Is she attractive? She'd better not be attractive.'

'Sally.'

'Sally!? Like in the song: Queen of our alley?'

'And I've no idea how old she is. A good bit older than me.'

'I asked if she was attractive.'

'I didn't really notice.' He lied.

'Well you'd better not.' She drained the glass, slid one hand beneath the sheets, gliding like a snake with a prey in its sights, placed the other around his neck, and pulled him down towards her. 'And, just in case you do, let me remind you what you'll be missing.'

14

It was quarter to one when the plane left Heathrow. With a time zone difference of eight hours, they were due to land at Pudong International airport, at a quarter to ten the following morning, Shanghai time.

'What do you do for jet lag Tom?' Superintendent Sally Yeadon asked, waving the in-flight magazine as the plane levelled up, and headed out across the Channel. 'It says here that avoiding stress, getting your affairs in order, getting plenty of exercise, and getting a good night's sleep before you leave, is really important.'

'Bit late to tell me that,' Caton said, looking out of the window at the cotton wool clouds obscuring the sea below. And in my case, he reflected ruefully, it was either exercise or sleep; and exercise had won.

'At least it's a day flight,' she continued. 'That's supposed to be better than flying at night. And plenty of liquids, especially water. When you think about it, it's a bit daft telling you to avoid alcohol, and then providing it free. What is that all about? And exercise. Walk up and down the aisle, it says, and do some stretches and side bends. I can see the stewards loving that when they're trying to shove their trolleys up and down.'

Just fifteen minutes into the flight, and Caton was already considering making use of the complimentary ear plugs and blindfold. 'Have you brought a book with you?' he asked with as much innocence as he could muster.

She fixed him with a quizzical stare. The corners of her mouth curled just enough to suggest that he had one chance to redeem himself. 'Are you telling me to shut up before we've barely left the ground, Chief Inspector? This doesn't bode too well for a twelve hour flight, let alone a close working relationship.'

'I'm sorry,' he said. 'I didn't mean it like that. You don't seem to have a book. I wondered if you wanted to borrow one of mine?'

'What have you got?'

'Samuel Pepys - The Unequalled Self, by Claire Tomalin, and The Tango Singer by Tomas Eloy Martinez.'

Her smile widened. 'My, but you have an interesting line in light reading. What do you read with your serious hat on; Homer's Iliad in the original Greek?'

Caton had to laugh. 'No, I did that at school.' He decided to come clean. 'Look Sally, to tell you the truth I didn't sleep that well last night. I just know it's going to catch up with me.'

'Fair enough,' she said. 'I tell you what. As soon as we've had lunch you can tell me your life history, I'll tell you mine. Then I'll let you get your head down. Who knows, I'll probably need a sleep myself by then.'

And so it was, by three o'clock in the afternoon, that Sally Yeadon was only the second person in the world, after Kate, to have uncovered so much of Caton's life. The story of his parent's death. How he had survived the accident, and gone to live with his mother's sister, and her husband. Of his time at the prestigious Manchester Grammar, and the culture shock it had been after eight years in the State system. She knew about his former sporting prowess; his commitment to keeping fit; his monthly sessions with The Alternatives Reading Group in the Old Nags Head that explained The Tango Singer – this month's choice. She was not surprised that his passion for the job had helped to undermine a marriage entered far too young, and was aware of his commitment to his team, and lack of further ambition. She was disappointed to discover that he had been hooked – more she suspected than he realised - by a senior lecturer in Forensic Psychology at the University of Manchester.

For his part, Caton had learned more about Sally Yeadon than he had of any woman other than Laura his ex wife, and Kate. Not that there was that much to learn. The daughter of a miner and a doctor's receptionist, she and her three brothers and two sisters had not had an easy time. Not that they ever wanted for the basics, but after the miner's strike, and the closure of the pits, things became tight; and not just financially. Her father never recovered from the blow to his pride, and the sense of betrayal. She was the eldest, and was expected to muck in with the housework, help bring up the others, and sacrifice her own youth to the needs of the family. When she decided to join the police it was as though she had slapped her father in the face, and put the boot in all over again. Every time he saw her in uniform, he was back on the picket lines facing the enemy. It was inevitable that she would leave home before he threw her out. From that point on, the story was one of total immersion in the job; ruthless ambition, rapid promotion. There had never been a husband, and little time for boyfriends. She was still young enough, Caton pointed out. There was still time. But she'd already raised one family, she wasn't sure she needed another one.

Caton put the ear plugs in, and picked up the blindfold. He looked across at her, already fast asleep beside him. He had been right. She was as close to Helen Gates as you could get. Younger, a little more attractive, and much, much, more lonely. If it wasn't for Kate... He pushed the thought aside, placed the blindfold over his eyes, and prayed for sleep.

It was ten degrees centigrade on the ground, the pilot had said. Light drizzle. Sufficient to deny them their first sight of Shanghai, a twenty first century phenomenon rising ever skywards on the banks of the Huangpu river. Caton pressed close to the window as the plane scythed through a layer of cloud the colour of Welsh slate. Suddenly there was grey blue sea beneath them that changed to swirling green and yellow swathes. They crossed one finger of land dissected by the great Yangtze river, and then another. The same approach path, from the north, over the delta, as the last time he had been here.

Sally Yeadon leaned as far towards him as her seat belt would allow; her chest against his. Her hair brushed his cheek as she strained to see. One hand was on his thigh supporting her weight. He felt her fingers tighten as the wheels hit the runway, bouncing once before the brakes bit.

'God, that's amazing' she said. A loose curl tickled his ear as she nodded at the building past which they were taxiing. A massive undulating wave of electric blue, picked out in a string of bright white pearls.

'The Terminal Two building,' Caton said. A Richard Rogers creation. It's due for completion later this year. They're building it, among other things, to cope with the visitors for the Beijing Olympics in 2008, and the World Expo here in Shanghai in 2010.' She straightened up, and started checking the pocket on the back of the seat in front. Caton craned his neck for a final glimpse of the building. 'I can't believe how far it's come on since I was here last year,' he said. 'Welcome to China.'

The Terminal One building was modern, if unspectacular. Unfortunately, the way in which customers were treated was every bit as bad as Caton remembered. They waited ages for immigration control which was not helped by the virtually nonexistent command of English, and the consistent bad manners, of the airport staff. 'It's not like this everywhere,' Caton told her. 'Far from it. But this airport is still state controlled. You'll find a lot of the privately managed concerns, including the hotels, are courteous, helpful, and desperate to please.'

'I'll have to take your word for it,' she rubbed the calf on her left leg irritably. 'I thought someone was supposed to be meeting us.'

As if by magic, a man approached the meeting point and headed directly for them. He was six foot tall, Chinese, with platinum blonde hair and eyebrows to match.

'Mr Caton, Ms Yeadon I'm so sorry to have kept you waiting. An accident on the ring road,' he held out his hand. 'Steven Yung. Mr Munby, the Resident, sends his apologies. He'll join you this evening. '

They shook his hand in turn, unable to tear their eyes away from his hair.

'Don't ask,' he said grinning. 'It's for a job I'm on. I'll tell you later.' He signalled to the porter lingering out of view behind him, to load their cases on the trolley. Without waiting to see that it was happening, he set off at a brisk pace towards the car parks. 'Hope you had a good journey?' he said. 'It's rush hour, but then it always is here. Still, we should have you in your hotel within half an hour or so.'

Simultaneously Caton and Yeadon glanced nervously over their shoulders, and were relieved to see their luggage following behind.

Only when they were settled in the back of the Lexus RX 350, did Agent Yung relax. 'Sorry about the Mr and Ms, but you never know who may be listening. Right now it wouldn't be good for someone to see me meeting two police officers from the UK. Best if you just call me Steven in public. Definitely not Agent.'

'Fine by us Steven,' Caton said. 'I'm happy with Tom,'

'And Sally's fine by me,' Yeadon said.

'I'm impressed that a SOCA Agent is driving a car like this,' Caton said.

'Yung laughed. 'We'll don't be. This is part of my cover. When the job's done it goes back, and they've told me that if I have an accident I'll have to pick up the excess.'

'Interesting cover,' said Yeadon, fishing.

'It's a major financial investigation,' he said. 'Involving some of the bright young things in the financial district. High living, high spending, way beyond their considerable salaries, and yearly bonuses. Everything points to money laundering for criminal syndicates through the companies they work for. There are direct links to London, so I'm working with the authorities here, and the SOCA intelligence and enforcement teams at home. There's no link with your investigation, so that's as much as I can tell you I'm afraid.'

He was polite but very firm. They turned their attention to the sights as they sped along the Ying Bin Outer Ring Road. The rain had ceased, and the sun had broken through.

'I had no idea there would be so many parks.' Sally Yeadon said as they passed immaculate pockets of green spaces between the glass and steel skyscrapers. Magnolias and flowering cherries provided graceful sprays of white and pink above the banks of gaudier bulbs.

'China has more land devoted to growing plants and flowers than any other country on this planet.' Yung replied without turning his head. 'A third of the world's total. Only we are not very good at it. Cultivation is so inefficient that only a small fraction reaches the market. It's a metaphor for the nation really. But in ten's year's time all that will have changed. Take this city for example. At the beginning of the 20th Century it was the greatest commercial and financial centre in the East; second only to London and New York. The whole of China suffered badly in the

1930's and 40's through the wars with Japan, and the civil war between the Nationalists and the Communists. But when the Communists came to power in 1949 that marked a disastrous period for Shanghai. Heavy taxes, the purging of the majority of the businessmen, and entrepreneurs, and the cutting off of relations and trade with much of the West spiralled her into decline.' He stopped talking while they exited the A20 and dropped down to the Longdon Lau. Sally Yeadon waited until he'd turned left onto the road, and entered cruise mode, then asked.

'So how did they get from that to this?'

'In 1992, the Government decided it was time to come out of the dark ages. They passed a decree allowing what they called market economic regeneration in Shanghai. The rest, as they say, is history. You are in the largest city in China; the eighth largest in the world. It's the largest cargo port on the planet, and the engine room and heart of China's economic, commercial, and financial revolution.' They saw his eyes smiling at them in the driver's mirror. 'Think of the Gold Rush in California; that's Shanghai today.'

Caton was thinking of Manchester in the heydays of the Industrial Revolution, and of her new financial and cultural revolution. She was never going to rival a city such as this. But then neither, in ten years time, would any other city in Europe.

'Is English spoken at all in Shanghai?' Yeadon wanted to know.

'It's only spoken well by those older people who were university educated before the cultural revolution; most of whom will be seventy or over.

And also by anyone who works for a foreign company, or does a lot of business with them. But all of the children are taught English from the primary school onwards, and have been for the past quarter of a century. Although Mandarin is the official language now, everyone also speaks Shanghaiese dialect. It's a sign of their independent spirit. But you've no need to worry, the hotel staff all speak passable English, and you'll have an interpreter when you get permission to meet the families.'

'You already know who they are?' Caton asked him.

Yung shook his head, his eyes on the busy junction where he was turning right. 'I don't know. You'll have to ask Mr Munby.' He pointedly changed the subject. 'We've just passed the industrial and hi-tech districts. This is the Expo Centre on your left. In a minute we'll cut past Century Park and we'll be in Pudong; the Financial District. Wait till you see it. Canary Wharf eat your heart out.'

They were not disappointed. In this architectural playground, slim towers of glass soared skywards. There were cylinders, and cones, cubes and pyramids, prisms, tetrahedrons, octahedrons, and shapes that Caton's 'O' Level maths had left him ill equipped to recognise.

'I thought Manhattan was amazing, but this...' Sally Yeadon searched in vain for an alternative superlative. 'There's just so much more green and open space between them.

'Coming up on your left the Bund Food Hall,' Yung told them, sounding ever more like a tour guide. 'You can't really tell from here but there are seven spokes radiating from a central wheel that is crammed with retail food outlets and restaurants. Up ahead, is the Pearl of the Orient Television tower.'

Oblivious to the horns of impatient drivers in a permanent state of road rage, he circled the roundabout slowly several times, giving them a better chance to see it from a comfortable distance. Rocket-like, it stood head and shoulders above the rest. Three pink and steel coloured globes of diminishing size, encircling it at intervals, gave it the appearance of a planetary minaret.

'And now,' he said, 'I'll run you along the east bank of the river. We're going to cross at the Yangpu Bridge, just a bit north of here. I'm afraid there are always hold ups on the bridges. People keep taking overloaded vehicles across, and either breaking down or smashing into the infrastructure. And the tunnels are chock-a-block all the time. They're building another six as I speak. The plan is for twenty tunnels under the Hungpau by 2010. State of the art, and you can bet they'll be finished on time.'

'There must be problems that come with growing this fast?' Caton said.

Yeung nodded his head vigorously. 'Tell me about it. Thirteen million people, going on twenty. The two big problems – apart from the congestion – are the massive wave of internal worker migration as people are drawn from the rural areas to the honey pot, and the massive wealth gap that goes with it. The criminal elements are having a field day. What you're experiencing back home is part of their export drive.' At which point he fell silent, taking his place in the queue waiting to get onto the bridge.

177

They crossed the broad Huangpu, and followed the river West before crossing the much smaller Wusong river, and skirting the northern perimeter of Old Shanghai. As soon as they hit the Nanjing Road they found themselves back in the twenty first century. Traditional stores selling jade and silk, embroidery and clocks jostled with vast department stores, with Tiffany and Armani, Dunhill and Mont Blanc. Exotic looking Chinese restaurants, cinemas, open air bars, and modern street cafes mingled with McDonalds and KFC. This was the first time, other than at the airport, that Caton had seen anyone of Western appearance. Here, on Nanjing Road, the world came to play just as they did on Oxford Street, and Kensington High Street. Through her window Sally Yeadon was taking in the fashions worn by the young and wealthy Shanghaiese. Many of the clothes and shoes would have originated on the Paris, London, New York and Milan cat walks. Steven Yung's extreme appearance was no longer out of place, she decided. It was de rigueur.

The car pulled up outside another gleaming tower; all angles and points. Their driver turned in his seat, and beamed at them.

'End of the tour folks. Welcome to the Hotel Sofitel Hyland. Only four star, but that's all a public service budget runs to I'm afraid. Although I think you'll find it more than adequate. The staff will help you with your cases. A taxi will pick you up at seven pm. In the meantime, have a look around. You couldn't be better placed. All the sites – old and new – within a mile in any direction. And if you have to, you can shop till you drop.' His smile disappeared, his voice became serious. 'Whatever you do though, take one of the hotel cards with the name on in Mandarin, and Shanghaiese. If you get lost, there's no telling that anyone will understand you, taxi drivers included. You'll find men and women trying to persuade you to patronise their bar or coffee shop. In your case, Mr Caton, some of them will suddenly spring female companionship on you.' He raised his platinum eyebrows. 'Just think Soho, and you'll know what to expect. Watch out for pick pockets, and stay on the main drag. No wandering off exploring dark passageways, and cute courtyards.' The grin returned. 'Listen to me,' he said. 'Dishing out the standard tourist warnings to a pair of police officers.'

The hotel was newly decorated. Bright and airy, spacious and tasteful. They were booked in efficiently, and whisked off to their rooms, agreeing to meet up in an hour and a half. Caton's room was a superior double he decided. The king sized bed had two double sets of plumptious pillows, white cotton sheets, and a white dimple coverlet with another, in soft grey, folded across the bottom. The walls appeared to be veneered in rosewood. A bowl of exotic fruit stood on the table. He crossed to the window and raised the cream Venetian blind. In the middle distance the sun slanted off the towering Pearl of the Orient. It was easy to imagine how spectacular this view would be at night. The only thing missing was Kate.

'Your taxi is here Mr Caton' The woman on reception told him. 'I have already called Ms Yeadon. She says she will meet you in the lobby.'

Caton had a quick look in the mirror, and walked over to the window. As far as the eye could see there was a geometric gem fest of blue and white, and pink and purple; amethysts and diamonds shimmering against the night sky. He lowered the blind, and collected his BlackBerry from the bedside table. He tried Kate's number for the third time since they'd arrived. Still no international connection. He placed it in his inside pocket, and let himself out.

Dave Munby was much closer to the stereotype that Caton had in his head. At a guess, the Resident Agent was in his early to mid fifties. The same height as Caton, a touch under six foot, he had an almost military bearing, but moved in an unhurried way that spoke of hard earned confidence. Ex MI6, was Caton's guess; straight out of a John Le Carre novel. He could easily have been the resident spook in the British Embassy in Beijing during the difficult days, or possibly in Hong Kong before the handover. Munby held the chair for Sally Yeadon as she slid gracefully into place, brushed back a strand of silver hair that had fallen over his forehead, and sat down. Yeadon looked surprisingly attractive Caton thought, in high heels and a red fitted three quarter length silk dress that revealed a firm full figure that came as a complete surprise. She had taken the trouble to straighten her hair through a visit to the hotel hair salon, and it suited her.

'I hope you like it here,' the Resident said in a rich and mellow voice. 'It's a bit corny really, bringing you into the Old Town, but I don't suppose you were expecting a hotel?'

'It's amazing,' Sally Yeadon said again. Caton wondered if it was the only descriptive word in her vocabulary. 'All lit up in gold, and those curvy roofs like a pagoda. Brilliant!'

That makes two, Caton acknowledged. Amazing and brilliant.

'What about you Tom?' Munby asked as the green tea arrived, and the waiter poured them each a cup. 'What do you think of the Shanghai Classical Hotel?'

'To tell you the truth, I've been here before,' Caton replied. ' But only for a drink in the bar. We did the obligatory tour of Yuyuan Gardens, and it looked really attractive. It's the oldest hotel in the city isn't it?'

'I don't know about that, but it's certainly one of the oldest; 1775. The real reason I brought you here is the food; It's Classical Shanghai cuisine. Ben Bang they call it. It translates as local. Loads of fresh fish, bright colours and strong flavours. I particularly recommend the Eight Auspicious Pepper Sauce. Not a sauce at all. Succulent pork, chicken, shrimp, bamboo shoots, peanuts and tripe, in a fragrant sauce. Then there's the braised silver carp, crisp baked eel, slow braised lamb in a pot..."

Two hours later they were sated. Although the number of dishes Munby ordered had seemed excessive Caton already knew that the Shanghaiese were the butt of jokes elsewhere in China for how little, in relative terms, they ate. The portions were smaller than normal, but the important word was relative. He was still bursting at the seams. Sally Yeadon, on the other hand, seemed to have paced her food well, but not her drink. Caton had stuck with the

Chinese tea and Tsung Tao Beer. Munby had plied Sally with Chinese white wine. He'd started with the fermented huangjiu at eighteen percent, but with a bottle of that emptied between them she was now cradling her second glass of distilled shaojiu, at somewhere between thirty and forty percent. Caton had been wondering if the man from the Agency had an ulterior motive. He still couldn't make up his mind.

'You said the photos Ray Barnes faxed you had come up trumps. ' he said. 'How exactly?'

The Agent put his glass down. His hand was steady, his gaze clear. It was as though he'd only been drinking water. 'Well for a start Tom, your man has been identified. His name was Feng Yi. We've also identified three of yours, Sally. And it looks like you were both right. They are linked. They all set off together, from Fuzhou. As soon as the photographs were printed in the local rags, four of the families came forward. Seems they'd started worrying because none of them had had a phone call since two days before the bodies were discovered. They knew their sons had arrived in Holland, and they had all promised to ring as soon as they were safe in England. They never did. It looks like all the families paid the same snakeheads to take them.'

'And the parents are willing to speak to us?' Caton asked.

'Not just willing, they're desperate to. They want to know what happened. And they want the money back from the snakeheads. Seems they've already given the local police some names.'

'So we're going to see them in the morning?' Sally Yeadon asked, with some difficulty.

'If you'd asked me that when you arrived in Shanghai, I'd have told you to expect to wait at least a week. As it is, you happen to be right. Permission came through this afternoon. I've already booked the seats. Ten thirty in the morning, which means leaving the hotel at eight I'm afraid.'

'How did it come through so quickly?' Caton asked.

'Partly because they remembered you from last time Tom. You must have made quite an impression. But also, because the Government are determined to do something about this. Nothing is quite as embarrassing as lorry loads of dead bodies turning up in the West. Makes it look like citizens of the People's Democratic Republic are literally dying to get out. It doesn't square with the stories of amazing economic progress, or the claims of rapid democratisation. They're extremely frustrated. I think you'll find them a hundred percent behind you. If anything, your main problem might be that they've put so much pressure on the provincial authorities that the local police and internal security might be a little too enthusiastic.'

'Enthu…siastic?' said Yeadon, slurring the word.

'They don't exactly have a police and criminal evidence act over here.' Munby reminded her. 'Nor a European Court of Human Rights.'

'You don't mean torture?' Sally Yeadon said.

'Lets just say, methods of interrogation that wouldn't go down too well with Amnesty International.'

'That's all we need,' Caton said, 'It would make any evidence we get inadmissible in court.'

'Precisely. So you'd better hope you get to any suspects before they do, or at the very least, at the same time that they do. Then all you you've got to do is pray that you're lucky with the police that you're dealing with, and that they understand that you need them to do it your way.'

'How do we do that without making it obvious we're criticising their methods?' Yeadon asked.

The resident Agent picked up his glass and drained it. 'You can't,' he said. 'But I can. That's why I'm coming with you.'

The short ride back to the hotel was interesting for all the wrong reasons. Sally Yeadon only discovered how much she'd drunk when she tried to stand. The high heels made it even more problematic. They had to pour her into the taxi. As the taxi door closed Caton could tell from the twinkle in Munby's eye that he had known exactly what he was doing, and had enjoyed every moment of it. Now he had taken his leave, and Caton had to get her back to the hotel, and up to her room unaided. Instead of taking in the neon technicolor lights of the Nanjing Road Caton was forced to concentrate on keeping her upright on the back seat, and stop her banging her head on the glass partition every time the driver was forced to brake; which was often.

From the concierge to the check-in staff, it was all the hotel employees could do to hide their amusement as he led her towards the lifts. His right arm was around her waist, the other holding her left arm firmly across his shoulders. When they reached her room he had to bend almost double to support her weight across his back as he fumbled in her clutch bag for her room key.

The room was a mirror image of his own, except for the contents of the make up bag strewn across the table top, the discarded towel on the carpet, and the sheer black silk nightdress folded neatly on the pillows by the turn down staff. He led her across the room until she had her back to the bed, and lowered her carefully down. He slipped off her shoes and put them beside the fitted wardrobes. There was no way he was going to risk removing anything else. He stared at her, wondering if it was safe to leave her. He went into the bathroom, and filled a glass beaker with water. She was going to have a hell of a head in the morning, but if he could just get this down her. He turned, walked back into the bedroom and almost collided with her. She was leaning on the door jamb for support. Her free arm brushed the glass aside splashing the wall with water.

'Tom. I knew you'd come,' she slurred, wrapping her arms around his neck. 'Kiss me.'

Caton felt the panic rising inside him. He tried to prise her arms apart but found it impossible to do so without hurting her. Supporting her under each arm he shuffled forward towards the bed, hoping to repeat his earlier manoeuvre. Instead, this time she pulled him down on top of her, clamped her lips on his, and shifted her hands to his buttocks. He placed his hands on the bed on either side of her, and managed to prise himself loose; like pulling a plunger from a sink.

She lay there moaning. 'Come on Tom. You know you want to...'

He went into the bathroom and grabbed a towel. He used it to dry down the wall. Then he refilled the glass, and placed it on the bedside table. He got onto his knees and approached cautiously from the foot of the bed. She opened one eye, and completely misunderstood.

'Oh yes plee…ase Tom…you beast.'

He grabbed her feet, swung them up on to the bed, and dragged her far enough towards the centre to limit the chance of her rolling onto the floor. Her skirt had risen half way up her thighs. Her arms were flung on either side as though in gay abandon, pushing her breasts invitingly towards him. Caton suddenly knew how easy it must be to cross that blurry line between consensual sex, and date rape. He backed towards the door.

'Goodnight Ma'am.' he said. He heard her moan something unintelligible, switched off the light, and closed the door.

There was a string of texts on his phone from Kate; wanting to know if he'd arrived safely. He cursed. Now she would be wondering what he'd been up to all evening. He looked at his watch. It was nearly one o'clock. About nine thirty in the morning in Manchester. She would probably be giving a lecture or a seminar, or in a tutorial. He decided to send her a text. There was less chance of her picking up on the fact that he'd been drinking, no chance of detecting the merest trace of guilt in his voice. Not that he had anything to feel guilty about. Or did he? He lay back on his bed. Women. They were just like the buses on the Wilmslow Road; none for ages, then two come along at once.

15

Caton stared into the shaving mirror, and saw the shower proof clock on the bathroom wall reflected there. Six forty five in the morning. That was three pm in England. 'Bugger!' he said out loud. Kate would be wondering why he still hadn't called. He dashed into the bedroom and tried her number. This time he got through. She answered immediately.

'Hello?'

'Kate. It's Tom.'

'Tom! Thank heavens,' she said breathlessly, 'I was really worried. When you didn't answer my calls, I looked up your flight on the internet, and it said you'd landed on time.

'I couldn't get a connection,' he said. 'It obviously took longer than I expected for them to sort out the mobile link up. I did keep trying. I knew you'd be worried. And by the time I got back to the hotel last night it was too late to call you from the hotel phone.'

'So how is it? What did you do last night?'

'Business. Had a meeting with the SOCA Resident Agent.'

'In a restaurant?'

'That's right.'

'Was Sally Yeadon there?'

'Superintendent Yeadon? Of course.' He tried to sound casual, but felt sure he sounded defensive.

'Good meal?'

'It was very nice. I'll have to bring you here sometime Kate. You'd love it. Amazing place, fantastic shops.' He was beginning to sound like Yeadon. Kate, on the other hand, was hurtling down a single gauge track.

'What time did you get back?'

'Midnight.'

'Long meeting.'

'They might eat fast, but the service is unbelievable. It comes in dribbles.'

'Have a night cap did you?'

'No way. The taxi's coming for us at eight o'clock this morning, and I needed a clear head.' In the time it took her to weigh up whether to risk carrying on with this line of questioning, Caton got in first. 'How was your day? Were you at the university, or over in Ramsbottom?'

He could hear the resignation in her voice. 'I held a seminar. But there's been some good news on the rapist front. One of the best fits with my profile has done a runner. Left home the day he got the letter about the DNA test.'

'Do they know where he's gone?'

'No, but he didn't have any friends, so he hasn't got too many options, and his mother's been co-operative. Mainly because she's in denial; adamant her son is innocent.'

He checked his watch on the bedside table. 'Look, I'm sorry Kate, but I've really got to get a move on.'

'I understand,' she said, although it sounded as though she didn't, but was trying to. 'Where is it you're going?'

'A place called Fuzho. It's south of here. We should

be there by lunchtime. It seems the local police have made some progress.'

'Does that mean you'll be back soon?' He caught the shift of emotion in her voice.

'I don't know Kate, I hope so.'

'I hope so too. I miss you Tom.'

'I miss you too. I've got to go.'

'I know. I love you.'

'I love you too. I'll ring you when we land.'

'Don't promise that Tom, I'll only worry if you don't manage to. Just send me a text, and give me a call when you can.'

'I will. Bye Kate.'

'Bye Tom.'

The silence left him feeling hollow. It was a sensation he hadn't felt in years. That call had been so important, but the words had been all wrong. There was a sound like a waterfall. He'd left the tap running in the wash basin. He rushed in and turned it off. The overflow had done its work. He poured some shaving oil in his palm, and slapped it on his face. The razor was poised in his hand when he remembered Sally Yeadon. He put it back down on the basin, and rushed to the bedside phone. It seemed to take for ever before she picked up.

'He...llo?' She sounded like a bullfrog with a sore throat.

'It's Tom. I just rang to see if you were up.'

'I am now. So you can stop shouting.'

'I'm not shouting Ma'am.' After last night best to keep it formal.

'Well how come your voice is bouncing around the inside of my head?'

'Because you've got a hang-over.'

'Whose fault is that?'

'Look,' he said as calmly as possible. 'We don't have time for all this. The taxi will be out front at eight o'clock. We can't afford to miss it. Will I see you at breakfast?'

'What do you think?'

'I'll give you a knock as I go down,' he said. 'After that, you're on your own.'

'This plane is about as good as it gets on a short internal flight,' Dave Munby told them. 'They're usually OK.'

Usually, didn't inspire a lot of confidence. Caton was wishing they'd gone by train. Yeadon was past caring. She looked like death, and the turbulence wasn't helping. He just hoped she wasn't going to need the sick bag. She pulled the sliding blind down over the window, and closed her eyes.

'We're flying straight down the coast,' Munby told Caton. 'Inland, because air space between the Mainland and Taiwan remains an issue. The province is mountainous and hilly, and there isn't a lot of farmland. Yet they produce a lot of food; rice, seafood and shellfish mainly, although there's a good chance the lychees and the Chinese tea you get at home has come from here.'

'So it's relatively poor?'

'On the contrary. There's quite a bit of money been poured in over the past ten years, by the Government, and by investors in Taiwan. In relative terms, it's one of the wealthier provinces in China.'

'So why are people so desperate to leave?'

'Because whatever the Government would like to believe, this is a capitalist expansion. The money goes to the speculators, the government officials who oil the wheels, the big merchants, the corporations, and the criminal gangs. If you're not working for one of them, you're going to be poor. Especially if you live in one of the mountain villages. Fujian is also a historical jump off point for the internal migrants who have come here from the rest of China across the centuries. When it didn't turn out to be the Eldorado they expected, they'd head for America, Australia, Canada, and Hong Kong. Nowadays they fancy Europe, and England in particular. There are thirty million Chinese living abroad.'

'I know,' Caton said.

Munby looked at him approvingly. 'Done your homework then.'

'They told us at a SOCA seminar.'

The agent smiled. 'Nice to know we're having an impact,' he leaned across the aisle and looked through the window on the opposite side. 'Speaking of which, we'll be at Changle in about five minutes. I wouldn't bother to wake Ms Yeadon up. Best to wait till we land.'

Changle airport was nothing like Pudong. Apart from the fact that it was half the size, Caton thought its best architectural feature was a control tower shaped like a stage microphone. The kind that singers hold in their hands. Like a torch with a wire golf ball on top. On the positive side, they were whisked through arrivals by airport officials primed to receive them as VIPs, and straight into the back of a police car. It was thirty four kilometres to Fuzhou City. Yeadon slept all the way.

'The Golden Resources International Hotel,' Munby told them as the car pulled up outside the twenty storey blue glass tower. 'Five star. But at only a hundred and nine US dollars for a whole suite I can't see the accountants bothering. There's a health club, including a swimming pool and gymnasium, indoor golf, indoor rock-climbing, a shooting gallery where you can hone your skills. And,' he said looking pointedly at Yeadon. 'A beauty spa. Only you'll have to wait till we get back from the station. I think we should get to these families as soon as possible.'

She picked up her room key, and stabbed in his direction. 'You pull another trick like that one last night,' she said. 'And you'll need more than a beauty spa to sort you out. More like a face transplant.' She spun on her heel and headed towards the lifts.

'And there was I wondering if she had the balls for this,' Munby said as he watched her go.

'You'd better believe it.' Caton told him.

The three of them had been waiting for fifteen minutes in an office with an oval table. They each had a glass, and a bottle of mineral water. It was obvious to Caton that the SOCA agent was becoming increasingly frustrated.

'What do you think's happening?' Caton asked.

'God knows. I'm worried they'll want to suck them dry before we get to them. Put the fear of God up them. Make our job harder, not easier.'

'Sometimes I think a bit of fear is what we're missing back home.' Said Sally Yeadon. They both stared at her. She lifted her glass to her lips. 'Let's face it. A bit of respect would be a start.' She emptied the glass, and half filled it again. 'But it's never going to happen is it? Gone too far.'

'When we've a moment, I'll tell you some stories about interview techniques in this station over the past few years,' Munby said. 'It may just change your mind.'

The door opened, and a man walked in; Chinese, in his late forties, dressed in a smart blue uniform with a leather belt that ran diagonally across his chest from his shoulder, to meet the belt around his waist. He had three gold circlets around each arm, and a crest on his epaulets. Wedged under his left arm was a broad blue cap with a large silver badge, and thick gold braid across the centre of the peak. His hair was short, and brushed forward without a parting. His eyes moved to each of them in turn; coolly appraising them. They stood to meet him. Munby introduced himself in Mandarin. The two of them had a brief conversation.

'This is Chief Sergeant Wang Shouwen.' Dave Munby told them. 'He's in charge of the case.'

The policeman stood before Sally Yeadon, placed his right hand over his left breast, and made a short bow with his head, before shaking her hand. He did the same with Caton.

'Apparently there are several provincial officials we have to meet,' Munby told them. 'Protocol really; they're probably curious as much as anything. Then he'll take us to the interview room. They've already interviewed the families I'm afraid, but he says they've been very co-operative,' he cocked an eyebrow, in what by now was clearly an habitual expression, and said as an aside. 'Whatever that means.'

They followed Chief Sergeant Wang from the room. The SOCA agent paused in the doorway, allowing the policeman to get a few strides ahead of them.

'Don't assume,' he told them quietly. 'That because the people we meet don't appear to speak English, they don't actually understand every word we say. A pound to a penny there will be someone in the room that does.'

The meet and greet was exactly as he had predicted. Five minutes of introductions, followed by mutual expressions of concern, and heartfelt co-operation. They were told that President Hu Jintao had pledged in his New Year's address a commitment to deal with transnational crime. This was a commitment strongly supported by the autonomous provincial congress here in Fujian. Caton detected an undercurrent of nervousness behind the bonhomie. He put it down to the presence of a tall thin man who sat on a chair in the corner of the room, was not introduced, and took no part in the proceedings. It was the way in which the others studiously avoided looking in his direction, and his eyes bored holes through their backs; a spectre at the feast.

They were taken directly from the meeting room to another on the second floor. Caton had been expecting an interview room like those at home or, in the worse case scenario, a cell. It came as a surprise to find himself in a room approximately six metres long, and four metres wide, with a rectangular wooden table running down the centre. The reason was immediately obvious. Aside from themselves, there were eleven other people in the room. A male and a female police officer stood on either side of the door. On the side of the table nearest the door sat another police officer, and three official looking men in civilian clothes. On the other side of table sat three men and two women; aged between forty five, and fifty five. One woman was crying; there were streaks down the face of the other one. Her eyes were red raw, and she twisted a sodden handkerchief between her hands. Both women were being comforted by the men beside them. The remaining man stared vacantly into space. It reminded Caton of every time that he had broken unwelcome news to unsuspecting parents. But in this room there was something more. A sense that they felt complicit in the death of their children. Sat in this room, surrounded by policemen, how could they not.

Only when they were seated, did Caton realise that the tall thin man had followed them and had taken a seat in the corner by the door. Dave Munby sat between Caton and Sally Yeadon, the better to translate without having to raise his voice. Chief Sergeant Wang began to introduce the people in the room.

'The policeman beside him is his boss.' said Munby. 'Two of the guys in the suits are from the border police. They are responsible, among other things for preventing illegal immigration. The third one is from the People's Congress here in Fuzhou.'

'What about the one in the corner behind us?' Caton asked.

Without looking, the agent replied quietly. 'Beijing. Ministry of State Security. Probably the First or Second Bureau; domestic or foreign intelligence. The woman who is crying and the man on her right are the parents of a man called Jin Chen. He was one of those found dumped in the sand pit. The other couple, are the parents of your man in the canal Tom; Feng Yi. The man on his own at the end, is the father of another of your victims Sally; Li Bai.'

Chief Sergeant Wang turned, and pointed with an open palm towards Caton, Yeadon and Munby. Everyone else in the room stared at them closely.

'He's introducing us now,'

Without warning, the miserable calm of the room was shattered. Both of the women began to shout and gesticulate. The mother of Jin Chen attempted to rise from her chair, and was held back by her husband. The officers already on their feet made to cross the room and intervene. The one beside Chief Wang waved them back. He let it run its course, waiting until the two of them subsided, sobbing.

'They want to know what happened.' Munby said. 'Have we caught who did it. And most of all, when can they have the bodies back. Don't worry. You won't be asked to respond. Except about the release of the bodies.'

When calm had been restored, Chief Sergeant Wang spoke to the relatives.

'He's telling them that their sons had been murdered by those who had smuggled them into England.'

'We don't know that for certain.' Caton whispered.

'Doesn't matter. It serves their purpose to believe that for the moment.' Munby told him.

The parents turned to them expectantly.

'What do I tell them?' Munby asked.

'We've had all the post-mortem results, and all the forensics we need. I can get the inquest brought forward.' Sally Yeadon said. 'So, we should be able to release the bodies by the end of this month.'

Munby turned to Caton. 'What about Feng, Tom?'

'I'm not sure. But I can try to arrange that. It'll help if there's a strongly worded request from the Government.'

The translation was met with nods of gratitude as the women dabbed their eyes and blew their noses. Then the part for which Caton had come all this way began.

'I'm sure they've asked all these questions already,' Munby warned them. 'So it's mainly for our benefit, as well as to check that the stories stay the same. Either way, you only need to take essential notes. He's assured me they're taping this, and we'll get a copy. Best that I translate verbatim. You'll get a better feel for it.'

'Why did your son wish to go to England?'

The question was addressed to the parents of Jin Chen. The father hugged his wife, and looked down at the table top, avoiding their gaze.

'We live in hardship. I earn less than nine thousand yuan in a good year. We can save nothing for our old age. All around us in the village there are people whose children are abroad, and send them three times that amount every year. They have fine houses, and money for their old age. We only wanted that for ourselves.'

'And a better life for our son.' His wife added through her handkerchief.

'You know this is against the law?' snapped the man from the People's Congress. 'The People's Congress is against this. You must know that.' His voice rose in pitch until it became a tirade. 'Your son is dead. You have brought shame on yourselves, and on your village. What were you thinking?' The father's head bowed lower. His wife shrank back from the assault. The senior police officer leant across Chief Sergeant Wang and whispered in the official's ear.

'They've been doing this for centuries,' Munby said quietly. 'One in three Fujianese lives abroad. Poor bastards probably didn't think they were doing anything wrong.'

'Tell us how you knew who to contact,' Wang said, taking some of the heat out of the moment.

'Everyone in our village knows,' replied the father of Li Bai, taking them all by surprise. 'Even the police.' His voice was powerful, though his demeanour spoke of resignation. His words reverberated around the room, causing a stir among those sitting opposite.

'That is a serious accusation.' The senior officer said.

'It is the truth.'

'Then it will be investigated.'

Wang directed his question back to the parents of Jin Chen. 'How much did you pay?'

'The husband looked up. 'Twenty five thousand dollars.'

'And you?' the Chief Sergeant asked the Fengs, and the father of Li Bai. They nodded in agreement. 'That is a lot of money,' he said. 'How did you get hold of it?'

'We borrowed from our relatives, and also from a moneylender,' said Mr Wu. 'Now they want it back. We have nothing to give them.'

'Me too,' said Mr Feng.

'I started saving when my son was born,' said Mr Li. 'When will you get our money back?'

From across the table, five pairs of eyes searched the face of Chief Sergeant Wang. He looked for support to his superior officer who whispered in his ear. Caton could see the local official going red in the face; fit to burst.

'We will do our best,' said Wang. 'But first we must catch the snakeheads. You mentioned a name before. Please repeat that for us now.'

The women clung tighter to their husbands. One of them was shaking her head back and forth. Caton wondered at their reluctance. Perhaps it was because the foreigners were present. Then he remembered the tall thin man from the Ministry of State Security.

'Yu Lai!' said the father of Li Bai. 'Yu Lai was the one who agreed the price, took the money, and gave us the details of the pick up point.'

'He lives in your village?'

'The next village. He has a nice big house, and a new car every year.'

'He is a snakehead?'

'I don't know. It is clear he works for them. Now can you get us our money back?'

'If what you say is true, the court may confiscate his house. That will help.' Said Chief Sergeant Wang.

'And can you bring my son back?' asked Mrs Feng through her tears. 'Can you do that? Bring back my son? She pushed herself erect, turning to address the three foreigners. 'I sent my son to your country full of hope for a better life. And you now send him back to me in a wooden box. How can this be?'

16

'God, that was awful,' said Sally Yeadon in the car back to the hotel. 'It was one thing to see those bodies, another to meet the mothers'.

'Think yourself lucky that wasn't all of the families, confronting you on the streets of their own village,' said Dave Munby. 'Imagine how you'd feel then.'

'Will they get their money back?' Caton asked

'I doubt it. The last snakehead they caught doing this got a two year sentence, and a twenty thousand dollar fine. By the time they've deducted the court expenses that wouldn't compensate one of the families, let alone all of them.'

'But seven people have died so far,' said Yeadon.

'That we know of,' added Caton.

'I suppose that would up the ante,' the agent agreed. 'But they'd still have to catch the whole gang, and not just the middleman.'

'So where do we go from here?'

'Wang says they'd already got Yu Lai under observation. They'll pull him in tonight. Bring him down to Fuzhou, and interview him in the morning. He's promised we can be there from the start this time.'

'Already under observation?' said Caton. 'So it's true. He is known to them.'

'Has been for three years or more. Him and a dozen others like him.'

'So why haven't they pulled him in before now?'
Sally Yeadon asked.

'Because some of the local officials are on the take,
and in any case, regardless of what I said about
methods of interrogation they still need evidence that
will stand up in court. There's no way the families
are going to admit to what's going on. Least of all
in court.'

'Until something goes badly wrong,' said Caton.
'Like now.'

'Exactly.'

'So in a way this has become an opportunity for the
authorities?'

'A mixed blessing more like. They have to balance
their loss of face, against a successful prosecution. On
one hand, the Fuzhou People's Congress has to be
showing Beijing that they're doing something about
it, on the other hand, every funeral is a public
reminder that it's far from under control.'

'And we're just a further embarrassment?' Yeadon
said.

'That's about the size of it. But they'd much rather
you got it sorted at your end, and out of the glare of
Western media.'

'That's exactly how DCS Hadfield put it.' said
Caton

'It's the last thing DCS Speed said to me as I left the
office,' Sally Yeadon chuckled. 'Perhaps we could get
them both a transfer to Beijing.

They agreed to spend the afternoon doing their own
thing. All of them needed to use the business
broadband link in their rooms to catch up on their

emails. It was too late for Caton and Yeadon to contact their teams back home, but not to keep a hold on their virtual in-tray.

'Why don't we meet up later on to write up our report on this morning?' Yeadon suggested to Caton as they rode the lift together. 'Might save us some time, and they say two heads are better than one.'

Caton thought about it for a moment. It made sense. 'OK, how about four o'clock, and then we'll have plenty of time to get ready before dinner?'

Her face lit up. 'Great. Your room or mine?'

Caton managed to keep his face deadpan. 'I was thinking about the Business Centre. Then we could print it out, fax it, whatever.' It was a lame excuse, and she knew it. To her credit, she didn't let it show.

'Good idea,' she said. 'Give me a ring when you're going down.'

The lift arrived at her floor, and the doors opened. She stepped out without a backward glance.

The first thing he did was text Kate. She would probably be in bed, but at least she'd know he hadn't forgotten her. Fifteen minutes later his mobile rang.

'Tom. I finally got your text. And the one you sent from the airport. How's it going?'

He looked at his watch. 'It must be midnight in Manchester.'

There was a smile in her voice. 'Quarter past, actually. Midnight in Manchester. Isn't that a record?'

'You're thinking of Midnight in Moscow. Midnight in Manchester, is a poem actually. It's by Tony Connor, an American. How come you're still awake?'

'I was reading.'

'Since when did you read 'till that time?'

'Since you waltzed half way round the world.'

'A third of the way, actually.'

'You're turning into a nerd Tom Caton.'

Must be catching, Caton thought, I can't believe I've just done a Yeadon.

'What did you do today?'

'Met some of the bereaved families at the police headquarters. It was hard.'

'I can imagine. Did you get any new information?'

'They gave the local police the name of the fixer. The man who set up the arrangements, and took the money.'

'That's good isn't it?'

'It's a start.'

'What are you doing now?'

He could picture her. Curled up in bed, a pillow tucked beneath her elbows, the phone to her ear. 'Chatting to you,'

He heard her laugh, happy, crystal clear from fifteen thousand miles away. 'I love you Kate,' he said softly.

'I love you too. Now answer the question. What are you going to do when you put down this phone? I need to picture it. It'll help me get to sleep.'

It was Caton's turn to laugh. 'I doubt it. I shall be logging on, dealing with a load of emails; checking if I've got any text or phone messages; then writing a report on today's meeting.'

'And then?'

'Going for a swim.'

'You took your swim shorts with you?'

'I always do. Anyway, you can usually buy a pair in the hotel.'

'And then?'

'Have a drink in the bar, followed by a meal in the restaurant.'

'On your own?'

It had taken her longer this time, Caton reflected, but she'd got there in the end. 'Of course not. With the SOCA Resident Agent, Dave Munby and Superintendent Yeadon.,

'Very nice. I'd hate to think of you eating alone.'

Caton decided to face it up.

'You're not jealous are you Kate?'

She laughed again. A little too forced this time.

'Of Agent Munby? Should I be?' she said.

'Of Detective Superintendent Sally Yeadon. She's not only older than me, she's a superior officer.'

'Superior,' she said mischievously. 'That sounds interesting. Are we talking S&M here by any chance?'

'Don't be daft.'

'Did you see Disclosure Tom? Michael Douglas and Demi Moore? Very nasty. Lock your door before you go to bed is all I'm saying. You might not be able to trust either of them.'

He was able to laugh at that, and found her joining in. 'I'll do that,' he said. 'And I'll put a chair against the door just in case.'

'Now I shall be able to sleep easier,' she said.

Caton could tell that she meant it.

According to the emails progress had been slow. Gordon Holmes had been as good as his word, sending a one page report. Despite the involvement of Immigration, and threats of deportation against the remaining kitchen workers at the Drum Mountain takeaway, and of obstructing the police against the family, no names had been forthcoming. He reckoned that the gang that had attacked them was unconnected with the one that called once a week to collect what they owed. So they probably didn't know the names anyway. And if there was a third party, they weren't admitting it. There had been one development though. Caton's hunch that Feng had been at the takeaway was now confirmed. His fingerprints were all over the place. Along with another set of prints they hadn't been able to eliminate. Caton emailed him back, telling him to send a faxed set to the hotel business centre for his attention, and to email them as a jpeg file. There was someone out there. And if they didn't find him, or her, before the snakeheads did... well it didn't bear thinking about. He logged off, and looked at his watch. It was ten to four.

'Look Tom, before we start, can I just say something?' Sally Yeadon said tentatively. 'I've been waiting for an opportunity all day?'

'Fire away,' Caton said, knowing full well what was coming.

'I wanted to apologise for last night.'

'What for?'

It was the first time he had seen her looking anything approaching sheepish.

That's the trouble. I'm not sure. But I have a feeling I made a complete fool of myself.'

Caton smiled reassuringly. 'Don't worry about it. No harm done.'

She grimaced. 'So I'm right; I did make a fool of myself.'

'Not really.'

'What happened?'

Caton really didn't want to get into this. 'Mainly, you just passed out.'

'Mainly?'

'That's it. You had too much to drink, and when you got back to the hotel, you passed out.'

She searched his face for clues. 'In my room?'

'Well, yes.'

'You put me to bed?'

'On the bed. I didn't think you'd thank me if you woke up in the morning to find I'd removed all your clothes, and tucked you up.'

She grinned. 'Oh, I don't know.'

God, I walked into that one Caton thought. His discomfort must have shown because she realised she had gone too far.

'No, seriously,' she said. 'I'm sorry I put you in that position. And I'm really grateful. And before we leave I'm going to get that bastard Munby. You wait and see if I don't.'

With the air cleared, they rattled off the report. Caton went off for his swim while Yeadon decided to visit the hair salon. The three of them met for a drink in the bar, and decided on the Japanese restaurant for a change. Yeadon declined the rice wine, sticking instead to mineral water. She insisted on buying a round afterwards while they talked tactics for the following day. Caton left the bar at ten thirty, rang Kate, and was in bed by eleven. Alone, unless you counted Clare Tomalin, and her biography of Samuel Pepys.

Yu Lai, middleman, profiteer, and member of a snakehead Triad, sat on a wooden bench bolted to the floor. He was short, and stocky; running to fat. He wore a white tee shirt, and loose blue linen trousers. Opposite him, across the table, sat Chief Sergeant Wang, and his boss. Yeadon, Munby and Caton, sat on simple plastic chairs behind the policemen; their backs to the wall. On their way in they had passed, on his way out, the tall thin man.

It had long been known by the police that Yu Lai was a member of a Triad, but for the sake of the angmo visitors, he was forced to remove his shirt and reveal a plethora of tattoos across his back, chest, shoulders and arms. Not that this in itself was proof, Munby had told them.

'There is a myth,' he said. 'For example In Hong Kong, that all Triad members have a tattoo of a white tiger on their right bicep, and of a black dragon on their left. Apart from the fact that there is more than one Triad, many men in Hong Kong have adopted these tattoos. In all probability, just to look tougher than they really are.'

Caton could see a tiger leaping across the centre of the man's back. Gold, with black stripes, green eyes, and yellow teeth, it was almost lost among the sweeps and swirls of complex abstract designs in blue black ink. There was a feng-like dragon on his right shoulder, and snake on his left. But it was the smaller tattoos - Chinese characters Caton assumed - to which the policeman pointed.

'This is the sign of membership of an affiliate of the 14K Triad,' Munby translated. 'He says it shows he is an ordinary member. Don't read too much into that, it just means that he doesn't hold one of the positions of authority within the Triad.'

Caton could make out bright red weals across the man's back, shoulders, and wrists. Chief Sergeant Wang followed his gaze and spoke immediately to the SOCA agent.

'He says the man attempted to resist arrest. It was necessary.'

Caton looked sceptical.

Probably close to the truth.' Munby told him. 'A bit of rough handling when they took him. Probably tied his wrists as well. If he'd been tortured, or really badly beaten, he'd look a damn sight worse than this.'

The prisoner was told to put his shirt back on. Then the questions started.

'You know why you are here?'

'No.'

'You have been told why you are here!'

'Something to do with helping people.'

'Something to do with taking money from poor people, sending their sons abroad, and killing them.'

For the first time Yu Lai's sullen countenance gave way to a combination of surprise, and fear.

'Killing? I know nothing of that.'

'How can we believe that, unless you tell us what you do know? Do you know what the penalty for conspiring to murder is?'

'Lethal injection. Immediately following sentence,' Munby added as an aside. 'No appeal.'

Yu Lai blanched visibly; there was desperation in his voice. 'I don't know anything about that.'

The Chief Sergeant's colleague leaned forward. 'It is for you to convince us that you did not have a hand in the deaths of these people. Not for us to prove that you did.'

'No presumption of innocence here then,' Sally Yeadon whispered.

'Tell us about these people you say you helped. What were their names?'

The prisoner squirmed, bowed his head, and shook it. 'I don't know. They came to me. I took the money, and passed them on.'

'Can he ask how many of them there were?' Caton said to Munby. Before the agent could do so, the other policeman rattled out a question.

'So he does understand English, probably speaks it well too.' Munby muttered. 'Incidentally, the prisoner says there were eight.'

'Eight!? Caton and Yeadon said simultaneously. 'That means,' Caton said. 'There's not just one more out there, but two.'

'And according to our friend here, one of those two must be female.' Munby told him. 'Seven men and a girl,' he says.

'A girl? Did he say how old?'

'Hang on,' the SOCA Agent said, 'Let them do their work. They'll get there in the end.'

Thirty minutes later the prisoner was a sobbing wreck. This was not what Caton had expected of the fearsome Triads. But then, faced with a choice between torture, public humiliation, and a lethal injection, or a few years in prison, a hefty fine, and throwing oneself on the mercy of the gang any one of whom could face a similar dilemma, he knew what he would choose.

'I thought that it was more than their life was worth to give away any information about the Triad.' he said.

'That's also something of a myth,' the agent replied. 'They'll often get away with it. Just so long as it's poor quality information already known to the police, and only exposes low level expendable members of the gang; temporary members for example.'

The Chinese police now had the name of the contact to whom the money had been paid, and from whom the instructions came. Munby said it would almost certainly prove to be another minnow; a middleman. They were about to apply more pressure, make more threats, when they were interrupted by a knock on the door. Chief Sergeant Wang left the room. Raised voices, and a heated debate, could be heard through the walls. Caton doubted that this room would be used for more robust interrogation. Wang re-entered the room, spoke with his superior, who then got up and left. This time the debate was short and sharp. He came back in and sat down.

'What was that all about? Caton asked.

'A solicitor has turned up out of the blue. Says he represents this man. He wanted to consult his client, and then sit in on the interview. He got short shrift.'

'Can they do that?' Sally Yeadon asked.

The agent's smile bordered on the patronising. 'They can do what the hell they like, my dear.'

Yeadon's eyes flashed. He's made a big mistake there Caton decided.

'It's rare that lawyers get to even see their clients before the trial.' Munby continued. 'And even then, their contact is very limited. What's interesting is that he's got representation at all, especially this fast. That's exactly what these two are discussing right now.'

Another twenty minutes, and it was clear that there was nothing more Yu Lai could tell them. Not without stronger methods of interrogation, Caton reflected ruefully. But then there were still two people missing, one of them they now knew was an eighteen year old girl. There were those back home who would still argue that in a case like this the means justified the ends. Caught between two cultures he was beginning to wonder himself, but there was no way he wanted to be part of a system of justice hinged around brutality, and the presumption of guilt. In any case, fear and honesty were poor bedfellows. At least that was what they told you on the training courses.

The prisoner had been shown photographs of the five men dumped in the Eggborough Sandpits, and a face shot of Feng Yi. There was no way they wanted him to see what had been done to his torso. He needed to be more scared of the police than of Triad retribution. On the strength of that, he had been able to give a sketchy description of the seventh man, and the girl. But still no names. Caton knew it would not be enough.

Caton and Yeadon skipped lunch back at the hotel, and shared instead a sandwich and a bottle of mineral water in the Business Centre while they wrote up their report.

'Just like home,' Yeadon mumbled through a mouthful of bun stuffed full of pork tenderloin, green onion, and Hoisin sauce. 'A working lunch.'

'How did Ray seem to you this morning?' Caton asked, pouring himself a glass of water.

'How do you mean?'

'I don't know if you noticed, but he was a bit hot under the collar when he arrived at the station. First thing he did was to ask for a bottle of water. I'm pretty sure he used it to wash down a couple of pills.'

She wiped the lingering crumbs from the side of her mouth with her serviette.

I don't suppose it had anything to do with his coffee last night,' she said feigning innocence.

'What did you do?'

'Well, you remember I insisted on getting the last round, and Munby said he'd have a chaser?' Caton nodded. 'Well I think he was expecting another brandy. What he actually got was a rather special four times distilled Chinese spirit the barman keeps in the freezer part of the fridge. You won't believe the alcoholic strength.'

'So why didn't he leave it?'

'Because when I came back he was speaking to you. I just tipped it into his coffee.'

'Tut, tut. That's an offence Superintendent.'

'So arrest me Chief Inspector.'

'He must still have known.'

'Male pride. He wasn't going to let me get the better of him.'

'Looks like you already have.' Caton said grinning. 'You'd better watch your back.'

Zheng Hu sat on the bench in the dark watching the moonlight slant through the trees in the rear garden of the house on Beardsworth Brow. It was cold out here, but he had his parka on, and he needed to think. The accountant and his wife had been so hospitable. They knew that he was hiding, and he guessed that they would have put two and two together from the stories in the newspaper, and on the television. They had assured him that they would not tell anyone that he was staying in the house, and he could stay for as long as necessary. But they had two young children under five, and he could not bear to think that he might bring down on them the violence that had exploded at his previous refuge. It was time to ring home. To reassure his parents. To seek their advice. To get help. It would be midday back home. He flipped open the mobile phone and pressed the speed dial number.

17

'I wouldn't mind the recipe for this,' Sally Yeadon said topping up her bowl. 'What was it again?'

Caton consulted the hotel menu. 'Fuo Tiao Qiang. In brackets it says Buddha-Jumps-Over-the-Wall. To you and me, it's a soup made with clams and chicken.'

'And Munby recommended this? There'll be a sting in the tail somewhere.'

Caton pulled a face. 'Wait till you get the bill,' he said. 'We'll have to fly economy on the way back.'

'Speaking of which,' she said between mouthfuls. 'Was he able to get us a flight?'

'Not direct from here to London for another three days. But there's a fast train to Shanghai the day after tomorrow, and a flight out that afternoon. I agree with you, there's not a lot of point in hanging around here any longer. Even if they do come up with the names of the two missing illegals we've still got to find a way of getting to them, and if they get us a lead on the Triad contacts at our end, we know they're as much in the dark as we are as to where they are hiding. Anyway, whatever they do find out, Munby will pass on straight away.'

'Do you believe that snakehead didn't know the names of the people he was helping to traffic?'

'He must have known the ones in the next village. For a start, he would have had to be able to make contact with the people who were paying him, if only to collect the money, and to give the pick up details. On the other hand, the less he found out, the less he would be able to implicate others.'

'I don't suppose the accomplice Yu Lai gave Chief Sergeant Weung is likely to just come out and give them the people at our end,' she said, her spoon suspended in mid air. 'That would be like committing suicide surely?'

'Even assuming he has their names,' Caton said. 'Which I doubt. If he doesn't, my guess is that they'll give him the death penalty anyway. You saw the look on the faces of those officials. They feel angry and humiliated. They've lost face in front of foreigners as well as their own government. Over here, that doesn't bode well for leniency. '

'Not anywhere, for that matter.'

'Yes, but not everywhere has mobile execution units, and the second highest proportion of death sentences in the world after Singapore...'

She interrupted him. 'I thought Munby said he had some work to do?'

'He did. Said he'd ring down for room service.'

'Well don't look now, but he's just entered the dining room, and he's coming over.'

Munby pulled up a chair from the neighbouring table and sat down. 'Mind if I join you?'

'Do we have choice?' Sally Yeadon asked him, 'How's your headache? She added solicitously. 'I must say you're looking a little less peaky.'

'Touché,' he said with surprisingly good grace. A waiter appeared, intent on laying a table setting for the surprise guest. Munby waved him away politely. 'It's alright thanks, I shan't be staying.' He watched

Sally Yeadon trying to extract the last traces of the main course with her spoon. 'You took my advice I see,' he said. 'What do you think?'

'It looked terrifying, but it tasted absolutely fantastic. I was telling Tom, I'll have to get the recipe.'

'You'll be lucky. Close guarded secret. If you ask me, that's what the terracotta army was all about.'

'Well,' she said giving up, and wiping her mouth with the serviette. 'If I was Empress of China I can only think of a couple of other ways the fittest young men in the Empire could be put to good use.'

'I'll arrange for one of our deep undercover agents to get you the recipe.' Dave Munby said. 'As long as you can get shark's fin, abalone, scallops, chicken and sea cucumber, you should be able knock it up yourself. Incidentally, go easy on the sea cucumber, it's supposed to be an aphrodisiac.' He smirked outrageously, then winced as the toe of her shoe made contact with his ankle.

'When you two have finished playing footsie, are you going to tell us what you're doing here Dave?' Caton said.

'Well I've got some good news.' The agent replied. 'It looks like they've got a lead on the missing girl. As far as I understand it, a teacher found her younger brother crying in school. She got him to confide in her. He's says his sister went away, to another country, and his mum and dad are worried because she promised she would ring when she arrived, but they haven't heard from her for over a week. The teacher said it was far too early to be worrying, and then he disclosed that he had heard them talking about some of the people who had gone with her being found dead. He thinks his sister is dead too.'

'How old is he?' Caton asked.

'Seven'

'Poor little devil.' Weadon said.

The school told the police, and by some miracle they suspected a connection, and rang Fuzhou.'

'She's not from Fuzhou?'

He shook his head. 'Meicheng. It's a small town on the Min river, about fifty five miles West of here. Chief Sergeant Wang is going up there first thing in the morning. He's offered to take us with him.'

'This means we should be able to get a photo, a good description, maybe a video appeal from the parents.' Caton reflected. 'At least we'll know who we're looking for at last.'

'Well don't get your hopes raised too far,' Munby told them. 'Hundreds of girls leave, or go missing from this region, every month.' He eased his chair back, and stood up. 'I've got some work to finish so I'll leave you two to enjoy the rest of your meal. I reckon I can manage an hour in the bar later. I'll pass on the coffee though this time,' he said pointedly. 'But I'm afraid it will be an early start. Wang Cheung is picking us up at six thirty in the morning, so I for one will want my beauty sleep.'

'In your case, wouldn't that be a lost cause?' Sally Yeadon said mischievously.

The agent put one hand lightly on her shoulder. 'You never know, my luck might turn one day,' he said, squeezing gently, before replacing his chair at its original table, and walking away.

I don't know about sea cucumber, Caton thought to himself, but I am beginning to feel like a gooseberry.

Neither Yeadon nor the SOCA Agent were down at breakfast. Caton found himself in the awkward situation of having to wait with the increasingly impatient Master Sergeant in the vast atrium of the hotel foyer, dwarfed by the golden pillars supporting a domed roof that would not have been out of place in the Great Mosque in Istanbul. Over the hotel public address system the missing pair were paged for the second time. It was as a pair that they arrived, relaxed, and evidently unaffected by the thought that they had kept the others waiting almost ten minutes.

'Sorry about that,' drawled Dave Munby, without the slightest trace of remorse. 'Decided to save time by ordering room service, and then had to wait for ever for it to arrive.'

'Same here.' Sally Yeadon added with a perfectly innocent smile, while the agent repeated himself in Mandarin for Wang's benefit.

The look the two of them received from the Chinese policeman got Caton's day off to a good start. Somehow it managed to convey two messages at once: I've heard better excuses from illiterate street urchin pickpockets, was the first; brazen hussy, the second. Wang Cheung he decided was very far from enigmatic; more "Disgusted of Fuzhou." So much for the inscrutable oriental, not that Caton had ever subscribed to that particular theory.

As he watched them walk side by side towards the hotel doors Caton reflected that not only was it none of his business but, if anything, it took the heat off him. In any case, Munby was divorced, and Yeadon single. Two consenting adults, and not even on each other's doorsteps. I suppose, he reflected, if it hadn't been for Kate then it could quite easily have been me.

The first ten miles were by road, out of the city to Shangjie, six miles or so up stream. Here they transferred to a small police launch for the forty five mile trip west along the Min river to Meicheng.

'Setting the purpose of this trip aside,' Munby said as they walked towards the jetty. 'You don't know how lucky you are. Trips up this river are the number one tourist attraction in the region. I should just sit back and enjoy it while you can.'

Even as they stepped into the boat Caton could see why they were not travelling by road. On either side of the river, beyond the stone houses and other buildings that crowded the flat alluvial banks, the ground rose. Gradually at first, and then as sheer cliffs, beyond which densely wooded slopes pointed the way to mountain peaks. Munby followed his gaze.

'That one there,' he said, pointing over Caton's shoulder. 'That's Drum Mountain. Three thousand two hundred feet. I've been to the top. There's a thousand-year-old Buddhist monastery up there. It's an amazing potpourri of halls and towers. They call it the Gushing-Spring Temple. You can guess why. If you ever come back, make sure you get up there. Only two things you have to look out for: crumbling rock faces, and the snakes.'

'Snakes?!' cried Sally Yeadon with what Caton perceived, probably unfairly, as more to do with affectation for Munby's sake than out of genuine fear. 'Poisonous snakes?'

'Deadly,' the agent replied. 'King cobras, pit vipers, bamboo snakes, ladder snakes. These hills are teeming with them. Well, to be more accurate, they *were* teeming with them. Such is the appetite for snake products all over Asia, some of them are being hunted to extinction.'

'Products?' said Yeadon.

'Apart from the obvious – snakeskin – they're used extensively for health products,' he turned to Caton and grinned. 'Snake penis for example, is particularly prized as an aphrodisiac. You should take some back with you,' he paused for effect. 'I'm sure you wouldn't need it, but they'd make great presents.'

'You've got a thing about aphrodisiacs, haven't you Dave?' Caton replied. 'First the sea cucumber, now the snake penis. What do you do, personally I mean? Use the cucumber as a splint, and slip the other one in the lady's soup?'

Sally Yeadon's neck flushed red. She punched his arm, and had to steady herself as the boat rocked. 'Tom Caton, for God's sake!'

Munby laughed it off. 'Speaking of soup,' he said. 'They reckon that well over ten thousand tons of snakes are used in stir fries and soups alone, and in this part of China they even flavour the wine with snakes' blood.'

'Enough Dave.' Yeadon said. 'I get queasy on boats at the best of times. Let's just look at the scenery shall we?'

That was fine by Caton. The river was the nearest thing to turquoise he had ever seen outside of a gem. So clear that he could see the sun's rays reflected from the scales on shoals of darting fish. Cranes stood guard on the bright white limestone sandbanks. Every so often a heron would rise at their approach, glide leisurely ahead, and alight on another bank. Waterfalls of pure crystal water cascaded from the cliffs above, tumbling into the river, their roar distinctive above the engine's tone. Where the river had been deepened by the swirling current, dark green pools punctuated the blue. Where the two met, fused, and reformed, the colour graduated through green, to yellow, and then to a deeper blue. From time to time, a long broad barge would pass by on its way down to the City and the sea, a reminder that this winding river with its dangerous shoals, and deep pools, was an artery that continued, as it had for centuries, to carry the economic lifeblood of the region. Caton wondered if it had also carried some of the young Fujianese on the start of a journey that would take them across Asia, the Middle East, and Europe, to end their lives in a desolate sand pit fifteen thousand miles away. Caton told himself that the only way that he could justify being here, seeing the beauty of the land that they had left, staying in hotels that when they lived here were way beyond their wildest dreams, was to bring them back.

The living, as well as the dead.

It was close to midday, sixty seven degrees Fahrenheit, and getting warmer. The boat swung under a bridge, and into a tributary of the Min River that took them directly into the heart of Meicheng, past the remains of high stone walls with holes that Caton assumed were constructed to let defenders fire out against assault from the river. This was an ancient town, wrestling with modern needs and manufacture. Stone houses, centuries old, with decorated curved tile roofs that would have graced the set of Crouching Dragon, Hidden Tiger, cheek by jowl with concrete factories and storehouses. They waited on the quayside while Master Sergeant Wang engaged in heated discussion with two uniformed policemen and an older man – in his sixties Caton thought – in a grey suit, white shirt, and silver tie. When Wang returned he was less than pleased.

'He says we have to wait here for a few minutes,' Munby told them. 'A car will take us to the family house. It seems they refused to come to the station. They either have some good connections, or it's because the local police knew that you and I would be here, because normally nobody gets away with refusing a request like that.' He stopped talking, the better to listen to the flurry of conversation going on a few yards away between Wang Cheung, and the pilot of their boat. Munby stepped away from the quayside, and motioned them to follow him.

'What's going on Dave?' Caton asked as soon as they were out of earshot.

'Curiouser and curiouser,' the agent said. 'Our Mr Wang can't understand why they couldn't force them to come to the police station instead of making us trail up there. Particularly, he says, since they're Falun Gong.'

'What's that when it's at home?' Sally Yeadon wanted to know.

'It's a religious sect isn't it?' Caton said. 'They were giving out leaflets around Manchester during the Chinese New Year celebrations.'

'Got it in one.' Munby said. 'To be precise, they're a prohibited sect. Forbidden to practise in public here in China since 1999. Anyone who does, can be expected to be imprisoned, tortured, and in some cases murdered.'

'Murdered?' Yeadon exclaimed. 'What kind of sect is this?'

'One that's got the Government running scared. It only started its revival a couple of decades ago. Now there are over a hundred million adherents, world wide, in over fifty countries. The powers that be see it as a challenge to their authority. They've put over a hundred thousand in forced labour camps. Their own figures show more than fifteen hundred a year are killed; some by organs of the state, some by vigilantes spurred on by the government's propaganda machine.'

'So it's anti-communist?' Caton said.

'It's actually not anti-anything. It's for, Truthfulness, Benevolence, and Forbearance; or depending on the translation, truth, compassion and tolerance. The nearest way I can describe it is a combination of Buddhism, and Tai Chi, only there's a bit more to it than that. Basically, its meditation and exercise for a healthy mind, a healthy body, and a moral life.'

'That doesn't sound like much of a threat.' Yeadon said.

'It does if you're running the country, and you're not particularly noted for truthfulness, compassion, and tolerance,' Dave Munby said, lowering his voice as the policeman came towards them. 'Looks like our car's arrived. Another ten minutes, and you'll be able to judge for yourselves.'

The house of Wu stood on the side of a hill, on the outskirts of the town. Like those around it, it was built of limestone. Unlike those around it, its walls had been newly whitewashed and shone brightly in the midday sun. It had an apex roof clad with ancient decorated tiles. Vegetables grew in a small plot at the side.

'Wang says the father works as an overseer in the local ceramics factory, and the mother is an accounts clerk in an electronics firm,' Munby told them as they climbed the stone steps. 'Well educated by all accounts.'

'If they were reasonably well off why would they want to take the risk of paying to have their daughter taken abroad illegally?' Caton asked.

'Probably because she's Falun Gong too. There's no way the Government would allow her to emigrate legally, and this might be her best chance of avoiding the persecution.' He lowered his voice as they caught up with Wang Cheung, and the civilian in the grey suit who accompanied him. 'There is another possibility. If she was pregnant, and wanted to keep the child, this might be the only way. If she was caught having a child without authorisation, it would be a fine, and a spell in a work camp for her, and curtains for the kid. Even if she was married.'

Sally Yeadon was appalled. She was about to say something when the door swung open.

Mr Wu Shen was a stately looking man in his late forties. He stood tall, close to Caton's height, in a short sleeved light blue shirt, and matching trousers. His eyes were sharp, and intelligent. His face betrayed the tell tale signs of grief, barely held in check. He led them through a small hallway into a room dominated by a large but simple bur ash table set out with six accompanying ladder backed chairs. A single black vase, filled with white lilies, stood atop a black lacquered box. Behind the table, as though deliberately putting distance between them, stood a woman much his own age, dressed in a navy blue high necked jacket, trimmed in gold at the collar and the sleeves, over a pair of blue denim jeans. Wu Shen rounded the table, and stood beside her. She barely reached his shoulder. Despite a brave attempt to smile it was evident that she had been crying. They introduced themselves in turn, placing a hand over their hearts, making the short bow with their head and shoulders.

'This is Mr Wu Shen and Mrs Wu Chua, the parents of Wu Ling.' Munby translated. 'They welcome you to their house, and wish to offer you tea after your long journey.'

Caton, and Yeadon sat in silence, together with Mrs Wu Chua, drinking refreshing green tea from delicate porcelain cups. An argument raged in the room next door, between her husband, Master Sergeant Wang and the man in the grey suit. Every so often they heard the calm tones of Agent Munby, though whether in mediation, or supplication, it was impossible to tell. They were on their second cup when they heard the front door slam. Agent Munby returned with Mr Wu. They were alone.

'They're terrified of speaking to us in front of the police,' Munby explained. 'Mr Wu has agreed to answer any questions they may have, but only with us present, and only after he's spoken with us on our own.'

'What is he hoping to gain from that?' Caton said.

'The snakeheads have warned them not to contact

the police. I also have a feeling that they are hoping we can use our influence to protect them from any subsequent action from officialdom when we've gone.'

'Can we do that?' Yeadon asked.

'If the officials here are led to believe that we have to make this family – and the others we've already met – part of a media operation to help us find the two that are missing, and track down the perpetrators, then yes, I think we can. They'll think twice about mistreating them in the glare of a global spotlight. But it will need careful handling.'

'In what way?' she asked.

'We have to make it look as though it's their idea, to show how determined their government are to stop the people trafficking, and how concerned they are for the families. It's all about face. Don't worry, that's one of the reason's I'm here. Leave it to me.'

18

It transpired that Mr and Mrs Wu spoke English. Seated at the table, she confirmed the SOCA agent's theory. They were terrified of what would happen afterwards, but just as scared that heavy handed intervention would prejudice the safety of their daughter. Reassured, they admitted that they had used their savings, and taken out a loan to send their daughter to England where a group of Falun Gong adherents had promised to look after her, and find her suitable work and opportunities to extend her education. At the same time, they would pursue a case for asylum status on account of the persecution in the region. Yes, their actions did not sit easily with their morals, but Wu Ling was everything to them.

'When did the snakeheads first make contact with you?' Caton asked gently.

'Four days ago, by phone,' Mr Wu replied. 'We thought it was Wu Ling. It was her phone they used. They even let her speak to us so that we would know that they had her, and that she was alive. '

Caton noted the past tense. This man knew that whatever her captives said, she could already be dead.

'What did she say?' he asked.

The mother stifled a sob. Her husband placed his hand over hers. 'She said Mother, Father, it's me, your delicate lily, Wu Ling. I love you. Then the phone was taken from her.'

'Delicate Lily, it is our pet name for her,' Wu Chu Hua said softly. 'Ling, it means delicate.'

What did the snakehead say then?' Caton asked.

'He said that harm would come to our daughter if we did not tell them where Feng Yi, and another man – Zheng Hu is his name – were hiding. Feng Yi is distantly related to our family. When he discovered that Wu Ling was travelling with him he promised to look after her. He told his family this, and Wu Ling told us. But we have not heard from him at all. Zheng Hu we did not know. I told them that. I said how could we know where they were all these miles away. The snakehead said we must contact the families of Feng Yi, and Zheng Hu, and persuade them to tell us where their sons are hiding, or they would kill our daughter...' he squeezed his wife's hand tightly, dropped his head and whispered. '...eventually.'

Sally Yeadon took up the questioning. 'Mr Wu, how many times have they phoned since then?'

'Every day, twice, sometimes three times, but now they only seem to be interested in the whereabouts of Zheng Hu.' He looked at Sally Yeadon, and then at Caton, wondering if they might enlighten him. Neither of them obliged. At this point in the interview Caton knew that it would be unhelpful to reveal that Feng Yi was dead.

'And the message has been the same each time?'

'Yes, but with increasing violence and threats.'

'And you have not given in to their demands?'

For the second time the mother decided to respond. 'How could we trade our daughter's life for that of either of these two young men.' She said. 'We could not set out to deceive these families to protect our own.' She searched their faces for understanding, for approval. Caton could see it written on her face that she desperately needed to believe her own justification.

'And you did not feel that you could go to the police?' Said Yeadon.

The father replied. 'Leaving China illegally is an offence, albeit a minor one, but we are Falun Gong. We do not practise in public, but this would be just the excuse the authorities need to arrest, beat, and torture us; imprison, and possibly kill us. How would that help our daughter? In any case we are warned each time not to contact the police. We were told that if we do, Wu Ling will be killed.'

'Might not the police be able to help find her?'

He shook his head, weary of the impotence of the questions, and of his own answers.

'She too is Falun Gong, why would they bother? In any case they would rather sweep it under the carpet; leave the three of them to their fate, and pretend that it had never happened.'

'How did they get your number?' Caton asked.

'From our daughter's phone.'

'And is that how they still contact you?'

'No, because we have tried to return the call, but the phone they use withholds the number. It is not our daughter's phone.' Suddenly his words came out in a rush, as though a dam had broken. 'They say we have until the end of the week, and then they will send another video of our daughter. They say it will break our hearts. They say we will get a new one every two days, each worse than the last. The final one will be our chance to say goodbye. There will be no grave for us to visit, no ashes to scatter on the wind.' His wife

230

dissolved in tears beside him. He placed his arms around her shoulders and spoke into her neck. 'But they are wrong. Our hearts are already broken.'

Had they been in Manchester, Caton would have insisted on a break. Instead they sat in silence for several minutes allowing husband and wife to compose themselves. When he judged them to be ready Caton asked the most obvious question.

'Mr Wu. You said another video. You have already been sent one?'

Mrs Wu seized her husband's hands, and shook her head violently. Without translation it was obvious that she was pleading with him not to co-operate. With soothing words, and firm demeanour, Mr Wu pulled himself loose, rose and crossed to the black lacquered box. He picked up the vase, placed it on the floor, opened the box, and took something out. He returned to the table, and placed a shiny, slim, red mobile phone between them on the table.

'We found this in our letter box yesterday morning,' he said. 'We do not know who put it there.' He picked up the phone, and handed it to Sally Yeadon. 'Please,' he said. 'No one else. Just you.' Only when she had nodded her understanding did he let it go.

Yeadon pushed back her chair. She walked across the room, and stood with her back towards them in the shadow of the small stone window. More than a minute passed before she turned and looked at them. Her mask of professional detachment had slipped over the edge of empathy, into gut wrenching pity.

'I am so sorry, Mr Wu,' she said. 'But if you want us to find your daughter I must show this to my colleagues.'

Caton sees half of a window, net curtains drawn, an old iron bedstead lit by a table lamp. A young woman lies naked on the bed, her arms and legs tied to the rails with what look like white scarves. The camera zooms in slowly. Her face has a perfect bone structure, her dark hair fans out around it on the pillow, like a halo. Her almond shaped eyes are open, but vacant, her lips parted slightly, as if about to speak. The camera lingers for a moment and then zooms out a little. It pans insolently across her breasts, over her stomach, and mound of Venus. Twenty seconds of poorly lit footage in all. More than enough. Too much.

Opposite them Mrs Wu began to sob quietly. Nobody spoke. Sally Yeadon broke the silence. 'I am sorry to have to ask you this. This is your daughter?'

'It is Wu Ling.' The father whispered.

Dave Munby seemed uncomfortable with their helplessness. He said something to them in Mandarin that caused the mother to nod her head as though acknowledging a crumb of comfort. The father stared at him coldly.

'What did you say Dave?' Yeadon asked.

'She doesn't seem to have been hurt,' he said.

Caton felt some the father's anger. Here was their daughter, fifteen thousand miles from home, kidnapped, drugged, splayed out naked like a piece of meat. In what way was she not hurt?

'Have they contacted you today?' he said, needing to raise their spirits somehow. The father nodded. 'At eight o'clock this morning. They asked if we had received the video. They wanted to know if we had made contact with the families.'

'What did you tell them?'

'That I was trying. They said trying was not good enough. They would ring back this evening. If I did not have the information for them by then, the next video would be less pleasant,' he looked up at them, his face a picture of disbelief. 'He actually used that word; pleasant.'

'Do you know how to contact the parents of Zheng Hu?'

The father nodded in sudden resignation. 'He is a friend of Feng Yi's. His family will be able to tell you.'

An hour later Master Sergeant Wang and his companion had been apprised of everything that had been shared in the room. After a long and apparently tortuous three-sided conversation with Agent Munby, they had had the opportunity to interview the family while Munby looked on. Assurances, it seemed, had been given on both sides. The result was better than Caton had anticipated.

'I'll say this for them. They're really moving on this.' Munby said, as they walked across the quay towards their boat. 'They're going to set up a trace on all incoming calls, and record them. Whoever the snakehead's service is with the calls are going to have to come through one of the two major Chinese providers. They will be able to get us not only the UK provider, but the number of the phone. We'll also get a copy of the tapes for voice recognition purposes. Then it's down to our people. Our Office in Beijing will liaise with them, and with Ray Barnes, and he with your people. And there's a bonus of having The Agency involved. One of our partner agencies is GCHQ. All we need is an incoming call.'

Caton's spirits lifted. He had been to the Cheltenham Headquarters of the Government's Communication Intelligence gathering agency. No longer just a code breaking, and electronic intelligence gathering arm of the state, GCHQ was also at the forefront of the battle against organised crime. Munby was right. There was no way that they would have agreed to use their sophisticated listening and tracking capacity for this case without it being facilitated by the Agency. It would only be a matter of time before they pinpointed the location of whoever was making these calls. The unanswered question, was how much time Wu Ling had left.

'They're also checking the origin of the phone with the video on,' Munby was saying. 'They've already emailed us a copy of that.

'And what was that all about?' asked Yeadon. 'Why not just send the video to the Wu's own phone.'

'Perhaps they tried, and found that Wu's phone wasn't configured to receive videos. Or perhaps they wanted to send another message: *We're right there, and we're watching you'*. Caton said. 'More to the point, won't whoever delivered that mobile phone know that the police have become involved?'

It's too late to worry about that now,' Munby said. 'Our friend in the grey suit has finally come out of the closet. He's with the Ministry of State Security, Bureau One, Domestic Intelligence. They're going to handle the surveillance, and the phone trace. And you can take my word for it, they're every bit as sophisticated as we are, and a damn sight better resourced. If anyone comes back to the Wu household, or even starts to keep an eye on it, they'll pick them up; and God help them.'

Their journey felt shorter because it was familiar. It was approaching six o'clock in the evening when they arrived at their destination. Master Sergeant Wang had phoned ahead. The parents of Feng Yi, confronted with the knowledge that the police already knew about Zheng Hu, had provided an address for the family. It was in Shad Village, on the outskirts of Shangjie Town where they had first embarked, some twelve kilometres from Fuzhou city centre.

'Another example of the two faces of modern China,' Munby told them as the car sped along No.316 National Highway 'It hosts some really poor housing alongside one of the best golf courses in South East China. Amai Golf Club. Designed by an American, it's what they call an eco-resort. Apart from the golf course, there are other sports and leisure facilities, commercial premises, and smart new homes. According to Wang Cheung, the golf course is amazing. It's divided into three different areas, each of them following the various land forms; a seaside area, a garden area, and a forest area. He says it's a pity we won't have time to explore it.'

Caton had never felt less in need of a round of golf. At the best of times he could think of better ways of using up half a day. Right now was far from the best of times.

In their mid fifties, the parents of Zheng Hu were considerably older than the Wus. Mrs Zheng worked as a contract cleaner at the golf club; Mr Zheng in a local Fireworks Factory.

'Not the safest of occupations.' Munby confided. 'In China as a whole, fatalities in these factories average four to five hundred a year. Only four years ago they had just such an explosion in Mr Zheng's factory. No wonder he didn't want the same for his son.'

This time the interview was easier, not least because these parents knew that their son was still alive, and safe. They shared the sorrow of their friends, the Fengs, for the loss of their son. The reason they had not come forward and told the police was because they too had been threatened. They had also been told that Wu Ling – who they knew only as a distant relative of the Fengs – would be killed if they did. Following assurances that they would not be prosecuted, and that the Chinese police would provide protection for them, and the British police for their son, they were close to agreeing to co-operate. They tried to bargain for the promise of asylum in England for their son; something which they were told was not in the gift of Caton, Yeadon or Munby. Although they appeared to resign themselves to giving in, Caton also detected a sense of relief.

'Yes our son has been in contact,' the father said, his thick black eyebrows etched with grey, arching dramatically above sad eyes that seemed perpetually perplexed. 'He telephones or texts us each day to let us know that he is safe. And there was a letter.' He nodded to his wife who left the room, and returned with a standard airmail envelope. She handed it to Caton. The post mark was Preston; the date three days ago. Caton handed it to Munby, who passed it in on to Wang.

'I may be able to speak Mandarin, and understand Fujianese,' the agent said. 'But that doesn't mean I can read them both that well. In this case it looks like a Min dialect. Might as well be in code.'

Caton and Yeadon waited for the Chinese policeman to read it out, and for Munby to translate.

'Father, Mother, as you can see I am safe. It is better that you do not know where I am staying. Not because I do not trust you, heaven forbid that I would ever fail to do so, but in case this letter should fall into the wrong hands. You may know by now that most of those with whom I travelled are dead. Among them, my friend Feng Yi for whom I grieve. I tried to save him but he ran away to find his distant cousin Wu Ling. Please tell his parents it was a heroic act. I pray for them. I hope that Wu Ling is still alive, but there is nothing I can do for her. It is not that I cannot be a hero; rather that I would not know where to begin. I can stay here for a little while, but I fear that I am placing my hosts in danger. If I go to the police they will deport me, and then the snakeheads will get me; if not in the detention centre, then when I am back in China. I tell you honestly, I do not know what to do. I need to be able to change my identity, get false papers, get away from here. I cannot ask my hosts to help with this. They are honest law abiding people. But then so I know are you. It breaks my heart to ask you this, but, as you love your son, can you think of anyone who can help me?

I will call you soon.

I love you

Your loving and obedient son

Zheng Hu'

'You said you have been threatened,' said Master Sergeant Wang. 'How exactly?'

'By phone. Four days ago, and then each day since.

Usually around four o'clock in the evening, and in the middle of the night.'

'First thing in the morning, and early evening, back home.' Caton observed.

Wang Cheung pressed on. 'They rang today?'

'Yes.'

'What did they say?'

'That we had better tell them where our son is hiding, or it will be worse for him, and for us, when they catch up with him. Today they say that they are running out of patience.'

'Do they say why they are looking for him?'

'No.'

'What else do they say?'

'That they have a girl, Wu Ling. A friend of our son. That every day until we tell them where he is, she will suffer. And then it will be our turn. They say unspeakable things. Things I cannot tell my wife.'

'And have you told the snakeheads that your son has been in contact?'

Both he and his wife shook their heads. 'No.' he said. 'No we have not.'

Within the hour, arrangements had been made for an identical tap and trace operation to be put in place. Caton had provided the parents with a contact number for them to give their son. It was one that Ray Barnes had given him; staffed twenty four hours a day.

'This is the opportunity we need.' Caton said. If we can get their son to tell us where he is, then when he's safely in our hands we can set up a sting operation. We can get the parents to give them a false address, where the Tactical Aid Team will be waiting.'

'Won't that put the girl at risk?' Yeadon wondered. 'If we don't get all of them, and the others think we're closing in, they may kill her, and dispose of the body. Without a body it becomes that much more difficult to convict.'

'If you find the premises, there should be enough forensic evidence. Put that together with the phones, and the voice recognition, and most juries are going to convict,' said Munby.

'Sally's right though, about putting the girl at risk,' Caton said. We need to try and co-ordinate whatever action we take. But first of all, we need both their son, and the snakeheads, to make contact.'

'Well there's nothing more we can do here,' Munby said. 'We may as well head on back to the hotel. I'll make sure your flight is still on for tomorrow.'

Caton looked at his watch. It was eight in the evening. Mid morning in England. Time to bring the team up to date.

19

They had stripped the bed bare. Wu Ling lay on a sheet of rubber, staring at the ceiling. Each time she tried to move, her body slid on a slick of sweat. In this moment, one of the too brief periods of cruel clarity, she understood that they had always taken her in that alternately wakeful and drowsy state following the initial euphoria of a hit; her senses dulled by the drug's depression of her central nervous system.

It had finally dawned on her that this was rape; beyond her control. She had no choice other than to endure the education on which Johnny had embarked; including the insatiable appetites of the other members of his gang. But when she recalled, for the first time, that in her drugged state she had not fought it - more than merely compliant, had responded - then she had experienced a different kind of pain. One that drilled into her mind; deep into her soul.

She did not know if it was the heroin, the stultifying effect of the twice daily repetition of the act, or a defence of her own making, but eventually, all that remained was a deep ache. She would have preferred the pain to that acceptance. When he told her what would happen next, somehow she had found the strength to resist. She told Johnny no. He said she would be punished. Explained why he did not want to mar her looks. Told her that he didn't need to. He had a better punishment. Cold turkey.

Her stomach went into spasm, forcing her to retch; to vomit what little stomach juices her body could muster. Her legs began to twitch uncontrollably. The pain in her bones intensified to a searing heat, contrasting unbearably with the freezing cold of her skin. The voice in her head screamed at her. Give up, give up. She knew that unless she did, her life would become this vicious cycle; an hour of euphoria, followed by days like this. She would rather die. But Johnny will not let you, the voice was telling her, and this was worse than death.

In the room next door, Cheng Jun – Johnny to friends - was on his mobile phone to the Lady White Snake Sauna and Massage Parlour.

'Nearly there,' he said. 'The package will be delivered in the morning.'

'Open house?'

'No, Chinese only. Regulars…ones you know. With this one we take no risks. You take no risks. Tell them newly arrived. Very special…at a special price.'

'Special price?'

'That's right. Start at ten a day; one hundred pounds a time. I want one rest day a week for the first two weeks.'

'Rest day? You want a rest day?'

'That's right.'

'Ten a day. Won't be able to keep that up for long.'

'I know, I know. Five weeks and the novelty value will have gone. Drop the price to fifty, and double the number per day.'

'When they stop asking for it – we sell it on to the Albanian?'

'No. When they stop asking, we'll have no use for it. I'll come and get it.'

He put down the phone. Less the cost of the drug, the money for the housekeeper, and for the woman who minded the girls, ten weeks would pay back the money the Triad had lost on the other seven illegals, and turn a handsome profit for himself. He looked towards the bedroom door. By then she would be unrecognisable in mind, or body, as the virginal innocent they had brought to this flat. What he would find it difficult to do right now, in ten weeks time would be no less than a kindness.

I'll have to say goodbye here.' Dave Munby told them, pushing his cup and saucer aside. 'I'm flying from here to Beijing. Your little visit has really set the cat among the pigeons. Not a bad thing as far as I'm concerned. The Chinese are still trying to work out what the Agency actually is, and how it fits into their pigeon holes. Before I go,' he continued. 'I've got two little presents for you both. Number one, our friend from the Bureau gave me a slip of paper just before he left. Very mysterious. Just said this may be of interest to us. It's the name of a firm; The Manchester and Shanghai Trading Company. Offices in Shanghai, Fuzhou, and Hong Kong, and in Amsterdam and Manchester. Manchester is the European Headquarters. I've spoken to Ray Barnes. It's already on our radar, but only as one of about a dozen where there have been whispers; nothing concrete to go on. Now we'll take a closer look. I suggest you do the same Tom.'

Something nagged in Caton's brain. It was not so much the name as the initials; MSTC. He'd seen them somewhere before. Holmes would know. As soon as he got back he'd check it out.

'And number two,' Munby was saying. 'The Chinese Government has agreed that if you ever get to the point where you have someone to prosecute, they will allow members of these families to testify in person in England regarding the threats and intimidation. That's only ever happened once before. He must have been really impressed by you two,' he grinned. 'Though I can't think why.'

'That was the kidnap in 2003,' Caton said. 'Two of my colleagues from GMP came over. Five snakeheads were given a total of forty two years.'

'Well let's hope we can emulate that.' The SOCA agent said.

In the silence that followed Caton sensed an awkwardness had fallen upon them. Yeadon and Munby had full on eye contact, yet stood well apart.

'I'll just have a look round the Duty Free,' Caton said. 'See what catches my eye.' He shook Munby by the hand. 'Thanks Dave, it would have been a nightmare without you. Any time you're back in the UK look me up. I'll see if I can return the favour.'

'I'll do that,' Munby replied warmly.

It was obvious his thoughts were somewhere else. Caton had a pretty good idea where. He headed for the Duty Free.

By the time he got back to the café Sally Yeadon was alone; reading a magazine, aimlessly turning the pages.

'Are you ready to go through to Departures?' Caton asked. 'It'll probably be a bit more comfortable in there, and anyway, we can use the Executive Lounge.'

'Good idea,' Yeadon said, leaving the magazine on the seat, and picking up her flight bag. 'I could do with some pampering.'

Caton feels safe, cocooned in this cabin. There is a murmur of voices, hushed and reassuring. Somewhere in the background music is playing. Images creep across the screen before him. A body floats face downwards in the swirling current of a river. A vulture lands on the corpse, and begins to tear at the open wounds. A snake slithers through the water; an emerald green ribbon in a turquoise torrent. It coils itself around a careless arm, and writhes towards the vulture. With a flap of its wings the raptor rises, and blots out the moon. In the centre of the darkness a point of light appears. The light grows brighter, wider, until it shines upon a bed on which another body lays face down; naked, white, and unmistakably feminine. There comes the sound of beating wings, hurrying towards this place. On the bed the head begins to turn. He sees an eye - green, flecked with brown - and auburn hair. Kate's face. A flash of light, then darkness. He is falling into an empty silent chasm, arms pinioned to his side, spiralling downwards. He struggles to fight free, the panic rising in his chest to choke him.

'Tom ,Tom…wake up! Wake up!'

He woke to find himself sitting upright, straining against the seatbelt, Sally Yeadon's arms encircling him. Sweat poured down his face. He forced himself to breathe from his diaphragm; slow and deep; to relax his hands, his arms, his legs. He sank back into the seat. Across the aisle, passengers craned forward more concerned than annoyed to have been woken from their slumber. An anxious stewardess hovered in the gangway.

'Are you alright sir?' she asked .

'He'll be fine now, thank you,' Sally Yeadon said. She cautiously loosened her grip. 'You will won't you Tom?'

'I'll be fine,' he said, smiling weakly at the stewardess. 'Really, I will.' He undid his seat belt, reached into his pocket and found his handkerchief. He wiped his forehead, the sides of his face, and his neck.

Conscious that they were still under scrutiny from the aisle across, Yeadon leant close, and whispered. 'What was that all about Tom? You had me really scared there for a moment.'

He mustered an embarrassed grin. 'You and me both. Just a nightmare.'

'Just a nightmare? That was a full bloodied horror movie. I'd just dozed off myself. I thought the plane was going down.'

'It won't happen again. I wasn't planning to sleep; just dropped off.'

Yeadon was about to say something when the stewardess reappeared carrying a bottle of mineral water and a plastic beaker.

'It's still, and ice cold,' she said.

Caton took it gratefully. It felt like nectar as it went down, cooling him from the inside out.

'Does this happen very often?' Yeadon asked.

'Occasionally. Not that often.'

'Always the same dream?'

He had to think about that; even with this one still vivid in his conscious mind. 'It used to be. These days

245

it tends to feed on what's uppermost in my mind. But the underlying components are the same.'

'Fighting, fleeing, falling, tunnels, claustrophobia, agoraphobia, aliens?'

'What is this?' he said. 'The Spanish Inquisition? Or are you doing an Open University course in Jungian Psychology?'

She laughed gently. 'No, just a dabbling amateur.' Her voice took on a serious tone. 'But I'm right aren't I? You know where this is coming from?' She hesitated, wondering if she was overstepping the degree of intimacy they had established in just four days. 'Is it what happened to you, and your parents? The car crash?'

Caton looked out of the window. He'd always known he had this weakness for confiding in emotionally intelligent women. He put it down to losing his mother when he did. On one level, he found it cathartic; on another, he felt it disempowering. Big boys don't cry. He nodded. 'It started out as flashbacks. Now it rarely happens. Once or twice a year maybe. But when it does, it's always triggered by something I'm working on. Usually something traumatic. Not so much what happened, as what might happen. The accident, my parents' death, being trapped, gets mixed up with what's going on in my life, my work.'

'Have you seen anyone about this?'

'I saw the school doctor. He said they would gradually disappear. Which they did.'

'But now they're coming back.'

'Yes.'

'Don't you think you should see someone again?' she asked.

'Funny,' he said. 'That's what Kate said.' He turned back from the window to face her. 'Look, I appreciate your interest Sally, but if you don't mind, I'd rather not talk about it. I know we're in different forces, but it's difficult. You being a superior officer. The circles you move in. The people you meet on courses, at conferences.' He left the rest unspoken. Embarrassed to have started down this route.

'Tom, I know where you're going with this. And I understand. I think you know that we've become good enough friends, not just colleagues, to keep each other's secrets. And I promise I won't mention it again. But I still think you should take Kate's advice. It sounds to me like you've found a cracker there.'

'I have,' he said. 'Both personally and professionally.' He checked his watch. There were three hours left of the twelve hour flight. They were due in at Heathrow at six fifty pm. The shuttle to Manchester would be leaving just thirty minutes later. That sounded like they were pushing it. He just hoped the twenty past eight was still operating. He retrieved The Tango Singer from under the seat in front where it had fallen, found the page marker, and picked up where he had left off.

They caught the final shuttle with three minutes to spare. Because of the luggage they were carrying they'd missed the baggage clearance for the penultimate flight. Yeadon was coming with him. She had left her car at Manchester Airport.

'I'm more or less equidistant between Leeds International and Manchester,' she explained.

'Where exactly?' Caton said as they strapped themselves in.

'Calderdale. I've just bought a large stone cottage in Stainland,' she said. 'Down in the valley, a few miles off Junctions 23 and 24 of the M62 motorway.'

Caton nodded. 'I did a circular hike from there; via Barkisland and Greetland. You like it there?'

'I love it. After a day like the one we had out at the sand pits, I can come home and leave it all behind. I could be on the other side of the world.'

'Not China though.'

She laughed. 'Not China.'

'Have you found that fabulous restaurant in the village,' he said. '1885 - The Restaurant?'

She shook her head.

'Family run, it's Yorkshire's best kept secret. You should give it a try.'

'I tell you what. You should take Kate there. We could make it a threesome'.

'I might just do that,' he said.

He was less sure about the threesome.

As they came into the narrow Arrivals hall Kate was waiting for him. She rushed forward and flung her arms around him. They kissed, oblivious to the tide of weary passengers that wove around them. Until Yeadon arrived at his shoulder.

'So this is Kate,' Yeadon said. 'I can see why you were in such a hurry to get back Chief Inspector.'

The three of them walked beyond the simple barrier of tape to find a space where Caton could make the introductions.

'I hope he behaved himself Superintendent?' Kate said as she appraised this cool professional woman who looked as though she had just stepped from a taxi for a night on the town.

'I think I can safely say he did,' Yeadon replied. 'And call me Sally. It's only we colleagues that have to stand on ceremony.' She looked at her watch 'Look, I'm sorry, but I'm going to have to rush. Tom, I'll give you a ring in the morning when we've both had a chance to catch up with our teams. And Kate, get him to tell you about the 1885. We should meet up there some time, the three of us, when all of this is over.' With that, she was gone.

'1885?' Kate said as she linked his arm, and led him towards the car park. 'What was that all about?'

'Just a restaurant I know of near where she lives.' He looked down into her sparkling eyes, green, flecked with brown. 'Anyway, you're looking amazing. Is it just because you're pleased to see me, or is this there something else you're dying to tell me?'

'Tom,' she said. 'You're a mind reader!'

'A face reader.'

'OK. A face reader. It's the Ramsbottom Rapist. They've got him. He was in London, dossing down near Kings Cross station.'

'Kings Cross? That proves he's off his head. I bet there are more transport police, anti-terrorist, immigration, and vice squad officers there than anywhere else in Britain.'

'Well that's where he was.'

'And he fits the profile you gave our people?'

'Like a glove.'

'No wonder you're chuffed.' He took her face in his hands, and planted a kiss on her impatient lips.

Kate had prepared a chicken salad. Caton returned from the wet room to find a bottle of Veuve Cliquot chilling in an ice bucket.

'It's a good job I stayed off the alcohol on the plane,' he said. 'Incidentally, I didn't know I had an ice bucket.'

'You don't, I brought it with me.'

'Well I've brought you a little something too.' Caton took a small package from the pocket of his dressing gown, and handed it to her. 'I couldn't find anything that would go with your black and white minimalist décor.'

She unwrapped the outer layer and opened the box. 'It's Vera Wang! My favourite perfume. How did you know?'

'I'm a detective, remember?'

She put the bottle on the table, pulled him to her, placed one hand behind his head, and drew it down until their lips met. When they finally came up for air she pushed him away playfully, and began to open the champagne.

'But I'm disappointed in you Tom Caton. I was expecting something Chinese.'

'It is Chinese. Vera Wang.'

'She's American.' The bottle opened with a sigh.

'Chinese American. And how did you do that, with the bottle?'

'Years of practice. And I had a boyfriend who was training to become a sommelier. Hold the cork, turn the bottle.'

'Is that all he taught you?'

She filled the glasses, and handed Caton his. 'If you play your cards right, you might find out.'

Caton's plate was still half full; the champagne bottle empty. Kate tipped the remains into the waste bin and put everything into the dishwasher. Caton had gone through to the bedroom. She went into the wet room, checked her make up in the mirror, fluffed her hair to loosen up the strands that Caton loved to twine between his fingers. Back in the lounge, she sprayed a minute amount of perfume at the base of the neck, touched the wetness with her index finger, and dabbed it in the cleft between her breasts, and behind each ear. It had been just five days, and seemed like an eternity. She had never felt like this before. She was certain that Caton felt the same. Kate switched off the light, and slowly opened the bedroom door.

'Coming…ready or not.'

The bedside lights were on. Caton lay on his back, his head against the pillow. The book had slipped from his lifeless hands. To add insult to injury, he had just begun to snore.

20

Caton's in-tray was piled high. There was an FMIT quarterly monitoring report two days over due, and DC Dave Woods' self-appraisal report with less than three days before the final meeting at which Caton had to decide whether to keep him on, or recommend he be sent back into uniform.

His email in-box was just as bad. It was only forty eight hours since he'd cleaned it up from the hotel business centre, and now there were thirty seven new ones. Two of them were reminders from Hadfield that the quarterly report was overdue. No allowance made for the fact that he had been in China. For all that the internet had revolutionised his working life, it was also a curse. If he was on the moon, Chester House would still expect him to hit every deadline. There was even a reminder from Nick Bateson, the conscience of his reading circle, The Alternatives, that they were due to meet as usual on Sunday evening at the Old Nags Head. A list of the questions each of them had posted for the discussion, except for Caton's, was attached. He was tired of telling Nick not to email him at work. But his frustration was as much to do with the fact that he hadn't finished the book, and had completely forgotten the meeting. He'd already agreed to go to the Bridgewater Hall with Kate, to hear the Verdi Requiem. Life was getting complicated.

There was a knock on the door. Gordon Holmes came in carrying a cup and saucer.

'I've brought you a drink Boss.' He put it down on the place mat. 'Make you feel at home.' He tapped the cup, and achieved a pleasant ringing tone. He grinned, lopsided, as only Holmes could grin; like a prop forward who's just collapsed the scrum. 'Nice piece of China.'

Caton reached for the cup. 'Alright Gordon. It's good to see you too.'

'How was the trip Boss?'

'Interesting. I'll tell you about it when we've time. Is everybody in?'

'Yes Boss. They're raring to hear how you got on.'

'And I can't wait to hear how you've wrapped it up while I've been away. You have wrapped it up?'

Holmes grimaced. 'Bit like my Cha Cha; two steps forward, three steps back.'

'Give me five minutes.' Caton said, 'And I'll come through to the Incident Room. See if we can't turn it into a Quick Step.'

The Incident Room was full. A spontaneous round of applause told him they were glad to see him, but left him worried that someone had gilded the lily, and given them the impression that his trip had been more successful than it really had.

'We're taking orders for lunch. Anyone fancy a takeaway?' Dave Woods called out from the back.

'What was it like Boss…up the Yangtze without a paddle?' said a voice he couldn't place.

Caton took centre stage. 'Alright, alright,' he said. 'Very funny. Now settle down.'

He waited for the banter to subside, and looked around at the flip charts and whiteboards behind him that traced the progress of the investigation. Holmes had done a good job. The faxes and emails had been busy between England and China. Beside the images from the four deposition sites, and the mortuaries, fresh photographs of each of the ill fated immigrants had been pinned. Caton made a point of scanning each of them in turn. Michael Chan and James Lee, from the original Chinatown Investigation; Jin Chen, and the other four recovered from the sandpits; Feng Yi at Lock 12; the kitchen porter from the Drum Mountain. He dwelled on the final two; the ones that that might still be alive. Nine dead, and two waiting to be saved. He turned back to face a silent room.

'Inspector Holmes will have told you already. We've got two illegal immigrants still missing. We're now pretty certain that they came in on that lorry, or at least that they were part of the group.'

He pointed to photographs. 'We have positive identifications; Wu Ling and Zheng Hu. She's nineteen, he's twenty seven. We know that she's being held somewhere against her will. We have no idea where he is, although we do have a copy of a letter he posted in Preston four days ago. It's obvious that the same people who are holding her, who killed Feng Yi, our victim at Lock 12, and wreaked havoc at the Drum Mountain takeaway, are looking for Zheng Hu. He has, or knows, something they are desperate to get, or to conceal. We have to reach him before they do. As for the girl, I'm afraid that if we don't find her before the gang realise that her parents can't help them to get to Zheng Hu, then she's going to end up like Feng Yi.'

He paused, and scanned the faces in front of him. They were ordinary people doing an extraordinary job. Clearing up the detritus of other people's lives. Trying, and failing, to live their own lives as though none of it existed. 'I've met this girl's parents. I've seen where she comes from. This is an innocent child fleeing persecution, who thought she'd be safe in Britain. I don't care what it takes; we're going to find her. Alive. Have you got that?'

He looked out at a sea of nodding heads; heard a chorus of approval.

'OK,' he said. 'Where are we up to?'

DI Weston stepped up to join him. 'SOCO have come up with a wide strip of plaster from the wreckage at the Drum Mountain,' she said, holding up a ten by eight photograph showing a bloodied strip of the kind of orange plaster used to cover large wounds. 'As you can see, it's soaked in blood. The victim's blood. Apparently they like to wrap it around the handles of their cleavers. Its soaks up the blood, and stops their fingers from slipping on the handle. Only this one must have got so wet that it lost its adhesion. The Forensic Science Service are trying to extract fingerprints or a trace of DNA from it. Other than the victim's, obviously.'

As she turned to pin it to one of the boards, Carter came forward.

'The lorry found in Newhey Quarry was bought from a scrap yard nine months ago, for cash,' he said. 'It was taxed and insured using a stolen identity. The person whose identity they stole wasn't even aware of it. He's a Chinese business man. It just so happens that he frequents casinos, here in Manchester, and in

Bolton. That's probably where they got his details from. He has a tab with them The credit check they'll have run would have been enough to apply for cards, and documents, in his name. They've been clever. Haven't bothered with the cards. Just documents. It looks like the Ministry Of Transport certificate of road worthiness was a cash unseen job, but we can't prove it. The garage have got the paperwork, but have amnesia when it comes to describing the owner. Same with the insurance. They got it through a broker in Liverpool's Chinatown. He remembers it as a cash transaction. And, surprise, surprise, he doesn't remember what the guy looked like.'

'In that case,' Caton said. 'Let's get the Vehicle Operators Services Agency onto him. Threaten to have his licence to carry out MOTs revoked. See if that jogs his memory.'

DS Joanne Stuart and Duggie Wallace were up next.

'We've got details of all of the BMWs and Black 4x4s and MPVs registered in the past five years,' Stuart began. 'Using VODS – the vehicle owners' descriptive search - we've sorted them into two sub sets: those registered or kept in the North West, and those registered or kept by someone with a name which is, or could be, Chinese. We've divided those up into ones registered or kept on Merseyside, in Greater Manchester, in Leeds, and in Birmingham. When you put those categories together, we're looking at just over four thousand BMWs, and one thousand three hundred 4X4s and MPVs.'

'That sounds a hell of a lot.' Caton reflected.

'There are over 400,000 people of Chinese heritage

living in the UK.' Wallace told him. 'That's just over one percent of all the people who own vehicles of this type.'

Caton nodded. That seemed about right. Joanne Stuart picked up the thread.

'Well the 4X4s and MPVs are likely to be our best bet, simply because there are less of them. But even when we do get a handle on the ones whose owners are either already known to us, or have dodgy occupations, we still have to have due cause to pull them in Boss.'

'You narrow them down,' Caton said. 'And leave the due cause to me.'

Gordon Holmes took over. 'We've not a lot more on the Drum Mountain incident. The family, and the remaining kitchen worker, have seen the photos of Zheng Hu we were sent. They positively identified him, but claim they have no idea where he's holed up. For what it's worth, I believe them. The neighbours are still playing silly beggars. Heard something, saw nothing. We've tried putting the squeeze on all of the other takeaways in the area, to see if we can get a lead on the gangs working the protection rackets. They're all scared witless. After what happened on Plodder Lane, who can blame them?'

'That only leaves what we picked up in China,' Caton said. 'You'll have probably heard that threats have been made to the families of Zheng Hu and Wu Ling. If they don't establish, and reveal, the whereabouts of Zheng Hu, then the girl will be tortured and killed, in much the same manner as Feng Yi. The families have been told they can expect a similar fate. We have no idea why the Triad – and we can't even be certain which one it is – wants so desperately to get its hands on this young man. Be that as it may, this gives us a real opportunity to intercept the snakeheads, and find both him and the girl. The Chinese police, and their Intelligence Service, have placed taps on the phones at their end. GCHQ is working with SOCA at this end.'

A murmur ran around the room. Someone gave a soft whistle.

'I know,' Caton said. 'It's not often we get that kind of support, but now we have it, let's make sure we're ready. I'm going to arrange to have the Tactical Aid Group, and the Tactical Firearms Unit, on high alert. Now that we have the co-operation of his parents, we have a real chance of locating Zheng Hu. When we do, I want a small group from our team to pick him up, and take him to a place of safety. Then I propose to mount a sting operation. We'll suck these thugs in, and take them off the streets for good.'

'What about the girl, Wu Ling, Sir?' Joanne Stuart ventured.

'I've already spoken with Rebecca Sharp, the SOCA Agent in charge of their Sexual Crimes Liaison Unit. She's going to liaise with our own people running Operation Talon. They'll be geared up to move in as soon as they, or we, have a lead. In the meantime, I'd like you to crack on with what you're doing. Catching them is one thing, but tying it down to the satisfaction of the Crown Prosecution Service is another. The more connections we can make between the perpetrators and the deaths, the better.' He looked around the room. The atmosphere had changed markedly through the course of the session. There was a real optimism about the team. 'Any questions?'

A hand went up near the back of the room. It was Dave Woods. Caton felt his heart sink. 'DC Woods?' he said, against his better judgement.

'All this presupposes that they'll actually make contact again Sir.'

Everyone swivelled to look at the detective constable. Caton was beginning to wonder if this was Woods' underlying problem; the need to be a centre of attention.

'And your question is, DC Woods?'

Under the concentrated glare he seemed to hesitate. When he did speak his voice had an uncharacteristic waver. 'What if they don't...Sir?'

If looks could kill, he would have died a thousand deaths.

Caton, took a deep breath. 'They will, DC Woods. They will.'

'But if they don't?' he persisted.

'Then we'll cross that bridge when we come to it. Anymore questions? No? Right, let's get on with it.'

Caton had watched, and heard, and felt, the room deflate. It was like a punctured balloon. One minute they were riding high, ready to take off; the next, sad, sorry, squashed. Woods was right of course, they had to have a back up plan, a contingency. But there wasn't one.

'I don't know why you put up with him Boss.' Holmes said as he closed the door.

Caton put down his pen, and eased back his chair. 'Sit down Gordon,' he said. 'He was right though wasn't he, we don't have any other leads.'

'Not yet we don't. But so long as we keep at it, we'll turn up something. The last thing we need is everyone thinking it's a waste of time.'

'On the other hand, maybe I just made them complacent.'

'Sorry Boss, but you know as well as I do, you had them raring to go. Now it's like a morgue out there.'

'It can't be that bad?'

'No, I suppose not. Everybody's going at it. They all think the calls are going to come. They've just got that what if nagging away at the back of their minds.'

'In that case, they're not alone.' Caton leant forward. 'Tell me you've got some good news Gordon.'

Holmes consulted the printouts in his hand. 'You asked if I remembered MSTC; the Manchester and Shanghai Trading Corporation. I said it rang a bell. Well that's because it was one of the businesses that were part of James Lees' Inland Revenue caseload. There was no evidence that he had anything on them. No case notes, special files, nothing like that. Nothing to suggest that he'd begun an investigation. They were just there on his list.'

'But he was in the investigation section. The company must have been referred for a reason?'

'Apparently not. They came up as a random selection. Bit like a random breath test. Just a quick check to make sure there was no reason to enquire any deeper.'

'And was there?'

'Well, when we started the Chinatown Investigation we asked the Financial Investigations team to give all the firms on his case load a health check. And you asked the Inland Revenue to check them out.'

Caton nodded. 'I remember.'

Holmes passed him the two sheets of paper. 'They both drew a complete blank.'

Caton read the two pages twice. The reports were brief, anodyne, bland, insipid. Worse than that, there was no evidence that anyone had gone beyond a simple scrutiny. A company of this size was hardly going to make it easy for professionals to spot its misdemeanours.

'Well SOCA are going to have another look. And they'll be involving the Serious Fraud Office, the Department of Trade and Industry, the Inland Revenue, and Immigration. For our part I want the GMP Financial Investigations Branch to get involved,' he said. 'Between them they're bound to find something we can use as a starting point. And Gordon, I want you to put a couple of people on going back over the witness statements we took in connection with the murders of James Lee and Michael Han. We know these are all linked in some way. Right now the only connection appears to be this MSTC. I want those statements scoured for any reference at all to either HXL or MSTC.'

'And if there isn't one, Boss?'

Caton handed back the reports and scooted his chair close enough to his desk to press his space bar, and bring the screen back to life. 'You're beginning to sound like DC Woods,' he said. 'If there isn't one, get out there and find me one. And Gordon, use DS Stuart. She has an eye for these things.'

Caton spent the next half an hour on the quarterly report. When a new email alert appeared, he clicked on his mailbox, grateful for the diversion.

To: *Detective Chief Inspector Tom Caton*
From: *Detective Superintendent S. Yeadon.*
Subject: *Help*
Tom,

During our absence my team have been going through all of the records of incoming freight to the North East, and East coast ports, for the forty eight hours prior to the discovery at the Eggborough sand pits. We've established that no lorry matching the description of the one found burnt out on your patch entered any of the ports, inbound, in that period. Interestingly, three MSTC Containers, and two MSTC freight trucks, appeared on the automatic number plate scanner records for Hull on those consecutive days. The port authorities tell us that there is nothing unusual about that. Apparently they book regular shipping slots about eight times a month. Have been doing for the past three years. I've got my people going over the specific details, and manifests, for each of those five vehicles. They are also looking at seven others which are owned by, chartered by, or were delivering to, Chinese companies. On the assumption that some kind of switch took place, our next move will be to apply for search warrants. I know it's asking a lot, but is there any chance that you could provide forensic officers to help with the ones on your ground?

S.

He fired off a reply. He'd have to get Gates to agree, but given that this was a shared investigation, he doubted there would be a problem. It came as no surprise that five minutes later he had a call from Ray Barnes.

'For the past two months,' the Agent told him. 'Our Proceeds of Crime operations team have had an agent inside the casino that your Michael Han was working at when he died.'

'The Arch Casino.'

'That's the one. Well our woman is working as a croupier.'

'Isn't that dangerous?'

'I would think so. But she volunteered for it, and she's a bloody good croupier by all accounts. Worked on the big cruise ships before she joined the Agency.'

'Seen the world, now needs to live dangerously?'

'Something like that. Anyway she's been keeping an eye on the comings and goings. Do you recall that Chan had been investigating a company called HXL?'

Caton sat bolt upright. 'Hang Xian Lo? He got threats, was warned off. But the investigation came to nothing.'

'That's the one. Well one of their senior executives is a regular. On occasion he's brought the company's Chief Executive with him. On those occasions, they didn't appear to come to gamble, but to meet with the Casino Management. And from your point of view, this is where it gets really interesting. A week ago, they had someone else with them. She managed to get a photo. You'd be surprised where they can put a camera these days.'

'Actually, I wouldn't.'

'It was only a couple of days ago that they put a name to the face. And you'll never guess. The guy's name is Wang Yi. And this is the good bit...he's the Chief Executive of the European Division of...'

Caton joined in; they chanted it in unison, like a mantra. '...The Manchester and Shanghai Trading Corporation.'

'And it gets even better,' Barnes told him. 'They dug a little deeper, and guess what?'

'Just tell me Ray.'

'HXL and MSTC are joined at the hip. HXL is a subsidiary. Very cleverly disguised, through a convoluted chain of partnerships, corporations, and loose associations, but take it from me. Hang Xian Lo is owned, lock stock and barrel, by MSTC.'

'And your people think that the casino is being used to launder money from the companies?'

'We don't think there's much doubt about that. The next question is, how are they generating dirty money in the first place. It's too much of a coincidence for it not to be connected with the deaths you and Sally are investigating, and with the kidnaps.'

'Lee was getting too close, and Han must have stumbled onto something.'

'We're working on the premise that he may have been feeding information to Lee.'

'We had a look at that too.' Caton said.

'But you didn't have someone on the inside.'

'True.'

'We don't have enough even to apply for search warrants. And an investigation like this can take months.'

'The girl, Wu Ling, can't wait that long.' Caton pointed out.

'I know. But if we blunder in like this, it might rattle a few cages, but they'll just stonewall us. Worse, it'll put them on their guard. And they may just decide to get rid of the girl now.'

'If they haven't already done so.'

They contemplated that in silence. Barnes was the

first to speak. 'Look Tom, this investigation touches every one of our core targets. I've persuaded my group leader to deploy all the resources we can spare. If we get any leads, you'll be the first to know. We're doing all we can.'

'I know, Ray, and I'm grateful.'

'I'll speak to you soon.'

Caton wondered how best to use this information. Perhaps he could get some observation set up on M&STC and explore the possibility of covert communication surveillance. Phone tapping, would be a start. Anything that might lead him to the snakeheads, or the street gangs. The door burst open, and Gordon Holmes charged in. He filled the room with anticipation.

'We've got a number Boss. From China. Zheng Hu's family got a call. It's been traced to an owner with a Liverpool address. The UK service provider is emailing us the phone records.'

Caton was already on his feet, snagging his jacket as he tugged it from the back of his chair.

21

'I'm sorry Sir. That phone has been cloned.'

Duggie Wallace handed him the details.

'This guy is legit. He's a junior doctor at the Royal Liverpool University Hospital. Someone's cloned his phone. They've been using it for the last two months. He probably wouldn't have found out till he got his next quarterly bill.'

'How the hell do they do that?' Carter asked.

'Take your pick. As long as it's a first generation GSM phone, all the hacker has to do is either have your phone in his possession for a couple of minutes, or wait till you're using an infra red hands free system within a few metres of him. Then he can carry out a partitioning attack. He'll ask your phone a series of questions, guess the PIN – and since most people never bother to change the default that's as easy as falling off a log – then he'll configure a blank chip, and insert that in a cell phone of his own.'

'It's that easy?'

'There's an even easier way. Very popular in the Far East. Korea in particular. And China. Every phone has an electronic serial number that's factory set. Unique to that phone. All they do is manufacture phones which they then programme to have the same number as a legitimate phone.'

'So our suspects could all be using cloned phones?' Caton said, suddenly feeling the need to sit down.

'I'm afraid so Sir.'

'So we won't be knocking on doors, and hauling them in?'

'Not immediately. You can forget all that stuff you see on TV programmes like Spooks. It's not going to be possible to pin point, for example, that they're at the Tesco supermarket check out, unless they're using the latest GPS phones. And this one isn't. Even GCHQ would be hard pressed to improve on the basic triangulation method used by the service provider.'

'So what can we do?'

'Well it will be possible for the service provider to go over the calls that have been made in past few months, and find out approximately where they were made from. They should be able to narrow that down to within a radius of fifty metres.'

Caton visualised a circle a hundred metres across, in an urban area. Maybe not the check out, but certainly somewhere within the store, or the car park.

'So if there are a cluster in the same location, we could set up an observation.'

'Oh yes. And put a detector van in there. Next time they use the phone from that location we'll be able to narrow it right down.'

'But first we need the patterns.' Said Holmes.

'Don't worry Sir.' Wallace replied. 'I've already asked them to get on with that.'

'Don't we need a warrant for all this?' Caton asked.

Wallace smiled. 'SOCA have already sorted that out.'

'Right, Gordon,' Caton said. 'SOCA have agreed to concentrate on the intelligence surrounding MSTC. They've left us to concentrate on the kidnaps. I want you to work with Duggie on isolating the user of this phone, and setting up an observation and detection operation. The snakeheads said they would ring back in four hours. I'm going to talk to Superintendent Gates about putting together a decoy operation.'

Superintendent Helen Gates sat on the opposite side of the table. Things were moving so fast she'd judged it appropriate to come to Caton rather than expect him to trail across the city to Chester House.

'Have you had any word from the Chinese about calls to the family of this girl?'

'Wu Ling, Ma'am, Caton replied. 'No we haven't. Not yet.'

'And do you know for a fact that the same people are holding her?'

'No we don't. But it's highly likely. At the very least, the two are connected.'

'And if they're are, don't you think that going after the people who are holding Zheng Hu might just lead their colleagues holding the girl to kill her, just to dispose of the evidence?'

Caton had been thinking long and hard about that. 'Yes Ma'am, it is a possibility. The only way I can see round it is to make sure we lift the people looking for Zheng Hu, fast and clean, before they have a chance to contact their accomplices.'

Her forehead furrowed. He found it unnerving that her eyebrows met in the middle 'Easier said than done,' she said. 'All it takes is a speed dial on a mobile phone.'

'That's what was bothering me. We could wait and see if any of the clusters of calls give us a clue as to where they may be holding her,' he said without enthusiasm. 'Or we could hold fire in the hope that her parents get another call that might give us the other location.'

'What about raiding the brothels and massage parlours? You must have thought of that?'

Caton ran his hands distractedly through his hair. 'Yes Ma'am. Firstly, we know that she's being held, but we have no evidence that it's a brothel or a massage parlour. The video suggests a flat. Which could be a brothel of course. Nevertheless, I alerted the officer commanding our own Operation Talon as soon as we knew she was being held. They're the experts on kidnapping, and trafficking for sexual exploitation. They tell me she could be being held anywhere.'

'You'd start with the ones in Chinatown surely?'

'Officially, there is only one massage parlour in Chinatown, it's supposedly regulated, and they're certain she's not being held there. All the illegal massage parlours, and brothels, keep themselves well hidden. Half of them at least, operate out of flats and council houses. Some masquerade as speed dating centres, or dance clubs. They reckon they only know about a quarter of them at any one time. They've promised to deploy some officers to see if there's any word on the street, but they're not hopeful. And right now, they're really stretched trying to reduce the amount of night-hiking that's going on.'

'I know,' she said wearily. 'Single female clubbers, out of their skulls on drugs or alcohol - or both - standing in the road in the middle of the night, flagging down any old car because they can't get a taxi; they may as well be holding up a sign saying rape me. The trouble is that if they are attacked, and it comes to trial, that's exactly what will be going through the minds of some members of the jury.'

She stood, picked her cap up from the table, and gave it a routine brush with her gloves. 'So what do you propose to do Tom?'

Caton stood facing her. 'I'd still like to go ahead with a decoy operation Ma'am. That way, we should definitely save the young man, and if we get it right, we should be a step closer to finding Wu Ling.'

Gates thought about it for a moment. She placed her cap on top of the crown of raven curls. Grasping the peak from either side she adjusted it so that the peak was in the centre. 'In that case.' she said. 'You had better get it right.'

It took less than half an hour for Sarah Finch, the Head of the Tactical Firearms Unit, to choose a spot they could both agree on.

'Indigo Mill,' she said stabbing a finger at the map. 'Scheduled for re-development by the council. Empty, and derelict. We used it for a night exercise a couple of months ago, so it wouldn't require much additional planning. We'll just pull out the report, and send someone down to make sure nothing's changed in the meantime.'

Caton knew it well. The path at the rear of the mill followed the bed of the old Manchester, Bolton and Bury Canal. It was now a Heritage Trail; thirteen miles of forgotten history he had walked a couple of years ago. If he remembered rightly this stretch down to Indigo Street was bounded by high walls, open space, and railway lines.

'There's a partially enclosed space at the back, iron railings down the side of the adjacent factory, a stretch of concrete, and a green space out front?' he said.

'That's the one.'

'But isn't there a row of houses opposite?'

'Two sixties semis, and a row of terraced houses built at the same time. There's a fence, trees, and gardens, in between them and the road.'

'But they're still well within range.'

'That's true, but the idea is to get the targets round the back of the mill where there's nowhere for them to go, and no risk of stray bullets. Once they're there we can block them in.

Caton was still not convinced. 'They're bound to have someone parked out front as a lookout, and in case Zheng Hu tries to break out that way.'

'We'll get everyone in the front row of the houses to move to the back of the house as a precaution. I won't have any of my people in those houses. We'll use stingers on the road to disable their vehicles, and place our own vehicles to block off any retreat from the front of the building. We won't give them any reason to fire in the direction of those houses, and our own field of fire is going to be inbound. In any case, from what you tell me, there's no evidence this lot even carry firearms.'

Caton stared at the map; calculating the possibilities. 'There's no evidence of them having used them,' he said. 'But that doesn't mean that they don't carry them. Let's face it, these days everybody does.'

'Look,' she said. 'There's no way we can use a completely isolated spot. They'd smell a rat at once. Those kind of places are also impossible to contain. There are just too many exits. We'd need an army to cover them. Don't worry Chief Inspector, I'm not about to take any unnecessary risks with my people, or members of the public.'

Caton had to agree that it made sense. There was a limit to how far Zheng Hu might have travelled once he'd left the Drum Mountain takeaway. Indigo Mill was just under six miles away, and on a reasonably direct route. In the minds of his pursuers that would have been feasible. It would also make it easier for the snakehead gang to check the place out, and mount an attack. It would also be much easier for GMP to manage on their own patch, but he knew from his own attachment to the Firearms Unit how easily these things could go wrong. And he desperately needed to take everyone alive. On the other hand, it was his best, and currently his only, chance of finding Wu Ling in time.

The phone call from Munby came through. The snakeheads had been in touch, and Zheng Hu's parents had kept to the script. His father admitted that he'd spoken to his son, but would not reveal his whereabouts without assurances. In the background, but loudly enough to be heard, his wife had entreated him not to trust the snakeheads; not to tell them anything. Her husband had bargained patiently, with just the right degree of desperation in his voice. Had listened to their honeyed promises. Had closed his ears to the wailings of his wife. Had said the words they'd written down for him to say.

'I told you, I don't know where. An old building he says, in Salford. Near a graveyard. Indigo Mill. Please do not harm my son. I will pay you whatever you want. However long it takes. Please do not harm him.'

His wife screamed at him. The line went dead.

Agent Munby had told them they'd done well.

The call had been timed at ten pm Shanghai time.
Caton looked at his watch. It was now three o'clock
Greenwich Meantime. An hour since that call had
been made. The teams had been in position for almost
two hours. Caton looked at the monitors that were the
focus of everyone's attention.

The first covered the rear of the mill. The broad
tarmac path, bordered by a stone wall, was topped by
a flat grassed bank from which rose a red brick wall,
eight feet high at its shortest point. On top of the wall
bristled a four foot high steel fence, erected by the
council to keep out the vandals. At one point the
horizontal strands of wire slumped drunkenly,
leaving a gaping hole. A testament to failure.

The second monitor, positioned at the top of the
ramp, looked down the street at the rear of the
property showing the slope up which any vehicles
would have to drive; the rear elevation of the Axion
Works; the high bank, strewn with rubbish left by fly
tippers, the concrete panelled wall dividing it from the
derelict land, and the railway beyond.

The third showed the side of Indigo Street, the only
route to the rear of the building. A cobbled street gave
way to patchy tarmac alongside the maroon walls of
the single storey mill. An arched doorway, long
bricked in, and a twelve foot high steel gate covered
by a horizontal ladder fence, challenged those seeking
easy access. On the opposite side of the road, safe
behind the three metre high turquoise green steel
fence, Caton could see DC Woods and DS Carter,

dressed in white overalls bearing the logo of Axion Polymers, busy inspecting huge white bags stacked on wooden pallets.

The fourth, and final camera, covered the front elevation of the mill, and the street outside. A wide triangle of grass, with a tree at its centre, separated the mill from the road. A cobbled path, wide enough for a car, ran from the street between the grass and the front of the mill. The original doorway, marking the grand front entrance, was only distinguishable by the relative newness of the brick with which it had been filled. Above the doorway a large sign - bold black letters on a white background - reminded the world that this had once been the famous Indigo Mill. A row of skylights running the length of the corrugated gable roof, shone like a river in the sharp spring sunshine. Caton detected an air of dreary decay, and casual abandonment.

They were parked out of sight, on the far side of the Polymers factory, and behind two of the delivery trucks. There were eight of them in the mobile command centre. Caton had immediate control on the ground as the Bronze Commander. Gordon Holmes was his deputy. Superintendent Sarah Finch, had her own direct and separate communications channel with her firearms officers. Chief Inspector Trevor Barrington headed up the arrest team from the Tactical Aid Unit. One officer operated the video cameras, another two the radio communications with Gold Command at Chester House, and Silver Command – the Salford Divisional Commander – at the new Salford North Station on Chorley Road, in Swinton, to which anyone arrested would be taken, and from which, the back up traffic teams, and other uniformed officers, had been deployed. The seventh officer – a uniformed inspector – was taking note of every decision made, command given, action taken. When it was all over Caton knew that this written record, together with the audio and video tapes – regardless of the outcome - would be subject to intense scrutiny. The pressure on everyone was relentless; on him above all. Despite the calm, quiet, professionally controlled voices, the atmosphere was tense with concentration. The temperature, notwithstanding the air conditioning and the fan, was already uncomfortable. Caton had no idea how long they might be here.

One by one the wireless operator observer accompanying each rifle officer reported in to their commander using the colour coding system to identify their position, and target field of view.

'Everyone is still in position,' she said. 'Hunkered down, and ready to go. The biggest concern now is going to be boredom setting in. But don't worry, they're used to it. It's what we train for.'

Caton thought about the SAS observers, dug into their hides in the sodden field margins of Northern Ireland, the mountains of Croatia, and the dust bowls of Iraq and Afghanistan. By comparison this must seem like a picnic.

He looked at his watch. It was now four forty five. Some of the factory workers had already left. The rush hour traffic had picked up; an endless river of commuters using it as a rat run out of the city to Bolton and Bury. If they decided to come now it would be a nightmare. He thought it unlikely. It would be that much harder for them to get away, and too many people who might remember their vehicles, and their faces. Suddenly, a voice came over one of the radio channels.

'Bravo Charlie One, this is Sierra Uniform Two. There is a black Bravo Mike Whisky, westbound in your direction. Two up. I repeat. Two Up. Over.'

Gordon Holmes pointed to the magnetic marker on the wall map showing the location of Sierra Uniform Two, the officer in an unmarked car. He's right there Sir...Orchard Street. They should be with us in less than a minute.'

Caton turned to watch the monitor for the camera at the front of the mill trained on Langley Road South. The target vehicle appeared, sandwiched between a white delivery van, and young woman in a Renault Clio.

'September 2006 registration, 325i Sport. About twenty six grand second hand Holmes muttered.'

As it passed at about forty miles an hour they could see two men of Chinese heritage in the front seats.

'Did anybody see them looking across towards the mill?' Caton wanted to know. Nobody had. They had stared straight ahead, if anything a little too fixedly Caton thought. Ten minutes passed. The traffic increased. At times it even slowed to match the thirty miles an hour limit on this stretch, as the vehicles ahead of them backed up from the junction with Agecroft Road. They had almost begun to relax again when the radio crackled into life.

'Bravo Charlie One. This is Sierra Uniform three. A black Bravo Mike Whisky, is eastbound in your direction. Two up. I repeat. Two Up. Over.'

Holmes pointed to the Northern Cemetery. 'They're coming back. Traffic's moving faster into the city.' he said. 'They'll be with us any moment now.'

The BMW sailed past, and kept going.

'He looked, didn't he?' Caton said, trying hard to control the effect of the adrenalin beginning to course through his veins. 'Please tell me I didn't imagine it. The passenger…he leant forward, and looked across at the mill.'

Sarah Finch and Gordon Holmes nodded in unison. 'You didn't imagine it,' Holmes said. 'And it wasn't just a glance. He had a real eyeful.'

With both eyes on the screen, Caton waited to hear from Sierra Uniform One that the car had reached and driven past his position in Orchard Street, but the message never came. Instead, the BMW came into view heading back towards them. The driver indicated left, and pulled off the road, onto the cobbled section along the front of Indigo Mill. Superintendent Finch calmly informed her Unit of the car's arrival, Caton and Barrington did the same with their teams. All the while their eyes remained glued to the monitors as the car cruised slowly past the bricked up door, and turned left into Indigo Street. They watched on the other monitors as it turned left again taking it behind the building, cruised up the incline to the top, went as far as it could go, turned, and paused at the top of the ramp. They watched as the front seat passenger pointed animatedly at the wall, and the gap in the fence. The driver nodded, and coasted down the slope, and around the corner. The car stopped yet again, this time outside the tall steel gates. Again they conversed. The driver pointed across his passenger towards the Polymer factory where only minutes before Carter and Woods had been completing their tally for the umpteenth time, but had since departed to the comfort of a van adjacent to the command post. He was pointing, Caton guessed, to the security camera, high on the wall beside the sign on the company logo, that was positioned only to cover the yard of the factory itself. Within the space of twenty seconds, the car had accelerated away, swung out across the sea of traffic, and headed back towards the city centre.

'They'll be back.' Gordon Holmes felt impelled to say. Caton had no doubt that he was right. The question was, when. And with how many others.

22

Caton glanced at the clock again. It was fifteen minutes past nine in the evening. The sun had set three hours ago. By agreement, the security lights on the Polymer factory had been switched off. The twilight gloaming had given way to that quarter-light where the combined efforts of moon, and street lamps, enabled shapes to be discerned, and detail blurred. In the windows of the houses, there was a muted glow behind the curtains; except in the occasional upstairs window where, acting on his instructions, the curtains had been left open.

The road was quiet now. Commuters long gone; pleasure seekers already returned to the city centre cinemas, theatres, restaurants and bars. Too early for the service vans and lorries bringing in the fresh produce for the morning. Every minute or so, a set of headlights would cast strange shadows on the face of Indigo Mill. In two of the skylights a faint light could be seen by anyone sufficiently interested to seek it out.

The air conditioning that had only just managed to keep them cool was failing now to cope with the chill of this evening, late in March. Caton thought about the rifle officers, and their buddies, huddled on the roof of the factory, and the cramped conditions inside the cars and vans tucked out of sight. Here, in the control centre, spirits had flagged, not helped by the angst that was building up in Chester House, and Swinton nick, where Caton could imagine the Gold and Silver Commands kicking their heels in frustration.

'Bravo Charlie One, this is Golf Charlie One.'

It was Gold Commander, the Assistant Chief Constable Special Operations, right on cue. 'Bravo Charlie One, still nothing?'

Caton suppressed the urge to remind him that if there had been anything he would have been the first to hear. Instead he forced his lips into something resembling a smile, in the hope that it would imbue his voice with a semblance of positivity.

'Golf Charlie One. This is Bravo Charlie One. Nothing yet. Over.'

'Bravo Charlie One. How long do you intend to sit this out?'

Caton gritted his teeth, aware that the others in the van were watching him; wondering the same thing.

'Golf Charlie One. Until dawn, was the limit that I thought that we'd agreed. Over.'

'Bravo Charlie One.' This time the frustration had been replaced by thinly veiled annoyance. 'That was in extremis. I do not think that any of us envisaged that it would go that far. Over.'

'Golf Charlie One. Nor will it. Over.'

'Bravo Charlie One,' There was a pause, a slow exhalation and then a phrase that Caton was hearing for the second time that day. 'Golf Charlie One. You had better be right. Out.'

'There was no way they were going to come waltzing in here in broad daylight, Boss,' Gordon Holmes said to cheer him up. 'And you were dead right about the fact that they'd want to check it out. If we hadn't been here when that BMW came by we

would never have known that they'd taken the bait.
And once we were here, we could hardly wander off
for a spell, and come back when it went dark.'

He was only stating the obvious, but Caton was
glad of it. He was about to say so when the radio
crackled into life again..

'Bravo Charlie One, this is Sierra Uniform Two.
You have a convoy: One Bravo, Mike, Whisky - two
up; one silver Audi - two up; one black Mike Papa
Victor, with tinted glass. Over.'

It was as though the mobile control room had been
struck by lightning. Everything, and everybody, burst
into action.

'This is it.' Caton said. 'I want India 99 airborne,
now.'

On either end of the roof of Axion Polymers, pairs of
tactical firearms officers wriggled out of their two-
season camouflage bags, and checked their equipment
for the final time. In the unmarked vehicles, stab and
bullet proof vests were tightened, and helmets placed at
the ready. In the van they watched on monitor four as a
pair of bright halogen headlights signalled the vehicles'
approach. There was less than a car's width between
each of them. With almost military precision, the leading
car – the black BMW - swung left into Indigo Street; the
silver Audi peeled off, and came to a halt on the cobbled
section outside the bricked up entrance to the mill. A big
black MPV with tinted windows followed the BMW to
the end of Indigo Street, where it turned left, and
stopped on the furthest side of the tarmac, opposite and
horizontal to the mill wall.

'That's a Chrysler Grand Voyager,' Holmes said in
a hushed voice as though fearful that those outside

would hear him. 'Seven seater, in three rows, with variable configurations; the rear five seats fold away into the floor well.'

The BMW continued up the ramp until it reached the barrier and gates of another industrial unit. Caton watched it slowly turn, and come back, until it was level with the section of wall where the wires of the fence on top had been breached . Then it stopped. A moment later, the lights on all three vehicles were simultaneously extinguished.

'They're in communication,' Holmes observed.

As if to prove him right, the front passenger door on the BMW, and the doors on the passenger side of the Chrysler, opened. In the absence of headlights, the night vision cameras gathered the ambient light, flung it against a phosphorous screen, and delivered clear, green-hued, images. One figure emerged from the car, and five from the MPV. Two of them wore balaclavas; the others had baseball caps with broad, low, peaks. The favoured outer garments appeared to be bomber jackets, and quilted anoraks.

'That leaves the driver in each vehicle,' Caton said. 'But if you're right, there could be up to two more in the Chrysler.'

'That's true,' Holmes agreed. 'Equally, they may have collapsed the remaining two seats to give them more room to store the man they've come to get.'

'Can anyone see any weapons?' Caton asked as the passengers from the MPV walked up the slope to join their colleagues.

They craned forward, scanning the screens closely.

'These two here.' Superintendent Finch said, pointing to the two at the rear of the group from the Chrysler.

The technician zoomed the camera. Each of them held something in his right hand; dangling at the end of a straight arm. As the camera focused a shaft of moonlight sent a silvery green flash into the night.

'Chopping knives.' Finch said, with certainty. They passed the news to the waiting officers. At the front of the building the doors of the Audi remained closed. No one had moved. The six strong group at the rear appeared to be taking stock. One of them broke away from the huddle and walked to the boot of the car. He opened it up, took out several objects, closed the boot, and walked back to join the others. Then they began to troop up the incline to the point where the sloping stone wall was at its shortest.

'Let's remember,' Caton said. 'There is no one in the factory to protect. It's just us, and them; no innocent victims, and no bystanders. I want every one of them taken alive. And no heroics. We keep our distance until it's safe. There's nowhere for them to run.'

They watched as the men vaulted onto the wall in turn, and began to walk in single file along the grassy bank beside the high brick section, towards the point where the steel fence was compromised. The camera zoomed in again.

'Those look like wire cutters, and that's some kind of blanket,' the technician said.

'Stand by,' Caton ordered. 'Any second now. On my command'

He waited until the one at the front of the group had reached the spot beneath the gap in the fence; had made a back for the next man to climb on; had handed up the tool. As the first of the wires was cut, he slapped the palm of his hand on the table top.

'GO,GO,GO!' he ordered.

Floodlights came on, bathing the area in a pool of bright white light. With a squeal of tyres, a van and an unmarked car raced along the top tarmac road, and braked broadside to seal the head of the ramp. On Langley Road South two unmarked cars screeched into place at either end of the cobbled street, and a van pulled up on the road itself covering escape across the large triangle of grass. The gates of Axion Polymers slid back on their rollers. A large delivery van emerged to completely block the width of Indigo Street. Above and behind it, on the roof of the factory, the two rifle officers made their presence known, emerging from the v section between the pair of sloping roofs and yelling their commands.

'Armed Police! Throw your weapons on the ground, and place your hands on your heads. Do it Now! Do It Now!'

They were joined by a further two firearms officers who appeared above the wall on the other side of the tarmac road, immediately opposite the group of stranded men transfixed in the pool of light, nine feet from the ground, with their backs against ten feet of wall, and a further four of steel fence.

Caton had arranged for the same commands to be broadcast over the loudspeakers in Mandarin and Cantonese. It was impossible to decide which had had the most effect. Caton didn't care. All that mattered was that in the glare of the spotlight, they had frozen like frightened rabbits. And now they were complying. The one on whose back his companion was still standing, could not decide whether to stay as he was, and risk being shot in the backside, or stand, turn, and place his hands on his head. In the event, that was exactly what he did, leaving his unfortunate colleague to hang desperately from the top of the wall, until he lost his grip, and plummeted down, throwing them both to the ground. Two armed officers advanced downhill from the unmarked car towards the BMW. They ordered the driver to get out, and lie on the ground. At the same time the driver of the Chrysler got out of the MPV, placed his hands on his head, and began to advance up the tarmac slope.

'Looks as though he's been here before,' Holmes said, barely able to hide his excitement.

Two armed officers and two members of the Tactical Aid Team turned the corner by the Chrysler. They yelled at the driver to stop, and lay down on the floor, following him up the slope until he did so. While the armed officers stood to right and left, the other officers began to check for weapons.

Caton could see from monitor four that both of the occupants of the Audi at the front of the mill were already lying face down on the grass verge, arms behind their heads. Officers approached them from the left and front, leaving their colleagues on the right flank safe from friendly fire. It looked like a text book operation. Overhead, the force helicopter, call sign India 99, having made record time from its base three miles to the East, began to circle; its searchlight pinpointing the line of suspects now shuffling, hands on heads, in single file along the top of the wall towards the small army of officers awaiting them. Switching his attention back to the rear of the building it suddenly struck Caton that nobody had checked, and cleared, the Chrysler.

'The MPV,' he said to Superintendent Finch. She nodded, ahead of him, already issuing instructions. Two more armed officers emerged from the delivery van. Another officer, who had come out of the gates to the factory, raced ahead of them up Indigo Street.

'Who's that, and what the hell is he doing?' Caton asked.

'It's one of yours, DC Woods,' one of the communication's officers told him.

'He's says he's just seen someone slip up by the wall at the back of the MPV.'

'Tell him to wait for the firearms officers.' Caton instructed.

They watched as Woods disappeared around the corner, and off the monitors.

'Can anyone see what the hell's going on behind that MPV?' Caton demanded. Superintendent Finch, still engaged in conversation raised one hand to indicate that one of her officers could.

On the roof of Axion Polymers, Hotel One, and his buddy, watched DC Woods clamber over the huge stone blocks that had been used to section off the dismal, disused, ramp that led towards the polymer processing tanks and the railway beyond. Ahead of him, a solitary figure emerged from the shadows of the wall that he had used for cover, and made for the point where the fence and railing met, beyond which lay waste ground, and the railway tracks. Behind him, they watched Woods negotiate the sodden mattresses, and piles of fly tipped rubbish, and start to sprint. Suddenly, the figure ahead of him became aware of his pursuer, and began to run. The Observer shouted the standard warning, commanding him to stop, but to no avail.

Hotel One concentrated his night sight on the centre of the man's back. It was only a precaution. His instructions were clear. All suspects to be taken alive. No shots unless an officer is at risk. Even if this man managed to scale the fence, the helicopter would be able to track his progress. In any case, there were three police vans with dog handlers on the other side of the tracks. What he didn't need, was this joker charging up the ramp. At the bottom of the ramp, the two armed officers were just negotiating the pile of rubbish.

The gap between DC Woods, and the suspect, was down to just two metres when he launched himself. A perfect rugby tackle, just above the knees, sent the suspect crashing into the railings. Hotel One cursed silently, and raised his sights, needing a clear and certain target. The two bodies rolled along the foot of the railings, kicking and scrabbling. The helicopter wheeled in their direction, its searchlight strafing the ground. The other officers were less than fifteen metres away, weapons at the ready, when Hotel One saw the suspect's arm break free, and a flash of steel. As he exhaled, his finger squeezed the trigger. The head flew back, the arm dropped. Moments later, the beam from India 99 found its target. DC Woods lay pinioned beneath the body of their suspect; his arms still clasped around his assailant's waist. Above him, two officers stood yelling commands, their pistols raised. Hotel One lowered his weapon, and cleared the breech. Clearly, and calmly his Observer spoke into his radio mike. 'Hotel Two,' he said. 'One man down. I repeat. One man down.'

'Your man is alright.' Superintendent Finch informed him. The suspect however, is not. He is dead.'

'The stupid bastard.' Caton said, partly out of relief, but mainly out of barely controlled anger.

'Very brave though,' Holmes said lamely.

'No, simply foolish.' Caton responded.

'Not to mention perilously irresponsible.' Finch added. 'You have no idea how my officer will be feeling now, not to mention the amount of paperwork this is going to generate.' She turned away, switching her attention back to her own officers.

Caton could only imagine. But he had other concerns now. Not least, what difference this would make when he came to question the others.

'Keeping them apart was a logistical nightmare.' Gordon Holmes told him. 'We've got four here from the MPV, and the two from the BMW. The two from the Audi, and the remaining two from the MPV are at Collyhurst. Eleven men, to take one frightened illegal.'

'Their street gangs always like to go mob handed,' Caton reminded him. 'Even more than our own indigenous gangs.' It suddenly struck him that in all probability these *were* indigenous gangs. The days when gangs of black youths in Moss Side, and white ones in the rest of the city, were all they had to contend with were long gone. In common with other cities in the UK they now had Asian, mixed race, Turkish, and Chinese gangs, with East European gangs coming up on the blind side. 'We've got one interpreter in each of the stations?' he asked.

'Yes Boss. Which means we'll have to see the suspects in rotation. It's going to be a long night.'

Detective Inspector Sarah Weston, and DS Carter, were handling the interviews at Collyhurst, he and Holmes the ones here in Swinton. DS Stuart had taken the evidence bags of confiscated possessions back to Longsight, where she, and Duggie Wallace, were checking the numbers on all of the cell phones. The body still lay at the back of Indigo Mill, while the independent investigation team looked into the circumstances of the fatal shooting. Ray Barnes had been informed that the operation had gone, more or less, according to plan. Caton could think of nothing else that needed to be done.

'Right,' he said. 'Let's get started.'

They were using three interview rooms. Moving between them on a strict rotation, taking their interpreter with them. Three hours into the process, not one of them had given so much as his name. Nor had they responded to any of the questions put to them, first in Mandarin, then in Cantonese, and finally in Fuhianese. It was only through their body language during questioning that Caton, Holmes, and the interpreter, had agreed that it was likely that all of the prisoners were from Fuzhon Province, except for the two that had been in the BMW. It was clear, even though they had tried to hide the fact, that those two alone had understood the test questions put to them in Cantonese. Sarah Weston reported a parallel situation at Collyhurst, except that none of hers appeared to understand Cantonese.

'I'll lay good odds that what we've got here is a Fujianese street gang working with several members of a Triad who are pulling the strings.' Caton said, as he placed the mug of coffee on the table behind the two-way mirror.

'Sounds right to me Boss,' Holmes replied taking a pull at his bottle of Red Bull. 'The burning question is, how are we going to get any of them to talk?'

Caton looked at the three men sat at the table in the room next door. He marvelled at the discipline that meant that even on their own like this, none of them had spoken a word since the door had closed. They might have suspected that they were being watched – at the very least being listened to – but there had not been so much as a whisper, or a gesture. They sat heads down, staring at an invisible point on the table top.

To make matters worse, there was a limit to how long he could reasonably hold them. So far, they had been charged with possession of an offensive weapon, contrary to Section 1 Prevention of Crime Act 1953; suspicion of wounding and assault, causing grievous bodily harm, contrary to Section 18 of the Offences Against the Persons Act 1847; and conspiracy to commit murder. The latter two still carried the possibility of a maximum sentence of life imprisonment, and would certainly entail remand awaiting trial. But to achieve that he knew that had to link each of them to the death of any one of Michael Han, James Lee, Feng Yi, or the kitchen worker at the Drum Mountain takeaway. Or, even the five Eggborough victims. And that meant either forensic matches or confessions. Swabs and fingerprints had been taken for each of them, but it would take at least seventy two hours to get all of the results. In the meantime, Wu Ling was at even greater risk.

Particularly when the news of their capture broke.

'What do we know about the dead man?' he asked, swirling the coffee around the mug.

Holmes began to count it off on the fingers of his left hand. 'Smartly dressed; he had a Furi Fillet knife; ten centimetres of wicked blade that would have done for DC Woods; he was the only one carrying a firearm; he was the only one to stay in the vehicle; it looked as though the driver of the MPV got out and walked up the ramp as a diversion, so he could slip away unnoticed.'

'And, though I hate to admit it, if it hadn't been for Woods he might have made it,' said Caton. 'Although he didn't need to go after him himself,' he added in case Holmes concluded that he was going soft. 'What did Superintendent Finch have to say about the gun?'

Holmes consulted his notebook. 'It's a Heckler and Koch, USP45CT. That's a model modified for American Special Forces. The CT apparently stands for counter terrorist. The main reason for the modification was to make it easier to conceal,' he looked up. 'It's the first one she's actually seen outside of a manual.'

'What does all that suggest to you Gordon?'

'That he was numero uno on this operation. He was very well connected. Highly professional. Not someone you'd want to mess with.'

'That's what I thought,' Caton said. 'And now he's dead. I think we can use that as a way in. Let's give it a try.'

They chose the one from the MPV who had shown the highest levels of anxiety. He couldn't have been more than twenty one years of age. His hair, thick, black, and shiny with sweat, hung down to his shoulders, in stark contrast to the papery white all-in-one that had replaced his clothes.

'Just use the Fuhianese dialect,' Caton told the interpreter. 'And let him know that we've spoken to the others, and we know that he understands.' The interpreter looked at him quizzically.

'Just do it please,' Caton said.

Holmes began by reminding him of the charges against him, then Caton leant forward, deliberately seeking eye contact.

'Tell him that we're about to charge him with murder. Multiple murder. The murders of Feng Yi, and of the kitchen worker at the Drum Mountain Café.'

He waited and watched, as the eyes flicked nervously from side to side, the pupils narrowed, and sweat began to breakout on his forehead.

'Tell him that we have found forensic evidence at the canal, and in the takeaway.' It was true, and although it might seem that he was stretching the truth, Caton had been careful not to say that the evidence, such as it was, pointed directly to him. It didn't. Not yet, anyway. The young man's head jerked up. He stared directly into Caton's eye. Seeking the truth. Hoping this was a lie. Instead he saw implacable assurance.

'Tell him,' Caton said. 'That he has this one opportunity to tell us what happened to those young men, or I shall charge him, and leave his fate to the courts. A life sentence here, or, more probably, conviction, followed by a decision to seek deportation into the hands of the Supreme People's Court of the Democratic People's Republic of China.'

Once again, the interpreter hesitated. 'Please,' Caton said. 'Repeat my words exactly as I said them, and I'll explain to you afterwards.'

Even before the whole of the sentence had been translated, the young man became agitated. He wrung his hands, and for the first time a torrent of words began to flow. So fast the interpreter had difficulty keeping up.

'Please no. You cannot do that. Please, I beg of you. It wasn't me...I didn't want to be part of this. Please you cannot do that...I had no choice. My family...Please.'

In just twenty minutes they had his name, the name of the dead man, and more importantly, a detailed description of the death of Feng Yi; the disposal of his body at Lock 13; the attack on the Drum Mountain takeaway; and the briefing that the gang had received for the assault on Indigo Mill. This was the key that would unlock the tongues of most if not all of the remaining suspects.

'But you cannot do that Chief Inspector,' the interpreter said as they took a break in the observation room. 'If you send him back to China he will be executed. We have no death penalty in this country. It would be immoral.'

'But that's not what I said.' Caton reminded her. 'I only said the courts would *probably seek* a deportation order. What I know, and he doesn't, is that the courts would turn it down unless there was a guarantee – that we could trust – that he would not be executed.

Everything that I told him was true. He simply filled in the gaps that he thought were there.'

'I'm sorry,' she said.

'Don't be, 'he told her. 'Just remember. In that room you do exactly as I ask. No questions, no hesitation. If you have any reservations, you can raise them outside. It's all on tape and camera anyway. It's up to the defence team to question my methods, not you.'

'I understand,' she said. 'And I am truly sorry. It won't happen again.' She started to leave, to freshen up, then turned in the doorway. 'Incidentally, I thought you might be interested. The name of the dead man. The man he said was responsible for the murders, and for everything else that happened.'

'Chu Wan?'

'Yes, but just once he also referred to him by another name; Tu Po Sin. In Chinese, it means... Slaughter Man.'

23

They had been working all night. It was now ten past four in the morning. This was only the second break Caton had had since the arrests had been made. Chester House had managed, thus far, to put a press blanket over the whole operation, but it was only a matter of time before someone broke ranks. There were too many people, in the houses opposite Indigo Mill, and at the Axion works, who would know that something big had gone down. Not only that, but there would be others, associates of the men they had in custody, who would have known about the raid, and have missed them already. He had an uneasy sense that time had already run out for Wu Ling.

His belief that the first confession would unlock the other tongues had been confirmed, at least in part. All but one of the Fujianese had proved willing, desperate even, to talk to save their necks. It was now clear that they were a rag tag street gang brought in to do the dirty work for a Triad. Two of them had given detailed descriptions of the capture, death, and disposal of Feng Yi, and the attack on the Drum Mountain. They were adamant that the murders had been committed by the man whose body now lay in the mortuary. As for the other deaths, they had denied any knowledge of them, let alone any involvement. The driver and the passenger from the BMW, whom Caton's team had identified as Cantonese from a driving licence, and the name of the registered keeper, had remained silent as the grave.

'What do you think, Boss?' Holmes asked as he carried his bacon bap, and steaming mug of coffee, over to the canteen table.

Caton pulled up a chair and sat down. 'About them only providing the back up, and the muscle, for the operation?' he said. 'I'd go along with that. The ones that DI Weston and DS Carter have been working on have told a consistent story. And let's face it. Do they strike you as the brains of the operation? No, the Cantonese are the ones pulling the strings. They have Triad written all over them.'

'Nice one Boss,' Holmes gave one of his classic grins. 'They have, quite literally, if those tattoos turn out to be what we think they are.'

'They're still accessories to murder though, the Fujianese,' Caton pointed out. 'And you can bet that they were involved in checking out that takeway, especially given that it's run by members of their own community. And I wouldn't be surprised if they were involved in some of the taxing – the protection racket; making threats, and collecting the payments on behalf of the Triad.'

'Only accessories? What about the torture Feng Yi suffered, and all those slashes to his body?'

Caton shook his head. 'But according to the post mortem, that's not what killed him. It was the blows to his head, against a hard surface.'

'Just like the first two; Michael Han, and James Lee.'

'Exactly.'

'Too much of a coincidence.'

'Precisely.'

'So if they're saying that Chu Wan, or Tu Po Sin, or whatever his real name was, killed Feng Yi…'

'Then it's odds on that he killed the other two as well.'

'Banging heads against brick walls is his MO.'

'More like his signature.' Caton observed, sipping his third mug of double strength coffee of the night. Holmes raised an eyebrow. 'Come on Gordon,' Caton urged. 'He's carrying a specialist filleting knife, a semi-automatic pistol used by US special forces, and his name – one of several – means Slaughter Man. What does that suggest to you?'

'He's a professional hit man?'

Caton rolled his eyes heavenward. 'Hallelujah.'

'There's one thing about it,' Holmes reflected brightly, 'If we can tie him in to what little forensics there are from those deaths, or any of those earlier ones, it means we'll have cleared up seven murders in all. That can't be bad.'

Caton was thinking about the video that he had watched on a cell phone, fifteen thousand miles away. 'Ordinarily, I'd agree with you,' he said. 'But right now my first priority is to prevent number eight.' His own phone began to ring. It was DS Joanne Stuart.

'Jo,' he said. 'Are you still at it too?'

'Yes Sir,' she was trying to sound bright, but Caton detected an underlying weariness. 'Mr Wallace asked me to let you know that one of the phones was definitely used to ring two of the numbers in China.'

'Which two?'

'The parents of Feng Yi and Zheng Hu.'

'You mean it's the phone that was cloned using that doctor from Liverpool?'

'Yes Sir.'

Caton began to work his way through the implications. They now had in custody the person who had been terrorising those families. That meant they could no longer track that phone, and follow its owner, in the hope that it would lead them to her whereabouts. But he did not have the one belonging to whoever had been phoning the parents of Wu Ling.

'Who does the phone belong to?' he asked.

'It was in the BMW Sir, when they searched it.'

'Where exactly?'

'On the floor behind the front passenger seat.'

'So it belongs to one or other of the Cantonese we've got here in the cells. Tell Mr Benson, I want the fingerprints matched as quickly as possible,' he said. 'And tell everyone well done, Jo, and to keep at it.'

'Hang on Sir,' she said before he could ring off. 'I've dug something up myself. Inspector Holmes asked me to go over the statements in the original file on the Chinatown investigation. Well I felt some of the background statements made relating to James Lee may have been taken at face value, so yesterday afternoon I decided to revisit some of them. After he'd had those threats, and was moved to the Stockport office, he took to drinking heavily.'

'I remember, it was all in the dossier,' Caton said, the combination of caffeine and hours of frustrating interviews making him impatient to get to the point. He heard Gordon's phone ring, and saw him rise from the table, and head to the other end of the canteen.

'Well it seems that in the Tong,' DS Stuart was saying. 'Of which he was a long standing member, he'd actually been making some rather colourful accusations about the Manchester and Shanghai Trading Corporation.'

'How come none of this appeared in the original statements?'

'Because none of them mentioned it. Partly because they felt sorry for his family; partly because none of them believed it could be relevant to his murder; mainly, I suspect, because several of their members are senior executives of the company.'

Face again, Caton reflected. 'So how did you manage to change their minds?'

'I mentioned something about needing to interview all of their members in turn. Possibly getting a warrant to have a look at their membership records. Next thing I know, the Vice President agreed to meet me at ten o'clock last night. He is only too happy to set the record straight. I think he genuinely believed there could be no connection, so there was no harm in him telling me about it.'

'Did they raise it with James Lee at the time?'

'Yes. He was actually called before the President, who pointed out that slagging off other members of the Tong was a breach of the rules, and that he would be well advised to moderate his drinking.'

'What did he say to that?'

'Nothing. He just stopped going there.'

'How long was this before he was murdered?'

'Ten days. The President got the Secretary to check in the appointments and meetings book.'

Caton breathed in deeply, and heaved a sigh. 'And they didn't think there could possibly be a connection.

'I would have told you sooner Sir, but you were a bit tied up to say the least,' she said.

Thanks Jo,' he said 'You've done a brilliant job. You won't be able to do much more till the rest of the world wakes up. Why don't you get your head down for a couple of hours, then freshen up, and grab some breakfast. '

'Thanks Sir. I may just do that.'

He was putting the phone back in his pocket as Holmes came crashing across the room pushing aside the chairs in his way.

'Zheng Hu has made contact with the number we told his parents to pass on to him,' he said, excitedly. 'They've been able to convince him that we've picked up the gang that were after him, and he's given his location; somewhere in Blackburn. A car is on its way over there to collect him. They're taking him back to Longsight like you asked. What do you want to do now Boss?'

Caton felt like he was juggling the spinning plates again; placing a new one on a stick, twirling those that were just about to fall, judging how long it would be before others began to wobble. 'I think we've got about as much as we can reasonably expect from this lot,' he said. 'You can only wring a sponge so far. In any case the custody officer is already asking when he can have his cells back. No doubt it's the same over at Collyhurst. I think we should all get back to Longsight. Prepare the paperwork to get them remanded later this morning. And welcome the elusive Mr Zheng Hu. Let's just hope he can give us something that might shed some light on the whereabouts of Wu Ling; though to be honest, I doubt it.'

There were five of them in the interview room. Zheng Hu had been provided with a solicitor; primarily as an assurance. He had, after all, entered the country illegally. There was an outside chance that his co-operation with the authorities, and the threats to his family, might just persuade the Home Office to regularise his status. Caton doubted it, but the possibility was worth dangling. In view of the relevance to her investigation, he had invited Sally Yeadon to join them. Holmes sat at the end of the table nearest to the tape and videotape controls. The very first question they put to him was related to the whereabouts of the girl, Wu Ling. This time they had the advantage that he spoke good English from his high school education, polished through a part time job in the golf-pro shop at the Ami Golf Resort. Once again, Caton's prediction proved accurate.

'I am sorry,' he said. 'I have no idea. I wish I did.'

'Was there nothing she said during your journey together that would suggest where she was heading for; where she might have gone?' Caton asked.

'No,' he said. 'You don't understand. She did not run away like us. They said they were going to kill everyone, except her. Wu Ling they kept.'

Caton and Holmes exchanged glances. They had assumed all along that she must have escaped, and then been recaptured.

'Right.' Caton said. 'In that case I think you had better start at the beginning.'

For the next twenty minutes, he led them step by step through his family's negotiations with the snakehead Yu Lai; the tortuous journey by road across countries he had only seen on maps; the additional sums that they were forced to pay to local couriers at every other change of vehicle or border crossing, until all of the money he had brought with him was gone. He told them of the hurried switch from one sealed container to another in Rotterdam; the dash for freedom at the Hull depot; hitchhiking on the motorway until they reached the Drum Mountain takeaway in Bolton. He choked back the tears as he recalled how Feng Yi had berated him for their abandonment of the young woman he had sworn to protect; of his shock and fear when he discovered that his friend had disappeared. The story of his journey to Blackburn, and his sanctuary there, felt like an anticlimax to the officers. It was evidently a painful source of guilt for him.

'Did you, at anytime, hear anyone call your courier by his name?' Sally Yeadon asked.

He shook his head. 'No. Only by what we took to be his alias; Three Fingers Meng.'

'Did he only have three fingers?' Holmes asked, expressing an interest part professional, part prurient.'

'No. One thumb, four fingers, on each hand. It was the first thing I checked.'

Holmes pressed him 'So how do you think he got that name?'

Zheng shrugged. 'I don't know. Possibly because he had once severed three fingers from the hand of an enemy. Or perhaps he just wanted us to think that.'

From what he had learned about the Triads Caton was inclined to believe the former.

'What about the man who met him at the depot; who said that he would kill you all, except for Wu Ling?' Yeadon probed. 'Did you hear his name?'

'No.'

'I still don't understand why, having brought you all that way with money still owing, he had decided to kill you all.' Caton said.

'I don't either,' the young man said. 'It doesn't make sense. Just because of some logo.'

Caton, Holmes and Yeadon froze; did a double take; looked at each other, then back at the young man across the table from them.

'Logo? What logo?' Caton said as calmly as possible. 'You didn't mention a logo.'

'Didn't I? I thought I had.' He looked from one to another, puzzled by the concentration on their faces. 'It was on the side of the container we were made to transfer to in Rotterdam. The one in which we arrived in England.'

Caton pushed a pad and pencil across the table. Zheng Hu wrote it down for them and slid the pad, still upside down, back across the table...

'They were in an oval.' He said. 'Gold characters against a dark blue background.'

Even before he spun it round Caton could see what had been written. MST&C.

24

Ray Barnes leant back in his chair in Caton's office, and folded his arms. 'Well, thanks to Zheng Hu, the young man you so dramatically saved from harm, the link between the Eggborough Five, and the gang you now have in custody is clearly established as the M&STC container truck. The problem, of course, is that any direct connection remains purely conjectural, and the evidence really shaky. Until, and if, we find the girl.'

'Wu Ling,' Caton reminded him.

'Wu Ling. Until then we've only got his word for it that that's what was on the side of the container.'

Yeadon was unable to restrain herself. 'We've got the licence plates of all of their vehicles in and out of Hull on the days in question. I still believe we should carry out simultaneous raids on the company's haulage depots, and on any of their trucks and containers on the road, or at the ports.'

Barnes remained unruffled. His reply was measured and professional; in no way dismissive. 'That's a very tempting suggestion. The logic is inescapable. Unfortunately, I'm told there are a number of problems. The container, in which they were shipped, may no longer be on one of the truck beds for which we have the registrations. The logistics involved in searching every single truck and container owned, or leased, by the company, would be considerable, and the cost difficult to justify. By the time we've got the company's transportation schedules, and moved on those at sea or abroad, any evidence would almost certainly have been destroyed. And to be honest, the Agency has to look at the bigger picture.'

Sally Yeadon all but exploded. 'The bigger picture!? What could be more important than the deaths of the five people dumped on my patch?'

The Agent calmly opened the document case on the table in front of him.

'I'm not attempting in anyway to diminish the importance of clearing up those murders. What I'm saying is that establishing the motive behind it is just as important, if not even more important. Because if we don't eliminate whatever it is that drove them to cold bloodedly snuff out those lives, then what's to stop them doing it, again, and again?' he unfolded his arms and spread them in a gesture of appeal. 'Look, we've spent months building a case on the Manchester and Shanghai Trading Corporation. We suspect them of tax avoidance, the laundering of money from criminal enterprises: drugs, people trafficking, prostitution, illegal gambling; counterfeiting. We don't know for certain, but it is possible that the prostitution may not even be directly linked to the company. It could be the case of a Triad seizing on the opportunity presented by the people trafficking, to engage the girls in their own little enterprise. Either way, we think there are two mechanisms they are using to do this. One theory is that they are avoiding tax by inflating their cost structure; specifically, by paying over the odds to their suppliers.'

'How can they get away with that?' Caton asked. 'Surely the figures from their suppliers would give the game away?'

'Not if the suppliers collude. After all, they're going to be paid at cost for goods and materials they don't even have to produce. Why should they complain? In any case, a pound to a penny the factories are owned by M&STC. We also have reason to believe that their associate company, Hang Xian Lo, is showing an exaggerated trading loss – also by falsifying their costs on the supply side. In both cases this is particularly difficult to track, because the firms they buy from have a habit of declaring themselves insolvent, disappearing, and remerging under a different name. Corruption in the regulation and monitoring of these companies in China makes it almost impossible to prove.

And then there's the thorny problem of laundering the cash payments from those other activities: money from the dealers, pimps, repayment of loans by the illegal immigrants, and from the illegal gambling. That hidden profit – none of which is taxed - will have to be cleaned through the casinos.'

'And how exactly, do they do that? Helen Gates asked.

'With collusion from the casino operators. We also believe a holding company related to M&STC actually part owns two of the casinos. All they need to do, is claim to have made significant winnings equivalent to a proportion of their dirty money, and actually lose the rest in the casino where some of it acts as a pay off to the casino operators, and some goes straight into the holding company.'

'Don't the company have to keep records of major players?' Sally Yeadon asked.

Barnes nodded. 'Over a certain limit. And those records are supposed to be available for scrutiny. But all they have to do is have a number of players, each of whom shows winnings up to, but just below, that limit. Then there's no way we can access those records, or question their claims.'

Caton had been thinking it through. 'And,' he said. 'If the middle men involved in their illegal activities were to have regular gambling accounts at either of these casinos that would be a way of them getting their cut safely, and cleaning the money at the same time.'

'That too.'

'And that's what you suspect James Lee, through his informant Michael Han, may have stumbled on.'

'Exactly.'

'What about the three killed in the other cities?' Yeadon asked.

'No,' said Barnes. 'As Tom will know, there is nothing to link any of those three to either company. We believe they were all down to Triads fighting over territory, but in this case hiring an assassin to do their dirty work, and enabling them to claim they had nothing to do with it.' He turned to Sally Yeadon. 'I know this is asking a lot, but if you can just give us another week or so we might be able to tie this up together.'

'But none of this gets us any closer to solving my case.' Sally Yeadon pointed out.

'I'm afraid you're right.' Barnes said. 'What we now need is a little more time to build our case. The Agency doesn't want to compromise that by blundering in without the evidence to make it stick, and the excuse that would give us to dig deeper.'

The Agency, Caton reflected. The way that Barnes had said those words implied an importance, a weight, far greater than that of a mere regional police force. If SOCA were not careful, he could see troubled waters ahead.

'That's all very well,' Yeadon was saying. 'But we can't just sit on our hands and twiddle our thumbs waiting for you to build that case.'

Caton smiled. Now that would be difficult. Sitting on them, and twiddling them at the same time. Yeadon had spotted him.

'Do you find something amusing?' She stormed.

But Caton had already moved on. He was thinking about Wu Ling, and how none of this bigger picture seemed to include her.

There was a knock on the door. Not for the first time, Ged came to his rescue. 'I'm sorry Sir,' she said, picking up on the atmosphere straight away. 'I've brought the drinks. Where would you like them?'

'Just leave the tray on the coffee table Ged,' he said. 'We'll help ourselves.'

She put the tray down, and straightened up. 'There was just one other thing Sir. You've had a phone call. From the Chief Executive of the Manchester and Shanghai Trading Corporation. He would like you to meet with him. He says it's very urgent. In view of...'

'Yes, thank you Ged,' he said, cutting her off, not in bad way. 'You did right to let me know. Just give us a few minutes and I'll ask you to ring him back. And when you do, please put the call through here.'

When the door had closed her turned to the others. 'It looks like they've decided to take the initiative. Shall we get our drinks before they get cold, and talk about how we're going to respond?'

The speaker was switched on, and the sound turned down. Caton thought it likely that it would be obvious to the caller, just from the hollowness of the tone, that others were listening in. That couldn't be helped. If he was going to commit himself, he needed to know the rest of them were happy.

'Chief Inspector Caton?' The voice was cultured and urbane.

'That's correct.'

'Please excuse me for disturbing you,' said the caller. 'My name is Ying Zheng Xiong. I would be happy if you were to call me John, or Mr Ying. I am the Chief Executive of the Manchester and Shanghai Trading Corporation. The Head Office of our European Operations is here in Manchester. You may know of it?'

'The name of your company seems vaguely familiar,' Caton said, receiving a nod of reassurance from Agent Barnes. 'But I have to admit I don't know where your offices are.' The nod became enthusiastic.

'I see,' the pause was pregnant with disbelief. 'Well…no reason that you should. We have just moved to a new suite of offices in the Beetham Tower. Perhaps you know where that is.'

The irony wasn't lost on Caton, or any of them for that matter. It was not a building one could easily miss.

'Very impressive Mr Ying Zheng Xiong. And what is it I can help you with exactly?'

'Ah, well, a very sensitive matter,' he lowered his voice. 'One I would prefer not to discuss over the phone. May it suffice to say that we have discovered that our company has been infiltrated by criminal elements. Ones that have been using our resources for their own wicked ends.'

'I see. And what led you to contact me sir?'

'Ah, well, it was not the sort of thing I would feel comfortable sharing with an anonymous operator on the end of your Crimestoppers telephone line.'

'I am sure that would have proved perfectly satisfactory sir, but why me?'

'I spoke to the President of our revered Chinese Business Forum, and he assured me that you would be just the right person. For a matter of this gravity.'

'I see. It would be really helpful, Mr Ying Zheng Xiong, if you could give me some indication of the nature of your concern.'

Agent Barnes now resembled one of those nodding dogs that people place on the parcel shelf of their cars. This time there was a long pause before the reply.

'Perhaps if I say that it involves breaches of security involving one of our containers? A tragic breach, as it turns out.'

Caton looked across at the others. Ray Barnes was shaking his head in disbelief; Sally Yeadon mouthing a great big YES.

'When would you like to meet sir?'

'As soon as possible. Today. This afternoon.'

'I think I can manage that sir,' Caton said. 'I could send a car for you.'

'No Chief Inspector,' his voice shifted suddenly from silky smooth to hard as steel. 'I do not think that you understand. I am willing to share this information with you, voluntarily. On the understanding that you will meet with me here. Shall we say 2pm?'

Out of the corner of his eye Caton could see Sally Yeadon gesticulating madly.

'I think I can manage that sir, as an *initial* meeting,' he let the words sink in. 'I should like to bring a colleague with me.'

'Of course, Chief Inspector. Thank you. Until this afternoon then.'

'Goodbye, Mr Ying Zheng Xiong.'

Ray Barnes was the first to speak. 'The cunning bastard,' he said. 'As soon as he found out we had Zheng Hu, he knew we were onto them. This is just a way of getting in first. Protesting his ignorance, innocence, and outrage.'

'It gets you in there though; into his cave.' Caton reminded him.

'Only I'm not ready to go in there yet. With what we've got so far he'll just chew us up, and throw us out.'

'I'm coming with you Chief Inspector.' Sally Yeadon told him.

'Of course you are Superintendent.' Caton said. 'This is what you've been waiting for.'

25

'I don't know if I love it or hate it.' Sally Yeadon said.

They stood at the traffic lights on the opposite side of Deansgate, staring up at the one hundred and fifty seven metre high ice blue tower, and the narrow blade of glass rising a further twelve metres beyond it.

'You've got to admit though, it's impressive,' Caton said. 'Manchester's done it again. It's the tallest mixed use building outside of London, and the highest residential space in the United Kingdom.'

'Only because the architect has got his penthouse right at top. I bet it's windy up there.'

'Perhaps, but he's got palm trees on the rooftop garden, and the views across to Snowdonia must be stunning.'

'But do you like it?'

Caton shook his head. 'Not really. I can admire it as an achievement; as a piece of urban sculpture even. But I don't like the way it's dwarfed historical buildings like these behind us.' He pointed over his shoulder to the former Urban Heritage Centre and the procession of buildings from the Air and Space Museum down to the original offices and station of the Liverpool and Manchester Railway. 'Call me a dinosaur if you like.'

'You're a dinosaur,' she said, as the lights turned to green, and the two of them began to cross the road. 'How high up that thing do you think his office will be?'

'I don't know,' Caton said. 'But given that the apartments and offices were built above the Hilton Hotel Sky Bar, and that's on the twenty third floor, I just hope you've got a head for heights Ma'am.'

'You call me Ma'am in private again,' she said. 'And I'll punch your lights out.'

'This is really impressive, Detective Chief Inspector.' He could tell that she had chosen her words carefully, conscious that the room might well be bugged.

'Something of an understatement Ma'am.' He replied playing along. And it *was* an understatement. The office spanned the entire width of the tower, with pale blue windows from floor to ceiling at either end. The two remaining walls were clad with a rich red veneer, to match the solid rosewood desk, ten foot table, and matching chairs. The table sat in the East window, with bronze pieces inlaid in the corners, and at the foot of each leg. They could quite easily have been on the Bund in Shanghai. Caton could imagine people with their backs to the room gazing out over the Pennine hills; those opposite them, ever mindful of the three hundred foot drop behind them.

'I wonder what that represents.' Sally Yeadon said, pointing to the huge tapestry hanging behind the desk. A white tiger moved stealthily through slender blades of grass, muscles tensed and bulging on its back and shoulders, ice blue eyes wide and alert, lips drawn, revealing vicious yellow teeth.

'The king of all beasts. The guardian of the West.'

Caton recognised the voice from the telephone. They turned to find that he had entered unheard. The door was already closed behind him. How long he

313

had been there it was impossible to tell. He wore a mid-grey herringbone double breasted suit in wool and cashmere, and a gold tie against a crisp white shirt with an Oxford collar. In his left hand he held a black leather folder. As he moved to meet them his suit moved softly with him; weighted for the Spring.

'During what we call the Han Dynasty it was popularly believed that when a tiger reached the age of five hundred years, its tail would turn white. Imagine how long it would take for the whole of the beast to turn white? Thus, for we Chinese, the white tiger is a creature born of myth. It was believed that the white tiger would only appear when the emperor was virtuous, and peace reigned throughout the world.'

Peace and virtue. Now that really is ironic, Caton was thinking. 'Mr Ying Zheng Xiong,' he said. 'It was good of you call us. This is Superintendent Yeadon, of the North Yorkshire Police Force.'

The Chief Executive made a short bow and shook their hands in turn. 'It was good of you to come. Please, take a seat.' He ignored the rich leather seats arrayed around the rosewood coffee table, and ushered them instead to the table by the window. Ying took the chair at the head of the table. The only one made of leather and capable of swivelling and reclining.

'I am a busy man,' he said without preamble. 'Both of you are, I am sure, at least as busy, if not more so. I will get to the point. We were shocked and disturbed by the discovery of the bodies of five of my fellow countrymen found close to the side of the M62 motorway. I immediately offered a reward within our community of fifty thousand pounds for information leading to the apprehension of those responsible.'

Caton and Yeadon glanced at each other. It was news to the pair of them.

'I also directed our own security team to ask among our drivers and staff if they had heard or seen anything suspicious. Imagine my surprise and distress when they reported to me that they had discovered that our organisation had been infiltrated by snakeheads. That is members of a Triad.'

'Yes we are familiar with the term, sir.' Caton told him.

'Of course. Well it seems that they had managed to bribe two of my drivers to allow them to delay a container, and modify it so that it could carry drugs, counterfeit goods, and illegal immigrants.'

'Where is this supposed to have happened?' Sally Yeadon asked. It was obvious from the time it took him to reply, that the directness of her question, the absence of any form of address, and in particular the use of the word supposed, had not escaped him.

'It happened' he paused deliberately, holding her gaze. 'Near Kara Bogaz Gol, on the border between Kazachstan and Turkmenistan.'

'How long ago was this?'

'A month ago, approximately. Such a thing has never happened before.' His eyes bored into hers, daring her to contradict him.

'But I assume that you have the drivers. That your security staff are holding them?'

He lay both hands on the table, palm upwards. 'I am sorry. As soon as questions began to be asked, they fled. Left their jobs and disappeared. You can imagine, it is a great embarrassment.'

'In which case, how did your staff come by the

information in the first place?' Caton asked.

His head remained still as his eyes switched to Caton's. If his intent was to convey contempt, it was highly effective.

'Those men had loose tongues, as well as loose morals. One of them told a drinking companion, who was also a colleague. You may speak to him if you wish.'

'Oh we most certainly do wish,' Sally Yeadon said. 'And we wish to speak with your security staff as well.'

Ying opened the black leather folder, and took out two identical brown envelopes. He slid them across the table. 'The details are all here. Photographs of the container, and its location. You will find it under guard by my staff in our compound in the freight yard behind Piccadilly Station. No doubt your forensics experts will want to look at it. You will also find the personnel files for the two drivers, including their photographs. More than that, my head of security has been very active. You will also find in there the names and descriptions of the courier who we believe accompanied the immigrants on the final stage of their journey, and the name of our agent in Rotterdam whom we believe assisted them in transferring the illegals to our container in the port itself. My head of security will be happy to answer any questions you may have.'

Caton picked up one of the envelopes. 'That's really helpful, sir,' he said almost choking on the words. 'Does it also include the details of the other vehicles? The one from which they transferred into the container, and the lorry into which they were moved in Hull?'

A bemused expression suffused his face. 'Chief Inspector, you have the advantage over me. I had no idea there were other vehicles. If there were, they were certainly not ones belonging to my company.'

'Mr Ying Zheng Xiong,' Caton said. 'If your container was modified half way between China and the Channel, why were those people not transferred to it then and there? Why wait until it reached Rotterdam?'

The Chief Executive of the European Division of M&STC, the White Tiger, Guardian of the West, raised his hands sideways, palms still facing the ceiling, like a priest at high mass.

'You're right,' he said, without a trace of sarcasm. 'It is indeed a mystery.'

Two miles to the East, Johnny Cheng flipped open his mobile phone. It was nine am. For the second time that morning he dialled the number. For the second time, he was informed that the phone had been switched off. It was odd. Hua Yu rarely switched off his phone. Perhaps the information he had received had been mistaken. Perhaps he was still hunting down the missing pig from Fujian. Johnny knew better than to leave a voice message. Instead he sent a text: Ring me.

He paced the flat, unsettled, observing with disgust the mess the others had made before they left. If he had heard nothing by midday he would have to think about moving the girl. Hua Yu was the only one beside himself who knew where she was working. If he had been taken, they would all be compromised.

The moment they entered the incident room Nick Carter, face beaming, launched himself out from behind his desk.

'You're not going to believe this Boss, 'he said. 'But one of the regular, and most recent numbers on that phone we got from the BMW, has tried to ring it twice this morning. The second time just a few minutes ago. Both times a text message was sent. It was one of the speed dial numbers in the address book; initials, CJ. We'd already found out that it was a one year pay as you go contract, paid for in advance, on another cloned phone. The Service provider gave us a rough triangulation on the first call. When the second one came through we already had a tracker van in the area. They've just pinned it down.'

'Where is it?' Caton asked.

'It's a block of flats in West Gorton.'

'Don't tell me,' Holmes said. 'The Wellington Estate?'

'Got it in one.' Carter replied. 'The ASBO capital of Britain!'

As good a place as any to hide, Caton reflected. He had just seen the statistics; twice as many anti-social behaviour orders per head of the population as anywhere in the country. Channel 4 had just had to move the filming of Shameless to another part of the city because the crew and cast were being targeted by mindless yobs. It was just about the only place in East Manchester that was yet to benefit from the physical and economic regeneration on the back of the Commonwealth Games.

'In that case we'd better get a move on,' he said. He turned to Sally Yeadon. 'Are you happy to carry on here Ma'am; see if there's anything more Zheng Hu can tell you about the people who brought them in?'

'No problem,' she replied. 'Just so long as we can agree about how we are going to move together on this; when you've sorted the girl out that is.'

'That was an unfortunate turn of phrase,' Caton remarked as he and Holmes hurried back towards the incident room. *'Assuming we get to her in time*; I've a feeling it's going to be more about putting her back together again.'

'Like you say' Gordon Holmes said, his voice laden with apprehension, 'Assuming we get to her in time,'

26

They crowded into the largest of the rooms at the Hough End Centre. There was no way that Longsight could have accommodated them all. Caton looked out at the sea of faces. Apart from his own team, there were three agents from the SOCA Sexual Crimes Liaison Unit, led by Rebecca Sharp their Agent in charge; nine officers from the Force Operation Talon, led by DI Chris Hall; three officers from the Force Sexual Crimes Unit; Doctor Peterson from the St Mary's Sexual Assault Referral Centre; twelve members of the Tactical Aid Unit, including four armed officers; and six members of the Force Motorcycle Unit. Over forty people in all. In addition, the drivers and crew of the transport vehicles were drinking coffee in the bar area. It might look like overkill, but this was one operation he had to get right first time.

'To summarise,' he said. 'We have a male target under observation in a flat in West Gorton. The girl we're looking for, Wu Ling, may be there, but we suspect that she may have been moved to other premises; almost certainly a brothel. Finding her is our primary target. We are hoping that the male target will lead us there. As soon as we have that primary target confirmed, we will move in on both sets of premises simultaneously. We can't risk those who are holding the girl being warned,' he paused for effect, looking around the room, making eye contact. 'At best, they'll move her, at worst, they may kill her. Assuming that we find any working girls on these premises they will be treated as victims, *not* as criminals. Unless, of course, it can be shown that they are actually involved in running the brothel. That's why Dr Petersen is here. I want to reassure them that our main aim is to protect them. Especially Wu Ling. She is potentially a crucial witness in a much wider investigation involving multiple murders. So, I'll say it again. Any women removed from any of these premises, not involved in running those premises, will be treated, from the outset, according to the procedures to be followed for the victims of rape, and of sexual exploitation. Does everyone understand?'

It was clear that everyone did. It was one of the advantages of dealing with specialist units. It had been a good briefing. Now they had to make it work.

High on the roof of the old Fujitsu building on Wenlock Way the observer, Echo Two, trained his high power Night Detective BPC 20X60 binoculars, on the windows of the fourteenth storey flat, just sixty five metres to the west. Had the windows not been covered with loose net curtains, and in one case a hessian blind, he would have been able to describe, in some detail, the tattoo on the back of the neck of the man who for the past ten minutes had been pacing back and forth across the main room. The detector van parked in the car park below, and its companion parked up out of sight on Bennett Street behind the impressive and imposing St Benedict's Church, had finally pinpointed this place. And the man in his sights right now had obligingly confirmed their analysis by making and ending calls on his cell phone that Echo One could observe, and they could track. There was no doubt about it. This was the flat. He watched as the man walked through the open door to what must be the corridor to the adjoining rooms. He saw the blind flutter in the smallest of the windows as the man placed one hand on the window ledge. He imagined him unzipping his flies with his other hand. Saw the blind move again as he straightened up. Thirty seconds passed. Suddenly, the curtain was pushed aside in the adjacent room, and the window opened, as though to air it. For a moment the man stood staring directly towards the building on which they lay. Neither of them moved. They doubted he would be able to spot them in the small building on the roof that housed the mechanism for the lift, but it was nevertheless a possibility. Echo Two froze. Echo One pressed the button on the end of the cable that started a continuous sequence of shots. These would be the best photos he had taken so far. In this enclosed space the noise of the shutter was magnified; causing them to wonder if the sound could be detected on the breeze that blew directly off the Pennines, and over their heads, towards the flats.

Johnny Cheng closed the window, and looked around the room. The stench of sweat and urine had all but disappeared, along with the sheets and mattress, into the skip behind the Wellington pub. The iron bed frame looked like a giant version of the cat's cradle with which his sister used to drive him mad on the deck of their floating home, as it rode the waves in the harbour at Aberdeen. That sampan, and Hong Kong, seemed a lifetime ago. It was at times like this that he wondered why he had ever left. He kicked the bed on his way out. It was a constant reminder and reproof. He hoped that he would never have to use it again. In his heart he knew that he would. He tried the number one more time. It was still switched off. None of the others, those whom he allowed on sufferance to use his flat from time to time, were responding either. There was no way that this could be right. The girl would have to be moved. He rang the Lady White Snake Sauna and Massage Parlour, and warned them to have her ready.

'Echo One to Papa One. Viper is on the move.'

From the safety of their unmarked car on the corner of Skarrat Close, and Wenlock Way, Echos Three and Four watched as the man left the flats and made for his car parked casually outside. That he dared to leave it here at all was an indication that he was not someone with whom to mess. They waited for him to start the engine and move away, before switching on their own engine and easing out from the curb. There was no rush. A second unmarked car was waiting on Gorton Road, and another at the far end of Bennett Street. Whichever way he went, they had it covered. Once he was moving, they would take it in turns to stay a couple of car lengths behind. If there was the faintest hint that he had cottoned on, there would always be a car ahead of him, where he would least expect it.

'Right,' Caton said. 'Listen up. Our target is on the move, heading towards town. He's just called a number in the city centre. One that's figured several times, and isn't known to us, other than that it's cloned. We're moving now.'

They approached the city centre in three small convoys. One travelled up Chorlton Road; one up Princess Road, and the third, along Upper Brook Street. There could be a dozen or more explanations for such a show of force. The residents of Manchester were used to seeing police convoys escorting high security prisoners to and from the Crown Courts, and visiting dignitaries speeding in from the Airport just six miles to the South. None, however, had been quite as impressive as those that had accompanied the Olympic and Commonwealth Games Committee Members on their fact finding visits to the city over the years. Nevertheless, Caton judged it best to err on the side of caution. Two of the convoys took up their holding positions in the maze of streets between the former UMIST buildings of the University of Manchester, and Whitworth Street; just a hundred metres from the place in which the first of the Chinatown victims had been discovered. The remaining convoy was a minute away from the West Gorton estate.

'What the hell's he doing?' Holmes muttered as they listened to the radio operators, and followed the route on the screen in front of them.

It was a perfectly reasonably question. Their target had eschewed the most direct route into the centre of the city, turning off instead onto the inner ring road at Great Ancoats Street.

'*Left into Ducie Street…Right,right,right, into Peak Street…Left, left,left, into Tariff Street…Left, left, left into Brewer Street…Right, right, right into Back China Lane … Right,right,right into Dale Street…*'

'He can't do that, that's a one way street!' Holmes complained.

'*Right, right, right into China Lane…*'

'He must have spotted them. China Lane for God sake. He's rubbing their noses in it.'

'Not necessarily,' Caton said. 'Listen to our cars. They keep backing off, and switching position. These guys are good.'

'*Left, left, left into Hilton Street… still on Hilton Street…Left, left, left onto Newton Street…straight over the lights into Portland Street…Left,left, left into Chorlton Street. Right, right, right into Chorlton Street Car Park… he's on the ramp, up into the car park.*'

'Clever,' Caton said. 'He's given himself a stack of options. He can drive around, park suddenly, and see if anyone's following him; he can come straight out again, and hope to lose whoever's following him; and if he leaves on foot, he's got three possible exits to choose from; he could even walk back down the ramp.'

Holmes nodded grimly. 'Then it's a bloody good job we've got four cars on him.'

Johnny Cheng sat in the car for five minutes. Just two others drove past; one, a young woman with a child in a car seat; the other a man in his late fifties driving a Kia. Finally, he got out, locked and alarmed the car, and made his way to the exit ramp. It was easier this way to spot if anyone was following him, or watching the exit ramp from below. He could see people making their way to and from the bus station. A homeless street beggar lay sprawled in a doorway opposite the ramp, a scruffy black and white terrier beside him, a plastic supermarket bag and a can of lager by his feet. A white delivery van was just moving away from the kerb and heading off towards Canal Street. He felt a little reassured. Even before he left the flat he had had an uneasy feeling that he was being watched. At one point on the journey into town he had seen the same car several times; initially behind him, then falling back, then behind him again. It was why he had turned off onto Ancoats Street. When the car had sailed past as he turned off into Ducie Street, he had felt a rush of relief. It was too early to drop his guard however. He turned left at the bottom of the ramp and crossed over the road, the better to be able to pause occasionally, and check in the plate glass windows of the offices if anyone behind him had also stopped. Proceeding in this manner, it took three times as long as it should have done for him to reach and cross Portland Street, and melt into the back streets of Chinatown.

The followers watched as he entered the White Snake Betting Shop. They walked purposefully towards the nearest dim sum restaurant, leaving Agent Gerry Ng, ten paces behind them, to peel off, and open the door of the shop. To anyone watching here was a man intent on changing his fortune.

It took Agent Ng less than ten seconds to observe that not only was the target not in the room, but also that this tawdry shop was nothing but a front for something else. There were betting slips indeed, and odds on the most bizarre of possibilities chalked on a board; but not a television screen in sight, nor anything resembling a point at which to bet, or to collect your winnings. Instead, a discreet sign in Cantonese, over a doorway immediately ahead of him, read Lady White Snake Sauna & Massage Parlour.

The man perched on a stool behind the excuse for a reception counter followed his eyes. 'What would you like?' he asked. His large square head barely cleared the top of the counter.

'What can you offer?' the Agent asked.

The man observed him shrewdly, assessing expertly, through half closed eyes, what this customer's desire might be, and how thick his wallet. 'Sauna; full body massage; very special massage. Up to you.'

'I hear you may have something really special. Recently arrived. Thought I'd give it a try,' said Ng knowingly.

The man stiffened, and rose from his stool. What he lacked in height, he made up for in breadth. His neck was thick and wide, creating a perfect triangle with bulging shoulders. He had the torso, arms and stance of a wrestler. 'Where did you hear this?' he asked.

Ng smiled innocently. 'Someone at work. Comes here a lot. You may know him as Kenny.'

The man advanced towards him, arms like the branches of an oak tree outstretched, shepherding him towards the door. 'You come back with Kenny, then maybe we see about something special.'

Ng turned in the doorway. 'If I do…you do have something special? Young and fresh?'

The man scowled and pushed him towards the door. 'Come back with Kenny, then you see.'

Out on the street a smartly shod and trousered man in an ill matching raincoat brushed past him on the pavement, and ducked into the shop he had just vacated. Ng needed no further confirmation. He scratched the back of his neck, brushed his hand twice through his hair, and set off down the street.

In the doorway of the dim sum restaurant one of the followers spoke into his radio mike.

'This is it,' Caton said. Let's go.' The engines started simultaneously. Less than fifty seconds to contact.

Johnny Cheng watched from behind the curtain in an upper room as Agent Ng walked away from the shop, crossed the road, and disappeared around the corner. Goose pimples began to appear, and the hairs on his arms stood on end. He raced down the stairs two at a time, and into the narrow hallway.

'Where's the girl?' he shouted. 'I said to have her ready.'

'We got rid of her client, and made her get her things together,' the feisty madam told him. 'But she's locked herself in the toilet.' She pointed down the corridor.

Cheng took two strides and hammered on the door. Barely waiting for a reply, he leaned his back against the wall and kicked the door with all his strength. The wood splintered around the handle, and the door burst open.

The girl cowered in a corner, wedged firmly

between the toilet and the wall. The left side of her face was badly bruised; a livid red from her cheekbone to her chin. Her left eye was puffed and closing; her lip split. In her hand she held a steel comb; the long thin handle pointed outwards in desperate defence.

'Who the hell did this?' he demanded.

Behind him, the woman shrugged. 'An over enthusiastic client…this morning. It happens. Don't worry, he won't be coming back.'

Cheng's head was spinning. If his instincts were right, it was too late to get a car to pick them up. In any case, who could he call when none of them were answering? Nor could he risk trying to walk out of here with her like this. He slid his hand behind his back, beneath his jacket, and grasped the handle of the knife. As he began to slide it from its sheath he sensed the madam beside him edging away; distancing herself; physically, emotionally, legally.

Cheng looked again at the girl. Her eyes were hard as glass, and just as vacant; the pupils fully dilated. The only evidence of fear, the whiteness of her knuckles where she gripped the comb, her bloodied lips withdrawn, exposed anaemic gums. Such a short time since he had brought her here; already she was barely recognisable. He heard a squeal of tyres, and a curse from the front of the shop. He pushed the knife back, spun, and hurried to the end of the passage, turned right, and hurried up the stairs.

On the landing he pushed open a door, and flung aside a naked man in the act of reaching for his trousers, sending him crashing into the woman kneeling beside the bed. He ducked behind the curtain hanging over a small space containing a toilet, shower cubicle and wash basin. He stood on the toilet seat, pushed hard against a panel in the ceiling, and levered it aside to reveal an opening. He teetered perilously on the toilet cistern, and hauled himself into the loft. He slid the panel back into place, crawled across the roof space, clambered through the small opening in the breeze block wall, and scattered the dusty pile of boxes until he found the trap door of the adjoining property. He lowered himself into the void, and let go.

Vaulting down two flights of stairs, he shrugged off his jacket as he went. Pausing on the second landing, he pulled his tee shirt from his trousers to hide the knife, and walked as casually as he dare down into the restaurant proper. The restaurant manager and waitresses were standing in the window watching the line of riot helmeted policemen racing past. Every head in the room had turned to watch the spectacle, or to listen to the shouts and screams from the house next door. Cheng chose a yellow waiter's jacket from the coat stand, and slipped it on. As he passed the bar, he picked up a bag containing takeaway meals awaiting collection, carried it to the door, and slipped out.

To his right, the last few officers were disappearing into the betting shop. Another group stood in a cordon around the door. Behind them two unmarked vans and a marked police van were drawn up, their rear doors open. A little further on an ambulance stood ready. Cheng could see that either end of the street was blocked by police cars and motorcycles. He stepped out into the street, and crossed purposefully to the far side, expecting a challenge at any moment. He reached the pavement, and pushed his way through the people standing two deep, gawping, slack jawed; snapping with their mobile phones. Behind him, on the pavement he had just vacated, uniformed officers had begun to push back the crowds, funnelling them towards the end of the street.

He pushed through the crowd on the opposite pavement and slipped inside another restaurant. He handed the parcel to the only member of staff who had the wit to challenge him, and hurried into the kitchen, most of whose staff were already out in the dining room watching the show. He dropped the yellow jacket into the laundry basket at the far end, replaced it with a grease stained kitchen worker's jacket, opened the backdoor, and slipped out into the empty alleyway beyond.

'Nine girls, Boss. Apart from our one.' Holmes reported.

Caton had just seen her being carried into the ambulance. 'Wu Ling.' He reminded him, steel in his voice.

'Sorry Boss,' he said sheepishly. 'Wu Ling. Apart from her, it looks as though three of them are Vietnamese, one Chinese, and five are Eastern European; Lithuania and Albania they reckon.'

'I can confirm that,' Rebecca Sharp said as she joined them. She had Doctor Petersen with her. 'No surprises there. It's what we're finding nationally. These poor girls are almost all the victims of trafficking specifically for this purpose. About two thirds of them arrive legally, and end up hoodwinked, or coerced into prostitution to pay off the villains that loaned them the money for their trips.'

'We've also arrested a man of Chinese heritage, and a woman they reckon is Albanian,' Holmes said. 'The pimp and the madam. They should be able to tell us something.'

'But our other target got away?' Caton already knew the answer; he just needed to be sure.

'I'm afraid so Boss. We've no idea how. Tactical Aid went in the back at the same time they went in the front. He either went through the walls, or through the ceiling. We'll find out which.'

'Not soon enough to catch him,' Caton said, looking at the crowd being funnelled through the search and question area at the end of the street. 'Unless he's among that lot...which I doubt.'

'But at least we've rescued Wu Ling,' said Holmes 'That was what this was all about.'

'You're right.' Caton agreed, recalling the quiet dignity of her parents as they stood discussing the fate of their beloved daughter on the hill overlooking Meicheng. 'How is she?' he asked Dr Petersen.

'For all of the girls,' the doctor said. 'There'll be a gradual and sensitive process of detoxification and debriefing. Of them all, Wu Ling's condition is the poorest. Physically, she's suffering the short term effects of what I'm almost certain is heroin addiction. Here in the brothel, it seems to have been replaced by crystal methadone.'

'Why crystal meth?' Holmes interrupted

'Because,' she replied patiently, despite her wish to get on with the real work of helping the girls. 'It raises levels of energy, and can significantly increase libido. If your workers have to have the ability, and the need, to engage in sexual activities for extended periods of time, what better than a drug that not only does that, but which actually leads to sexual compulsivity?'

'There are side effects.' Caton said. 'How is it going to affect her?'

'Fortunately, she's been on it for less than a month. Long term use would have challenged her kidneys and her heart. Her teeth would almost certainly have rotted. She would have been at risk of hypertension and stroke. As it is, she'll suffer severely from withdrawal, although we can help her with that. Her body, including her brain, will struggle with the loss of Dopamine, Norepinephrine, and Serotonin. At first, her thinking will be slow, and confused. Her body will recover from all of this over the course of several months. Good nutrition will build it up without too much short term damage. But emotionally, and psychologically, she'll be a mess. She'll suffer from psychotic delusions; feel guilt and self loathing because of the activities in which she's been forced to engage; be terrified of having to face her parents, family and friends. Typically, she'll feel anger because of what's been done to her. The total loss of control she's experienced will have erased every vestige of self-confidence; she'll have been stripped of her self esteem. There is a very real prospect that she'll revert to drug use to shut out all of this. She may even attempt suicide at some point in the future. Not as a cry for help, but to escape from a world that's made a mockery of her past, and has taken away her future.' She raised her eyes to meet Caton's. They were dark with anger, though not with him. 'Other than that Chief Inspector? She's fine.'

As she watched the doctor walk off towards the ambulance, Rebecca Sharp shook her head. 'And to think, there are thousands more girls like this out there, and more arriving by the day. I'm glad I only have to track down the bastards who are responsible. I don't think I could cope with what she has to put up with.'

'I've got a feeling she'd swap with you any day,' Caton said. 'And I'd give anything to be there when she got her hands on them.'

As he crossed the bridge, Cheng Jun - Johnny to his friends, Viper to his latest enemies – dropped the cell phone into the water without breaking stride. The greasy kitchen porter's jacket lay at the bottom of a black wrought iron bin, with a golden bee moulded on the side, at the end of Canal Street. By the time they discovered it, he would be long gone; not back to the flat, but far away from here. If things were indeed as bleak as they now appeared, there would be no point in trying to contact the other members of the Triad. Any that had not been taken would be looking out for themselves. As for those for whom they had been working, he had a feeling that any contact at all would be unfavourably received. Particularly since the girl was still alive. Thus far today, his instincts had not let him down. Right now, they told him to disappear.

27

Caton made a mental tick list. The pimp and the madam had been processed, questioned, and locked up for the night. The Sexual Crimes Unit had reassured the girls, housed and fed them in safe and secure accommodation, and arranged with Dr Petersen for medical examinations. The interviews would begin in the morning. Joanne Stuart would be there to represent his team. Wu Ling was sedated, and as comfortable as could be expected. The man they had code named Viper had slithered away into the subterranean underbelly of the city. Even with the photos, Caton had no expectation that he would be found anytime soon.

It was ten o'clock when he finally met up with Kate. Desperate though they were to spend a night together, Kate could see the tell tale signs. Not so much the drooping eyelids as the glass of wine he knocked off the table, splattering the light oak laminate flooring with a crimson stain.

'Look Tom,' she said. 'You're exhausted. You're in no state to hold a conversation, let alone anything else. Let's leave it till the weekend.' She sensed him avoiding her gaze. 'You will have some time at the weekend?' She said.

He turned to face her. In his eyes she read weariness, and guilt. 'Whatever happens I'll make the time.' He replied.

She took his hand and squeezed it. 'I know it's not your fault. It's just that what with China, and the last few days, we've hardly seen anything of each other.'

He wrapped his arms around her, and pulled her to him. 'No, you're right,' he said. 'I'm forever preaching about work life balance; it's time I did something about it. I'll make it up to you, I promise.'

She tilted her head up towards his, and they kissed. It was only when she felt his lips stop moving, and the sudden weight of his head, that she pushed him off, and sent him packing.

Caton opened the blind to find the dazzling sun melting a frosting of snow on the roof of the Y Club, and on the barges moored on Potato Wharf. With a cracking sound, like intermittent gunfire, a cold wind tore at the taut canvas canopy over the arena steps. Mini tornados swept spirals of discarded wrappings across the sandstone flags. Yesterday had marked the Spring solstice. The clocks would go forward at the weekend, and March – having come in like a lamb - was going out, true to form, like a lion.

Washed and showered, he went through to the kitchen, and opened the fridge. He had not had time to stock up since he'd come back from China. To all intents and purposes the cupboard was bare. Not even a carton of juice. He picked up the bottle of milk and the tub of margarine, and took them over to the bread bin. Circles of green mould dotted the loaf like fairy rings. He threw it in the bin, and poured himself a glass of milk. Even before it reached his lips he could tell it was off. He poured it down the sink, and washed away the curdled residue clinging stubbornly to the stainless steel. The first appointment of the day was the remand hearing at the magistrates' court. There was no way he wanted them to walk out of that court on bail. And if there was an application for bail, he wanted to see from whom it came. The courts were just four minutes walk away. Plenty of time for a quick breakfast at Katsouris.

It was almost midday in Caton's office. DI's Holmes, and Weston were there from Caton's team, together with Agent Barnes, and Detective Superintendents Yeadon and Gates. Helen Gates had come because the operation was at a pivotal point, and also to pass on the congratulations of the Chief Constable and DCS Hadfield on the progress made over the past two days.

'It's rare to have two operations take place within twelve hours of each other, with such positive outcomes,' she said with genuine enthusiasm. 'And all the more impressive because it's been the first time that Greater Manchester Police have had the pleasure of mounting such operations in collaboration with the Serious and Organised Crimes Agency,' with a smile and a nod towards Sally Yeadon, she added. 'Not forgetting our colleagues from the North Yorkshire Police Force.'

'Not exactly flawless though Ma'am,' Caton pointed out, worried that this would turn into a self congratulatory session. 'Granted, we've recovered the missing persons, but we still don't know who brought them into the country, nor why their travelling companions were murdered, or by whom. Nor have we any idea what happened to that 'special cargo'.

Or for that matter, what it was. Although, at two million pounds, the odds are that it was a drug consignment. And whilst we got the man we suspect of having murdered Lee, Han, Feng, and the other three in London, Birmingham, and Liverpool, we still haven't the faintest idea who paid him to do it, or why.'

Her expression barely changed. It was only by the controlled manner in which she spoke that Caton knew just how irritated she really was. It was one thing, he realised too late, to speak frankly to her in the privacy of her own room, quite another to do it in front of strangers.

'Thank you Chief Inspector,' she replied icily. 'I was going to come to that. And to the target who mysteriously disappeared from the place you were raiding when you supposedly had it surrounded. I had hoped to give due weight to the positives first. But, since you seem to be in a hurry to get on… please do proceed.'

He felt someone kick his ankle under the table. He looked up and saw Sally Yeadon, sitting opposite, raise her eyebrows, and give him half a wink. Beside her, Gordon Holmes stared fixedly at the table top; a curl at the edges of his mouth. Caton was glad someone was enjoying it. He opened the file.

'Following your lead, Ma'am, I'd like to ask Inspector Weston to tell us the good news concerning the forensics.'

DI Weston passed printed copies around the table. She was looking a little brighter Caton realised. He wondered if Mike had finally seen the light about babies, and caved in.

'As you can see,' Weston said. 'We have a positive match to the soles of the shoes belonging to the man referred to as Tu Po Sin. '

'The man shot dead at the back of Indigo Mill?' Helen Gates asked.

'Yes Ma'am. They are a perfect match to one of the sets recovered from the grassy area adjacent to Lock 12. What's more, there were traces of dried blood on his shoes, and on those of three of the men we have in custody, that belong to the same blood group as the victim, Feng Yi. DNA tests are being run on all the samples, and on the sticking plaster recovered from the Drum Mountain takeaway. The pollen and spores recovered from the clothing have been sent away for comparison with those gathered from the scene.'

'What about the bits of fur and fabric recovered from the bushes alongside the path they took to the canal?' Holmes asked.

She shook her head. 'Nothing yet. Some was from cats and dogs, rats, even a fox. The fabric could have come from any manner of people who'd used it as a short cut.'

'It sounds as though,' Gates said, 'You've got enough to partially substantiate the accounts they've given us so far. Especially if the DNA comes up trumps.'

'That doesn't tie Tu Po Sin in to the other deaths, about which they claim to be ignorant,' Caton reminded them. 'The only link is the way in which they were killed. And that's purely circumstantial.'

'Not good enough for the courts, I agree,' said Helen Gates. 'But good enough to enable us to close the files on the others. I call that a result.'

Caton was still not satisfied. He found it difficult to believe that Lee, and Han, and the other three, had been lured to unfamiliar territory, and murdered, without the involvement of at least another one or two accomplices. His money was on the two Cantonese; the Triad members. If he could tie them in, he might just break the conspiracy of silence, and find a motive behind these otherwise senseless killings.

'Chief Inspector?' Helen Gates voice broke into his reverie.

'I'm sorry Ma'am, I was thinking.'

'Yes, well try and do it out loud,' she said. 'It's unnerving when you sit there with that far away look.'

'Inspector Holmes,' Caton responded. 'Perhaps you could tell us what we have from the further questioning of those arrested in both operations.'

'There's not a lot to tell Sir,' Holmes replied, replacing the title Boss in deference to the assembled company. 'Apart from a few more details about how they got hold of the meat van, and the place where they held, tortured, and killed Feng Yi. They told us it was the old Renolds Chain Factory.'

'The one at the junction of Burnage Lane and Lane End Road? The one the residents have been complaining about for the last fifteen years? The one that holds the record for call outs in South Manchester?'

'That's the one Ma'am.'

'I thought Tesco were supposed to have started building a supermarket on the site?'

'Within the month, apparently Ma'am.'

'About time,' she said.

'Not soon enough for Mr Feng Yi.' Agent Barnes said dryly.

'We've got a Scene of Crime team down there at the moment,' DI Weston told them. 'It might just throw up something new.'

'Presumably that information came from the Fujianese street gang members,' Caton said. 'What about the two Cantonese? The Triad members?'

Holmes shook his head. 'Not a peep from them. Tighter than a...drum.'

'And nothing from the brothel keepers?'

'Just their names. They know nothing. Never saw our secondary target enter or leave the premises. And this is a good one: the girls turn up of their own volition. They don't solicit on the street, or advertise their services. All very discreet. They have no idea where the girls come from. They're horrified at the suggestion that they might have been trafficked. They've no idea where the drugs we found on the premises came from. The girls must have brought them in themselves; or the clients.' He shook his head. 'I can tell you that these two will happily go down for a stretch rather than grass on their associates. It is, literally, more than their lives are worth.'

Caton knew he was right. In their shoes he would have done the same. And Gates was right. This was as much as they'd get. It was time to put it to bed. For now.

28

'How on earth did you find this place?'

It was a large stone cottage, at the end of a tiny terrace, on the edge of the village of Stainland. Above the door, the date 1885. Where the cottage ended, the ground fell away abruptly to accommodate a bowling green, and tennis courts, then dipped into the valley proper, beyond which the Pennines rose majestically. Forsythia were flushed with golden flowers; buds on the wild pear and cherry trees hinted at blossom just around the corner. In that respect alone it reminded him of China in the Spring.

'I left the motorway, headed for Halifax, turned right, turned left, and there I was.' Caton pushed the door open for Kate, and stepped aside.

'Sometimes you're just infuriating,' she said.

Before he could reply, Julia, the owner, maitre d', and genius behind this place, came forward smiling brightly.

'Tom. It's good to see you again. This must be Kate?'

Introductions made, they settled by the bar with their drinks.

'She's very nice,' Kate said. 'And she owns the restaurant?'

'And her sons, Nathan and Matthew, run the kitchen. Nathan trained at the Auberge Du Lac and Matthew worked on the Oriana. It shows in the food.'

'That was a hell of risk she took when we came in. What if I'd been someone else? How embarrassing that would have been.'

'Not so much of a risk,' he said. 'I've never brought another woman here. And you're the only one I ever talk about.'

She studied his eyes, trying to work out if he was telling the truth or simply winding her up again.'

'Besides,' he said, sipping his drink to prolong the moment. 'When I reserved, I told Julia you were coming.'

She laughed, and prodded him in the chest. He lifted his glass away and steadied it to stop it spilling on the stone flags.

Julia Evans appeared with the menus. 'I'm glad to see you two are enjoying yourselves.'

'Never a dull moment with Tom,' Kate said. 'When he's a moment to spare.'

'Ouch.' Caton said with feeling. Not least because it was true. Just to rub it in, his phone began to ring.

'I hope that isn't work?' Kate said, as Mrs Evans moved discreetly away.

Caton looked at the number. 'I'll have to take it, but I'll be quick, I promise.'

He stepped out into the street. 'Gordon,' he said. 'This had better be good.'

'I'm sorry Boss, but I thought you'd want to know. Ray Barnes has just been on. The Dutch police have pulled two bodies out of a canal in Rotterdam. Both of them slashed to beggary, just like Feng Yi. Very conveniently, they still had their papers on them.'

'Don't tell me. The two names the CEO of M&STC gave us; the courier and the contact?'

'Spot on.'

'They've tied up the loose ends. Dressed it up as a Triad blood feud.'

'That's the way it looks. And one other thing. The DNA came through. We got a match on Tu Po Sin – The Slaughter Man - with Feng Yi, and with The Drum Mountain takeaway. Hadfield says well done, and we're to close the case. Leave the rest to The Agency.'

'But it isn't closed, is it Gordon?'

'It is for us Boss. You know the score. Sometimes this is as good as it gets. Three murders off our books, five off Yeadon's, and three other city forces saying thank you very much. I call that a result.'

'A pyrrhic victory Gordon.'

'What's that when it's at home?'

'A victory offset by major losses. Like winning a battle with heavy casualties, but the war goes on.'

'So what's new? Sounds to me like you need a rest Boss. I suggest you get back to whatever it is you're doing. I'll see you on Monday.'

Roles reversed, it was just the kind of thing Caton would have said.

'I'll do that,' he said. 'And Gordon, thanks for letting me know.'

'Bad news?' Kate asked, as he took his seat.

'Not really. Mixed I suppose. Nothing that need spoil our evening. I'll tell you about it later.' He picked up his menu. 'Have you chosen?'

'Of all the places, in all the world…'

Caton could hardly believe it. Julia had led them to a cosy corner table, perfect in every way, except that on the opposite side of the restaurant sat Sally Yeadon and Agent Dave Munby. Munby rose from his seat, threatening to come over. Caton decided to head him off.

'You stay here,' he said to Kate. 'It'll be quicker.' He crossed the room to shake their hands. Sally Yeadon insisted on a hug. He wondered what Kate would make of that.

'I bet you'd forgotten you'd told me about this place,' Yeadon said. She looked across at Kate and waved. 'Good choice.' It wasn't clear if she was talking about Kate or the restaurant. 'I hope we haven't spoiled your party?' She said.

'Not unless you're intending to stay the night,' Caton replied. 'Because we are.'

She laughed. 'No need. There's plenty of room at my place, isn't there Dave?'

'What are you doing here Dave,' Caton said. 'I thought you were in China?'

Munby grinned. 'Evidently not. I'm over here trying to help tie things together. No doubt you've heard about Rotterdam?'

Caton nodded. 'It was inevitable I suppose. A pre-emptive strike. Zheng Xiong threw us a bone he'd already chewed. They'll close down that route. No doubt another will open?'

'No question about that, and this time they'll be more careful.'

Caton thought back to the SOCA briefing at the Radisson Hotel. What was it they had called their overarching investigation? 'Operation Tiger,' he said. 'Those two in Rotterdam, and the ones awaiting trial; they're just the cubs.'

Munby smiled. 'I know. We haven't got the tiger; not yet. But now we know where his cave is, it's only a matter of time.'

Caton stood looking out across the bowling green and the fields, to the hills beyond. The moon was new and lustrous, like the sheen on Kate's hair. The lights on the road, climbing the distant hillside, glowed like a tiny string of pearls.

He had been thinking about this for some time. Trying to set aside the dark thoughts that had dogged him in the years following his divorce. It wasn't Kate he doubted, but himself. His obsession with work had ruined his last marriage; he didn't know if he would be able to stop that happening again. Kate shivered in the cold evening air, and nestled closer; strengthening his resolve.

'How do you feel about us moving in together?' he asked.

She pulled away a little, and looked up at him; her eyes bright, and searching. 'Where did that come from?'

He had no idea what she was thinking. He looked out over the valley, not wanting to see disappointment in her eyes. 'I've been wondering about it for some time.' He said.

'You're a deep one, Tom Caton,' she snuggled close again. 'Your apartment isn't big enough, neither is mine.'

'We could get one together.' He said, knowing full well where he was taking this.

'That's a big step.'

'I hope so.'

346

'Are you sure?'

'The one thing that my life, and this job in particular, has taught me,' he said. 'Is that nothing is certain. I don't want to end up a sad bastard, drinking himself into oblivion; dreaming of what might have been.'

He felt her pull away a little.

'That makes me sound a bit like a pension plan,' she said.

Mortified, he turned to face her. 'I'm sorry Kate. You know I didn't mean it like that.' Then he saw that she was smiling, and cupped her face in his hands. 'I love you Kate,' he said. 'You make me feel...complete.'

'There will have to be some rules.'

'Toilet seats and toothpaste caps?'

She levered his hands apart, and put on her serious face. 'About work. A Detective Chief Inspector, and a Home Office profiler. That's a hell of a combination as we've already discovered. Rule number one is we only discuss our work when it's absolutely necessary. When one or the other of us needs some healing. We do not bring it home.'

'Agreed.'

'We share all the costs straight down the middle.'

'I wouldn't have it any other way.'

'What if it doesn't work out?'

'It will.'

' O.K. What if it does work?'

'When it does, I think we should make it permanent.'

Her eyes widened; liquid pools of green and brown. 'Is this a different proposal Tom Caton?'

Caton couldn't decide if he had been manoeuvred into this, or if he had been heading for it all along. Either way, it wasn't the way he wanted to propose.

'Can we just work on living together first?' He said. 'If you still feel the same when you've had a few months of me twenty four seven, I promise you won't have to ask that question. You'll know.'

'If you still feel the same Tom.'

'I will,' he said. ' know I will.' As he kissed her she clasped her arms around his neck, and drew him close.

Thirty eight miles to the South, the Father of Wu Ling exits the arrivals terminal at Manchester Airport, to be taken by taxi to his daughter's bedside. His wife has been refused a visa; remaining at home on surety of their return.

Three thousand four hundred and thirty seven miles to the west, it is five thirty in the evening. Cheng Jun, Johnny to his friends, Viper to his enemies, leaves the apartment and sets off down Huron to walk the three blocks to Grange Avenue, and his new place of work in the heart of Toronto's Chinatown. The Big Circle Boys, the largest players in the importation of heroin from South East Asia to the whole of America, with a growing share of the trafficking of South American cocaine and marijuana, long established in the American and Canadian sex slave rings, have welcomed him with open arms. The pokey flat in the Manchester tower block, Wu Ling, and the Lady White Snake Sauna and Massage Parlour, are distant memories.

Fifteen thousand miles away, at Changle Airport, it is six thirty in the morning. Hidden away behind the arrivals building seven large wooden crates are being unloaded from a cargo plane. A line of fork lift trucks are waiting to carry them to the unmarked vans beside the perimeter fence. Officials prepare to make a cursory customs check. No ceremony, no witnesses, and definitely no press. Once inside the vans, the crates will be removed to reveal the simple coffins. Five bodies will travel by land into the suburbs of Fuzhou; thence into the villages beyond. One will take a final journey up the Min River. One will transfer to an internal flight, and thence to a province in the north of the country where, in accordance with tradition, a group of snakeheads have offered to provide a ghost bride to accompany the young man on his journey to the after life.

Whether the girl had died of natural causes, or been selected for the purpose, the family would never know, or question. In their grief, they would promise to pay another sum they could not afford. One more link in the chain of evil.

Another mother shedding tears into the barren earth.

The Author

Formerly Principal Inspector of Schools for the City Of Manchester, Head of the Manchester School Improvement Service, and Lead Network Facilitator of the National College of School Leadership, Bill Rogers is currently a Fellow and judge of the Teaching Awards. Bill has numerous publications to his name in the field of education. For four years he was also a programme consultant and panellist on the popular live Granada Television programme *Which Way*, presented by the iconic, and much missed, Tony Wilson. He has written six crime thriller novels to date – all of them based in and around the City of Manchester. His first novel *The Cleansing* was short listed for the Long Barn Books Debut Novel competition. His Fourth novel *A Trace of Blood* reached the semi-final of the Amazon Breakthrough Novel Award in 2009.

Also By Bill Rogers

The Cleansing
The Head Case
A Fatal Intervention
A Trace of Blood
Bluebell Hollow

www.billrogers.co.uk   www.catonbooks.com

If you've enjoyed

THE TIGER'S CAVE

You will certainly enjoy the novel that first introduced
Detective Chief Inspector Caton

THE CLEANSING

Christmas approaches. A killer dressed as a clown haunts the streets of Manchester. For him the City's miraculous regeneration had unacceptable consequences. This is the reckoning. DCI Tom Caton enlists the help of forensic profiler Kate Webb, placing her in mortal danger. The trail leads from the site of the old mass cholera graves, through Moss Side, the Gay Village, the penthouse opulence of canalside apartment blocks, and the bustling Christmas Market, to the Victorian Gothic grandeur of the Town Hall.

Time is running out: For Tom, for Kate…and for the City.

Short listed for the
Long Barn Books Debut Novel Award

Available in Caton Books paperback
ISBN: 978 1 906645 61 8

www.Amazon.com
www.catonbooks.com
www.billrogers.co.uk

Also Available in EBook format

Lightning Source UK Ltd.
Milton Keynes UK
UKOW040234051212

203192UK00001B/8/P